Dear Reader,

Welcome to another month of exciting romances from ***Scarlet***. From your letters to date, for which I thank you, it seems as though you are enjoying my monthly choice of new novels.

I wonder, have *you* ever thought of writing a romance? We are always looking for talented new authors here at ***Scarlet***. Do you think you could produce 100,000 words of page-turning storytelling which readers such as yourself would enjoy? Don't worry if you're not a professional author, as we're happy to help and advise you if your work shows promise. If you *are* interested in trying your hand at writing for ***Scarlet***, why not write to me at Robinson Publishing (enclosing a stamped addressed envelope) and I shall be happy to send you a set of our guidelines?

Keep those letters (and manuscripts!) pouring in!

Till next month,
All best wishes,

Sally Cooper

SALLY COOPER,
Editor-in-Chief – ***Scarlet***

About the Author

Brought up in the market town of Ormskirk, Lancashire, **Margaret Callaghan** trained to teach in the West Midlands. She met her husband Rob at her first teaching appointment and, like all good romance stories, it was a case of love at first sight!

Margaret took a career break to have her daughter Laura, now a teenager. Then she did several years short-term contract teaching before accepting a full-time position back at her first school in West Bromwich, where she currently teaches 11-to-16 year olds.

In her spare time, Margaret enjoys good food, good wine, foreign holidays and spoiling her cats. Margaret had her first romance novel published in 1991 and her last ***Scarlet*** novel, *Devlin's Desire*, won her rave reviews.

MARGARET CALLAGHAN

MASTER OF THE HOUSE

Enquiries to:
Robinson Publishing Ltd
7 Kensington Church Court
London W8 4SP

First published in the UK by Scarlet, 1997

A copy of the British Library Cataloguing in Publication data is available from the British Library

ISBN 1-85487-928-6

Printed and bound in the EC

10 9 8 7 6 5 4 3 2 1

For my parents
Ron and Winifred Heath,
with my love and thanks.

CHAPTER 1

'No, Ella! No!'

He woke with a jolt, jerking upright in the bed, the image in his mind so clear that he couldn't be dreaming. But he had to be dreaming, since the room was bathed in darkness and he was alone – alone with the nightmares of the past. The past. Gone. Over and done with, he insisted, willing himself to believe it as he pushed back the duvet and padded naked to the window, where he nudged aside the heavy folds of curtains, gazing out with unseeing eyes, his mind locked in the past.

He could see her, smell her, touch her almost. And why, why after all this time should the sordid mess of the divorce flood back to haunt him? Ella. He'd loved her, and he'd taken her. And for three glorious years they'd been happy. Ella. The most beautiful woman in the world. And he'd lost her. No. He pulled himself up sharp. No regrets. No futile meanderings down memory lane. The past. Over and done with. He'd moved on and he'd forgotten her.

Liar, the voice inside his head pointed out, and Jack smiled despite himself, checked his wristwatch in the faint silver light thrown out by a waning moon and recognized the truth. Not forgotten. Because he'd loved her, once. And sleep, he acknowledged wryly, was the last thing he'd manage just now.

Wide awake and stone-cold sober, Jack felt the sudden need for a drink. It carried him across the hallway. Brandy. Candy is dandy but liquor is quicker, he recalled with another tight smile as his bare feet sank into the thick pile of carpet. And it had been true. He'd seduced her, taken advantage of the unaccustomed effects of alcohol and taken her. And he'd loved her. And he hated her. Cradling the glass in his palm, he carried it across to the low-backed settee and then sat, the distinctive aroma of the brandy filling his nostrils as those last, dreadful-scenes began to replay in his mind . . .

'What are you doing?'

At the sound of her voice he halted in the doorway, spun round to face her, smiled bitterly. 'Surely it's obvious. I'm leaving. Walking out. Going. I've had enough, Ella, and now I'm leaving. Hence the suitcase. I'll pick up the rest of my things later in the week.'

'But – why?'

'Why? Come now, Ella, don't sound so naïve,' he scorned, sharp blue eyes flicking over her, logging the shabby bathrobe that gaped across her cleavage, giving more than a glimpse of the body beneath, a body he knew inside out and had revelled in – once. His gaze moved down, over the generous swell of hips and belly, his lips twisting in disgust – a disgust he took no pains to hide, though, heaven knew, Ella's fuzzy mind wouldn't notice or care – and, yes, he could hardly miss the glass, empty now but with the faint smell of spirits lingering on the air between them. 'It's over. It's been over for months. Don't pretend you haven't noticed.'

'But – you can't,' she said stupidly, hazel eyes widening in fear. 'You can't leave me, Jack. You're my husband. You love me. You *love* me. You can't.'

'Wrong, Ella. I not only can, but I am. I'm going. Face it, Ella, there's nothing to keep me here.'

'No,' she acknowledged bitterly, the once beautiful face beginning to crumple, and as Jack turned away her voice sliced across to halt him. 'That's right. Go. Walk away. Walk away, Jack Keegan, and may you rot in hell for the rest of your days.'

He swung round, eyebrows arching in surprise. Anger, not tears, he noted. She had guts, he'd grant her that. And he was wrong. She might have been drinking but for once she was very much in control. But they were through. It was over. It had been over for months and now it was time to go. Better for both of them.

He needed space and Ella needed help. And, since she refused point-blank even to acknowledge that she had a problem, maybe, just maybe, leaving her alone would force her to face the truth. Ah, yes. Mustn't forget that other reason – the real reason, if he was being honest. Hardly altruistic, hey, Jack, he needled.

Because he'd had enough. Cold-blooded and selfish. Just a simple matter of survival, really. Because if he stayed, Ella would drag him down too and they'd both go under. Brutal but honest. And if he hated Ella, right now he hated himself more.

'Since I've been living in hell with you,' he told her tonelessly, 'I guess I can take my chance out there in the big, bad world. Who knows?' he tagged on bitterly. 'It might even be an improvement.'

She flinched. 'So cruel, Jack. That isn't like you.'

'No? Well, I've changed,' he told her, closing his mind to the flicker of pain that crossed her face. She was playing for time and he was anxious to be off. Escape. Start living again. Shed the millstone and start to enjoy life.

But she's your wife, your responsibility, the voice of his conscience pointed out, unlooked for and unwanted. To love and to cherish. In sickness and in health. Sick. Ella is sick. And you're walking out on her.

But she won't let me help, he argued, beginning to weaken. Because he'd loved her once and she needed help, and, heaven help him, he wasn't such a bastard that he could walk away without a backward glance.

Hell, but he needed a drink. Dropping the suitcase, he headed for the sideboard, had reached for the decanter before he remembered. No alcohol. In an effort to keep her sober he'd purged the house. Another futile gesture since she'd clearly managed to find another source. The local off-licence, at a guess, and he should have known, should have called in when he was passing, had a discreet word with the manager.

And the next off-licence and the next? Have some sense, man, he chided. He could close the whole town and still she'd manage to track it down. And, since the empty glass she was clutching to her breast had been refilled with the familiar amber liquid, there had to be a bottle stashed nearby.

'Drink?' she enquired, reading his mind, and, like a magician producing a rabbit from a hat, she whisked a bottle from behind a cushion.

'No.' His need for a drink died suddenly. One drunk in the family was more than enough. And that was another mistake, he realized at once. He should have said yes, seized the chance to take it from her. 'Give me the bottle, Ella,' he urged softly, moving close.

Hazel eyes narrowed slyly. 'Mine,' she told him, clutching it to her chest, brandy slurping over the rim of the glass and splashing the front of her robe.

'I know, sweetheart. But you've had enough now. Give me the bottle and I'll put it away safe for the night.'

'Ha! You'll pour it down the sink. Don't think I haven't watched you,' she told him accusingly.

'If you give me the bottle, I promise I'll put it somewhere safe.'

'And then you'll come to bed?' she coaxed, with a calculating smile.

His heart sank. Bed. With Ella. That enormous double bed that was made for love. Love. They hadn't made love in months. Not since she'd lost the baby. Because every time he'd reached for her she'd frozen him out.

'Bed?' she repeated, and she was suddenly close, the bottle and glass discarded on the table as she crossed the room and sidled towards him. The waves of revulsion rippled through him – revulsion, and another emotion he'd thought was dead and buried.

Coming to a halt in front of him, she plucked at the fastening on her robe, the brandy-stained fabric falling open to allow her breasts to spill free – such wonderful breasts, he remembered, struggling to hold his ground, to mask the panic, the distaste, the unexpected surge of heat. His Ella. His love. Only not any more. She'd killed the love. No – circumstances had killed the love. She'd lost the baby and she'd gone to pieces, and nothing he could do or say had seemed to help. She'd frozen him out. *Her* pain, *her* grief, *her* need.

And what about *my* pain, *my* grief, *my* need? he railed silently, closing his eyes, aware of her hands, magic hands, sliding round to hold him, to touch him, to tease him, to touch him again. And hell, how he needed her. Needed her, loved her, wanted her. Even now, he realized, despite the angry scenes, the bitter words, the cold and lonely nights back to back and miles apart in the depths of their bed. He wanted her.

'Bed,' she murmured, her mouth against his. The whiff of brandy was a sickening reminder of his failure. He should have tried harder, insisted she saw the doctor sooner, dealt with the problem at the start. Only he hadn't. He'd been numb, too caught up in his own grief to notice. He'd failed her. And if he turned her down now, heaven alone knew how much more damage he'd inflict.

She was his wife. And for the first time in months she was allowing him to touch her. You can't say no, man, he reasoned as the needs of his body began to override the dictates of his mind. He needed a woman and, though he'd never been short of offers, he'd stayed faithful to Ella.

Wonderful, wonderful Ella, he told himself, weakening, pulling her into his arms and nuzzling the corners of her mouth. It wasn't too late. They could start again. The first flush of love had gone but they were good for each other. They could laugh together, cry together, make love together. Love.

She was moving against him, her hips describing erotic circles against his, and he was responding, rising, groaning, moaning, and he was kissing her, tasting her, his mind blocking out the sour taste of alcohol.

One last try. She deserved that at least. Was it really so much to ask? And he'd loved her once, could love her again. Had to try. Not so hard, since the love hadn't all died, had simply damped down like the embers of a fire. He wanted her. Never too late. Love her, kiss her, hold her, rekindle the love.

His mouth moved down, nuzzling the hollow in her throat, and down again, his tongue sliding into the valley between her breasts. His hands closed round her breasts as Ella plucked at the buttons of his shirt, and she was pushing against him, rubbing her breasts against his chest – wonderful, wonderful breasts, each with a dark areola, an even darker pink bud at the centre, and he dipped his head again, his mouth closing round, tongue teasing, lips sucking, teeth nibbling as his hands slid round into the curve of waist and hip.

She'd changed, he realized with a shock. He'd have had to be blind not to have noticed how she'd let herself go over the months, but just how far hadn't registered. Until now. Always a generous size twelve, he wouldn't mind betting she'd struggle to fit into a sixteen now, and yet he shied away from the thought. She was his, and she wanted him, and the long, lonely nights had left him hungry. He needed her, he wanted her, and tonight wonderful, wonderful Ella wanted him.

'Easy sweetheart,' he murmured as her hands travelled downwards, brushed against the front of his trousers, registered the bulge and began to tug impatiently at the zipper. And she laughed as he snared her wrist, pulled her towards the bedroom. The urge to place her down on the floor and take her there and then had almost gained the upper hand.

Easy. He had to take things easy. Rush her now and he'd be back at the beginning. And, yes, she seemed as eager as he, but she'd been as changeable as the wind over the past few weeks, was clearly in need of help. But she might just be receptive to suggestion if he handled things right. Love. Make love. Man and woman. Husband and wife. Normality. The first tentative steps on the long, hard road back to normality.

He placed her gently on the bed, his blue eyes smoky with desire as he shrugged himself out of his shirt, discarded socks and trousers. Ella lay back on the sheet, not the sleek and inviting Ella that he'd married, but she was his and she wanted him, and he buried his face in the mass of black hair that spread out across the pillow, felt the warmth of her body against his and his mind soared.

And then he was kissing her, his tongue sliding through into the secret depths of her mouth, the battle for patience lost because she wanted him every bit as badly. She arched against him, her breasts brushing the mass of golden hair across his chest, a strange, erotic sensation that sent rivers of heat pulsing through him, and he reached down to part her legs, caught her groan of delight as his fingers found her moist, paused to touch, to probe, to incite, and then they were moving together, the rhythm building, the heat building, until Jack couldn't hold back any longer – and then the waves were breaking over him, a wonderful tidal wave of pleasure, an explosive, mind-blowing crescendo that carried them both into a whole new dimension.

'Happy?' he asked a lifetime later, propping himself up on an elbow and gazing down at her.

'Very happy. We should have done that weeks ago,' she acknowledged, hazel eyes thoughtful.

'We certainly should,' he agreed with a smile. 'But we'll soon make up for lost time, hey, my love?' He bent to kiss her, to nibble at the corners of her mouth.

'Jack?'

'Mmm?'

'As soon as I'm sure I'm pregnant, one of us should move into the guest room. We can't afford to take any chances. Not this time.'

He went cold. 'Pregnant?'

'But of course. What else do you suppose we're doing here?'

What else indeed? he asked himself, aware that stone-cold sober he'd been outmanoeuvred – and how! 'Is that what this is all about?' he asked carefully, not really needing an answer. 'The need to get pregnant.'

'But of course. What else?' she asked, wriggling into an upright position and pulling the sheet up under her chin, an unexpectedly prudish gesture that hurt more than he'd care to admit.

He counted to ten. He'd stay calm. After all, he'd come this far, he might as well see it through. And maybe he had his lever at last, the incentive to persuade her to see a doctor, accept the help she needed. And she certainly did need help, he realized starkly.

'What about us, Ella?' he asked, sharp blue eyes fastening onto hers, refusing to allow her to look away. 'What about our needs, yours and mine?'

'Meaning?'

'Meaning us. Now. Making love. Making love, Ella, not making babies.'

'But I want babies,' she told him fiercely. 'Lots of babies. Our babies.'

'All in good time,' he insisted. 'You're young, you've your whole life ahead of you. It's too soon, sweetheart. You need – '

'No!' She pulled away, shrank against the pillows, eyes wild, twin spots of colour staining her cheeks. 'I need a baby. My baby. My beautiful little boy. Such a beautiful little boy,' she said in anguish as the tears sprang, hovered on her lashes. 'And they took him away. Why did they take him away, Jack?'

'Oh, sweetheart, sweetheart.' He reached out to touch her, to pull her down into his arms, the anger dying, drowned out by the pity.

'No! Don't touch me!' she bit out, twisting free, springing out of bed and reaching for her robe. 'Are you listening, Jack Keegan? Don't touch me. You killed him. You killed my baby.'

'Now you're being ridiculous,' he countered, as patiently as possible. And as the last piece of the jigsaw dropped into place something vital in his mind died.

His fault. All these months she'd been brooding, blaming him. No wonder she'd frozen him out. How she must hate him. And yet she wasn't thinking straight. Grief, hormones out of rhythm, postnatal depression. He'd read up on it, of course, had even spoken to their GP, but until Ella was ready to face up to the problem herself there was little anyone could do.

'Not ridiculous. Truthful,' she insisted with a defiant toss of the head. 'You killed him. You lied.

You said it was safe. Let's make love, *you* said. Nice and easy. It can't hurt the baby. Such a beautiful little boy, Jack. And you killed him.'

'No, Ella. No!'

'Yes! I hate you. I've hated you for months and I'll hate you till the day I die. And I really do hope that I'm pregnant,' she explained, with a chilling lack of emotion. 'Because all I need is my baby. My baby, Jack. Not yours. Understand, Jack?' she asked, angling her head, her eyes nuggets of ice. 'It's over. You can go. And, since your bag's packed and ready in the hall, there's nothing to keep you. Run along, Jack,' she insisted frigidly. 'You've done your duty so now you can go.'

'For God's sake, Ella – '

'No.' She cut him off with an imperative wave of the hand. 'No more, Jack. It's over. We're through. Finished. I don't need you any more, you see,' she explained confidentially, folding her arms and leaning back against the doorjamb. 'Because, with or without you, I'll have my baby. One man, two, a dozen . . .' She gave disdainful snap of the fingers. 'It's all a matter of time. Now go. Get out of my life and stay out.'

'Ella – '

'No. No more. And don't pretend you care,' she derided. 'I've got eyes, and believe me, Jack Keegan, I'm no fool. Make love? Oh, yes, you wanted me alright,' she allowed, with a sneering curl of the lips. 'Any port in a storm, hey, Jack? But I saw the expression in your eyes. Fat and frumpy. But good enough for sex. Well, fine. That makes two of us.

Good enough for sex. But not any more. Like I said, I simply don't need you.'

She swung away before he could reply, and, left alone on the bed that bore the imprints of their bodies, Jack stared the truth squarely in the eye. He loved her. Always had, always would. And he'd lost her. But he wasn't about to go down without a fight.

He shrugged himself back into his clothes. A robe would have been quicker but instinct told him that his only hope now was to goad her, hit out, hurt her, make her face the truth. And being dressed for walking out, not for bed, would give a starker impression.

She loved him. He had to believe it. But she was hurting inside and needed to lash out at someone, at him, had to focus her anger, the hate, purge the hate. Hence the stinging remarks about a string of other men. Sheer bluff, Jack sensed, knowing full well that Ella was simply overwrought, would never dream of sleeping around. His Ella. Only his. Always his.

He found her in the kitchen, wasn't really surprised to find her pouring out a brandy – a large one.

'One for the road?' she asked over-brightly, tilting the bottle.

'Why not?' he agreed pleasantly, careful to avoid skin-to-skin contact as he took the glass from her. He raised his glass. 'A toast?' he suggested. 'To us? To the future and whatever it may bring?'

'We haven't got a future. Not together,' she reminded him, her mouth a thin and bitter line.

'No? No, I don't suppose we have – unless by some miracle a baby comes along,' he drawled, taking a long, hard slug and gasping as the raw spirit hit the back of his throat.

'Stranger things have happened,' she told him.

'Very true,' he agreed solemnly. 'And in that case, Ella, you're wrong. Our baby. Yours – and mine. If. A big if. But believe me, until I know for sure, like it or not, I'll stick around. You surely don't think that I could walk away and leave you now?'

'Why not? You were ready to do exactly that an hour and a half ago.'

'I see. So this is your strange idea of revenge? Make Jack pay. Give him a taste of what he's missing and then *bang*! Don't call me, I'll call you.'

'Like I said, you wanted out. You're free to leave whenever you're ready.'

'Only I'm not. I've changed my mind.'

'Fine. I'll make up the guest room.'

'If that's what you want?' he challenged softly.

'You know what I want.'

'A baby.'

'A baby,' she agreed solemnly. 'Not you. Not any man. Just my baby.'

'But aren't you overlooking one tiny but significant detail?' he enquired, sipping the brandy, slowly now, since he was already halfway down a very generous measure.

'Am I?' she queried over-brightly. 'I don't think so.'

'Making babies. Making love, Ella. One man, two, a dozen. Or me.'

'My choice, hey, Jack?' she needled.

'It's a free world,' he allowed, hurting inside, aware that Ella was right, that ninety minutes ago he'd been ready for walking out with never a backward glance. But he'd been kidding himself. He was wrong. He loved her. But how to convince Ella of that with the damning evidence of his suitcase packed ready and waiting in the hall?

'Exactly. I'm free to choose and you're free to leave. So why not get it over and done with, Jack, put us both out of our misery? Go, Jack. You're not wanted here. Not any more.'

'But I am free to stay?'

'Apparently. Though heaven knows why you should want to.'

'Don't you know, Ella? Can't you guess?' he asked, his voice carefully neutral.

'Not interested, Jack,' she countered brightly.

'I love you, Ella.'

'Liar!'

'I love you and you love me,' he insisted, flinching at the venom in her tone but ignoring the single brutal word. 'Man and woman, Ella. Man and wife. I love you and you love me.'

'And if you believe that, you're living in cloud-cuckoo-land,' she retorted coldly, hazel eyes darting round the kitchen in search of liquid comfort.

Spotting it where she'd left it, on the draining board, she shuffled across, her gait not quite steady, and, watching her, Jack felt his sinking heart settle somewhere near the floor. He was wasting his time. She wasn't drunk by any means, since she was sober enough to keep him in his place, but she was deaf to reason, to truth, to pleas. And as for declarations of love . . .

'That's right,' he goaded softly, the words an ironic echo of hers. 'Walk away, Ella. Walk away from me, walk away from the truth. Take the easy way out. Drink yourself into oblivion.'

'As if you care,' she bit out, swinging round, just the twin spots of colour in her cheeks betraying how the dart had hit home.

'Of course I care, woman. You're my wife.'

'And quite an asset at that, Jack. A disposable asset, since you're on the verge of discarding me.'

'Past tense, Ella. Oh, yes, it crossed my mind,' he allowed with devastating candour. 'But I was wrong. I want you.'

'Like the little boy who suddenly finds his toy snatched away? Want. Possession. Power.' She smiled, gave a theatrical twirl on the spot – a pirouette that wouldn't have disgraced a ballerina. 'Like I said, take a good look Jack. I'm quite an asset.'

'Not at the moment. Not if you want the truth,' he admitted with brutal honesty.

'So why stick around where you're not wanted?'

'Because I love you.'

'And love conquers all? Quite the romantic. And to think,' she scorned with a defiant toss of the head, 'I didn't know you had it in you.'

'No? Well, that makes us quits,' he admitted bitterly. 'You don't know me, and I sure as hell don't know you.'

'And that's the way it's going to stay.' She drained her glass, tucked the bottle under her arm and headed for the open door. 'Goodnight, Jack,' she flung out over her shoulder. 'Sweet dreams.'

'Hardly,' he sneered. 'But at least mine will be sober.'

'Meaning?'

'Meaning precisely that. Unlike you, I'll be thinking straight. And furthermore, Ella Keegan, I'll be making plans.'

'The blue or the pink for the nursery wallpaper, Jack? Or how about a sunny yellow? Nice and neutral.'

'Separation. Divorce. Custody of my child,' he slipped out softly. 'My child, Ella.'

'My baby, Jack.'

'Maybe. If you get that far.'

'Ah, yes. *If*. If we've managed to conceive. If I'm stupid enough to let you back into my life, into my bed. But don't forget, Jack,' she pointed out sweetly, 'you're not the only horse in the compound. If and when I need a stud, you can rest assured I'll find one.'

'And you such an asset. I can well imagine.'

'And what the hell is that supposed to mean?' she demanded, swinging round to face him.

He raised his head, locking his gaze onto hers, holding it for long, long moments. And then he smiled, his eyes travelling over her slowly, assessing, appraising, remembering, blocking out the reality, seeing the girl he'd married, the slim yet curvaceous

Ella, who could turn a roomful of heads simply by appearing in a doorway, not the woman who'd let herself go; until finally, inspection complete, he brought his gaze back to hers and smiled again.

'Use your imagination,' he invited. 'Or, better still, take a long, hard look at yourself in the mirror. Yes – why not do it now?' he snarled, and, spurred on by the idea, he moved fast, snaring her wrist before she had time to fathom his intentions, tugging her the length of the hallway and through the open doorway of the bathroom.

'Let go of me.' She squirmed.

'When I'm good and ready,' he insisted tightly, taking the brandy bottle and placing it out of reach. He twisted her round to face the full-length mirror, moving in behind, rigid fingers gripping her shoulders as she struggled to be free. 'Take a good look, my dear,' he entreated coldly. 'Take a good look and tell me what you see.'

'No!' Her darting eyes looked anywhere but at the bronze-tinted figures in the glass.

'No? But why not, Ella? Why not face the truth? The truth, Ella. After all, you're quite an asset.'

'Don't – '

'Don't what? Don't be honest, truthful, brutally frank? Does the truth hurt, Ella? Does it? *Does it*?' he demanded savagely, and when still she refused to meet her reflection, to even glance in the direction of the mirror, he slid a hand under her hair, rigid fingers gripping her chin, forcing her head up, the grip tightening as she closed her eyes, denying him, denying them both.

'Look at me, Ella,' he insisted, his head close to hers, his breath warm against her cheek. 'Look at me. Then look at yourself. Look at yourself and tell me what you see.'

'No!'

'Yes! Now. Or an hour from now. Or half a day from now. But you will face the truth, Ella. Once and for all.'

And she did. Opening her eyes, flinching at the fury in his, the disgust in his, seeing herself through his eyes and coming face to face with the unpalatable truth.

'Well?'

She dropped her gaze, the fight seeming to drain from her body, and, watching her, Jack couldn't begin to guess what was going through her mind.

'Quite an asset,' she allowed, in a voice devoid of emotion. 'Quite an asset for any man.'

'Only one. This man. To me you're the most beautiful woman in the world. I want you, Ella.'

'Then you're a fool. The truth, Jack. I've taken a long, hard look, so now it's your turn. Look at me, Jack. I'm a mess.'

'Yes.'

Her head jerked up, eyelids flying open in surprise.

'The truth, Ella,' he insisted softly, continuing to hold her, the fingers on her shoulder a gentle restraint.

'You said you loved me.'

'I do love you.'

'But I'm a mess.'

'Yes.'

'And I drink too much.'

'Yes.'

'And you still love me?'

'Yes.'

'Why?'

'Why? *Why?*' he repeated. 'Because the girl I married still exists,' he pointed out, aware that he was giving her the truth. Somewhere deep inside, the Ella Andrews that he'd known and loved was struggling to break free. 'But you need help – professional help. You've been to hell and back and now you need help. I've tried, but I don't have the expertise. Just the love. I want us to try again, Ella, but you must be prepared to ask for help.'

'I just want my baby.'

'Yes.' He masked the pain. A stud. A father for her baby. When, as she'd already pointed out, any man would do. But she did love him; he was sure she did. He had to believe it. 'Sweetheart, you can have your baby. Soon, I promise you. But a doctor first, hey?'

'I don't need a doctor. Just my baby.'

'No doctor, no baby,' he pointed out, hardening his heart to the expression in her eyes.

'Meaning?'

'The drink, Ella. The brandy. You have to stop. Carry on like this and you'll hurt the baby.'

'But there isn't any baby.

'Not yet.'

'So – no baby, no problem,' she said brightly. 'And the minute I start a baby, I promise I'll stop.'

'No.'

'No?' She frowned.

'Trust me, Ella. It's better this way. And there might be a baby,' he pointed out, his hands sliding down and over the curve of her belly. 'In here. Right now.' A long shot, he had to admit, but if it helped to convince her, bought him time, two or three precious weeks, surely the means justified the end? 'And you wouldn't want to hurt the baby, would you, my love?'

He saw the wonder in her eyes, the hope, the love – love for a baby that probably didn't exist, he acknowledged as the knife-blade twisted. But he had a chance to win the battle, would fight on for the love that he needed, that he believed – hoped – was buried somewhere in her heart. One day at a time, he realized, threading his fingers through hers and drawing her the length of the hallway and back into the subdued light of the bedroom.

And he paused, his gaze locking with hers, all the love that he'd ever feel for this woman, and more, pouring out from each and every pore. And he smiled, and he reached out to touch her, to brush her cheek with the palm of his hand. And Ella smiled, just like the sun coming out from behind a cloud, and she turned her head to nuzzle his palm with her mouth and he knew that she'd turned that corner, that, however long it took, everything was going to turn out fine.

It was all a matter of time.

CHAPTER 2

A bad dream, only a dream, Ella reassured herself as the familiar objects in the room emerged from the darkness, began to take shape – the bamboo wing chair in the corner, the matching stool and dressing table, the rickety-rackety wardrobe that threatened to topple and pin her to the floor every time Ella opened the door. Oh, yes, and the rocking horse, an extravagant gesture from Jack the moment they'd realized Ella was pregnant.

'For the baby,' he'd explained indulgently, over ruling Ella's objections that they couldn't afford it, and that since the baby was barely a twinkle in their eyes toys like this wouldn't be needed for at least a couple of years. But Jack had simply laughed, hugged her fiercely, kissed away her objections. And, taking her cue from Jack, Ella had ignored the chill shiver of premonition that was trickling down her spine, smiling despite herself.

The baby. And the next one. And the next. Tiny scraps of humanity that had never stood a chance, she recalled, the tears beginning to stream unheeded down her cheeks. No babies, ever, for Ella at least. Too cruel.

The past, over and done with. Gone but not forgotten, she recalled with a bitter twist of the lips, and, though she lay back on the tear-dampened pillow, willing herself to relax, to sleep, the memories refused to go away, her mind locked in the past. Her past. Her marriage. Her Jack. Only not any longer. Because she'd driven him away.

'One man, two, a dozen . . .,' she'd scorned in a particularly bitter moment. She'd needed her baby and any man would do. Only she'd been bluffing, of course, hitting out, hurting Jack. Ella's revenge for Jack's daring to walk away and leave her.

Not that he'd gone through with it, though heaven alone knew why, Ella acknowledged, remembering, seeing herself as Jack must have seen her, hating herself. Fat and frumpy, not to mention half-drunk. And Jack, wonderful, wonderful Jack, had tried so hard to save their marriage. How he must have loved her – once.

'One man, two, a dozen . . .' Sheer bravado at the time, but for years the hateful words had come back to haunt her in the dark hours of the night. Bad dreams, guilt-ridden nightmares and always the same unremitting scene, word for painful word, touch for touch, glance for glance, until time had begun to dull the ache, and, having finally reached rock bottom, there'd been nowhere else for her to hide.

Rock bottom and the only way was up. Too late for her and Jack, of course. But not too late for Ella to regain her self-respect. So – since she hadn't suffered the nightmare for months – why now?

Ella sighed, running her fingers through the tangle of her hair. Stephen. A thoughtful employer, a very good friend. Too good, Ella acknowledged wryly, aware that, whilst they hadn't come as a surprise, Stephen's words had unwittingly triggered the demons of the past. And tonight she'd be giving him his answer.

'Oh, Ella,' she murmured wearily, checking the time in the half-light and pushing the duvet away as she swung herself upright, thrust her feet into the mules parked ready beside the bed. 'What on earth are you going to say to Stephen?'

'But why, Ella? *Why*?' Stephen demanded incredulously. 'We're good together. We make a good team, and, damn it all, woman, you must have known the way we were heading. I don't understand. Why can't you marry me?'

Ella winced, hearing the pain in his words, seeing the pain in a pair of cloudy blue eyes and yet shockingly aware that in marrying Stephen she'd end up hurting him even more. She didn't love him. Never had, never could. And yet Stephen was right in a way. They *were* good together – but only as friends and colleagues. She could see that now. And, yes, she'd seen the way things were heading; Stephen had made no secret of his hopes.

So, whilst Gramps was the main reason behind her decision to move on, to find a job closer to the home she'd never known as a child, Ella was achingly aware that it was Stephen's growing attachment that had finally forced her hand.

How to let him down gently? She took a long sip from the glass of iced mineral water. Stalling, she realized, and, swallowing the water along with the lump in her throat, brought her gaze back to the man sitting opposite.

'I'm sorry,' she murmured, forcing a smile. 'I only wish I could. But it wouldn't be fair,' she pointed out softly, willing him to believe it. 'To either of us. Marriage is a serious step, an absolute commitment, and since we've both been married before – '

'It's a case of once bitten, twice shy, I suppose?' he interrupted bitterly, blue eyes pinning her. 'For you, at least. And to think I didn't have you down as a coward. Afraid, Ella? Of me, I wonder? Or yourself? Though on second thoughts,' he railed, with devastating insight, 'I guess you're still carrying a torch for that bastard who let you down in the first place.'

Ella flushed. 'Wrong, Stephen. Nobody let me down,' she said with a curious lack of emotion. 'Believe me, I managed that all by myself.'

'Irrelevant, since it's soured you for anyone else,' he flung out heatedly. 'And that's the real rub, Ella. You're stranded in the past, in love with a man you haven't seen in years, a man you stubbornly refuse to discuss. Such a waste, Ella. Such an awful waste,' he repeated, shaking his head, his reproachful gaze raking her face, searching for an answer and reading that answer in Ella's troubled eyes. 'You still love him, don't you, Ella?'

'In a way,' she acknowledged frankly. 'As a man that I've lived with and known, shared the good times and the bad. But not in the way that you mean. And it's over. He went his way and I went mine – my decision.'

Not quite true, of course, since the decision to part had been a joint one, but Ella had been the one who had finally walked out, for good that time, yet if the tiny white lie helped Stephen to understand then surely it could be forgiven?

Stephen smothered a sigh as the anger drained from his features, and, watching him, Ella felt herself beginning to waver. *Could* it work? she mused, aware that her instinctive refusal to even consider remarrying was based on self-disgust.

She'd failed once and she would never forgive herself for the pain she'd caused. She had been sober enough throughout the brandy-sodden haze to know she'd been an out and out bitch to Jack. But she'd been hurt, and confused, not to mention afraid – so afraid for the child she could never carry to term, for the man she loved and was terrified of losing. Because Jack had wanted their child every bit as badly as she had. And Ella had failed him – on every count – and then she'd driven him away with her taunts and her drinking and her hate.

No, not hate, she amended, even though she'd said the words more times than she cared to remember.

Only love. But Jack's love, like the babies, had died. Ella had killed it. And yet, she acknowledged frankly, marriage to Stephen would be based on a whole new footing.

With a son and a daughter he openly adored from his marriage to Louise, Stephen had no plans to expand his family further. So – could respect and affection rather than love form a sound enough basis for marriage? she mused, turning the idea over in her mind. There was no shortage of either, as the last couple of years surely must prove, and with Stephen's plans for expanding his chain of hotels the length of Britain and ultimately to Europe, their relationship would never lack challenge.

A relationship. Man and woman. A solemn commitment. Not love, she acknowledged sadly, not in the conventional sense at least. She didn't love Stephen, and the good-looking Stephen Tolland, for all his declarations, was too shrewd ever to allow his heart to rule his head. But a commitment to work together, stay together – and a physical commitment, Ella's racing mind tagged on, aware that Stephen's kisses in the past few weeks had been growing more and more heated, while exploring fingers had traced the curves of her body, urging Ella to relax, to respond, only slowly, oh, so slowly, as if Stephen instinctively knew that to move too fast would cause a terrified Ella to bolt.

And how ridiculous. A grown woman terrified of the responses of her body. A grown woman more skittish than a Vestal Virgin. One man, two, a dozen

. . . Her lips twisted wryly. An empty threat if ever she'd heard one. Only Jack. Only ever Jack. Unless she married Stephen. So – the sixty-four thousand dollar question. *Could* she marry Stephen?

Catching Ella's half-smile, Stephen visibly brightened. Crumpling his napkin into a ball, he reached out across the exquisitely set table. 'Come on,' he urged, long, tapering fingers closing round Ella's with a squeeze of reassurance. 'Since the night's still young, we might as well make the most of it,' he murmured, tugging Ella through the archway and across the expanse of carpet to the cushions of a generous sofa that beckoned anything but cosily in Ella's churning mind.

'You can make yourself at home while I make the coffee. And later,' he added, cupping her face in his hands and dipping his head to brush her lips – barely a touch but more than enough to set the adrenalin pumping madly through her veins. 'Later, you and I are going to have round two of our discussion. And I give you due warning, Ella,' he tagged on huskily, 'that this time I shall refuse point-blank to take no for an answer.'

CHAPTER 3

'Jack Keegan! I don't believe you've heard a word I've said.'

With a huge effort of will Jack brought his mind back to the present. Daydreaming. At his age. Better than nightmares, he supposed, aware that he was tired, bone-weary, the anything but restful night he'd just endured wreaking its revenge on the day.

He smiled ruefully. 'Sorry, Fliss. I was miles away. What were you saying?'

'It doesn't matter now. And don't call me by that ridiculous nickname. You know I can't abide it.'

'No.' Generous lips twitched, but the venomous glance she shot across the table put paid to the comment on the tip of his tongue. Wrong time of the month, he decided, turning his attention to the wine list.

'The Domaine Picquemal,' he ordered, sensing the wine waiter's discreet presence at his elbow.

'Wine? At this hour of the day?' Elegantly plucked brows arched their disapproval.

'It's lunchtime. We've just ordered a first-class meal and I, for one, need a drink.'

'Fine. I'll have a Perrier water, if sir doesn't mind?'

'Sir doesn't. But the wine wouldn't hurt. Not a glass, at least.'

'Calories,' she reminded him. 'One of us has a figure to think about.'

'She certainly does. And believe me,' he added, his appreciative glance travelling over her, lingering on the soft swell of breast beneath the fine lawn fabric of her blouse before homing in on the proudly jutting nipples, 'I think about it all the time.'

'Oh!' She coloured prettily and Jack swallowed a smile. Beautiful and vain she might be, but, like most of the attractive women he knew, Fliss was basically insecure. Hard as nails when it came to getting what she wanted, but soft and vulnerable deep inside. Just like Ella.

Ella. He froze, his glass halfway to his lips. Why now? he mused. He'd barely given her a thought in years but, having spent the night tossing and turning with images of his ex-wife running through his mind, he seemed to be having trouble banishing the shadows.

Ella. Pre-wedding jitters? he wondered. Hardly, since the wedding was months away and nerves were the prerogative of the bride. But something had opened the floodgates to the past. Exactly. The past. Over and done with, he reminded himself, switching his attention to the exquisite meal that had just been placed before him. Medallions of beef in a delicate pepper sauce. Pink and perfect.

'How's the sole?' he enquired, glancing across to find Felicity half-heartedly pushing a solitary mange-tout around her plate.

'Fishy,' she told him tartly, but she was smiling, and she obligingly took the hint, began to eat with a degree of enjoyment, aware that since he never ceased trying to fatten her up, her figure might well be on his mind. All skin and bone, he was apt to pronounce, only half-teasingly.

All skin and bone, he was indeed thinking. No chance of that lithe figure running to seed. Running to seed. What a strange expression. As far as Jack was concerned she was far too skinny – halfway to being anorexic, he wouldn't mind betting. All for the sake of fashion. Unlike Ella.

Ella. It was there again, that frisson of unease. Why now? he wondered, had been wondering all morning if the truth were known, but, topping up his glass, he took a long, hard pull of a very moreish wine and pushed thoughts of the past firmly back where they belonged.

'Do we have to drive up this afternoon?' Fliss enquired with a moue of distaste when Jack called for the bill. 'Can't we stay over, drive up in the morning?'

'No can do, honey. Interviews,' he reminded her. 'Nine o'clock sharp. And, since you'll soon be the lady of the house,' he told her, giving her shoulders a reassuring hug, 'you get to pick your staff.'

'Huh. Some perk. Though on second thoughts,' she added thoughtfully, 'that's not a bad idea. If it's left up to me, each and every female will be fat and frumpy and as old as the hills. Don't want the domestics getting their claws into the lord and master, hey, Jack?' she teased, with a playful dig in the ribs.

'Maybe I like my women frumpy and mature,' he retorted, laughing eyes sweeping the long, lean lines of her body.

To Jack's surprise, Fliss visibly bristled. 'Some men,' she reminded him acidly, her heart-shaped face fleetingly ugly, 'fancy anything in skirts. I trust you're not one of them?'

'And what do you think?' he asked, annoyed that she could even think it. Playboy he might have been dubbed in the press, but, like Ella, that was all in the past, and if the rat-pack of reporters had taken the trouble to delve a little deeper they'd have stumbled on the truth. His lifestyle was pure image.

An attractive woman on his arm, dinner in a high-profile restaurant, the latest West End show before dancing the night away at one of the top clubs. And then home. Alone. His lips twisted wryly. Some reputation. But then that sort of truth, he was all too aware, wasn't the kind to send sales figures soaring.

'Like I said,' Fliss repeated huffily, 'anything in skirts.'

'With a woman like you in my bed?' He gave an offhand shrug of the shoulders. 'No contest.'

He stood and watched as she sashayed across the marble-tiled foyer and a string of heads turned in her wake, focusing on that pert little bottom. Off to powder her nose. Literally, if he knew Fliss, but he'd caught the speculation in other men's eyes, the naked flash of hunger, envy, and he was smiling, the spurt of annoyance forgotten.

He'd packed and was ready to leave, suitcase stashed in the boot, but they needed to pick up Felicity's mountain of luggage before heading for the M1 and the leafy lanes of Staffordshire.

'A weekend,' he groaned, hauling yet another suitcase down the steps and wondering how on earth he would fit it in the car. 'Heaven help me when you finally move in. I'll need to hire a jumbo jet.'

'Just a private little plane,' she demurred. 'To whisk your loving fiancée back to the bright lights at double-quick speed. And if you're moving in,' she informed him sweetly, 'I'm moving in. Leave you alone with that harridan of a housekeeper?' she railed mock-severely. 'No chance. Besides, we haven't been together for weeks.'

'Very true, my love.' He leaned across to kiss her. 'And I'm glad. That you're moving in too. The house needs a woman's touch. And that "harridan of a housekeeper",' he reminded her, grinning broadly, 'must be seventy if she's a day, and retires at the end of the month.'

'Good. Next time we'll go for politically correct and hire a man. A male housekeeper. It has a certain ring to it, don't you think, and should be one in the eye for the neighbours?'

'I think they're labelled butlers, my dear. And, knowing our neighbours, someone's doubtless beaten us to it. Still, if it makes you happy, by all means hire yourself a dozen. As long as they're fifty, fat and frumpish,' he added acidly, 'I shan't have grounds for complaint. Mind you,' he mused with a flash of wry amusement, 'I think you're out of luck. Ian Sampson drew up the shortlist, and there's not a single male name to be seen, as I recall. Ready?'

'As ready as I'll ever be,' she agreed, climbing into the passenger seat and double-checking her appearance in the mirror on the flipside of the sun visor.

They lapsed into silence as Jack nudged the car into the busy London traffic, but once they reached the motorway and picked up speed Felicity perked up.

She'd been right about the wine, Jack decided, her constant chatter washing over him. Since he'd known he'd be driving, even a glass and a half had been a glass and half too much. But he'd needed a drink, hadn't needed a drink like that in years.

Ella, he acknowledged. Since the day she'd finally walked out, and he'd finished what was left of the brandy – more bottles than he cared to remember, even if most were half-empty – he'd gone years without so much as a sip of anything as innocuous as low-alcohol beer. Even now he drank sparingly, just wine with a meal mostly, and rarely in the middle of the day. So – just what was different about today? Why the sudden need?

Darting a glance at Fliss, he smothered a weary sigh. Ella. Heaven alone knew why, but she was eating away at his mind. Stupid, really, since they were all washed up years ago. And he was happy. For the first time in what felt like a lifetime he was content, and in six months' time he'd be marrying the woman of his dreams. Fliss. The Honourable Felicity Foxwood to be precise, elder daughter of Viscount and Lady Plumpton. And as different from Ella as chalk and cheese.

Felicity glanced across, caught his thoughtful gaze and smiled happily, her hand on his thigh sneaking imperceptibly higher.

'No, Fliss,' he almost growled, taking his hand from the wheel for a moment to cover hers.

But she simply laughed, leaned across and nibbled at his ear, her darting tongue sending shivers of heat running through him.

'You'll get us arrested,' he warned as the needle crept past seventy. 'Assuming we survive to tell the tale.' He signalled left, slowed, pulled into the middle lane and settled down to cruise before flashing her a warm, approving look.

Dynamite. And all his. Five feet eight inches of bubbly personality, with her hungry, elfin looks highly in demand and staring out week after week from the pages of countless glossy society magazines. Twenty-two and every man's dream.

He'd been amazed to discover they'd hit it off from the start. The same sense of fun, an interest in antiques, and, despite a love of the bright lights, a sparing approach to alcohol. She had an equally sparing approach to food that he didn't quite approve of, but he'd fatten her up in time. After all, she was young, still caught up with her image. She would be sure to relax when they finally settled down and the babies came along. Babies.

He froze, seeing Ella's stricken face when they'd given her the truth. No babies. Ever. The third miscarriage had put paid to that. No babies. No love. No marriage. No Ella. And heaven alone knew where she was now or what she was doing. She'd simply disappeared from his life the moment the divorce came through, and all his efforts to trace her since had been in vain. He'd failed her. He'd lost her. He'd loved her.

Past tense, he reminded himself. He had Felicity now. He loved Fliss. So why the sudden need to rake over the ashes of his marriage?

'Penny for them,' Felicity offered, breaking into his thoughts.

'Cheap enough at half the price,' he agreed, banishing the shadows with a massive surge of will. 'There's a service station coming up. I was thinking of stopping off for coffee. Interested?'

'I might be,' she acknowledged archly. 'But, since there's sure to be a travel lodge attached, why stop short at coffee? Let's go for the works. Bed,' she reminded him. 'After all, as long as we arrive before nine o'clock tomorrow morning . . .'

'Tempting. Very tempting.'

'But?'

'Did I say there was a but?'

'You didn't have to. It was written loud and clear in your big blue eyes. You've made other plans – have probably promised to speak to Ian ahead of the interviews if I know you. I'm right, aren't I?' she challenged as Jack's grin broadened. 'You're growing boringly predictable,' she told him huffily, folding her arms across her pert breasts. 'I can't imagine why I agreed to marry you in the first place.'

'Something to do with bed?' he suggested, not the least put out by her spat of ill humour. 'And my prowess between the sheets. And if my little tigress can be patient for just another hour,' he growled, 'I'll show her exactly what I mean.'

'Promises, promises,' she jeered, but she was smiling, as Jack was – though, disconcertingly, the thought of the night ahead wasn't enough to banish the shadow of Ella.

'Thank you, Mrs Murdstone. Coffee will be fine. If we need anything else, we'll help ourselves.'

'Well, if you're sure . . .'

Jack swallowed a smile. It didn't follow, but, fanciful or not, with disapproval oozing from every pore of the woman's thin and bony frame, the sniff did seem to hang on the air. 'I'm sure. And thanks again. It was an excellent meal.'

'Liar,' Felicity murmured only half under her breath, and Jack stiffened, his sharp eyes catching the dull flush that stained the older woman's face as she turned to leave.

'That was unkind,' he murmured, the moment the door closed.

'Unkind, but honest,' she allowed with brutal unconcern. 'Murdstone. With a name like that she could be straight from the pages of Dickens, and now that I come to think of it, she's probably just the right age to be exactly that.'

'Sixty-one,' Ian Sampson interposed, pouring himself another glass of wine and holding out the bottle in general enquiry.

Jack shook his head. 'Not for me, thanks. Wine, Fliss?'

'Felicity,' she insisted, the edge to her tone barely perceptible. Because he'd used the nickname she hated, Jack mused, or had his words of reproof hit home?

They moved through to the smaller of the drawing rooms to find the tray of coffee waiting.

'Progress indeed,' Felicity murmured with a pointed glance at Jack.

He ignored it. She was right. The house was a mess, despite the extensive redecoration, and the service anything but efficient. Still, things would change once the interviews were over and, with luck, by the end of the month the whole estate would be running like clockwork. And if Felicity really was serious about moving in, the management of the house would be in her capable hands as from tomorrow.

Yes, why not? Jack mused as the idea took seed. It would give her a definite stake in the place, underline her status with a batch of new staff, and might even keep the boredom at bay when Jack was abroad. A tall order, if he knew Fliss, but worth a try, and he made a mental note to have a word with Ian later, make sure the young estate manager allowed Fliss her head at the interviews.

Blissfully unaware of Jack's plans, Fliss curled herself up on one of the Chesterfields, Jack taking a chair to the side as Ian rummaged through his briefcase.

'I've made a copy each,' Ian explained, passing a glossy-backed wallet to Jack and placing Felicity's carefully on the cushions beside her.

She ignored it, thumbing through the pages of a society magazine while the two men perused the wad of information in a silence broken only by the soft rustle of pages.

'This is just a summary, of course,' Ian explained, pausing to sugar his coffee. 'And, though the final decision is yours, I've put an asterisk against the most promising. Most of the applicants are local, and with just the housekeeper's post residential that should please everyone. Don't want to start off on the wrong foot by antagonizing the village.'

'Oh, heaven forbid we put the peasants' noses out of joint,' Felicity put in, smothering a yawn, and, bored by her magazine, allowed it to close under its own momentum.

'Crude but succinct,' Jack acknowledged, his cold glance flicking over her. 'The estate won't run itself, Fliss. And, yes, the local economy will benefit, but we need them more than they need us, and only a fool would choose to forget it.'

'Whoops. Hit a nerve, did I?' she tossed out brightly. 'Sorry, darling. I simply wasn't thinking.'

'No.' His thoughtful gaze rested on her face, the classical angles and planes perfectly framed by the crop of silver-blonde hair. God, she was beautiful. Beautiful but spoiled. Hardly surprising given her privileged lifestyle. Lady of the manor.

Not for The Honourable Felicity Foxwood the relentless struggle to survive in a tied cottage, with indoor sanitation an unheard of luxury and the highlight of the year the hamper of food sent down from the big house on Christmas Eve. Until his father lost his job that was, and lost the roof over their heads that went with it, Jack recalled, scowling.

Sensing some of his mood, Felicity moved, leaning across to kiss him, and then, when Jack didn't respond, wriggled her pert body closer, her tongue darting between his clamped lips and into the secret recesses of his mouth, a long and leisurely exploration that set the blood pounding in his veins. 'Forgiven?' she murmured huskily, supremely aware of his reaction.

'You might be,' he conceded as Fliss smiled, stretched, almost danced across the floor to the sideboard.

'Scotch?' she queried, spinning round, her wide green eyes switching from Jack to Ian and back again.

Recalling that they weren't alone, Jack's gaze flicked to Ian, caught the flash of naked hunger on the other man's face as he locked his gaze onto Fliss.

A prickle of alarm ran through him. Jealous? he probed. Surely not. He loved Fliss, Fliss loved him, and the devastating effect she had on the male of the species hardly came as a surprise. So why the sudden concern? he mused, with that irritating line about while the cat's away the mouse will play running through his mind.

Not an impossible scenario, Jack could allow, but not the wisest of moves for an ambitious man. And if he hadn't known Ian Sampson long, it had been time enough for Jack to recognize a lot of himself in the younger man's drive to succeed. And as for Fliss . . . Jack shook his head, banishing the shadows. He was on edge, didn't like to admit to needing that whisky, but he took the glass Felicity proffered with a smile of thanks.

'And what happens to old Murdstone?' Felicity queried, flicking through the folder with as much interest as she'd previously given the magazine. 'After all, she's been here for years – was probably born here. Bad for the estate's image, don't you think, turning her out to graze at her time of life?'

Again, crude but succinct, only this time Jack recognized it for what it was – an olive branch, Fliss's way of making up for that earlier gaffe – and he flashed her a smile of approval as it crossed his mind that she'd done better than he. At sixty-one, the widowed Mrs Murdstone was clearly eligible for retirement, but beyond that Jack hadn't given her so much as a moment's thought, he realized with a stab of guilt.

'Don't worry,' Ian reassured them. 'She's moving to Devon to live with her sister. Miss Potts has been trying to persuade her for years, apparently, but, being a loyal and faithful servant, Mrs M had to put the house first.'

'And the pay-off?' Jack queried, aware that a state pension wouldn't go far these days.

Ian consulted his diary, named a sum.

'Double it.'

'Jack!' There was a pause, the estate manager's eyes locking with his in surprise, and then Ian smiled, shrugged. 'You're the boss . . .'

Exactly. And with his background he should have known, should have taken an interest. But he would have left the woman living in genteel poverty had it not been Fliss, and though Mrs Murdstone had come with the house, had technically been in his employ only for a month or two, that didn't entitle Jack to treat her like a worn-out glove.

'Andrews,' Fliss murmured, breaking the silence. 'Aileen Andrews-Watson. No relation to the first Mrs Keegan I suppose?' she enquired with sudden sharpness, darting eyes glancing from Jack's startled face to the neatly typed curriculum vitae in her lap and back again.

Jack went hot, then cold. Another ridiculous reaction since he and Ella had been divorced nearly eight years. 'I wouldn't have thought so,' he conceded carefully. 'Andrews is a common enough name, and this one sounds hyphenated.' And if his fingers shook as he turned the page, thankfully no one seemed to notice.

He found it. Aileen Andrews-Watson. Details brief even for a c.v. Thirty-one. Same age, then. Born in Stafford, lived and worked in Bristol. Hankering for home, at a guess. References impeccable, experience ditto, though the city hotel she was currently in charge of was a far cry from a former stately home in the depths of the country. Divorced, he registered. So, a Miss Andrews or a Miss Watson? he mused, assuming she'd linked her name to her husband's.

Yet definitely no relation to his ex-wife. Since Ella was an only child of ageing parents, and each of those an only child, he recalled, relatives of any sort had been thin on the ground for Ella.

'So what exactly happened to the former Mrs Keegan?' Felicity enquired deceptively mildly once arrangements for the morning had been finalized and a tactful Ian had made himself scarce.

Jack felt his colour rise. 'And what sort of question is that to pose after all this time?' he stalled.

She gave an offhand shrug of the shoulders. 'Just idle curiosity, I suppose,' she acknowledged, her skirt riding up as she stretched her legs the length of the cushions, allowing him a tantalizing glimpse of creamy white thighs above the tops of her stockings. 'Since you rarely mention the dear lady's name, I wondered what she was doing with herself these days. And before you ask,' she tagged on defiantly, 'with the wedding drawing close, it's hardly surprising she's on my mind.'

No. He supposed not. And he'd been dwelling on Ella himself over the past twenty-four hours or so. Uncomfortably aware of Fliss's unblinking gaze, he tugged at his shirt collar, dragging his tie free and loosening the top two buttons. 'Worried, Fliss? That's not like you.' He found himself goading her. Guilty conscience, he realized, though heaven knew he'd done nothing to feel guilty about. Apart from allowing himself to remember, dredging up the past with a relentless flow of images and thoughts once the dream had set them in motion.

'So?'

'So . . .' It was Jack's turn to shrug. 'Haven't a clue,' he conceded carelessly. 'And, since I neither know nor care, as far as I'm concerned, the subject's closed.'

'Why?'

'Why, what?' he heard himself bark edgily.

Expressive eyebrows rose. 'Another nerve?' she sneered. 'That's not like *you.* Something to hide, Jack?'

'Hardly,' he bit out. 'Since we've been practically living together for months and I can't make so much as phone call in private. No, Felicity,' he conceded coldly, 'I've nothing to hide, as well you know.'

'Just your resentment, apparently.'

'Meaning?'

'Meaning me. You and me. Living together. And your sudden need for privacy. Having second thoughts?' she enquired mildly – too mildly.

'What's the matter, Jack? Afraid the second Mrs Keegan will cramp your style?'

'You're not the second Mrs Keegan yet,' he rasped, hitting out without thinking. He was aware from the sudden surge of colour in her cheeks that he'd hurt her – dented her pride, more like, he tried to reassure himself – yet he hated himself, and wished the offending words unsaid. But it was too late. They'd spewed out loud and clear. Damage limitation, then. Apologize.

'Apologize for speaking the truth? Many a true word, hey, Jack?' she needled, stumbling to her feet and towering over him, five feet eight inches of quivering indignation.

Logging the stubborn set of her jaw, that steely glint of eye that past experience told him didn't bode well, Jack smothered a weary sigh. 'Don't niggle, Fliss. I'm not in the mood. The remark was uncalled for and I'm sorry. Let's leave it at that, hey?'

'My name,' she told him icily, 'is Felicity. Felicity Foxwood. And if you continue to push your luck, Jack Keegan, that's the way it will stay.'

He shrugged. An empty threat if ever he'd heard one. Call it off now, when the announcement had already gone to *The Times*, and with the church, reception and honeymoon booked and boasted about to her wide circle of friends? No chance. But he was tired. Too tired for the row he'd unthinkingly provoked.

He drained his glass, placed it carefully on the coffee table and then came lazily to his feet. Without so much as a glance in her direction, he headed for the door.

'Where are you going?'

He paused, turned, allowed his solemn gaze to travel the length of her, down one long, shapely leg, up the other. The hem of her skirt barely reached below the tops of her stockings, he noted subconsciously, and despite the weariness the muscles in his belly began to clench as his gaze climbed higher, in an almost tangible caress of thighs outlined beneath taut fabric. The thought of that luscious triangle at the apex of her legs set his pulse racing, and his gaze moved higher, pausing to focus on the rapid rise and fall of breasts beneath the flimsy blouse. She was angry. Or afraid. And he'd hurt her. And the dark circles of her jutting nipples were an eloquent reminder of the needs of his body. Oh, yes. Jack smiled. And hers.

'Bed,' he reminded her, piercing blue eyes switching to lock with hers. 'Remember?'

'I might do,' she conceded huffily. 'But maybe a girl needs a little privacy once in a while. Maybe I'd rather sleep alone.'

'Liar,' he said softly, and she flushed, her chin snapping up in defiance. Recognizing that mulish set of her mouth, Jack smothered his own annoyance. 'Come to bed, Fliss,' he said softly, coaxingly, moving slowly forwards. He paused when he reached her, close enough to reach out and touch, instinct telling him that she had to be the one to make the first move, physically at least. 'I'm sorry,' he insisted urgently, his piercing gaze pinning her. 'The comment was out of order and I'm sorry. Now come to bed and I'll prove it.'

'Like I said,' she reminded him, just those rigid nipples belying her words, 'maybe I'd prefer to sleep alone tonight.'

'Fine.' He swallowed a smile, caught a second flash of panic in her eyes and relented. Leaning forwards, and careful not to touch, he whispered in her ear. 'Bed,' he repeated. 'Sleep alone by all means,' he entreated. 'But later. Much, much later,' he growled. 'Love first, hey, my little tigress?'

'If that's what you want?'

'If that's what *you* want,' he demurred, his heated gaze sweeping over her again, and when still she didn't move, hardly seemed to breathe, just the parted lips and the rapid rise and fall of breasts betraying her, Jack dipped his head, running his tongue over the fabric of her blouse, homing in on the thrusting buds and logging her gasp of dismay as just as swiftly he pulled away.

'Bed,' he repeated huskily, snaring her wrist and tugging her to the door. And then he paused, cupping her face in his hands and gazing down at her, the expression in his eyes a solemn echo of the wonder in hers. 'Next problem,' he pointed out as he dipped his head again, this time to kiss her parted lips. 'Given this sudden need for privacy, my love, my room or yours?'

'A thorny problem indeed,' she conceded, head on one side as she made a pretence of considering. And then she grinned. 'Let's compromise,' she suggested impishly, already snapping the buttons of her blouse. 'My room – then yours.'

'Oh, good. A long night, then?'

'As long as a piece of string,' she informed him teasingly. 'Which means, Mr Keegan, that it lasts just as long as I want it to. Understand?'

'Perfectly.'

CHAPTER 4

As long as a piece of string. A very short piece of string. The drink, he decided, heading for the shower and careful not to wake her. The wine at lunch, at dinner, the unaccustomed Scotch. And he'd been overtired to start with. Hardly surprising he'd had trouble performing.

Performing? Jack grimaced as the cold jets of water punished his body. He wasn't a star turn at the circus, for goodness' sake. He was a man, with a man's needs, a man's pride. And he'd failed her. And for once Felicity had been perfectly understanding.

'Come and lie down,' she'd murmured, kneeling behind him, pushing her pert little breasts into the rigid muscles of his back. 'These things happen now and again. It's nothing to worry about. It's been a long day and you're tired. Now come and get some sleep. Sleep, Jack,' she'd repeated, her lips nuzzling the back of his neck as her hand reached round to scrunch the mass of hair across his chest. 'And in the morning . . .'

In the morning, he'd taken the coward's way out, slipped furtively out of bed, and he was fully dressed before he leaned across to kiss her awake.

'Eight o'clock,' he explained, closing his mind to her wide-eyed disappointment. 'And with the first of the interviews scheduled for nine, that just about leaves time for breakfast.'

'Not my idea of breakfast,' she pointed out sulkily, her hands snaking round the back of his neck, the threaded fingers refusing to allow him to pull away.

'Exactly.' He kissed her again, tugged gently but firmly free of her grip. 'You're much too good to rush,' he reminded, gamely resisting temptation as certain parts of his anatomy began to stir lustily into life. 'Later,' he insisted. Though not too much later, he silently amended. After all, for his own peace of mind, he needed to banish that faint but lingering doubt.

The phone call came through as he was pouring his second cup of coffee.

'Sorry, boss. Trouble.'

'Lloyd! What is it, man?' Jack demanded, his heart sinking. Lloyd Rafter was one of his top men, and, as a general rule of thumb, what Lloyd couldn't fix wasn't fixable.

'A walk-out. They've downed tools. Something to do with religion and the perils of the demon drink.'

The demon drink. Jack smiled despite himself. The way he felt this morning there was a lot to be said for giving the transient pleasures of alcohol the permanent cold shoulder. 'Can't you sort it, Lloyd? It doesn't sound like a major crisis to me.'

'Believe me, I've tried. But they're adamant they'll only deal with the Boss Man himself. Sorry, Jack, but the atmosphere's ugly, and it's my guess they'll raze the place to the ground if we don't give them what they want and soon.'

'How soon?'

'How does yesterday sound?'

Jack swore softly under his breath. The words might have been chosen to sound like a joke, but Lloyd wasn't given to exaggeration. And, since life in the Middle East was unstable at the best of times, it didn't take much imagination to picture the entire gleaming complex as a heap of burning rubble on the sand. A self-contained holiday village. In the middle of nowhere. Paradise on earth once it was finished. If it was finished. Jack had known he was taking the biggest gamble of his career in building it in a Moslem country.

'Boss?'

'Okay, Lloyd. I'll take the first plane out. Expect me when you see me.'

Easier said than done, he quickly discovered. Waste an hour and a half driving back to London to pick up a direct flight, or take the first connecting plane from Birmingham? Birmingham won. There was a flight to Frankfurt leaving in just over an hour and he booked himself on it. So – no time to waste. Thank goodness he hadn't bothered unpacking.

'Going somewhere?' Fliss enquired when he strode, grim-faced, into the bedroom. She was propped up in bed reading a magazine, the breakfast tray on the side ignored but for the cafetière of the coffee which she took strong, black and sugar-free, and, though his mind was several thousand miles away, his subconscious noted the untouched food congealing on the plate, the nakedness she'd made no effort to cover.

His already grim expression tightened. Disapproval. Mrs Murdstone's tangible disapproval at least. No wonder the old dear couldn't wait to retire. Tact. Never Felicity's strong point, although once they were married that particular bone of contention would disappear. Which led his thoughts neatly round to the interviews, and, since he'd already agreed with Ian that Fliss would take the lead, have the final say, one thing less to worry about. Not so the holiday village.

'Damn.' He'd been rummaging though his suitcase, double-checking for the passport and wad of travellers' cheques he carried as routine, and now he straightened, running his fingers through his hair.

'Trouble?' Fliss queried, raising an eyebrow.

He told her, logging her reaction, the furrowed brow, the sulky pout of the generous mouth.

'Sorry, darling. No time to explain. I'll phone,' he insisted. 'As soon as I can. And I'll be back before you've had time to miss me. A couple of days,' he added, fingers crossed that the infallible Lloyd might have read things wrong for once. 'And, since you'd already made up your mind about moving in, it looks like you're running the interviews. You're the lady of the house,' he reminded her, ignoring her scowl. 'So I'm leaving it all in your capable hands.'

'Ja-ack!'

'Sorry, darling. Can't stop.' He dropped a light kiss on the top of her head and slipped out of the room, closing the door quickly behind him, aware from the dull thud of impact that he'd managed it not a moment too soon.

He swallowed a smile. Knowing Fliss, he could probably count his blessings that the scalding jug of coffee hadn't followed the magazine across the room.

Two weeks. Two weeks of hell. Paradise on earth it would be once it was finished, but even life's little necessities couldn't be guaranteed in this sort of climate. What he'd give for the sheer joy of a cold shower, not to mention even half a mug of hot water to shave in. Jack grimaced as he ran his fingers over the three-day rasp of stubble. Still, nearly there. He'd be going home tomorrow – and not a moment too soon given Felicity's cold-shoulder treatment.

'A couple of days *you* said,' she'd pointed out coldly when he'd finally found the time – and the technology – to call her. 'You've been gone a week. A whole week, Jack. A whole week left alone in this God-forsaken place. I'm bored out of my mind.'

'With the lively Mrs Murdstone for company, surely not?' he'd teased, attempting to loosen her up.

'Since the dear lady packed and left the moment your back was turned,' she'd retorted huffily, 'hardly.'

Jack had gone cold. He might have known. 'What have you done this time?' he'd asked, not bothering to temper the note of condemnation.

'Nothing. Just told the old dear exactly what I thought of her slovenly ways. The place was a mess, the food overcooked and cold by the time it reached the table, and she didn't deserve so much as penny of that pay-off you insisted on making. You're a fool, Jack Keegan, letting the staff walk all over you. Luckily for you I'm not such an easy touch . . .'

The voice had gone on and on, rising and falling as the connection faded in and out. Only Jack hadn't been listening, his mind racing on, picturing Fliss, remembering the flash of naked hunger in Ian Sampson's eyes as he'd glanced across the room at Fliss; he had put Fliss and Ian together in the house, together and alone in the absence of a housekeeper.

A housekeeper. The prim and proper Mrs Murdstone. And Jack had smiled despite himself. He really was overreacting. Ian had a cottage in the grounds, for starters, and, as for Mrs Murdstone, a fine chaperon she would make if Fliss took it into her head to have a discreet fling. And she could be discreet when the fancy took her, Jack had mused. But the really awful thought that had just begun to dawn was that he wouldn't trust Fliss as far as he could throw her.

'So how are you coping?' he'd managed to put in edgeways, the idea of Fliss donning cook's hat and apron, not to mention dustpan and brush, banishing his scowl.

'Don't worry,' she'd pronounced airily. 'The Andrews-Watson woman was happy to oblige. She'd already worked her notice, so jumped at the chance to start straight away. Quite a coup,' she'd almost trilled. 'A double-barrelled housekeeper. It almost makes up for that bevy of butlers you promised.'

'And is that why you employed her?' he'd queried tartly. The decision to put Fliss in charge had clearly been the right one.

'Nothing to do with me, darling,' she'd laughingly demurred. 'I went shopping, gave the super-efficient Ian Sampson *carte blanche* to hire and fire the whole caboodle. But the woman's a treasure, as you'll discover for yourself – assuming you ever come home,' she'd needled, with a lightning change of tone. 'I thought we'd throw a party – a welcome-back-Jack-cum-housewarming. How does Saturday night sound?'

Dreadful. He didn't like parties at the best of times. Platefuls of nondescript food, warm, indifferent wine, even allowing for a raid on his cellar, and a houseful of strangers with their self-absorbed conversations. Give him a cosy dinner with friends any time.

But then he *had* let Fliss down, he reasoned, leaving her alone the moment she'd moved in, and they would need to invite some of Fliss's crowd sooner or later. And whilst never, rather than later, would still be too soon as far as Jack was concerned, he knew better than to push his luck with even a jokey reply.

'Perfect,' he'd conceded instead, expecting to be home and settled in plenty of time. Only he wasn't. But, with luck, he'd arrive before the first of her guests.

'Nice of you drop in.'

'I live here, remember?'

'Do you? Do you really, Jack? Or is this just your clever way of keeping the little lady safely out of sight?'

'Meaning?'

'Meaning me. Incarcerated in this mausoleum of a house in some dead-and-alive hole, leaving the lord and master free to play the field elsewhere.'

'And what's that supposed to mean?' he enquired, deceptively mildly, logging the high colour in her cheeks.

'You know. Don't add insult to injury by pretending otherwise. Insisting I move in and then leaving me alone while you fly away into the sunset.'

'You know where I've been and you know the trip was business,' he pointed out coldly, not bothering to add that the decision to move in ahead of the wedding had been hers and hers alone. 'Something came up, Fliss,' he reminded her, tugging at his tie and loosening his collar. And, though he'd taken the sting out of the dispute in the Gulf, he was sharply aware it was nothing more than a holding job.

A couple of weeks, a month at the most, and he'd have to go back and sort things out once and for all. He popped the buttons of a crumpled shirt. God, he was grimy. He needed a shave and a shower, and would sleep for a week once his head hit the pillow. But he'd the evening to get through first, or what was left of it, he conceded silently. He was late. Very late. Wouldn't have made it at all but for some clever juggling of connections and more money than he cared to remember greasing the right palms. But he'd made it at last. Logging the stubborn set of her mouth, the anger smouldering in a pair of green eyes, he was beginning to regret having made the effort.

'Sure. A two-week holiday, courtesy of Jack Keegan Holdings,' she sneered. 'You should do it more often; the tan suits you.'

'Since I left at the drop of a hat, the tan, as you so quaintly phrase it, is sunburn.'

'Poor you,' she jeered.

'Not really,' he conceded coolly. 'I run the show. I'm aware of the risks. I should have been more prepared.'

'Then let's hope you remembered your pack of three.'

'And what the hell does that mean?' he asked in a dangerous undertone.

Fliss had the grace to look ashamed. 'Nothing,' she said quickly, too quickly, swinging away and crossing to his wardrobe. 'We're late, Jack,' she reminded him from the depths of a suit rack. 'You take a shower and I'll pick out some clothes.'

'Thank you, but no,' he retorted politely, folding his arms and leaning back against the wall. 'I'm perfectly capable of dressing myself – always assuming I'm prepared to make the effort.'

The glance she shot across the room was wary. 'Fine.' She shrugged. 'Come casual, if that's what you want. Just don't take all night about it.'

'That isn't what I meant.'

'Oh?'

'Oh? Oh, what?'

She licked her lips. 'Just, oh,' she conceded uneasily, refusing to meet his gaze.

'Not good enough, I'm afraid,' he pointed out coolly.

'No.'

'So?'

'Are we arguing?'

'Apparently.'

'Why?'

'Something to do with an uncalled for remark about a pack of three.'

'Ah!'

'Yes. Ah.'

'Not very clever really, was I?'

'No, Fliss.'

'But you will forgive me?'

'Will I? Give me one good reason why I should.'

'Because you love me. Because you've missed me. Remember how you've missed me, Jack?' she pleaded softly, gliding across the expanse of carpet and coming to a halt before him.

And he looked at her, saw the shadows in her eyes, the hunger in her eyes, a hunger reflected in his own, and, yes, he remembered. He wanted her, and, but for that houseful of guests awaiting his anything but chirpy presence, he'd be able to take her now, swiftly, satisfyingly swiftly. Then he'd sleep the clock round and wake to find her dozing in his arms, and then the love making would begin in earnest and he'd take her again and again and again, and more than make up for the past two weeks of abstinence.

'Later,' he murmured, dipping his head to kiss her. 'Later,' he repeated huskily, 'I might just be in the mood to let a certain little lady beg nicely for forgiveness.' And though Fliss smiled her approval, the niggle conveniently forgotten, there was an enormous shadow hanging over the rest of the evening. In Jack's mind at least.

'It looks like our Felicity has fallen on her feet.' A disembodied voice, the words over-loud in the still night air.

'If I didn't know you better, Shelley, my love,' a deeper voice chided, 'I'd say that remark was bordering on the bitchy.'

The woman laughed, a high-pitched giggle that set Jack's teeth on edge. 'Oh, definitely bitchy,' she airily conceded. 'Bitchy, but truthful. Hunky Jack Keegan. Rugged good looks, a house fit for a princess – or in this case a viscount's daughter – and pots and pots of money. What more could a girl ask for?'

What more indeed? Jack echoed, smiling despite himself. Eavesdropping. At his age. And, since secret listeners rarely heard anything good about themselves, he moved swiftly and silently away from the open window.

He ambled away from the noise and the crowd, and, pausing at the top of the steps that led down to the ornamental pond, took a long, hard pull of the generous measure of Scotch he'd helped himself to before slipping almost furtively away, the mind-numbing and repetitive thump of the bass of what apparently passed for modern music still ringing in his ears.

Five minutes. A blissful snatch of peace and then he'd head back to the great hall, with its imposing oak panels, and dance the rest of the night away if that was what Fliss wanted.

A house fit for a princess. His house. A lifetime ambition realized. Because the grim years of his childhood were engraved on his mind. 'Here's to you, Dad,' he murmured with a sudden surge of pride, raising his glass in the gloom.

A stately home. Hardly Chatsworth or Blenheim. Not even close to the size and elegance of his nearest aristocratic neighbour just across the park at Shugborough. But all his. Bought and paid for by the sweat of his brow. A house fit for a princess. And if Felicity wasn't exactly dressed for the part in that skimpy froth of fabric, tonight she was the cat that got the cream – the centre of attention and loving it.

Catching the murmur of voices, and not wishing to be drawn into another mind-numbing conversation, Jack slipped soundlessly round the corner, leaning back against the wall, the chill of the brickwork seeping through his jacket. With a bit of luck the young lovers would find the early autumn air too cool for secret assignations and scurry away to find a cosier spot, one of the greenhouses, Jack hoped, knowing they wouldn't be locked.

Another vain hope. It wasn't so much a secret assignation as, like Jack, an escape from the noise, a gentle stroll about the grounds, the chance for a bit of a gossip no less. And his heart sank as he recognized the voices, recognized, too, that the original subject hadn't been exhausted.

'Oh, yes,' the faceless Shelley was explaining, faceless to Jack, at least, who'd long since given up trying to keep track of Fliss's wide circle of friends. 'Plumpton lost all his money. Gambling. He practically lives in the casinos. And our Felicity isn't the sort to sit back and let the vulgar matter of money come between her and an affluent lifestyle. Still, she might not be getting quite what she bargained for.'

'Really? This sounds intriguing. Isn't Keegan as well-heeled as she thinks?'

'Probably more so. Filthy rich. A self-made man. But a self-made man with a past.'

'You don't say?'

'I do. Wife number one. And when wife number two sues for that divorce, she might just discover it's a three-way split. That should put her pert little nose firmly out of joint . . .'

They drifted away at last, leaving Jack to stand and shiver. Wife number one. Ella. No matter where he turned he couldn't seem to escape from her lately. She was in his mind, inside his head, was dominating his thoughts.

Guilt, he decided, draining his glass and allowing reluctant footsteps to carry him back towards the house. Only natural, he supposed, since he was on the verge of getting married and needed to put his life in order. And the unknown gossips had been right about one thing. Money. Ella was entitled to her cut and yet had never claimed so much as a penny – was probably unaware that he'd finally made that dream come true, not so much by the wave of a magic wand as by sheer hard graft on Jack's part. But Jack knew he'd never have done it without Ella. Ella.

'Believe in yourself, Jack,' she'd urged all those years ago. 'If you want it badly enough, you can do it.'

He had, too. Unlike Ella. Babies. No babies for Ella. Babies for Fliss? he wondered, amazed they'd never discussed it. Engaged to be married and yet the vital matter of a family had never come up in conversation. And, yes, he wanted babies – eventually. He supposed Fliss did too. Only natural, being a woman, and, though she wasn't on the Pill, Jack had never taken any chances.

A pack of three. An unexpectedly bitter remark. A hint of resentment that he'd always taken charge? he mused. Or was Fliss hoping for an early baby? Still, if he didn't ask, he'd never know, and what better time than now?

'Babies? *Babies*?' she repeated incredulously. 'Are you mad? You drag me away from all my friends to ask if I'm ready for babies. What's the matter, Jack, fancy a bit of practice out here on the lawn?'

His face muscles tightened. 'Do you have to make it sound so crude?' he demanded. 'I'm talking about us, our future, our family. Not a quick tumble between the sheets.'

Or a tumble on the grass, he amended, but silently, aware that they were dangerously close to falling out, and how.

What was wrong with them lately? They'd been happy enough for months, had been engaged for three, but the past few weeks had been one long niggle – and he didn't need to cast his mind back to pinpoint precisely when it had begun. The dream. The night he'd woken up in a cold sweat and hadn't been able to catch his sleep. Ella.

The anger died. Ella. Heaven alone knew why, but whichever way he turned all roads seemed to lead to Ella, and it was suddenly vitally important that he made an effort to find her. Find her, pay her off, purge the guilt, he realized, running his fingers through his hair and wincing at the thought. Pay her off? Wash his hands of her once and for all was what he really meant. And to think he'd had the nerve to call Fliss crude. What a cold-hearted bastard he was turning into.

He swung away.

'Jack?'

He pulled up short. Engrossed in thoughts of Ella, he'd almost forgotten he wasn't alone. 'Fliss?'

'Let's go to bed.'

Bed. Sleep. A tumble between the sheets. Fliss's way of saying sorry. And right now he knew which he'd prefer. Stifling the panic, he spun on his heels.

'Tempting, very tempting, my love,' he lied, forcing a smile as her chin snapped up. For the truth was beginning to dawn in her eyes. It was little more than a fleeting shadow of doubt, but Jack knew he couldn't hope to hold that gaze and lie convincingly, and so he reached for her, held her, kissed her, nibbled at her earlobes, his words washing over her. Lies, all lies, he realized, hating himself, ducking the issue and sickeningly aware that sooner or later he'd have to force himself to face the truth.

'Later,' he reminded her, his hands absentmindedly caressing the warm, silky skin of her fragrant shoulders. 'We've a houseful of guests who'd doubtless understand if we disappeared for an hour or two, but leave it till later and the rest of the night is ours. Later,' he repeated, dropping a light kiss onto the tip of her upturned nose. And later, he vowed, if the effort half killed him, he'd give the performance of his life and be top of the bill in that circus.

A long night. As long as a piece of string, he recalled, his lips tightening at the memory. But if the party went on until the early hours, that would be one problem solved. Midnight. Too early to relax but at least there was no slowing of tempo, no flagging bodies. Bright young things. Like Fliss, twenty-two, twenty-three at the most and bursting with energy.

And why not? There wouldn't be one who'd risen before noon, Jack scorned, visibly scowling. And then he smiled. He wasn't being fair. Just because he was a self-made man, had worked his fingers to the bone, earned each and every penny the hard way, didn't mean he could condemn others for having been born into affluence. Even so, watching the mass of bodies gyrating on the dance floor made him feel his age all at once.

Loosening the knot of his bow tie, he snapped open the button beneath. God he was tired. And hungry. Hardly surprising given the iron rations of the past couple of weeks. And, having put the idea of food in his head, he wandered through to the dining room, his chin snapping up as his gaze swept the length of the exquisitely set table, logged the gleam of silver and crystal on a pristine damask cloth.

Pleasanter and pleasanter. Having steeled himself to face the debris and crumbs of the usual boring party fare – sausage rolls, quiche and the ubiquitous limp salads – arriving to find the chafing dishes on the sideboard hot, their contents recently replenished, not to mention first-class and varied, was a definite bonus.

Like a king alone in the throne room, Jack sat, pouring himself an excellent Chablis, an excellent *chilled* Chablis at that, as he tucked into strips of chicken in a delicate white wine sauce and the wild rice that proved the perfect accompaniment. He'd been spoiled for choice, lid after lid raised to reveal yet another piping hot and fragrant meal, and, almost like a schoolboy involved in a prank, he stole furtively back for seconds.

'Compliments to the chef, Jack?'

'Ian!' Jack beamed his approval, waved his estate manager to a vacant chair and poured him a glass of wine. 'Most definitely compliments to the chef,' he conceded, resisting the urge to reach for a piece of bread, wipe his plate clean. 'Mrs Andrews-Watson, I suppose? Or is she a thoroughly modern miss who goes by that strident handle, Ms?'

'You were right the first time. And, divorced or otherwise, there's a no-nonsense air of repelling all boarders.'

'Had your knuckles rapped already?' Jack teased, aware that, though he hadn't known Ian long, it had been long enough to detect his lady-killing instinct. 'Losing your touch, Ian? Dear me, things must be bad.'

'Just dipped a toe in the water, so to speak.'

'And she slapped you down?'

'She slapped me down.'

Jack grinned. Good. The last thing he needed was a housekeeper hungry for a man. Too many complications in a set-up like this. And with this fashion show scheduled for the end of the month, knowing the woman was efficient was a load off his mind. 'What's she like?' he mused, curiosity getting the better of him.

Ian shrugged. 'Difficult to say, really. Quite a looker, I suppose. Dark hair, almost translucent skin, and as for her figure . . .' He sketched an hour-glass with his hands. 'Hides it well beneath a voluminous starched apron, but an absolute stunner at the interview.'

Yes. Jack could imagine. Hardly the best of reasons for making the appointment, but Ian had been given *carte blanche*, courtesy of Fliss and her shopping spree, and, judging from the evidence so far, the decision had been a good one.

Jack had barely recognized the place when he'd walked in. The house was immaculate, lights that hadn't worked in weeks bathed forgotten corners in a warm, inviting glow, and if tonight's spread was anything to go by his new housekeeper was a treasure. He was looking forward to making her acquaintance in the morning.

'So what happened to Mrs Murdstone?' he enquired casually, discarding his napkin and leaning back in the chair.

'Straight up, Jack?'

'Straight up,' he agreed, already guessing what was coming.

'Felicity. They were never going to hit it off at the best of times, and without you to keep the peace . . .' Ian's voice trailed off apologetically.

'Yes. Still, she did accept that pay-off?'

'Quite touching, really,' Ian confided. 'Since she hadn't worked her notice, she wasn't expecting a penny.' He paused, shot Jack a swift, assessing glance. 'Under the circumstances, I took the liberty of slipping in two weeks' extra wages. I hope you don't mind?'

Under the circumstances. A tactful description of Mrs Murdstone's row with Fliss. 'You're the estate manager, Ian,' Jack reminded him. 'That's what I pay you for. And I'm beginning to see that you're worth every penny. Thanks. You don't know how good if feels knowing I can leave the place in your capable hands.'

'Leave?' The younger man frowned. 'But you've only just moved in. You're not thinking of moving out already, surely?'

'Not exactly. But, given the nature of my job . . .' Not to mention Felicity's hankering for the bright lights. Still, maybe she did have a point. A small private plane, a helicopter, even. He could more than afford either, could even afford the cost of a pilot since the idea of playing Biggles didn't appeal, and then the journey time to London would be negligible. He drained his glass. He'd make some enquiries first thing Monday morning, but in the meanwhile what he needed right now was a coffee.

Bang on cue, the door swung open.

'Katie! Good to know you're still with us.'

The young maid blushed to the roots of her hair. 'I'm working a month's trial, sir,' she explained, and, though it might have been sheer imagination on his part, Jack could have sworn she almost dropped a curtsey. Placing the tray of coffee on the table beside him, she backed to the door.

'The Andrews-Watson influence, I presume?' he enquired dryly, aware that being deferentially addressed as 'sir' would rapidly lose its novelty. And then there'd be a battle – his need for informality pitched against the housekeeper's need to keep up appearances. Inverted snobbery. But he was the boss, he'd make the rules – only gently.

'Got it in one,' Ian agreed. 'Since she was the first appointment of the day, it made sense to canvass her opinion.'

'And?'

'Most of the staff agreed to stay. On her terms.'

'Ah, yes, a month's trial. Inspirational. Disruption's kept to a minimum, the locals keep their jobs, and yet the new broom ensures the place functions like clockwork.'

'I'm glad you approve.'

'Like I said, that's what I pay you for.' And worth a pay-rise at the end of month, Jack added silently, making a mental note to make it a large one.

The door burst open and Fliss burst in. Jack's heart sank as he logged the expression on her face. 'We're moving on. One of the night-clubs in Birmingham,' she explained brightly. 'Might as well see what the provinces have to offer.' And, reaching his chair, she draped herself over his shoulder.

Ian, Jack noted, melted discreetly away.

'Come on, darling,' Fliss coaxed, sliding onto his lap and gazing up, green eyes dancing with excitement. 'Let's go and dance the night away. And before you complain you're in no fit state to drive, your ever thoughtful fiancée has ordered a fleet of taxis.'

'I can think of better ways to spend the time,' Jack stalled, craving sleep and beginning to feel trapped between the devil and the deep blue sea.

'Later,' she reminded him, her hands sliding round his neck as she urged his head down, her mouth warm and moist against his.

The weariness drained away as he felt himself respond. 'Now,' he contradicted thickly, the urge to place her on the table, spread her legs, push aside the flimsy barrier of her panties and, houseful of guests notwithstanding, take her there and then almost gaining the upper hand. 'I've waited long enough,' he growled. 'Bed,' he insisted, his tongue sliding between her parted lips, finding hers, entwining with it while his thumbs brushed against the soft underswell of her breasts. 'All night long. Or what's left of it.'

'Later,' she countered sulkily. 'I want to dance, Jack, dance, dance, dance till the sun comes up.' And she wriggled free and pirouetted across the floor, hands raised, her tall, lithe form shown off to perfection.

The long, long legs were encased in the sheerest of stockings, their lacy tops slipping into view as her hemline undulated in time to the music in her head. Jack's heated gaze climbed higher, sliding from the curve of her tiny waist to the swell of her pert little breasts, and, yes, she was braless, couldn't be anything but braless in that flimsy, halter-necked wisp of fabric, her nipples rigid buds that surely must ache for his touch as much as Jack ached to touch them.

His gaze moved on, fastening at last on her exquisite, elfin face framed by its silver-blonde crop, and the stubborn set of her generous mouth killed his need stone-dead. He couldn't win. If he capitulated and danced the night away he'd be in no fit state for love-play later, and if he was honest, brutally honest, the urge to take her now was nothing more than the need to prove himself, that single failure festering in his mind and eating away at his pride.

Pride. Nothing more, nothing less. A disconcerting thought, and since the implications didn't bear thinking about, Jack swiftly brought the shutters down.

'You're not coming.'

Statement, not question. Jack wasn't going and trying to explain would be a complete waste of time.

He shook his head. 'I'm bushed, Fliss. But don't let me stop you – '

'I don't intend to. Goodnight, Jack. See you in the morning – maybe,' she tagged on defiantly, already swinging away.

As the door clicked to behind her Jack slumped wearily in his chair, pouring another cup of coffee and sitting on for long, lonely minutes. He ought to go to bed. God knows, he was tired enough to sleep for a week. Only he didn't, sitting on, brooding, a million and one thoughts swirling in his mind.

And time and again he came face to face with the truth, and time and again he shied away from it. The truth. Pride. Self-respect. Nothing more, nothing less. Tired. Too tired to face it now. Time enough in the cold light of day.

A draught of air, a faint rustle of skirts and Jack froze, the thought that Fliss might have changed her mind anything but reassuring. Only she wouldn't have, of course, and so Jack didn't stir, knowing Katie would simply clear away around him.

'I'm sorry, sir. I didn't realize anyone was here.' A soft, melodic voice that certainly didn't belong to the young maid. 'I'll come back later – '

'No.' He cut her off, something in her tone triggering alarm bells, sending shivers of heat the length of his spine as his racing mind sifted the clues, the clues that had been staring him in the face for the past two weeks.

With a blinding flash of insight Jack knew, wanted to believe, hardly dared to believe, and, stumbling to his feet, he spun round, his gaze locking with hers across the bridge of time.

'Ella! Ella,' he repeated softly, wondrously, as the pieces of the jigsaw slotted into place. 'Oh, Ella, it really is good to see you.'

CHAPTER 5

Good to see me. I'll bet, she derided, but silently, logging the incredulity on his face, the look of sheer amazement. Because he hadn't known, hadn't the least idea she'd been on his payroll for the past two weeks. And though Jack might easily have been one of the guests, instinct told her otherwise. For if the Honourable Felicity Foxwood had been introduced as Ella's employer, the man standing before her was the power behind the throne. The boss. Her boss.

Only not any more. Because Jack Keegan was the last man on earth Ella was prepared to work for. So – that was it. She might have known the job was too good to be true. Have things go right for her for once? Her lips twisted bitterly. Oh, yes, and pigs might fly. Without a word, she spun on her heels, heading for the door.

'But – what are you doing?' Jack asked incredulously.

She halted, aware that she'd heard the words before, a long, long time ago. She sieved through the debris of her marriage and then she remembered.

Her words. That night he'd almost walked out on her.

And Ella smiled bitterly, giving him the answer he'd once flung at her. 'Surely it's obvious? I'm leaving. Walking out. Going.'

'But you can't.'

'Can't I? Arrogant as always, hey, Jack?' she needled. 'Well, have I got news for you. I not only can, but will, and am.' And, blinking back the tears, she reached for the handle, heard a rustle behind her and pulled up sharp as Jack's long, tapering fingers reached past to forestall her. Her head snapped up, and though the glance she shot back at him was venomous he seemed not to notice. 'Let me go, Jack.'

'No.'

'Fine. I'll go the long way round.' She side-stepped. An arm snapped smartly into place against the oak panel, pulling her up short and effectively cutting off the means of her retreat. Because to move would be to touch him, hardly skin-to-skin contact but more than she could bear, and, damping down the panic, she forced herself to take deep and calming breaths.

It didn't help. She knew this man and they could play this game all night if Jack was in tormenting mood, and, heaven knew, simply being in the same room as him was a torment she hadn't been prepared for. So – she licked her dry lips, a give-away gesture of nerves he'd be certain not to miss, and sure enough he smiled, that devastating smile that could turn her blood to water.

'Your move, I believe,' he invited, strange lights dancing in his eyes – such wonderful eyes, she acknowledged. The most devastating eyes in the world. The most devastating man in the world. Her husband. Ex-husband, she tagged on silently, bitterly, her lips twisting.

And, logging the pain, Jack felt his smile vanish, his whole expression softening as he took a step back, giving her space, the means to escape – though escape from Jack, she was beginning to think, was something she'd never do. 'Why, Ella?' he asked. 'Why?'

Why had she walked away? Why had she left him, disappeared without trace? Why had she loved him, rejected him? Or why had she walked back in without warning?

'Coincidence, Jack,' she told him coldly, taking the coward's way out. Besides, the past was dead and buried. He knew full well why she'd gone. The marriage had been over – dead. Just like her babies. She'd walked away because she loved him, because he deserved so much more than she could give. Babies. And sooner or later, despite the fine words, he'd have wanted that son and heir and then he'd have grown to resent her.

'Sheer coincidence,' she repeated, amazed she could sound so calm when her careful world had just come tumbling down about her shoulders. 'I was looking for a job in the area, and this one sounded perfect for my needs. But worry not,' she tagged on tartly. 'Give me ten minutes and you'll never even know that I've been here.'

'Why?'

'Why, what?'

'Why walk away from a job that's perfect for your needs?'

'You know very well why.'

'Because of me.'

'Because of us. Because I've got my life and you've got yours. And quite a life, too,' she added, the words spilling out and unintentionally bitter. 'Congratulations, Jack. It looks like you finally made it – and how.'

'Believe in myself, *you* said,' he tossed back accusingly.

'Yes.' The resentment died, had never really been there in the first place. Lord of the manor. He'd done well. Though, knowing Jack, he'd probably worked night and day to achieve it. He'd done it. And he'd done it alone. And yet with wedding bells in the offing, Ella amended, maybe he hadn't been alone.

Wedding bells. The knifeblade twisted. There'd been no hint of gossip downstairs, but as Alicia Murdstone had paused to wipe the dust of the place from her feet she'd seized her chance to have her say.

'It's indecent,' she'd muttered sourly, condemnation oozing from each and every inch of her. And, though Ella had done her best to ignore the bitter words, helping to carry the older woman's bags down to the waiting taxi had made her captive audience. 'That young miss cavorting about the house dressed in next to nothing. And as for sleeping together . . .' She'd sniffed loudly, thin lips pursed in disapproval. 'The wedding can't come soon enough if you ask me.'

Only Ella hadn't. Not knowing the 'young miss' or the master, she hadn't been interested – then. Jack. Yet another of life's devastating ironies. Jack, making love with another woman, married to another woman, fathering another woman's babies. And all with Ella practically within earshot. She felt the sudden sting of tears, dashed them away with the back of her hand and made to slip past.

'Ella?'

'Let me go, Jack.'

'Not like this. Not now. Not after all this time. Don't go, Ella. Not yet. Come and sit down. Come and have a drink.'

A drink. Her chin snapped up.

There was an electric pause and then, 'Oh, sweetheart, I'm sorry.'

'No!' She waved him away with an imperative slice of the hand. 'Don't. Don't say a word. Don't touch me, don't speak, don't even breathe. Just leave me alone. Are you listening, Jack?' she demanded frigidly. 'Just leave me alone.'

'Fine.' He ran his fingers through his hair in a strangely appealing gesture of distraction.

Not a grey hair in sight, she acknowledged, aware that time had been kind to the rugged Jack Keegan, that the laughter lines fanning from his eyes simply added character. The blond hair was slightly longer than she remembered, but still those wonderful silky tresses were just made for fingers to rake – her fingers

– and as for the mass that covered his chest – No. Her mind skittered away. Too much. Too much pain. Too much to have to endure it all over again.

'But I can't let you go. Not like this,' he added softly, almost pleadingly. 'Not yet at least. Sit down and I'll ring for Katie, order some coffee.'

'Katie's gone home.'

'Why?'

'Something to do with time, Jack. She works here, and, believe it not, slavery was abolished centuries ago.'

'So who's clearing away?'

'I am.'

'Alone?'

'Since everyone else went home hours ago, obviously.'

'Why?'

'Why, what?'

'Why leave yourself a mountain of work, a Herculean task? Good God, woman,' he berated unexpectedly, 'there's a houseful of guests. By the time you've cleared away, you'll be cooking breakfasts by the dozen.'

'I enjoy work.' True enough. It kept her busy, occupied her mind, drove her body to the brink of exhaustion. And by the time she was ready to drag herself to bed she might even manage a dreamless sleep. Dreams. Memories. Nightmares. And, for some inexplicable reason, after all this time, this man was at the centre of each and every one. Her lips twisted.

'Don't move. I'll make the coffee.'

Yes, sir. You're the boss, she might have retorted, snapping to attention, but didn't, half smiling at the thought. Her own sense of humour never ceased to amaze her. And, heaven knew, she'd need something to help carry her through the next few hours, the next few days. So, she'd drink her coffee, finish her night's work, have everything laid up and ready for breakfast and the moment Katie appeared she'd leave, take a taxi to Stafford and book herself into a hotel while she planned the rest of her life.

The rest of her life. Like the past eight years, glaringly empty without Jack. Jack. She felt the tears sting. Might as well face it, girl, you love him. Always have, always will. And knowing he was engaged to be married to someone else, that he'd been sleeping with another woman under the same roof as Ella, was surely the last straw. But, no. It might be a technicality, but since Jack had been abroad for the past two weeks, the fiery Felicity Foxwood had been sleeping alone. Leastways, Ella amended with a twinge of unease, that was the theory.

'She's very beautiful,' she acknowledged on Jack's return with the coffee.

'Who?'

'Don't play games, Jack, not with me. You know who I mean.'

'Yes.' A fleeting smile lit up his features. 'Fliss.'

Fliss. A pet name? A lover's name. Another knifeblade twisting. She accepted the cup of coffee, the brush of skin on skin almost causing her to drop it, but she recovered, just the give-away rattle of cup in saucer betraying her.

So – another deep breath. 'I hear you're getting married soon. Congratulations,' she said without rancour. Because she loved him and she did want him to be happy. She just didn't want to be around to witness the billing and cooing.

'Thank you. I guess I've been lucky. First you, now Fliss.'

'Lucky? Given the hell I put you through? Oh, Jack,' she scorned. 'Ever the gentleman. Or does looking at the past through rose-coloured glasses cancel out the pain?'

'Does it for you?'

'No. But then, I was the cause of it all. And most days,' she lied, swallowing hard, 'I don't even give it so much as a passing thought.'

'And me? Do I merit a passing thought or two?' he queried softly.

She dropped her gaze, focusing on the cup she was nursing in her lap. Coffee. Perfect coffee. Strong, white and sweet. He'd remembered. Or assumed.

'Do I, Ella?' he persisted. 'Do I?' Only she didn't speak, didn't breathe, didn't glance across. 'Ella.'

Soft, like the whisper of breeze on a summer's day. Soft, persuasive – dangerously persuasive. Because this man had loved her once and she'd never stopped loving him. She'd tried. Oh, yes, she'd tried very hard. But the very thought of other men touching her, kissing her, making love . . .

Even Stephen, she acknowledged sadly. For when it had finally come to the crunch, Ella hadn't had the strength to go through with it, not even to lay the ghost of her marriage once and for all. Because she remembered. Jack's touch, Jack's brand, every touch. Soft, persuasive, dangerous. Just like the words. 'Ella?'

Her head snapped up. 'No,' she told him brusquely, her tone unintentionally bitter. 'The past is over and done with. I've made a new life, and if the old one surfaces now and again, I simply put it down to one of those things. It exists but it doesn't impinge.'

He flinched, recovered fast, rugged features hardening. 'Good. You won't mind working here, then?'

'You are joking?' she queried politely.

'You know me better than that, Ella.'

'Apparently not, since the idea's ridiculous.' Unthinkable, unbearable, she tagged on, images flashing through her mind unbidden and unwanted: Jack and Felicity, together in marital bliss, frolicking round the house like the newlyweds they'd be, lying sated and naked in each other's arms when the dutiful housekeeper carried in the breakfast tray. The dutiful ex-wife.

Cruel, too cruel, and surely Jack must know he was asking the impossible. And when the babies came along – 'No, Jack,' she said harshly, placing the empty cup and saucer carefully down on the table.

'Don't ask – don't even think it. Like I said, give me ten minutes and you won't even know that I've been here.'

'But I do. And I will. And I want you to stay.'

'Why?'

He shrugged. 'Why not? You need a job. You're good at your job. Your references were excellent and the evidence here speaks for itself.' He waved an airy hand. 'You've turned the place around, Ella. You need a job and you said yourself this one suited your needs.'

'Past tense, Jack. I was wrong. I've given it a try and I was wrong.'

'Liar!'

She raised her eyebrows. 'So sure, Jack? You haven't changed one bit, have you?' she goaded.

'Maybe,' he acknowledged tightly, 'and maybe not. But you're ducking the question. You like the job. It suited your needs until I walked in. That's the real rub, isn't it, Ella?' And there was just the merest hint of a pause before he tagged on icily, 'Or should I call you Aileen these days?'

Her head snapped up, the sneer in his voice slicing through her. 'Call me what you like,' she invited coolly. 'It won't make a scrap of difference.'

'You're walking out?'

'Believe me, Jack, if I'd known, I'd never have walked in.'

'No, of course not. Like the failed relationships, what's another job or two in the space of a month? But take it from me,' he explained confidentially, blue eyes raining scorn, 'it doesn't look good on the c.v.'

'My problem, Jack. Like my private life. Private.'

'Maybe. But once you were my wife.'

'Exactly. Over and done with. Ex-wife. And quite a shock for the next Mrs Keegan when she discovers she's sharing you with me.'

'Hardly.'

'No. Quite.' Hardly. He'd hardly be interested in Ella with a girl like Felicity in his bed. Strange that in all this time he'd never remarried. Since he'd been the darling of the tabloids, the up-and-coming entrepreneur, rarely a week had gone by without his face appearing in one or other of the gossip sheets, and always with another bright young thing hanging on his arm. Only now he was engaged. And she was lovely. Young and lovely and fertile.

'So –.' He drained his cup, refilled it, held out the cafetière to Ella in silent invitation and simply shrugged when she shook her head. 'So tell me, Ella. When you walk out of here, what exactly will you do with yourself?'

'The same as before, Jack, survive. I managed then; I'll manage now.'

'Alone?'

'Of course alone.'

'No concerned Mr Watson lurking in the wings this time, then?'

She licked her dry lips. 'Mr Watson?' she queried carefully.

'But of course. Husband number two. A flash of inspiration adding his name to yours. It has quite a ring and creates just the sort of name that doesn't get forgotten. A definite advantage when applying for jobs like this. Much better than plain Ella Andrews.'

'Maybe,' she retorted warily. 'Though just for the record, Jack, I didn't walk out on you and straight into the arms of another man.'

'No?'

'No!'

'So tell me, Ella, just for the record, of course, if it wasn't another man, why did you walk out?'

'History, Jack. The subject's closed.' Had been closed for the past eight years.

'Damn it all, woman, you're not being fair.'

She raised a single, mocking eyebrow. '*I'm* not being fair?' she enquired with subtle emphasis. 'Well pardon me for breathing,' she sneered, hurting inside but damned if she'd let it show.

She had her pride; it was probably all that was left – though, heaven knew, it was more than she'd had in the dark days, the nightmare months of her marriage, and later, when the decree absolute had come through and the final link with Jack was severed.

'What exactly do you want, Jack?' she queried, saccharine-sweetly. 'A confession? A signed and sealed declaration that I let you down, failed you, made a mess of your life?' she berated, the swell of anger gathering momentum. 'Because if that's what you're expecting, you'll wait a long time.'

Guilt. She'd purged the guilt. Part of the therapy. Don't blame herself. No one to blame, not Jack, not Ella. No one to blame. Easier to blame, she'd realized. It had given her a focus. Hate. She'd hated herself, hated Jack, too, for a time. But most of all herself. Not guilty. Don't rake up the past, the guilt, the whole sordid interlude.

But how the hell not to with the past staring her in the face, large as life and every bit as devastating? Love. She loved him, had never stopped loving him. His angry face went out of focus, the well of tears taking her by surprise.

'Ella? Ella! Don't cry. Please don't cry,' he implored. And the soft words were almost her undoing. He darted forwards.

'Don't!' she insisted tightly, sniffing, needing a hankie. A large square of linen was pressed into her hand even as the thought occurred. 'Leave me alone, Jack. Just leave me alone.' Turning her back, she stemmed the tears with a massive surge of will, blew her nose, screwed the hankie into a ball and dropped it into the pocket of her apron.

'Ella.'

Close, so close. She could reach out and touch him. But he'd moved, giving her the space and time to pull herself together, only now he was standing behind her and Ella went rigid, every nerve, every instinct urging her to bolt, to put distance between them, a lot of distance. But, like an animal frozen in the headlights of a car, Ella couldn't move.

And again, so close she could feel the heat of his breath on the back of her neck, just the single word, 'Ella.'

A touch, a featherlight touch of fingers, almost sheer imagination, wishful thinking. Because she wanted him to touch her, and more, much more. She closed her eyes, clamping her hands to her sides in an effort to stay in control. Unfair, her mind screamed. He was touching her, caressing her, his words were washing over her and she was weakening, the needs of her body overruling the dictates of her mind.

Touch her, kiss her, take her. The very thought was enough to turn her knees to water. Stay strong. She had to be strong. She had to resist. How to resist with magic fingers raking out the pins of her hair, raking through the tresses, allowing it to tumble freely about her shoulders? And then Jack paused, such an exquisite, tantalizing pause.

'Ella – '

A discreet cough from the doorway, then, 'Boss?'

Jack swore, softly, eloquently, and Ella, suddenly free from the spell, seized her chance to swing away.

Jack's lightning reflex denied her as his hand snaked out to snare her wrist, her cheeks flaming as he pulled her up short. 'You, lady, stay right there,' he insisted when he finally released her, his expression grim as he turned to deal with the intrusion.

'Sorry, boss.' Ian Sampson's features were carefully neutral. 'I guess you didn't hear the phone.

Felicity called. The provinces are "dull", I quote, and she and a couple of others are driving down to London. You can expect her back tomorrow afternoon.'

'Maybe,' Jack tagged on acidly. 'And the rest of the guests? No, don't bother, let me guess. The minute daylight breaks, they'll be heading back here for a five-star breakfast?'

The younger man grinned. 'Got it in one. But if there's anything I can do to help?' he probed, his gaze flicking briefly, curiously, to Ella.

Jack shook his head. 'Thanks, but no thanks,' he insisted pleasantly. 'You've done more than enough already, and believe me, Ian, everything's under control.'

Under control. Ella turned the hysterical laugh into a genuine fit of coughing. Under control? The man was mad.

'Glass of water?' he enquired with a touch of asperity, once the door had closed behind the estate manager.

She nodded, watched as he crossed to the table to the jug of iced water she'd replenished less than half an hour ago – half a lifetime ago, she was beginning to think, so much having happened in a short space of time.

'Thank you.' No skin-to-skin contact this time. Deliberate? Ella mused, wondering if Jack had been as surprised as she at the heated scene Ian Sampson had unwittingly curtailed. And the muscles in her belly clenched as she remembered. Unfair. But then life generally was, she acknowledged bitterly, her lips tightening.

'So –.' The master of the house was back in control. 'To return to an earlier subject,' he murmured crisply, tugging his bowtie free and stuffing it into a pocket before casually snapping the top few buttons of the dress shirt. The shock of golden hair at his throat gave Ella a tantalizing glimpse of the mass that she was all too aware covered a powerful chest. 'I can't let you go. I need you here. You heard Ian. The gang will be back soon, and like pigs at the trough they'll expect to be fed before I send them on their way.'

'Fine.' Ella swallowed hard. Back to practicalities, the tender moment over, forgotten, doubtless regretted. 'I can go along with that.' And then she'd pack and leave, walk away – walk away from the man she loved. Brutal. But the story of her life, she was beginning to see. Only Jack was speaking, the words not quite making sense. 'What did you say?' she enquired politely.

'Daydreaming, Ella? That's not like you. You're doing too much,' he conceded on a lighter note. 'You've breezed in here like a breath of fresh air and transformed the place in the space of two weeks. No mean task, Ella, not to mention tonight's spread and the hassle of overnight guests. But carry on like this and you'll wear yourself into a frazzle. So the minute breakfast's over,' he smilingly insisted, 'take the rest of the day off and catch up on some sleep. In fact, why not take a couple of days? Leave Katie in charge. She's bright enough to cope, and if there's a problem – '

'No.'

'No?' He shrugged. 'Fine. On your own head be it. But you'll burn yourself out at this rate.'

'Unlikely, Jack. No job, no burn-out,' she explained. 'And, since I'm overdue a break, now's as good a time as any.'

'Meaning?'

'Meaning nothing's changed. I can't work here – '

'Can't – or won't?' he interrupted savagely.

She shrugged. 'Take your pick,' she invited sweetly, inwardly flinching as Jack closed in on her. But he didn't touch her this time, simply whipped her with that Arctic gaze, that rapier-sharp tongue.

'You're running away, Ella – again,' he castigated coldly. 'Running away from me, running away from life. And one day, believe me, you'll be forced to stand and face the truth.'

'Your version, Jack, or mine?' she sneered. 'Have some sense,' she berated. 'Think, man, think. It wouldn't work. You and me here. It wouldn't work. There'd never be a moment's peace. We'd be at each other's throats night and day, just like we are now. And what would the lovely bride-to-be think?'

'Leave Fliss out of this – '

'Keep her in blissful ignorance is what you're really saying. And that's the idea, isn't it, Jack? Heaven knows what's running though your mind, but it won't work. It's unfair. The idea's preposterous. It won't work.'

'Wrong, Ella. It's a job I'm offering. Nothing more, nothing less.'

'And the new Mrs Keegan? Will she approve? Will she even know, Jack? Or will this be our little secret?'

'Secrets? *Secrets?*' he hissed, his expression ugly. 'You've got a cheek. You turn up here with a whole new identity and have the nerve to hint about secrets. Aileen Andrews-Watson,' he sneered. 'Mrs Aileen Andrews-Watson. No wonder I couldn't track you down. You kept that one quiet, didn't you, Ella? Aileen. *Aileen*' he repeated incredulously. 'The new surname I can swallow, since you married the guy. But Aileen. Why the hell Aileen?'

'You wouldn't understand,' she murmured as his anger died.

'No, I don't suppose I would,' he conceded. 'And, since you're not on the verge of explaining, I don't suppose I'll get the chance. Unless – Ah, yes!'

He broke off, eyes narrowing suddenly, and, watching him, Ella went cold. 'Ella Keegan,' he murmured, as if testing the name on his tongue. 'Mrs Ella Keegan. My wife. To love and to cherish. Love. That's it, isn't it, Ella?' he demanded, angling his head, eyes as sharp as diamonds. 'You love me. And ditching my name was a desperate attempt to deny it. A new name, a new husband, a new life. Only it didn't work. Because you still love me.'

'No!' Cruel, too cruel. He was miles out in his assessment and yet devastatingly close to the truth, to forcing the truth from her. Only he mustn't.

'Yes!' he insisted, and he was touching her, fingers digging into the skin of her upper arms as he pulled her close, dangerously close, just a hair's breadth between them. The urge to give in, to sway against him, to feel the length of his body against the length of hers, have his arms close round her was a luxury she simply couldn't afford. Because then he'd have his proof. Jack wouldn't want her, but Ella would have given in, would have betrayed herself – and how! And she closed her eyes, praying for the strength to resist him, to deny him. He shook her.

'Yes, Ella,' he repeated. 'Yes, yes, yes!' And then he kissed her.

Her lids flew open in alarm, her eyes meeting his gaze, flinching from the knowledge in his, the knowledge and a fleeting surprise that he'd masked in an instant. And then he was holding her, kissing her, wanting her, the unmistakable hardness at his groin sending waves of heat running through her. She was drowning, drowning, drowning.

Resist. Be strong. He wanted her. Want. Not love. Never love. All gone. She'd killed Jack's love years ago. Want. Nothing more, nothing less. Resist, Ella, resist.

Pulling away, she logged his pain, the hurt, the sheer disbelief that she could choose to deny him. 'No, Jack,' she said without emotion, her eyes nuggets of ice – ice that was matched by the coldness in her heart. 'No, Jack.'

And she swung away before he could reply, head held high as she walked with leaden footsteps to the door, aware of the man and the screaming silence behind. But she would go. She had to walk away. Because she loved him.

'Proof, Ella,' he goaded, and she halted – only polite in the circumstances – but she didn't turn, didn't respond, simply stood and waited, the scalding tears coursing silently down her cheeks. 'Walk out on me by all means,' he entreated silkily. 'But at least wake up to the truth. You love me. Always have, always will.'

'No, Jack,' she repeated, fingers clenched as she struggled with the threads of self-control. 'No, Jack. What else can I say to make you believe it?'

'Not a thing, Ella. Not a single word,' he conceded tersely. 'But you can stay. Your contract, Ella. Three months. Three months and then you're free to go. Prove it, Ella,' he challenged softly. 'If you really don't love me, the easy way to prove it is to stay.'

CHAPTER 6

If. Such a little word, such huge implications. If. If she runs away, can't face him, then it's obvious she still loves him. And if she doesn't . . . What has she to lose by staying? If.

Too busy to think, thank goodness. Breakfast. The debris of the evening piled high in the kitchen. Seven o'clock. And she was tired, too tired to think. But Katie would be here soon, along with the others, and with a dozen or more breakfasts to cook, the next couple of hours would be fraught.

Nothing like as fraught as the hours leading up to them, Ella acknowledged, straightening, brushing a stray lock of hair behind an ear. Unhygienic, she knew, but since Jack had loosened it she hadn't had the heart to loop the long, flowing locks back into the prim and proper pleat she wore low at the back of her neck while she was working. But fraught nonetheless.

Decision time. If. Damned if she did and damned if she didn't.

Evidence. Jack Keegan's version of the truth. Only he was wrong. Clever Jack Keegan had sifted all the facts, put two and two together and – bingo! She must have remarried. Well, fine. If that was what he chose to believe, then let him. The c.v. didn't lie. Divorced, she'd stated, and divorced she was – from Jack. And the reason for her change of name was simply none of his business.

Breakfast. She kept it simple. Cereal, fruit, croissants and jam, and all the chafing dishes on the sideboard. Sausage, bacon, kidneys, mushrooms, tomatoes and scrambled eggs. Not the mountains of food she'd prepared the previous evening. Because the bright young things, her years in the hotel trade had taught her, would have burnt themselves out on the dance floor and in the bars. So, just enough to tempt the jaded palates of the hangover-free.

'Seems a waste of time bothering, if you ask me,' Katie murmured primly. She was still young enough to disapprove, the mellowing influence of age sure to prove elusive for a year or two. 'Not to mention the cost of the food. And with all those starving children in the world –.'

'Worry not, Katie,' Ella reassured her. 'Nothing will go to waste. Like last night's casseroles, we'll freeze what we can and use what's left in savoury dishes for the rest of the week.' Pancakes, risottos – a million and one ways with leftover everything and precious little waste. Cook, freeze, thaw, cook, serve. And all in small, manageable portions neatly stacked on the shelves of the huge walk-in freezers.

Katie shrugged. 'Well, if you're sure . . .' she allowed doubtfully. 'We've always thrown it away in the past. Mrs Murdstone was very particular about her food.'

Ella swallowed a smile. She could well imagine. Like her Dickensian namesake, Mrs Murdstone's views would be strictly Victorian. 'I'm sure,' she told Katie tartly. Only she wasn't. She simply wasn't sure of anything – not any more.

Taking Jack at his word, she slipped out after breakfast, wheeling her bicycle down the drive and then pausing to stand and look at the house, an impressive Jacobean reconstruction with intricately carved gables and ornate window bays.

Two weeks. Two whole weeks of living there without the least idea that Jack was the owner. Hardly surprising since the super-efficient Ian Sampson had conducted the interviews in the absence of Ella's employer, The Honourable Felicity Foxwood. And if her fun-loving employer was content to leave everything in Ian's capable hands, who was Ella to criticize? Besides, she'd been too busy settling in to give thought to the set-up.

Oh, yes, she'd known there was a man in the background – wasn't there always with women like Fliss? And had thought that no doubt he'd appear in the fullness of time. But in the meanwhile she'd had work to do – simply finding her way around the maze of corridors, for a start, not to mention whipping the place back into shape.

Yes, it was a magnificent house in a wonderful location, and, with Gramps's cottage just a ten-minute bike ride away, simply perfect for Ella. Then the catch twenty-two. Jack. Turning up like the proverbial bad penny. Hardly, Ella amended, since the house was clearly worth a small fortune.

Stifling a sigh, she threaded her hair through an elastic band before steadying the wobble on the handlebars and pushing down hard on the pedals. She'd spend the afternoon with Gramps, brush away some of the cobwebs and then head back to Sherbrook to supervise supper for whoever was in residence.

Decision time. And, rightly or wrongly, Ella had made up her mind. She was staying. For now.

'Just himself,' Katie explained on Ella's return. 'Everyone else was packed and gone by eleven.'

'Supper for two, then,' Ella said briskly. 'I'll cook, you can serve, and the moment they ask for coffee you can slip away. I'll take care of the rest. And thanks, Katie. You've worked hard these past few days, and don't think I haven't noticed.'

'Thanks. It's been hard graft but I must say I've enjoyed it,' Katie admitted, plump cheeks colouring at the unexpected praise. 'You're fun to work for,' she confided shyly, colouring again. 'And if it hadn't been for you, Mrs A, I wouldn't have had a job at all.'

No. Ella frowned. Ian Sampson had been given the power to hire and fire and, but for Ella's intervention, half the staff would have been out on their ears. And in a rural community like this the resentment would have festered. But if Ella had secured them a second chance, like Katie, then it was now down to each to prove their own worth.

'Supper for two?' Katie echoed absentmindedly, the carton of eggs she'd taken from the fridge clutched fiercely to her chest. 'No, Mrs A. Like I said, just himself.'

Mrs A. Ella swallowed a smile. She might have known her name would prove a stumbling block. Miss A would be more accurate, she supposed, but she wasn't about to provoke speculation by splitting hairs. And then Katie's words sank in. 'What did you say?'

'Just himself. For supper,' Katie added, sensing Ella's confusion. 'I told you. Everyone else has gone.'

'Yes, I know. I heard you. But – ' She broke off, caught Katie's curious gaze and forced a smile. 'Supper for two,' she repeated brusquely. 'Miss Foxwood's expected later, and as sure as eggs is eggs, the moment the meal is served is the moment she'll arrive.'

Katie shrugged, an eloquent lift of the shoulders that gave Ella the distinct impression she wasn't convinced. Progress of sorts, Ella decided, cracking the eggs into a basin and whisking them to a froth. After all, two short weeks ago Katie wouldn't have thought twice about airing her opinions. Not that she had need to. When the untouched omelette was returned to the kitchen, Katie's smug but silent I-told-you-so spoke volumes.

One down, eighty-nine to go. Day one of life with Jack. Yet not so much life with Jack as, like the past eight years, a glaringly empty existence. But the decision to stay had been the right one, Ella decided as the long day began to draw to a close. As long as Jack could be trusted to keep his distance.

'What are you doing, Ella?'

'Jack!' She swung round, almost dropping the bowl she'd been about to replace on a shelf, his appearance out of nowhere thoroughly unnerving. Keep his distance? She might have known she was asking for the moon. 'Do you have to sneak up on me?' she demanded tartly. 'And what on earth are you doing down here?'

'Would you believe, visiting the kitchen – my kitchen?' he emphasized slyly.

'I'm surprised you know the way,' she heard herself deriding, and, suddenly all fingers and thumbs, placed the bowl on the dresser before it could slip from her grasp and shatter at her feet.

'For your information, madam, I not only know the way, but am perfectly capable of making myself at home. Coffee,' he explained. 'Since the rest of the staff leave at seven, and *you*,' he reminded her grimly, 'were under strict instructions to take the day off, I thought I'd help myself.'

Ella shrugged. 'Be my guest,' she invited, waving an airy hand. And then she remembered. His house. His kitchen. His coffee. Her cheeks flamed. 'Though on second thoughts,' she told him brusquely, 'you pop back upstairs and I'll make the coffee.'

'Why?'

'You know perfectly well why.'

'Yes.' Generous lips twitched their amusement. 'Something to do with keeping up appearances and preserving the social order. Familiarity breeds contempt, and that kind of stuff.'

'Precisely. And, since the experience is new to us both, we might as well start as we mean to go on.'

'Cosily?' he enquired dryly.

'No, Jack, not cosily,' she retorted tartly. 'You're the master and I'm the – '

'Mistress?' he interrupted provokingly.

'Chief cook and bottle-washer,' she snapped, colouring again despite herself. 'Nothing more, nothing less. So in that case, sir, perhaps you'd care to return to the drawing room?'

'Not especially,' he conceded, but he obligingly took the hint, began to stroll leisurely back across the quarry-tiled floor. 'Only make it the den,' he tossed back matter-of-factly. 'Definitely cosier. And bring an extra cup.'

Two cups. So Felicity was back. Ella went cold. She couldn't do it. She'd thought she could but when it came to the crunch she was kidding herself. Sleep in the same house as Jack and his lover? Too cruel.

Straightening, she ran her fingers through her hair and faced the sobering fact. She'd have to leave – tonight. And Jack would know, would jump to his own arrogant conclusion. He'd know, and there was nothing Ella could do to convince him he was wrong. Ah, yes, but since he wouldn't be alone when she handed in her notice, he wouldn't be able to goad her.

A fleeting smile lit up her features. Thank heavens for small mercies.

Five minutes later she paused outside the door, bracing herself to knock. For if making the decision was one thing, following it through was something else again. Heart thumping nineteen to the dozen, she took a deep breath and stepped forward, almost dropping the tray as the door swung open on its hinges.

'Ella. I thought I heard your step,' Jack murmured pleasantly, taking the tray not a moment too soon and waving her through as a second wave of panic gripped her. 'Come in,' he urged. 'Don't stand on ceremony.'

And, steeling herself for the anything but pleasant sight of Jack and his fiancée together in domestic bliss, she hesitantly crossed the threshold.

'But – ' She flushed, spun round, eyes wild. 'You're alone?'

'Not any longer,' he pointed out smoothly. 'Take a seat, Ella, make yourself at home.'

Another surge of emotion – anger that Jack was back to playing games. 'Oh, no!' she rasped, annoyed with him, more annoyed with herself for jumping to conclusions. 'No way, Jack. What the *hell* do you think you're playing at?' she demanded. 'You and me and a cosy little chat over coffee? You can't be serious,' she railed. 'You're the boss, for heaven's sake. You've an image to project and I'm – '

'My wife?'

'Ex-wife,' she bit out, damping down the panic. Over, done with, finished. They'd gone their separate ways and life had gone on for them both. Until now. 'This isn't going to work, Jack,' she tossed out bitterly. 'I told you last night the idea was ludicrous.'

'Three months,' he reminded her silkily. 'Three months, you promised.'

'But that was before – '

'You realized you loved me?'

'Before I remembered your warped sense of humour.'

'So who's laughing?'

'Not me, that's for sure.'

'No. Yet you had a sense humour in the good old days.'

'Bad old days.'

'If you say so,' he murmured provokingly, pouring the coffee. 'Strong, white and sweet?' he queried politely, holding out the cup. 'Unless you've changed?'

'Of course I've changed,' Ella snapped, making no move to take the coffee, or the seat that he'd waved her to. 'Eight years, Jack.' Eight long, lonely years.

'That isn't a cue for me to say you don't look a day older, by any chance?'

'No, Jack.'

'No? Well, it's true. Oh, yes, you've changed; I'll grant you that,' he allowed, in response to her snort of derision. 'But you can take it from me, it's a definite change for the better.'

And those piercing blue eyes dropped from her face, sweeping the lines of her body in a long, slow perusal, an almost tangible invasion of her body as they lingered on the swell of agitated breasts that rose and fell beneath the crisp white cotton blouse, and then moved down, to the curve of her waist, and on, lower, assessing, appraising, touching almost. And then the gaze began its slow climb the length of Ella's long shapely legs, paused at the junction of her thighs, a tantalizing pause while Ella held her breath, felt the sudden dampness in her groin and knew that her need for this man had never gone away, would never go away.

His eyes moved on before reaching the now glowing cheeks, her frightened eyes. 'Oh, Ella,' he breathed, his eyes fastening onto hers and seeing to the centre of her soul. 'You really are wonderful.'

'And you're engaged to be married,' she bit out. 'Remember?'

'Jealous, Ella?'

'No!'

'So why the sudden concern?'

'A simple matter of fairness, Jack.'

'To Fliss? Strange,' he mused with a flash of wry amusement, 'I hadn't realized you two were friends.'

'You know very well we're not.'

'No. Just card-carrying members of the same exclusive club, apparently. Women. Females. Feminists. The sisterhood,' he needled. 'Shall I go on?'

'Trust a man to trot out that stale issue,' Ella scorned, more amused than annoyed. 'What's the matter, Jack? Feeling threatened? And in your own home at that.'

'Just trying to find my way around the tortuous maze of the average woman's mind,' he admitted.

'Since the average woman, like the average man,' she pointed out sweetly, 'doesn't exist, you'd be wasting your time.'

'Where women are concerned, average or otherwise, nothing is ever wasted, Ella. Like I said, anything that helps crack the code has to be a bonus.'

'My, my, you *do* feel insecure,' she scorned. 'Adoration in short supply, Jack? Feeling neglected? Or is one woman simply not enough to feed that ego?'

'Maybe it all depends on the woman in question, Ella.'

'Oh, I'm sure it does,' she demurred. 'Which brings us neatly back to where we started. Felicity. The loving fianceé. Absent, maybe, for now at least, but no less tangible.'

'And, let me guess, you've no intentions of letting me forget it?'

'If you were even halfway to being a gentleman,' she needled, 'you wouldn't need reminding.'

'Your definition or mine?' he queried, not the least put out by Ella's condemnation.

'Neither. Why waste time trading insults when a dictionary definition can provide the perfect answer?'

'And miss out on all the fun, Ella? Fun,' he repeated. 'A neat, three-letter word that can make all the difference in life. But if you've really forgotten what it means,' he scorned, folding his arms, blue eyes openly mocking as they raked the lines of her face, 'while you're thumbing through that word bank why not look it up? You'll find it under F. F for fun.'

'And what about F for Felicity?' she riposted.

There was moment's stunned silence, then, '*Touché*. I guess I should have seen that coming.'

'You should indeed,' Ella agreed, smiling broadly. 'But don't be too hard on yourself,' she soothed sweetly, leaning forwards and patting his arm. 'After all, you're only a man.'

'And you're back to spouting feminist views.'

'F for feminist?' she mused. 'F for fiancée? Or, at the risk of sounding repetitive, should it be F for Felicity?'

'And if Felicity wasn't in the picture?'

If. Such a little word, such a devastating meaning. And Jack was playing games, dangerous games, probing, testing. Because Jack was a man alone with a woman, and not just any woman. Oh, no, she conceded, folding her arms and returning his gaze with cold and steady defiance. A woman who'd walked out on him, rejected him, hit out squarely where it hurt, at his manhood.

Ella swallowed hard. 'Irrelevant, Jack, since she is.'

'Yes.' Another of those strange, fleeting smiles that seemed to tug at her heartstrings. 'And in that case, Ella, consider yourself safe. Sit down. The coffee's growing cold.'

Just like my heart, she acknowledged, perching warily on the edge of a chair. Safe. Trust Jack to know she was petrified. Jealous, yes. Hardly worth debating since she loved the guy. But safe? How could Jack have known she was so afraid, and afraid of what exactly? So, back to that resolution. Resignation time. Only Jack was alone, would know, would use that knowledge to taunt her.

Ella licked her dry lips, smiling inside despite it all. A neat alternative had just popped into her head. The coward's way out, she'd be the first to concede, but to borrow Jack's phrase, safe. She'd simply leave him a note. Only not tonight. She was tired, hadn't slept a wink in the past twenty-four hours. And definitely not when Jack was in the house. Instead she'd pick her moment. She'd pack, watch, wait, and the minute Jack was out of sight she'd leave, find another job in the area.

If all else failed, she'd simply swallow her misgivings and head back to Bristol. And if that took her away from Gramps for a while, Ella would make it up to him another way. Poor Gramps. She smothered a twinge of conscience. He'd been so proud to learn she was following in his footsteps, would be living at the house where as boy and man he'd given a lifetime's service. But there was nothing she could do about it now.

No guilt. Part of the therapy. She wasn't to blame herself when things went wrong.

Gramps. Ella's features softened. Gramps and Jack. Ironic, really. So much in common – Ella, for a start, not to mention that austere background. Only Jack had finally made it. And if the grandfather whose very existence had come as a surprise to her was proud to know Ella was working there, think how tickled he'd have been to see her installed as its mistress. Mrs Jack Keegan of Sherbrook. Ella could almost see the funny side. But where Gramps had nurtured a dream, Jack had made the dream come true, for himself at least.

'I guess you must have loved him.'

Jack's voice nudged her out of the reverie, soft, probing, the underlying pain taking her by surprise.

'Who?' she queried warily, draining her cup, the coffee long gone cold.

'The man you were thinking about just then – and it was a man,' he insisted with devastating insight, blue eyes brimming with hurt. 'Wasn't it, Ella?'

'Yes.' No point denying it. 'And present tense, Jack, since I always will love him,' she added without thinking as Gramps's weatherbeaten face swam into view. So many wasted years to catch up on, so few to come. Unfair. Just like everything else in her life, Ella railed silently.

'Tell me about him.'

'Why?' Wary now, she felt the shutters coming down. Because Jack had caught her off-guard and she'd already given away more than she'd intended.

'Call it idle curiosity,' he conceded almost carelessly. 'The prerogative of the first husband.'

The rejected husband was what he really meant. The only husband, if Jack but knew it. And, though she could explain, fill him in on the whole sorry tale,

Ella preferred to keep him at a distance. Safer that way. Because Jack would understand, would say all the right words, would break down her guard with his pity. Pity. When all she'd ever wanted was his love.

So, she licked her dry lips, blinked back the tears, eyed him uneasily. 'What exactly do you want to know?'

'Quit stalling, Ella. You know what I'm asking.'

Yes. How did he compare with Jack? Why had it gone wrong? And, since the second husband didn't exist, except in Jack's mind, what on earth could she say? 'He's – '

'A fool, Ella,' Jack interrupted harshly. 'But then I guess that makes two of us.'

'Oh?' she queried as tiny hairs on the back her neck began to stand on end.

'I shouldn't have let you go,' he surprised her by conceding. 'I should have put up more of a fight, stopped you walking out on our marriage.'

'But I didn't walk out on the marriage, Jack,' she reminded him softly. 'I walked out on us. You and me. It wasn't working.'

'Ah, yes. The relationship wasn't working. And why was that exactly? Because of us?' he queried nastily. 'Or because of him?'

Her chin snapped up. 'Oh, Jack. How could you? How could you insult me by even thinking it?'

'You're saying it isn't true?'

'Since that's what you clearly believe, why the hell should I bother saying anything?' she railed bitterly.

'The truth, Ella. I simply want the truth.'

The truth? A failed relationship with each of them forced to accept a part in it? Or Jack's twisted version? That Ella had found herself another man?

So easy to lie. One tiny little lie would keep him at that distance. No more lies, she told herself, no more guilt. She'd already shouldered more than enough.

'Like I said,' she repeated tonelessly, coming to her feet in a slow, unhurried movement that belied her inner turmoil. Because she didn't need to lie. She could tell by his face that he'd already made up his mind. Jack's truth. And it hurt; it hurt like hell. 'If that's what you want to believe,' she invited, 'don't let me stop you.'

'Afraid, Ella?' Jack challenged silkily. 'Running scared? Now, why, I wonder? Afraid to face the past?' he taunted softly. 'Or the future?'

'Neither. Believe me, Jack, I laid my ghosts years ago – eight years ago to be precise.'

'I see.'

'Do you? I doubt it,' she bit out, swallowing the pain, masking the pain, because she'd had a lifetime of practice – half a lifetime with Jack, half a lifetime without. Only she mustn't goad. Let sleeping dogs lie. Jack had his answer, and if Ella had any sense she'd leave it at that. Swallowing hard, she brought the subject to a close, in her mind at least. 'Good-night, Jack,' she murmured pleasantly.

'Ella?'

'Now what?' she pulled up short, hands stuffed into the pockets of her skirt, eyes fixed on the pattern of the carpet – rug, she corrected automatically. Persian, new, and worth a small fortune. She was beginning to crumple, the tears that had never been far away for the past twenty-four hours starting to sting. Only she wouldn't. Not again.

'Because of us?' he repeated softly. 'Or because of him?'

The truth. Because Ella had been wrong. The doubt was still there, was festering in Jack's mind, and Jack had a right to know.

'What do you think?' she responded, angling her head, meeting that gaze, seeing the pain and inwardly flinching. Because she loved him, had never, ever stopped loving him.

'My fault, Ella. Whichever way you look at it. My fault.'

'No!' She darted forwards, the knifeblade twisting. 'No, Jack. Not your fault, not mine. It simply wasn't working – '

'But it might have done, Ella. It wasn't too late. We could have worked at it, worked round the problems, found a way – '

'No, Jack. No, no, no,' she repeated urgently, tugging at his arm and forcing him to meet her gaze. 'No, Jack.'

'No.' He thrust her away, his expression hardening as the truth dawned – his truth at least. 'Of course not,' he conceded bitterly. 'I was right in the first place. Another man. Only that didn't last either,' he sneeringly reminded her. 'So, maybe not my fault after all – hey, Ella?' And then, inexplicably, irrationally, 'Why the hell did he make you change your name to Aileen?'

'Don't you like Aileen?' she queried absurdly.

'Yes! No! I don't know. Yes, if you must know,' he admitted wearily, running his fingers through his hair in heartbreaking distraction. 'Like the rest of your double-barrelled name, it has a certain style. But you didn't answer the question,' he pointed out tersely.

'No.' She smiled, caught another flash of pain in bottomless blue eyes and realized she wasn't being fair. 'He didn't,' she acknowledged softly. 'Force me to change my name, I mean. And, like I told you last night,' she reminded with the merest touch of asperity, 'Neither did he feature in the breakdown of our marriage.'

'But you love him?'

'Yes.'

'And he's hurt you?'

'No.'

'But – it doesn't make sense,' he conceded, slumping down into his chair and gazing up at her. 'I don't understand.'

Ella gave a mental shrug. Surprise, surprise. He'd been out of her life for the past eight years, hadn't given her so much as a second thought if the truth were known, yet all of a sudden arrogant Jack Keegan needed to understand. And then a snatch of conversation popped into her head out of nowhere: 'No wonder I couldn't track you down.' Jack's words less than twenty-four hours ago, not registering then but clearly stored away at the back of Ella's mind.

It was Ella's turn to struggle with the sense of things. He'd tried to find her. And, *yes*, she'd gone to ground, had needed time and space to lick her wounds. But why should Jack want to find her? Why?

'Why, Ella?' An unwitting echo of her mind, only this time, at least, she could give an honest reply.

'Simple, Jack,' she smilingly confided, and the need to keep it to herself was no longer eating away at her. Because Jack *had* cared once, must have cared since he'd tried to find her. 'I traced my roots – discovered Aileen had been my mother's name, my name on the original birth certificate.'

'And you liked it better than Ella?' he mused, reaching his own conclusion. 'And your mother?' he queried politely, angling his head.

'Long gone, I'm afraid,' Ella explained without rancour. 'Like the rest of the family.' Apart from Gramps, and she was keeping him to herself. 'She died. Soon after I was born. Father unknown. Hence the adoption.' And now she was sharply aware that she risked, though wasn't inviting, his pity.

'And did it help?' Jack probed, his expression carefully neutral. 'Discovering you had roots? Or did it hurt that the trail petered out before it had begun?'

'I found me,' she said simply. The truth. Aileen Watson.

She turned, began to walk away. The long day was drawing to a close and she was tired, so very tired –

would sleep for a week once her head hit the pillow. And she *would* sleep, she realized. Because in a strange sort of way she'd found peace.

'Ella?'

She halted, spun round to face him, saw the shadows in his eyes, and all the love she'd ever felt for this man came flooding back with a vengeance. Her expression was fleetingly tender, Jack's expression softening as his eyes locked with hers. 'Jack?' she queried softly, holding his gaze.

'Ella or Aileen?'

'To you, Jack?' she probed, instinctively reading his mind. And she smiled. 'Oh, Ella,' she told him simply. 'Your Ella. Always your Ella.'

And it was true. Because she loved him. Aileen Watson was the mother she'd never had the chance to love, and using the name that Ella had been given at birth was a way of giving pleasure to Gramps. But to Jack, to herself, if she was honest, she was Ella. Ella Keegan. And always would be.

CHAPTER 7

'Good morning, Ella. I trust you slept well?' Jack enquired, appearing bang on cue in the doorway.

'Like a log,' she told him sweetly, her heart leaping at the sight of him. Because she loved him. And if it wasn't quite the truth, then the dreams had unravelled all the gentle things, all the good things about their marriage.

Swinging away, she busied herself, placing the last of the breakfast things carefully in the centre of the table, using the few precious moments it gave to compose herself before turning back to face him.

'Are we short-staffed?' he enquired, frowning as Ella pushed the cafetière within reach of the single place setting. Not the oak-panelled dining room this morning, since Jack was eating alone, but the sun room at the side of the house, south-westerly facing and designed to catch the sun for as many hours as possible, especially in the dreary months of winter.

'Not that I'm aware of. Why?'

'Your job description. Housekeeper. And in need of modification, apparently. You're paid to manage, I seem to recall, to carry the can when things go wrong, not run around the house fetching and carrying. That's for Katie and the others to do. At least, that's the theory.'

'Thank you. It's nice to know I have my uses. But, as I told you the night of the party, Jack, slavery's illegal. And in case it's slipped your notice,' she pointed out tartly, 'There's a cunning little perk called a day off.'

Jack grinned. 'Let me guess – Monday is Katie's?'

'Got it in one. And, since it's barely seven o'clock, the others haven't yet arrived.'

'So what happens when there's a houseful?'

'Overtime. Time and half for Saturdays, double pay Sundays and evenings. Any objections?'

'To the way you seem to be running things? Not at all. The house runs like clockwork. Believe me, Ella, the lovely Mrs Murdstone didn't hold a candle.'

Ella swallowed a smile. So she'd gathered. Not that she'd listened to gossip, since gossip wasn't allowed when she was around, but, despite its recent redecoration, the state of the house when she'd first moved in had spoken volumes.

'So, when's yours?' Jack queried, shaking out his napkin.

'My what?' she enquired, running a critical eye over crockery and dishes, double-checking there was nothing she'd forgotten.

'Your day off?'

'Oh, I fit one in around and about,' she explained airily. 'As and when, you know.'

'As a matter of fact, no,' he contradicted her, blue eyes narrowing as he angled his head. And he sat back in his chair, folded his arms, refused to allow her to look away. 'You don't take one, do you, Ella?'

'Like I said,' she repeated, squirming beneath the frankness of his gaze. 'As and when. An hour here, an afternoon there. If and when I need a whole day, I'll work it into the roster.'

'Tomorrow.'

'I beg your pardon?'

'A day off. Work it into tomorrow's roster. If that isn't too much trouble?' he queried.

'No-o . . .' she conceded carefully.

'But?'

'Exactly.' She raised a puzzled eyebrow. 'But. But, why? Am I missing something here?'

'Time to relax,' he explained. 'If you've nothing special planned, you can spend the day with me.'

'That, Mr Keegan, sounds suspiciously like work,' she informed him acidly. And hard work at that. 'Thanks, but no thanks,' she told him sweetly.

'But I'm the boss,' he reminded her slyly. 'And that sounds suspiciously like insubordination.'

'So it does,' she agreed, completely unperturbed. 'But if the master of the house doesn't like it, he knows what he can do. You'll just have to sack me, won't you, sir?'

'Ella – '

'Telephone,' she interrupted as sharp ears detected the familiar trill in the room next door, and, smiling broadly, she made her escape.

The smile lasted all of twenty seconds.

'Ah, Mrs Andrews-Watson,' Felicity drawled with a yawn in her voice. 'Looking after my fiancé, I hope?'

'I'm doing my best, madam,' Ella replied carefully. 'Mr Keegan's in the breakfast room. If you'll excuse me, I'll tell him you're calling.'

'No. Don't bother disturbing him. I've a plane to catch. A spot of shopping for the wedding. First stop Rome. He'll know where to reach me. If you could just let him know? Oh, and Mrs Andrews-Watson?' she added musingly.

'Madam?'

'About my fiancé. Like I said, I hope you're looking after him. But just remember there are one or two, shall I say, little attentions, that I prefer to handle myself. You do catch my drift?'

'Perfectly,' Ella clipped out, indignation and amazement vying for position. 'But if I was as worried as you seem to be,' she pointed out sweetly, 'Italy's the last place I'd be heading, Madam.' And, without waiting for a reply, she cut the connection.

'Trouble?'

She jumped guiltily. 'Not exactly,' she stalled, wondering how long he'd been standing in the open doorway and how much he'd overheard. She delivered the message, the relevant part at least, but didn't stick around to log his reaction. His fiancée. His problem. And one less thorn for Ella to deal with. Italy. Her lips tightened. But safely out of Ella's hair for a week or two.

Not so Jack, who seemed in no particular hurry to go anywhere, turning up like the proverbial bad penny in whichever room Ella was working. And, since there were countless dozens to choose from, it was most disconcerting.

Pausing now outside the library, an arrangement of flowers weighing heavy, Ella strained her ears. Silence. Because Jack was elsewhere, she mused, or because Jack was engrossed in his task? Nothing ventured, nothing gained, she chided herself, and, levering the handle with her elbow, backed herself into the room. She was relieved to find it empty for once, just the dusty ledger propped open on one of the desks hinting at his presence. Dust. Ella's lips tightened. She'd have to speak to Millie, but, in the meanwhile, Ella had come prepared.

Estate accounts, she noted idly, whisking a cloth from the voluminous pockets of her apron and wiping the fragile leather binding. And, quite without realizing it, she'd turned the first page, losing herself in the past, in a fascinating list of names and figures and household expenditures recorded in the neatest copperplate hand. Ella smiled. Thank heavens she wasn't expected to keep accounts like these.

And then she found what her subconscious had been seeking all along. Peter Watson: under-gardener. And, a dozen years further on, Peter Watson: head gardener. The page blurred. Roots. Her roots. Right here in this house. Just another of life's little ironies.

'Hardly bedtime reading, Ella.'

'Jack!' She jumped guiltily, blushed to the roots of her hair, fumbling clumsily with the ledger as she made to close it.

Jack's lightning reflex denied her and she froze, focused on the hand, Jack's hand, palm-down on the right-hand page, the tiny golden hairs on the back glinting in a sudden shaft of sunlight. 'Nice to see you taking an interest in the history of the house,' he acknowledged dryly.

'Just idly flicking through,' she explained, crossing her fingers at the tiny white lie. And, with Jack's hand effectively covering up the give-away name, she forced herself to relax. Glaringly obvious though it might be to Ella, it probably wouldn't register in Jack's mind. Peter Watson, a humble employee, just one of many on the payroll and doubtless long forgotten over the years.

Not so the lists of distinguished guests.

'Quite a revelation,' she babbled in relief. 'When the Earl and Countess of Shrewsbury came to stay just before the war, the dinner they were served would have fed a marching army.'

'I can imagine. First catch your wild boar,' Jack teased, with echoes of Mrs Beeton. 'And, while we're on the subject, have dinner with me tonight.'

'Why?'

'Because I'm asking. And since I'm the boss,' he reminded her, rugged features impassive, 'you can take that as an order.'

Ella flushed. 'If you insist. Sir,' she added pointedly.

He moved, allowing the ledger to close under its own momentum as he reached out to touch her, his palm cradling her cheek as his thumb brushed the delicate skin beneath her eye. 'Oh, Ella, Ella,' he reproved, shaking his head. 'That sounds suspiciously like insubordination to me. Again.'

And he dipped his head, kissed her – the merest brush of the lips but more than enough to fill her with heat, fill her with pain. She tried to jerk away, but Jack's free hand was snaking round the back of her neck and holding her steady.

'You, madam,' he murmured softly, pulling out the pins from the neatly coiled tresses and allowing her hair to tumble freely about her shoulders, 'have a lot to learn about the master of the house. When I give an order,' he growled, the words punctuated by light but devastating kisses. 'I expect instant obedience. Instant, Ella,' he repeated solemnly. 'Understand?'

And then he smiled, nodded, kissed her again.

A lifetime later he raised his head, smoky eyes locking with hers.

'Not a good idea, Jack,' she reminded him shakily.

'The kiss – or the dinner?' he probed.

'Both.'

'A matter of opinion, Ella. The master of the house doesn't agree. Dinner,' he repeated. 'Cook it yourself by all means,' he carelessly conceded. 'But Katie can serve it. The experience won't hurt her, and with double pay for evenings the same can probably be said for the money. Seven for seven-thirty. Dinner for three.'

'Three?' She twisted away, the pain scything through her.

'But of course,' he confirmed with a devastating smile. 'You, me and Ian Sampson. Business. With a fashion shoot planned here for the end of the month, there are one or two things we need to discuss. Business,' he conceded carelessly. 'Nothing more, nothing less.'

Stone-cold sober, Ella nodded. Playing games. She might have known. And like a fool she'd let him.

'What would you like to drink, Ella?'

An innocuous question really, with just the hint of hesitation betraying him. Sheer imagination, she might have concluded, had it been anyone else. Only it wasn't, and, ever the gentleman, Jack didn't want to embarrass her – or have Ella embarrass them all, she added with a flash of wry amusement. Not even remotely funny, she decided, sobering fast. Given the shame of her behaviour in the bad old days, Jack was entitled to be worried. He was also entitled to the facts.

'Tonic water, please. No ice.'

While Jack crossed to the drinks tray Ella took her place on one of the richly upholstered armchairs, inhaling deeply as she forced herself to relax, allowing her gaze to travel round the room. Not a single speck of dust daring to defy her, she noted with another flash of humour.

The green room was the smaller of the drawing rooms and, like the rest of the house, elegant, spacious and sumptuously furnished. Money was clearly no object, judging from the beautifully preserved period tables and the delicate figurines that graced one or two. Exquisite and understated. No vulgar show of opulence here, just unerringly good taste. Fliss's taste? she wondered. Or had Jack's love of antiques kept pace with his growing fortune?

'Thank you.' She took the glass, careful to avoid contact with the long, tapering fingers. His generous mouth she couldn't help but notice, was twitching provokingly at the corners. Ella bristled. Trust Jack not to miss a thing. Trust Jack to ooze confidence, with the poise of a sleek cat as he took the chair opposite.

He raised his glass – a dry white wine that Ella had placed in the cooler less than thirty minutes ago. 'To business?' he challenged. 'Or pleasure?'

'Oh, definitely business,' she agreed solemnly. 'Why else would I be here?'

'Why else, indeed?' he needled, blue eyes narrowing as he glanced at his wristwatch. 'Ian must be running late.'

'Yes.' An awful thought popped into her mind. Running late, or purposely not invited? Jack wouldn't. Jack would.

Seeing she was on the verge of challenging him, Jack grinned. 'Worry not, Ella,' he lazily reassured her. 'Ian will be here.'

'Did I speak?' she queried, flushing despite herself. 'Did I say a word?'

'You didn't need to, my love, it was written loud and clear in those beautiful hazel eyes.'

Impossible man. Ella drained her glass, jumping up and crossing to the sideboard. 'I'll help myself,' she muttered stonily, adding as an afterthought, 'If I may?'

'Be my guest.' He folded his arms, sat back in his chair perfectly relaxed, perfectly at home, blue eyes dancing as they locked with hers, moved across the lines of her face, down to the hollow in her throat and lower, logging the heated rise and fall of breasts beneath the fabric of her dress – a dress that she'd chosen with care for dinner with the boss. Not too formal, not too casual.

Just like Jack, in a lightweight suit a far cry from the dinner jacket he'd worn with ease the night of the party, but nevertheless made to measure and expensive, charcoal-grey and the perfect foil for the shock of blond hair, those piercing blue eyes.

Those eyes had moved down and were now beginning to climb the lines of Ella's body, and though she froze the currents of heat were swirling through her.

Approval. Jack's approval. For the pale green button-through dress that hugged the swell of her breasts, the curve of her waist before swirling over her hips and ending a demure inch and a half below the knee? she wondered. Or approval for the body beneath, the body he'd once known as intimately as his own?

Somewhere in the distance came the faint sound of a bell – the doorbell. Ella's sigh of relief was almost tangible.

'The cavalry?' Jack teased, seemingly aware of every thought, every nuance. Then, logging Ella's glass with its chill of condensation, his eyes narrowed suddenly.

Ella's turn to goad. 'Worry not, Jack,' she sneeringly echoed, taking a sip of the excellent Chablis and savouring it on her tongue. 'There never was a problem.' Not to do with alcohol, at least. 'Ironic, isn't it?' she acknowledged with a defiant tilt of the head. 'For all my efforts to drink myself stupid, I simply hadn't the capacity to push myself over the limit.'

'Straight up, Ella?'

'Worried, Jack?' she needled, holding his gaze.

His lips formed the ghost of a smile. 'Not worried,' he acknowledged softly. 'Just glad. Very glad.'

But of course – one thing less on his conscience, she derided.

She enjoyed the meal despite the devastating company; Ian Sampson's presence did much to ease the tension. In a strange sort of way he reminded her of Jack – similar height, similar build, but with darker hair and skin. And there was that hungry look in his eyes that had haunted Jack's in the old days. Ambitious. A bit of a ladies' man, as she'd already discovered, given the opportunity. Recalling the cosy little dinners he'd shared with Felicity while Jack was abroad, she smothered a twinge of unease.

'More wine, Aileen?' Aileen. Ella started, her eyes darting from Ian's quizzical gaze to Jack's vaguely amused expression. Aileen. The name no one but Gramps used. On Ian's lips it was strangely incongruous, though not as incongruous as it would have been on Jack's. Thankfully Jack had managed to avoid calling her by any name. So far.

'Thank you. No.' She pulled herself together, determined to make the single glass last the rest of the meal. Reassurance for Jack, proof that even under stress she could remain stone-cold sober, and, since they'd been brought together for business, all the more reason to keep a clear head.

Yet it was not so much a high-powered business discussion as a progress report, as it turned out, with a bemused Ella discovering there was a lot more to running the place than simply paying the wages. And with the comments fielded back and forth across her, she wasn't so much piggy in the middle as umpire.

'Enough!' Jack groaned when Ian finally paused for breath. 'The place is a bottomless pit. At this rate I'll be pushing up daisies before it begins to pay its way.'

Ian shrugged. 'Five years,' he soothed. 'And you won't recognize the place.'

'More changes?' Jack challenged lightly. 'With, let me guess, more of my hard-earned cash disappearing down the plughole?'

'Could be,' Ian agreed, grinning broadly. 'But you must have known what you were letting yourself in for. The estate's been neglected for years, but with careful investment – '

'Courtesy of Jack Keegan Holdings,' Jack reminded him dryly. 'And with even better management, courtesy of you.' He nodded. 'You're right, Ian, of course. It will turn around in time.' He raised his glass. 'Here's to the future, and a healthy-looking bank balance. The farms, the stables, the trout farm – '

'And the house,' Ella cut in, with thoughts of the forthcoming fashion shoot. Though that would be confined to the grounds, and with half a dozen pantechnicons parked out of sight there'd be little enough for Ella to do. Just sandwiches, drinks and cloakroom facilities. The house itself would be little more than a luxurious backdrop. 'If you're really hell-bent on making it pay, the possibilities are endless – conference hire, themed weekends, shooting, fishing.'

'Possible, but unlikely,' Jack agreed pleasantly. 'We may be in business but the house is my home. The fashion shoot's a one-off,' he pointedly reminded her. 'A favour for a friend. Believe me, it won't be setting a precedent.'

Oops! Heaven forbid, Ella acknowledged sourly. Jack's reasoning came across loud and clear. Expect the lovely Fliss to live above the shop, share her home with the *hoi polloi*? Far too vulgar.

The phone rang. Ella rose automatically.

'Katie will answer it,' Jack reminded her. 'It's your night off, remember?'

'Business,' Ella countered primly. 'Purely and simply.'

'If you insist,' he allowed, equally tersely. 'But, as I'm sure Ian will agree, so far it's been nothing but a pleasure.'

A moot point, but hardly the time and place to argue the toss.

'Telephone for you, Mr Keegan,' Katie murmured, appearing in the doorway and bobbing a swift curtsey.

'Thank you, Katie. I'll take it in the den. Help yourselves to drinks, folks.' He waved an airy hand. 'I shouldn't be long.'

He wasn't, and the conversation resumed in the drawing room where Katie had served the coffee.

'If that will be all, sir?' Another dip of the knees and Katie's enquiring glance slid first to Ella, who nodded imperceptibly, and then onto Jack.

'Thank you, Katie. It there's anything else we'll help ourselves. Take yourself off home now. And thanks again,' he added warmly. 'You've done a first-class job.'

A blush, another bob, before she backed herself to the door. 'Thank you, sir.'

'Slavery's abolished, *you* said,' he challenged Ella the moment the door swung to.

'And so it is,' Ella agreed, puzzled by his train of thought.

'In that case, my dear, I suggest you cure a certain young lady of that weakness in her knees before the habit sticks. I can't think why you encouraged it in the first place,' he complained good-naturedly.

'Not guilty, Jack,' Ella demurred. 'I simply explained the need for more respect.'

'Fine. Respect I can handle; just make sure Katie and the others know where to draw the line.'

'Certainly, sir. Your wish is my every command,' Ella allowed as the imp inside her surfaced. She raised a hand. 'Now, let me get this straight. No curtseying, no tugging of forelocks – or should that be fetlocks?' she queried absurdly. 'No guards of honour and definitely no red carpets,' she added, ticking them off on her fingers. 'Anything I've forgotten?'

'With my new broom of a housekeeper the model of efficiency,' Jack drawled, taking the dig in good part, 'surely not.'

'Attention to detail,' Ella reminded him sweetly. 'And nothing's too much trouble for the master of the house.'

'And that's another – '

'Whoops!' she interjected. 'Wrong comment, sir? Or wrong tone of voice? A mite too deferential?' she queried, lowering her voice, fluttering her lashes, their audience for the moment forgotten. 'It's all a question of balance, really, but a fine line don't you think? Respect, deference, shades of familiarity? So easy to hit the wrong note.

'Now what does that remind me of? Oh, yes, I know,' she insisted, enjoying herself immensely by now, and stifling Jack's protest with an imperative wave of the hand. 'A poem I read at school,' she confided, the laughter gurgling in her throat. '*Dumb Insolence*. The teacher can rant and rave till the cows come home, but as long as the boy says nothing, he can't be done for cheek. It's written all over his face, of course, but that's something else entirely. And now I'm rambling. My apologies, sir, I guess I'm forgetting my place again.'

'You *have* quite finished?' he enquired drolly.

'Well, now that you come to mention it – '

'Enough!' Jack roared, just as he had done earlier.

'Why, certainly, sir,' she breathed, mock-contritely. 'Whatever you say. Like I said, nothing's too much trouble for – '

'El – '

A discreet cough from Ian was a timely reminder that they weren't alone, that Jack had come dangerously close to giving away her name – and not just her name, Ella realized, sobering fast. Ian Sampson was no fool. He'd be aware of Jack's history. And once Ian guessed, how long before Fliss was given the shocking truth?

She felt another twinge of unease, and a picture of Ian and Fliss flashed through her mind – heads and hands far too close together for a working dinner, a business dinner. And such a lot of business to discuss when Jack was safely out of the country, Ella tagged on silently, sourly. And, having set the thought in motion, she completely missed the cue that Ian was ready to leave.

'Dashing off already, Ian?' Jack queried as, too late, Ella realized the danger and scrambled hastily to her feet. 'But the night's still young,' he drawled with wry amusement, pointedly checking his watch. 'No, don't tell me – let me guess. The Bull in the village, perhaps? And the charms of a blonde and buxom barmaid?' His grin broadened. 'I only hope she's worth it, Ian.'

'She is,' Ian confirmed, taking the dig in good part, and then added, his glance sliding across to Ella, poised ready for flight, 'But don't let me spoil things here.'

'Worry not, Ian,' Jack reassured him airily. 'You won't.'

Silence. Just the granddaughter clock in the corner chiming the hour – the hour for Katie to take herself off home. Home. The safety of her own four walls – or, in Ella's case, the housekeeper's flat. Not exactly tucked away below stairs, but all of a sudden seeming to be miles away.

Jack smiled. 'Sit down, Ella. More coffee?' And, taking her compliance for granted, he placed the refilled cup and saucer on the highly polished table beside her chair.

Outmanoeuvred, Ella regained her seat, burning her tongue in her haste to finish the coffee. Cosy. Far too cosy, even allowing for a room as big as the average tennis court. Small talk. Nothing important – not even the forthcoming fashion shoot. Ella's turn to glance at her watch. Surreptitiously. Time for bed.

Bed. The very thought was enough to make her cheeks flame, and heaven knew she'd already spent a string of disturbed nights under the same roof as Jack, tossing and turning in her surprisingly generous bed, dreaming, wanting, remembering. Much better a hard and narrow cot, she decided waspishly.

So, nothing to fear in coming casually to her feet, bidding Jack a calm goodnight and taking herself off. Nothing to fear at all, she reassured herself, risking a glance through the veil of her lashes. Just the hunger in his eyes, the need, want, the naked emotion.

'Ella – '

'Goodnight, Jack,' she murmured calmly, her heart thumping nineteen to the dozen as leaden feet carried her across the room.

His swift and soundless counter-move caught her off-guard and Jack's powerful frame blocked the doorway.

Pulling up short, she raised her eyes. 'Let me go, Jack,' she said softly, imploringly. 'Let me go.'

'If that's what you want,' he acknowledged thickly. But he didn't move, simply stood, his blue eyes fastened on hers and seeing to the centre of her soul. Impasse. Not a word, not a sound, not a breath. And then he touched her, a single finger tracing the angles of her face.

'No, Jack,' she murmured, her head snapping back as if stung. 'No, Jack.'

No! No! No! Only Jack wasn't listening, and as his hands closed round her, pulling her against him, Ella's treacherous body was already responding.

CHAPTER 8

'Wonderful, wonderful woman,' he growled, his lips hungrily nuzzling the hollow of her throat as his fingers traced the nodular ridges of her spine, up and down and back again, such a searing touch that the barrier of her clothes was practically non-existent. 'Ella, oh, Ella,' he crooned throatily. 'My Ella. My wonderful, wonderful Ella.'

Rigid with fright, yet gripped by an emotion she'd thought was dead and buried, Ella shivered at the touch, remembering, wanting, needing, loving. Jack. Her Jack. Hands, fingers, lips creating havoc in her mind, triggering whirlpools of desire in a treacherous body.

She loved him, had never stopped loving him, needed him so badly the tears were stinging the backs of her eyes. Suddenly afraid that Jack would notice the salty trickle of moisture and jump to the wrong conclusion, Ella closed her lids, swaying dizzily against him, and the long, hard lines of his body moulded instantly to hers.

Ella gasped at the contact, waves of heat and pleasure turning the blood to water in her veins, and, sensing her response, Jack tugged her even closer, his hands splaying out across the swell of her bottom, urging, pushing, caressing, his manhood rigid against her, his need, like Ella's, spiralling out of control in a matter of seconds.

She was tinder-dry for love, hadn't made love for more years than she cared to remember, and this man knew the nooks and crannies of her body better than Ella herself. It was madness, but such exquisite madness that common sense was forgotten as Ella closed her mind.

'Jack. Oh, God, Jack,' she moaned as his mouth claimed hers, her lips opening like the petals of a flower as his tongue swept through into the dark, moist depths, finding her tongue and darting, dancing, entwining, teasing, sweeping on and round and – 'Jack!'

'Don't you like it?' he growled, the tiny, playful nip of teeth against her upper lip sending fresh darts of pleasure pulsing through her. Only Jack didn't wait for her response, simply laughed deep in his throat as his hands cupped her face, thumbs feathering the angle of her jaw as his eyes locked with hers in a timeless moment when the earth stood still.

Because the doubt was there – the merest wisp of cloud in a devastatingly blue sky. He wanted her, he needed her, but for once in his life arrogant Jack Keegan simply wasn't sure.

Ella smiled, banishing the shadows, and Jack groaned as he dipped his head to touch her lips, taste her mouth. Ella's arms rose instinctively and she plunged her fingers into the thick, silky tresses of his hair, urging his mouth to meld with hers, and as she raised her hands so her breasts rose, brushing against his chest. The contact was searing, not skin-to-skin by any means but with currents of heat swirling back and forth, the flimsy fabric of his shirt and the needlecord fabric of her dress with its lacy bra beneath proved scant insulation.

'Ella. I want you, Ella,' he breathed against her ear, his tongue darting into the swirls of skin, tracing the outer rim, the inner rim and back again, across the angles of her cheek to her mouth, down, round, skirting her lips, darting between her parted lips and just as swiftly moving on.

His throaty laugh was music to her ears as those lips swept on to the corner of her eye, tiny kisses punctuating her brow, and then down again, in a languid exploration of the angles and planes of Ella's face and neck. And if his lips caused havoc, the trail of devastation those hands could wreak was a bittersweet pill. Too much, yet nowhere near satiation.

Madness, Ella told herself in a fleeting moment of clarity. Madness, exquisite madness – so near, so far. The need was spiralling, the floods of heat drowning out the tiny voice of protest. No! Too good to be wrong, too wonderful to be wrong. And she wanted him, needed him, loved him, would love him till the day she died. Too right to be wrong.

Ella was moaning, shockingly aware of his lips nuzzling the hollow at the base of her throat, aware of his hands plucking at the buttons of her dress, nimble fingers descending, lips following the trail they blazed, into the hollow between her aching breasts, feathering the ripe curve of first one breast then the other, and on, downwards, skirting the dimple of her navel.

His tongue darted into that erotic pucker of skin, swirling, lapping, sending fresh currents of heat pulsing through her belly; hands simultaneously pushed her dress free of her shoulders, allowing it to land in a heap at her feet, unheeded, unneeded, a cloak of modesty just as redundant, and the triangle of lace at the apex of her legs, the matching scraps that masqueraded as a bra were both concealing and revealing.

'Oh, Ella. Oh, my God, Ella,' Jack breathed, pausing, holding himself aloof, his glance reverential as he traced the lines of her body. 'Oh, Ella, you're the most beautiful woman in the world,' he told her solemnly.

And when Ella shook her head, smiled her denial, he nodded, smiled, allowed his gaze to touch her all over again in a tangible caress from the top of her head to the tips of her toes. Downwards, slowly, eye to eye, eye to mouth, down the long column of her neck and on, to the half-moons of breast that peeped from their halters, nipples hardening at the touch that wasn't a touch, thrusting against the lace.

Their desperate juttings were noted, a much too sensuous mouth smiling its approval as Jack's gaze moved on, lower, then another pause, another moment to savour, at the junction of her legs with its dark mound of hair outlined against the lace.

And Ella didn't breathe, simply stood and waited, flooding in the heat of anticipation. And still Jack didn't attempt to touch her except with the reverence of his gaze, moving down, sweeping the lines of her left leg, climbing the curves of her right, and back up to the juncture of her legs, the seat of her emotions.

'I want you,' he told her solemnly as she began to tremble. 'All day I've wanted you. I've been living in hell because for each and every moment I've been aching to touch you, to kiss you, to make love to you. And now it's time. I want you. Understand, Ella? I want you and I've already waited too long.'

Ella smiled as Jack nodded. Too long. Much, much too long. Eight long years without Jack, without love. But he doesn't love you now, the voice of her conscience pointed out, and the pain came slicing through. Love, she derided, her lips twisting bitterly. A transient emotion. Want, need – the needs of her body. Eight long, lonely years.

Too good to be wrong, she argued inside her head as Jack smiled, held her gaze, snapped the buttons of his shirt one by one, with a slow deliberation guaranteed to inflame. A powerful chest. An inviting mass of golden hair. Itching to reach out and touch, but determined to resist to the point of exquisite pain, Ella clamped her hands to her sides, holding herself rigid as Jack tugged the fabric free of the waistband of his trousers and shrugged the shirt carelessly over his shoulders.

Naked, from the waist up at least, the muscles of his chest gleamed and rippled, and Ella smothered a groan. Wonderful, wonderful Jack. And she wanted him, and she needed him, and when Jack opened his arms in simple invitation it was the most natural thing in the world for Ella to step into them, to feel the heat of his embrace as he wrapped his arms around her, held her.

A fleeting moment of calm and then he was kissing her, lips hard and demanding as his hands planed the contours of her back, down and round into the curves of hip and waist, down and over the swell of her buttocks, urging her against him, Jack's own need every bit as urgent.

Giving instinct its head, Ella moved against him, her hips undulating slowly, her whole body swaying to the strains of a primeval love song as the erotic scratch of her bra against his naked chest drove Jack to fever-pitch.

A snap of the catch and the offending garment was gone, Ella's breasts spilling free, Jack's hands closing round. And Ella's gasp of pleasure was in total harmony with his as Jack took the weight of each ripe breast in his palms, allowed his thumbs to brush the delicate pink tips that hardened, darkened as the muscles of her belly clenched in reflex. God, how she wanted him – wanted him, needed him, loved him . . .

'Jack! Oh, yes, Jack!' she moaned as he dipped his head, his lips hungrily nuzzling first one breast then the other, and it was Jack's turn to groan as he pushed her breasts together, attempted to bury his head in the valley between, his tongue greedily lapping the slopes. And all the while those magic thumbs were coaxing the rigid nubs of her nipples and Ella was floating, floating away on a magic carpet of love . . .

Mouth to mouth again. Ella's tongue darted between his lips, finding Jack's tongue, weaving a love dance with Jack's tongue as her fingers raked the muscles of his back then down, across the tight swell of his bottom, where the texture of fabric beneath her hands was both unexpected and unwelcome. No time for even fleeting disappointment with the distraction of Jack's hands ranging her body, with each and every point of contact triggering the currents, nerve-endings tingling, straining, wanting.

So much pleasure and yet not nearly enough, and Jack swept her off her feet, carried her across to the hearthrug, kneeling to place her down with sudden solemn reverence, kneeling beside her, his gaze locking with hers and seeing to the centre of her soul.

'I want you, Ella,' he told her thickly. And he reached out to touch her, gentle fingers brushing her brow, her cheeks, her mouth.

Ella's lips parted to draw his index finger into her mouth, and it was her turn to suck hungrily, Jack's sharp hiss of indrawn breath thrilling her as he gently disengaged his finger and moved on, blazing a delicate trail the length of her neck, then another pause to pleasure the hollow, and then onwards, downwards, feathering the valley, skirting round and under first one breast then the other, and round again, sensitizing, tantalizing, with Ella's moans provoking a smile.

'Please, Jack,' she implored, eyes dark with passion. And, because she'd asked so nicely, Jack took pity, dipped his head to kiss the rigid buds, lips sucking hungrily, teeth nibbling gently, and then the magic finger was dancing on its way, down, slowly yet relentlessly, coming to a halt at the waistband of Ella's skimpy panties.

A lifetime passed as Jack paused. Electricity crackled on the air and Ella couldn't breathe, didn't dare breathe as Jack traced the pattern of lace, glided across the mound and paused again, a single finger sliding beneath the hem.

'Oh, Ella,' he breathed with veneration, parting the curls and finding her moist and ready. 'Oh, my Ella.'

'Oh, God, Jack.' She writhed as unerringly he sought and found the tiny ridge of pleasure, stroked and teased and stroked again. Ella closed her eyes, giving herself up to the moment as the tremors began to ripple through her, and, having carried her to the edge, so near, yet so achingly far, Jack paused, in bittersweet denial.

'Look at me, Ella. Look at me,' he commanded huskily.

And she did, raising her lids, her smouldering gaze locking with his, seeing the wonder, the love, the passion, and she smiled, arched against his hand, nudged the hand to continue. Jack laughed out loud, obligingly taking the hint as Ella stretched, smiled again. Yet as Jack lowered his gaze Ella's eye was caught by the smiling face in the silver-framed photograph on the mantelpiece behind him.

Fliss. Ella froze. Fool, fool, fool, she whipped herself viciously, silently. And as Jack reached out to tug the damp panties over her hips Ella's numb mind sparked painfully into life.

'No, Jack!' She twisted away, his hurt expression a knifeblade in her heart.

'What the hell – ?' Fleeting comprehension, then, 'Oh, no! Oh, *yes*, Ella,' he insisted, refusing to believe it, hands gripping her shoulders as he pushed her down, covering her lips with his own in a vicious exploration of her mouth that she barely had the strength to resist. Because heaven help her she loved this man, wanted this man, and the shame of knowing he was simply using her would live with her for ever.

He didn't belong to her. Her Jack. Only not any more. He belonged to someone else. And he was using her.

Shameless – through and through, Ella felt her resistance begin to crumble. She was drowning, drowning, drowning. Too good to be wrong. Too wonderful to be wrong. And she closed her mind, the last of the fight draining from her body as she melted against him, opened herself beneath him.

Only the moment she gave in, of course, Jack thrust her away in disgust. 'Why, Ella? Why, damn it?' he demanded frigidly, snatching at her shoulders and forcing her to sit, those piercing blue eyes daggers of hate. 'Why, Ella? Why?'

Too choked to reply, Ella shook her head, turning away and switching her gaze. A perplexed Jack followed the same line, and the sharp hiss of his indrawn breath was scant consolation. Guilt? she wondered vaguely as without a word he dropped his hands. Because of Fliss? Or Ella, perhaps? Or something much more basic? A flash of anger that something as incongruous as a snapshot should rob him of the pleasure he'd been dangerously close to taking?

Left alone on the hearthrug, naked but for that inadequate scrap of lace, Ella shivered, drawing up her knees and wrapping her arms around them, hugging them. She was cold, frozen deep inside. Love. Lust, more like, as far as Jack was concerned. And as for Ella . . . She blinked back the tears. She was shameless, or as near as made no difference. Wanting Jack, even now aching for Jack. And the knowledge that Jack had been the one to call a halt before he lost control was yet another coal to heap upon her head.

She'd wanted him, she'd fought him, and lo and behold she'd finally given in. Only Jack didn't want her. Not really. Oh, yes, he'd have taken her easily enough, but in the end it was a simple matter of pride. Jack had been making a point. An eye for an eye, no less. Ella wanted Jack, despite her seeming rejection, and, heaven help her, he'd proved it with brutal eloquence.

She was vaguely aware of a movement behind her; tiny hairs on the back of her neck began to stand on end. Another needless worry since, ever the gentleman, Jack had simply gathered her scattered clothes, now dropped them beside her before moving out of sight. Squirming at the sudden need for modesty, Ella shrugged herself back into the crumpled garments.

A chink of glass on crystal and then Jack's legs hove into view again.

'Here. Drink this,' he insisted, thrusting a goblet into her hands.

'I don't – '

'Yes, you do,' he contradicted her, retreating again as the distinctive aroma of brandy hit the back of her nostrils.

Ella closed her eyes. Brandy. Surely Jack couldn't have forgotten? Or maybe he simply didn't care. Ella sniffed, blinking back the tears. Well, that made two of them. Because Ella didn't care. Shameless she might have been, but at least her emotions were honest. She loved him. She was a fool, but she'd done nothing wrong. Unlike Jack, who'd been on the verge of being unfaithful to Fliss.

Fliss. Another shameless sniff. Young, beautiful and fertile. Every man's dream. Jack's love. And probably as faithless as Jack if the truth were known, Ella derided silently. So – maybe they deserved one other after all.

'Why, Ella?' Cold. Polite. Only vaguely curious.

'You know why.'

'Fliss.'

She nodded, took a tiny sip of the amber spirit and almost choked. Revolting. Ella grimaced. And to think she'd almost lived on the stuff in the past.

'But you wanted me.' Statement. The truth. Stark. Cold. Fact.

'For a moment,' she acknowledged, beginning to pull herself together, Jack's taut control goading her. 'For old times' sake,' she heard herself sneer. 'A fleeting moment of madness before common sense returned.'

'Oh, yes? And who do you think you're kidding?' he jeered. 'You wanted me, Ella,' he carelessly informed her. 'You might have pushed me away but it didn't take much persuasion to effect a change of mind. Face it, Ella. You wanted me all right.'

'What's the matter, Jack?' Ella bit out, stung onto the attack. 'Doesn't that over-inflated ego know how to cope with a spot of rejection?'

'It would take a better woman than you to dent my ego, madam,' he scathingly informed her.

'Come now, Jack, don't be modest,' she scorned in turn. 'You might as well admit it. There isn't a woman alive who could even come close. Invincible Jack Keegan. Self-centred Jack Keegan. Self-contained Jack Keegan. With an ego so big it's a wonder there's room for a woman – any woman – in your life. Only there is. Fliss – remember?'

'Since the woman in question is my fiancée,' he pointed out coolly, 'I'm hardly likely to forget. Jealous, Ella?'

'Oh, positively green with envy,' she agreed flippantly, swirling the amber liquid round and round the balloon of the glass before risking another tiny sip.

And, though many a true word was spoken in jest, Jack was hardly likely to have guessed. Easy enough to keep it that way. No overreaction. No walking out.

Three months, Jack had goaded, and three months Ella would endure. Proof. All the proof Jack was entitled to. And the truth? Ella probed, aware that, deliberately or otherwise, he'd managed to back her into a corner. She loved him. And packing up and leaving while Jack was away was tantamount to handing him proof on a plate.

Three months, she reassured herself. Ten weeks at the most and then she'd be free. Only she'd never be free, she acknowledged sickly. Not from loving Jack.

Placing the virtually untouched glass carefully on the marble-tiled hearth, she rose slowly to her feet, achingly aware of the man who'd flung himself down on one of the sumptuous settees and was sprawled, hands behind his head, his body language speaking volumes. Unconcern. Boredom. Indifference. Choking back the tears and clutching the remnants of her dignity, she moved slowly towards the door.

'Ella – '

Close, too close. That early warning prickle on the back of her neck had been nowhere near early enough. And how the hell did he manage to move so stealthily and so fast?

'Jack?' she queried politely, freezing.

'We nearly made it, hey, Ella?'

And what the hell was that supposed to mean? Ella railed with a sudden surge of anger. 'No, Jack,' she contradicted him coolly. 'Believe me, we never even came close.'

'Liar.'

'If you say so,' she demurred, too bone-weary to care any more. And then he touched her. Just the merest hint of a connection but more than enough to provoke a response.

'Like I said,' Jack crooned in triumph, spreading his hands. 'And next time – '

'There won't be a next time,' Ella bit out, hazel eyes spitting flames. 'Understand, Jack? No more. Pull another stunt like this and I'll pack and leave so fast you won't even have time to blink. Are you listening, Jack?' she demanded icily. 'No more.' And, secure in the knowledge that if nothing else, she'd had the final word, she swung away.

Jack's voice sliced across the room to halt her. 'You're running scared, Ella,' he told her with a curious lack of emotion. 'You're running away from me, but most of all you're running from yourself. And believe me, Ella, one day you're going to wake up old and withered and lonely and wonder where it all went wrong.'

'Wrong, Jack,' she retorted, not even bothering to turn. 'Believe it or not, that particular time and place is carved in stone upon my heart. December the thirty-first,' she informed him frigidly. 'When, fool that I was, I allowed a virtual stranger to see me home from a party and continue the New Year celebrations in my bed. Still, at least I've had the sense to learn from my mistakes. Like I said,' she repeated thickly, the tears threatening to fall, held at bay by sheer force of will, 'no more. Never again.'

Jack laughed. 'Never again,' he agreed nastily. 'Until the next time.'

CHAPTER 9

Next time. As if. As if Jack could possibly want her. But with Fliss away the mouse would play, and Jack, devastating Jack, knew every trick in the book. Because he knew Ella's mind and body almost as well as he knew his own.

Testing, always testing. A word, a glance, but curiously enough never a touch. So, maybe Jack knew that if he pushed his luck too far, Ella would be on her way. Yet why should Jack care? With housekeepers ten a penny, if Ella walked out today there'd be a dozen or more ready to step into her shoes tomorrow. What could Jack possibly have to gain from keeping Ella at Sherbrook?

Tweaking the duvet into place, Ella straightened, absentmindedly hooking a lock of hair behind an ear as she turned the question over. Until Fliss returned, probably little more than a well-managed house, she decided sourly, casting a critical eye about the room, searching for the tiniest speck of dust and nodding her satisfaction when she found none. Good. Millie was learning. And, since this was the last room on the floor, the wing was now complete.

Not that Jack seemed the least bit interested. His house, his prerogative, Ella scorned. His monument, more like – a palace of a place with ninety per cent of the rooms hidden beneath dust-sheets. Such a waste, in Ella's eyes, but hers was not to reason why. Jack's pride and joy. The finest wine, the finest food, a houseful of servants at his constant beck and call – and Ella.

Why Ella? Katie would do the job just as well, she was beginning to think. So – back to that earlier thought. Pride? she mused, since for all Jack's brave words Ella *had* put a dent in that ego, walking out on their marriage in the first place and then pulling back on the verge of making love. And, yes, she'd finally given in, allowing Jack his moment of triumph, but with an ego that stretched all the way to Mars and back, Jack wasn't in the mood to forgive and forget.

So, keeping Ella at Sherbrook had to be Jack's revenge. Ella smiled grimly. Fine. As long as she had it straight in her mind she could cope. And the moment her time was up, she'd be off.

'Playing hide and seek, Ella?'

'Jack!' Silently cursing his uncanny knack of appearing out of nowhere, Ella damped down the panic. It was the first time they'd been alone since that shameful scene on the hearthrug, and, determined to set the rules for their relationship once and for all, she took a deep breath. 'Mr Keegan. You gave me quite a turn. I didn't expect you back until lunchtime, sir.'

His mouth tightened. 'Don't be ridiculous, Ella. Jack will suffice – in private, at least. Naturally when we've guests – '

'Oh, naturally,' Ella echoed, aware that she'd never get away with calling Fliss by her given name, or Jack, for that matter, within the other woman's hearing. The wrath of Fliss. Instant dismissal? she mused. The idea was appealing, and, since Jack could hardly throw *that* back in Ella's face, the ideal solution in fact. Despite the unnerving company, Ella smiled.

'Something I've said?' Jack queried tartly, blue eyes narrowing. 'Something I've done? Forgotten to zip up my fly, perhaps?' And he a cast a critical eye over his clothes before double-checking his appearance in the dressing table mirror. 'Nope,' he finally conceded peering close. 'Everything's in place, and there isn't a spot the size of Mount Etna erupting on my nose. So come along, Ella,' he entreated lightly, folding his arms and dazzling her with the brilliance of his smile. 'Be fair. Share the joke.'

'It would lose a lot in the translation,' she conceded, aware of a subtle change in the atmosphere. Dangerous. Much better to keep Jack at arm's length, keep the antagonism simmering.

Wiping damp palms down the sides of her dress, Ella took what she hoped was an unobtrusive step away from him. His corresponding step forward was eloquent proof that he'd noticed. Unnerved, she stumbled backwards, was brought up sharp by the newly made bed behind her. Bed. Her cheeks flamed. She was alone in a bedroom with Jack, when, as she'd so recently proved, being alone with him in any room could have devastating results.

'So – ' Jack grinned, and, aware of the panic flickering in her eyes, chose to take pity for once, giving her space by crossing to the window with its views of the estate – a gently rolling landscape, each and every inch almost as far the eye could see belonging to Jack. 'What are you doing hiding away up here?'

'Double-checking on the staff, Jack?' Ella challenged defiantly. 'Keeping tabs on me?'

'As a matter of fact, yes,' he drawled, and Ella's audible gasp provoked another smile. 'You work too hard,' he pointed out mildly. 'And someone has to stop you burning out.'

'How very commendable.' She couldn't help but sneer.

'If you like. But dig a little deeper and the motive's much more basic. You do a first-class job, Ella, and I can't begin to think how we'll cope when you're gone.'

'Oh, I'm sure you'll get by,' she countered airily.

'And you, Ella?' he queried politely. 'How will you manage?'

'Perfectly well, thank you,' she reassured him, holding his gaze with a massive surge of will. 'Believe it or not, there's no shortage of jobs in the offing.'

'But you've a perfectly good job here.'

'For the moment,' she agreed reluctantly.

'Your decision, Ella, not mine,' he reminded her. 'Yet it doesn't have to be – hey, Ella?'

She swallowed hard. He'd turned and was leaning back against the windowsill, arms folded across his chest, blue eyes full of hidden knowledge. Jack. Her Jack. Only not hers any longer. And the torment of being under the same roof would shortly convert to the torment of separation. Together or apart. Hell on earth. Together, yet never together. Purgatory. And Ella was sharply aware that either way she couldn't win.

'Hey, Ella?' Soft, probing, persuasive. 'You don't have to go – not yet, not ever. Why, Ella? Why can't you stay? We – '

'No!' She waved an imperative arm as the pain sliced through her. 'Don't. *Don't*,' she repeated harshly. 'The idea's crazy, Jack. You're not being fair. It wouldn't be fair to any of us and surely you must know it. Three months,' she all but hissed. 'Three months we agreed; three months I'll do. But not if you make things difficult.'

Jack shrugged. 'Fine. But if you do change your mind all you have to do is say so.'

'I know,' Ella conceded tersely. 'But I won't, can't, shan't – and you might as well start to believe it.' She swung away, pointedly checking the time on her wristwatch. 'Now, if you don't mind,' she clipped out, praying he'd take the hint and drop the subject completely, 'despite the risk of burn-out, one of us has work to do.'

'Such as?' he queried, obligingly falling into step beside her, not touching by any means but in the confines of the narrow corridor far too close for Ella's peace of mind.

'Oh, you know. Lunch for a start. Instructions for Katie for dinner. Guest rooms to prepare. A dozen and one things, in fact.'

'Why?'

'Why, what?'

'Why the guest rooms? I wasn't aware we were expecting company.'

'We're not. I just like to be prepared. Who knows who might decide to drop by?'

'A marching army, judging from the evidence. Not just the guest rooms, hey, Ella? The east wing was pristine the last time I looked, and now these. I'm impressed.'

'Well, you needn't be; I'm simply doing the job I'm paid for.'

'And an excellent job at that.'

'You *are* checking up on me?' Half-question, half-statement, and a mildly offended Ella pulled up sharp at the top of the flight of stairs.

Jack swallowed a smile, raised his hands in a gesture of submission. 'Not guilty, Ella. I was simply nosing round, I promise you.'

'Why?'

'It is my house,' he pointed out mildly.

'Ouch,' she conceded, having the grace to blush. 'I guess I asked for that.'

'I guess you did at that, but it's a reasonable question. If you must know I was exploring, getting to know the place. It seems a waste, having all these rooms yet never setting foot in them from one month's end to the next.'

'Shades of Buckingham Palace,' Ella mused, only slightly tongue in cheek.

'Only a teeny-weenie little bit,' Jack allowed, taking the dig in good part. 'Though I do take your point.'

'So?'

He shrugged. 'I don't know, really,' he admitted frankly, resting his hand on the ornate banister, the covering of golden hairs on his lightly tanned skin drawing Ella's gaze. He shrugged again. 'Having set my heart on the place, I don't suppose I'd thought beyond acquiring it,' he finally admitted.

'And you – quote – "the shrewdest business man this side of the Pond"?' Ella scorned. 'Surely not?'

'You, madam, shouldn't believe everything you read in the morning papers.'

'I don't. But this was the Business Section of *The Times*. Hardly a scurrilous rag, Jack.'

'Definitely not a scurrilous rag,' he agreed, feigning horror at the thought.

Inhaling deeply, Ella took the plunge. 'The place is so big, Jack, and you've already admitted there's room enough to spare. You could hire out any of the wings and still keep your privacy.'

'Irrelevant. As I've told you before, Ella, the idea's off limits.'

'Your view, Jack – or Fliss's?' she heard herself needle.

Generous lips tightened. 'Like I said, it's my house, my decision.'

Ella shrugged. And clearly none of her business. The uneasy silence underlined that as they continued down the stairs.

He paused in the entrance hall, a magnificent room that spanned the front of the house, and, sensing he had something to say, Ella raised an eyebrow.

'Don't look so worried,' he teased, blue eyes dancing.

'So who's worried?' Ella scorned. 'I'm hardly facing the sack, and if by some miracle you came to your senses and allowed me to go, I'd simply fall back on Plan B.'

'Plan B?' he queried casually – too casually. Ella's sensitive ear was alert to the danger of giving too much away.

'Bristol,' she bit out. 'Just one of many options, I assure you.'

'Yes.' Jack's smile was grim. 'I can imagine.'

'So?'

'So?'

'You were about to say?' she prompted testily.

'Ah, yes. Like I said, nothing to worry about. I just thought I'd sit in on this afternoon's planning meeting – assuming you don't mind?'

Ella shrugged. 'It's your house, your business,' she pointed out coolly.

'Fine. Two o'clock, then. And don't bother about lunch. I'll grab a sandwich later in town.'

'Town?'

'London. Business. But I should be back first thing in the morning.'

'But if it's important why not leave straight away?' she pointed out logically.

'Trying to get rid of me, Ella?'

'Simply exercising a bit of common sense,' she demurred, blushing despite herself. 'Using my initiative, if sir doesn't mind?'

'Not at all. Using your initiative is part and parcel of the job. But I've a couple of loose ends to tie up here first. If madam doesn't mind?'

Madam didn't, but madam didn't suppose that it would make a scrap of difference if madam did, she tagged on silently, sourly, scurrying back to the safety of the kitchen.

Business. A cursory glance at the household accounts that Ella had drawn up for Ian – or in this case Jack's inspection – and little enough for Ella to do but listen to a surprisingly informed debate on the cost and relative merits of foodstuffs for the home farm stock and stables. A compliment, she supposed. The house, as Jack was so fond of reminding, was in her capable hands.

The duty roster, the meal plans, tentative arrangements for Fliss's return – whatever subject she raised, Jack simply smiled, nodded or waved another airy hand, and the sneaking suspicion lingered that Jack had graced them with his presence for no more pressing reason than to pin Ella down. No beds to make, no meals to cook, no burn-out. And, for someone as active as Ella, frustration.

'I'll make some tea,' she offered when the conversation switched from straightforward estate matters to Jack's involvement at the impending Tourism and Trade Fair at Birmingham's NEC.

'Katie will make the tea,' Jack insisted pleasantly, and, glancing across and seeing Ella about to rise, added, 'No, don't bother ringing. I'm slipping upstairs for a folder I need and will pop my head round the door in passing.'

And if passing the kitchens *en route* for Jack's suite of rooms was tantamount to travelling round the Wreakin, who was Ella to comment?

Outmanoeuvred, and tired of twiddling her thumbs, she spotted the folder Jack had left open on the desk and pulled it towards her, idly flicking through, just the soft rustle of pages breaking the silence. 'This conference sounds important?' she probed, glancing across at Ian, who sat, shoulders hunched, as he checked and initialled a batch of orders.

'That, Mrs A,' he murmured dryly, 'is the understatement of the year. It's not so much important as vital.'

Mrs A. Ella swallowed a smile. The name had stuck, tripped easily off the tongues of one and all. Understandable, she supposed, given the full mouthful, but, with Andrews the name she'd grown up with and Watson the name she'd been given at birth, combining the two had seemed the obvious thing to do.

'Oh?' she queried politely.

Ian filled her in – a thumbnail sketch of Jack's expanding empire, a fascinating resumé of Jack's expert finger in a diversity of pies.

'And since he's invested heavily in Sherbrook, with no chance of any returns for the next five years or so,' Ian reminded her, 'he needs to spread the risk of the Gulf scheme. Hence the Geraghty carrot.'

'The *what*?' Ella queried, wrinkling her nose.

'Paul Geraghty. The reclusive billionaire. If a man with his instinct for business can be persuaded to invest, the scramble from the rest will snowball. A personal endorsement from Geraghty is worth its weight in gold.'

'And Jack's sweet-talked him into attending? Ah, yes, I think I'm beginning to see,' Ella exclaimed, Jack's decision to take the entire top floor of Birmingham's premier hotel, suddenly making sense. 'It keeps Geraghty out of the limelight, yet allows the rest of the party access to the NEC. Clever Jack.'

'He hasn't pulled it off yet,' Ian warned her.

'Oh, but he will,' Ella murmured confidently as the door swung open and Jack reappeared.

'Trouble, boss?' Ian queried, sensing a change of mood.

Jack nodded. 'Trouble with a capital T. Lloyd's just come through on my mobile. It looks like I'm on my way again,' he explained briskly. 'But I'll drive down to London as planned and fly out to the Gulf first thing tomorrow. In the meantime, folks – ' he spread his hands, gave an eloquent shrug of resignation '– I'm leaving things here in two sets of capable hands. But if anything does crop up that you think you can't handle,' he added almost dryly, 'Lynette Kaye will know where to reach me.'

It was a strange few days in a surprisingly quiet house. Ella spent her time teaching Katie how to produce half a dozen classic meals that had the added advantage of going from freezer to oven to table with any last-minute touches kept to a minimum. Well-stocked freezers would help when Fliss landed back, complete with entourage – that there would be an entourage Ella didn't doubt – and once Ella herself moved on, Katie would be prepared.

Then came the first of the phone calls. The hairs on the back of Ella's neck prickled as she recognized the sneer in the younger woman's tone.

'Ah, Mrs Andrews-Watson,' Fliss drawled. 'Still holding the fort, I see. Such a lot to do, I expect, especially when there's no one home. And since no one's home,' she added with a barely smothered yawn, 'I might as well hang on here for a while. If you could let Mr Keegan know?'

'Mr Keegan's out of the country,' Ella reminded her politely.

'I know that,' Felicity scorned. 'But his mobile's not responding, and I've better things to do than hang around and wait. Next time he phones,' she explained, as if spelling it out to an unreceptive three-year-old, 'you can put him in the picture. You'd better jot it down,' she added, saccharine-sweetly. 'Knowing how busy you are, I should hate it to slip your mind.'

Ella counted to three. Slowly. 'You will be back in time for the conference?' she reminded her, aware that Jack was relying on Fliss to help entertain when business gave way to pleasure in the hotel's award-winning restaurant.

'I might be. Not that it's any of *your* business,' she pointed out, with all the charm of a rattlesnake. 'Just make sure Mr Keegan gets the message and ask him to give me a call.'

Yes, madam. No, madam. Three bags full, madam, Ella railed, only silently, her sense of humour bubbling as Felicity cut the connection.

Five minutes later, Jack's cool, calm and unflappable PA sounded anything but when she telephoned. 'His mobile's not responding,' Lynette Kaye explained tersely. 'If he does call home, ask him to give me a ring. It's urgent.'

'That sounds ominous,' Ella probed, vaguely alarmed.

'Worse than ominous,' Lynette groaned. 'I still can't believe it. It's Geraghty. He's pulled out. According to the fax we've just been treated to, a city-centre hotel, and especially in the provinces, is too big a security risk.'

'But he must have known that when he agreed to attend?' Ella pointed out, swallowing her disappointment.

'The prerogative of the filthy rich,' Lynette murmured dryly. 'I guess the guy's entitled to change his mind. Though with that sort of attitude, I only hope he can sleep at night.'

'A couple of nights,' Ella repeated, pacing up and down the estate office, a coiled spring of emotion. 'We can do it, Ian. I know we can.'

'Maybe so,' Ian allowed, folding his arms and leaning back, eyeing Ella warily. 'But Jack won't like it. You know how he feels about the house.'

'I know how he feels about this project,' she bit out. 'And having that prize ace he's holding up his sleeve turn into a joker isn't going to help. It makes sense, Ian,' she added less heatedly. 'And it isn't too late to organize. All we need is the go-ahead from Jack.'

'Which we'll never get.'

'We won't know unless we try.'

'But the whole world's been trying for days,' Ian pointed out patiently. 'Jack's out of contact. His mobile isn't responding, which means he's probably on his way. We might as well wait until he's back,' he added, visibly brightening.

'It will be too late by then,' Ella clipped out. 'And we're not just *running* out of time, we're clean out of it. Face it, Ian, it makes sense.'

'Agreed. But I don't have that sort of authority, and if you call Lynette Kaye she'll agree with me.'

'So – who does have the necessary authority?'

'Jack.' He gave an apologetic shrug of the shoulders. 'You know Jack. Some things he'll delegate, some things he handles himself.'

'But – ' Ella was growing more and more frustrated, the rogue strand of hair she was twisting round her finger getting tighter by the second. 'We can't just do nothing,' she wailed. 'Someone has to make the decision. If we wait until Jack flies in it will be too late to organize and he'll have lost Paul Geraghty's support.'

Ian shrugged. 'It's out of our hands,' he pointed out softly. 'And you might as well face it.'

'Oh, no, it's not,' she contradicted vehemently. 'We *can* still swing it. Think, Ian, think. We simply switch the venue. Thirty miles is neither here nor there, and it's a simple matter of diverting specialist staff and equipment from the conference room to here – *if* Geraghty agrees to our suggestion.'

She broke off, eyeing Ian shrewdly and allowing time for the idea to take hold. 'If I speak to Lynette and she agrees with me,' she probed, fingers crossed that he'd see things her way, 'can we do it? Please, Ian. You know what this means to Jack.'

There was an electric pause and then an almost imperceptible nod. 'But heaven help us if things go wrong.'

'Worry not,' Ella soothed, aware of the doubt clouding Ian's eyes. 'You run the estate, I run the house – and by my reckoning that makes it squarely my decision. And before you point out that I've bitten off more than I can chew, just remember my training. I've organized more conferences in the past five years than you've had hot breakfasts.'

'I doubt it,' Ian drawled, features relaxing, and then, 'Okay, okay, you win, Mrs A. But square it with the London office first, hey?'

So, which comes first, the chicken or the egg? Switch the venue or first catch her wild boar? In this case, the reclusive Paul Geraghty. Hardly a sprat to catch a mackerel but a very big feather in Jack's cap – *if* he could pull it off. Too many mixed metaphors, Ella acknowledged, too busy to worry that she might be making a mistake – and a disastrous mistake at that.

Geraghty first. Easy. Too easy. The first shock was managing to make contact with the guy at the very first attempt, and then for once in her life she must have said all the right things. But then, if Geraghty was half as shrewd as rumour had it, he'd be keen to be in on the investment, would view Ella's suggestion as a means to an end.

Lynette Kaye next. Taking a deep breath, Ella didn't so much square things as manage to imply Jack had given his blessing, and in no time at all the list of names Jack was targeting was spilling freely from the fax machine, galvanizing Ella into action.

Together with Sarah, the estate's part-time secretary, she spent the next few days liaising with the hotel manager, accepting his advice, for a guaranteed fee of course, not to mention underwriting the bill for an entire top floor that was suddenly redundant – and five-star hotels, as Ella well knew, didn't come cheap.

With a neurosis born from necessity, she checked and double-checked each and every arrangement. Surprisingly little equipment to hire: laptop computers, extra phone lines, fax machines and modems. Secretarial staff and anything else would come courtesy of the hotel. So, letters of explanation, invitations, and a fleet of plush cars to ferry people back and forth to the airport, Birmingham International and New Street Stations as well as the NEC itself. And, last but not least, the final touches at Sherbrook.

So, D-day minus one, and all that was missing was the great man himself. Oh, yes, and Jack.

Jack. Oh, hell, Ella railed with her first twinge of conscience. What if he hit the roof?

Only it was worse than that.

'You've done *what*?' he demanded, the expression on his tanned face black as thunder.

'We didn't have much choice, Jack,' Ian began mildly. 'And if we'd left it any longer – '

Jack cut him off with an imperative wave of the hand. 'You're fired. You can take two months' pay in lieu of notice and consider yourself lucky.'

'Jack!' Ella protested, stumbling to her feet, glad of the solid planes of the desk coming between her and this toweringly angry man. 'You can't. It had nothing to do with Ian. You don't understand.'

'Don't I? Then pray, my dear, do enlighten me.'

'Given the mood you're in? Where's the point?' Ella scorned with a defiant toss of the head. '*I* did what *I* thought was best, Jack,' she added less heatedly. 'But I should have known better than to think you'd be pleased.'

'Pleased? *Pleased*?' he repeated, leaning forwards, his balled fist hammering at the desk as Ella inwardly flinched. 'This is my home, damn you. You had no right.'

'Use my initiative, *you* said. And that goes for Ian too.'

'Oh, I think I'm beginning to see,' he drawled, folding his arms and dazzling her with the brilliance of his smile – only the row of teeth in question seemed about as innocuous as a shark's. 'Why didn't you say?' he entreated silkily. 'Housekeeper today, empire-builder tomorrow. Such a talented little lady,' he scorned. 'And to think I never knew.' And then his voice changed, any pretence at amusement banished in a trice. 'You run the house, Mrs Andrews-Watson,' he reminded her tersely. 'Not my business. You had no right – '

'Then it's a pity I didn't remember it sooner,' Ella bit out, the formal use of her name hurting more than she cared to acknowledge. 'Because believe me, Mr Keegan, if I'd known these were all the thanks I'd get, I'd have left you and your business to fry in the desert.'

'I doubt it,' he bit out. 'Since I've managed perfectly well without you in the past. Believe me, madam, I'd have worked something out.'

'Really?' she challenged, wincing again, the underlying barb triggering the sting of tears. Cruel, Jack, so cruel. 'At less than twelve hours' notice?' she scorned. 'Well, fine. Now's the time to prove it.' She checked the time on her wristwatch. 'Twelve hours,' she reminded him coolly, angling her head in defiance. 'Since you make it sound so simple. All it takes is a wave of that Keegan magic wand, and hey, presto, everything's sorted.'

'Things wouldn't need sorting if you hadn't interfered in the first place,' he hissed, leaning on the desk and cutting the space between them to a whisker.

'And how the hell would you know?' Ella rasped. 'Since you've been conspicuous by your absence.'

'On business,' he reminded tersely. 'Like tomorrow's farce of a conference, Jack Keegan business. Damn it all, woman, why the hell did you have to interfere?'

'It wasn't compulsory,' she pointed out flippantly. 'I didn't *have* to get involved – '

'Then more fool you for doing precisely that. Have you any idea what this could cost me? Have you? *Have you*?' he repeated, thumping the desk again.

'I can probably hazard a guess,' she allowed, with another twinge of conscience as the final invoice from the hotel swam into her mind. Lots of noughts, she'd registered, swallowing hard. Far too many to stop out of a housekeeper's wages. And yet Ella had blithely given the go-ahead.

Feeling suddenly faint, Ella sank down into her chair – another mistake, she realized at once, with six feet four inches of vibrant man, six feet four inches of power towering over her. The lightweight suit he'd travelled back in was straining at the seams as Jack continued to glower.

Anger and hate washed over her in turn. Unfair, her mind screamed. She'd done it for Jack, only for Jack, and, despite his reaction, she'd do it all over again tomorrow if she thought it would help.

If. If Geraghty turned up. If. She was shockingly aware that a verbal agreement to attend might be nothing more than ploy to appease a persistent woman. And, though Geraghty would never allow himself to be bulldozed, fine words would trip glibly off the tongue of a man like that.

Ella let out a sigh. Rightly or wrongly, she'd done it for Jack, but at the end of the day it could all be a huge waste of time. And money, she forced herself to acknowledge. Lots of money. Jack's money. A king's ransom, in fact.

She licked her lips, hazel eyes silently pleading. Jack's gaze was cruelly unbending. 'I – '

The phone rang, slicing through the tension. Quick as a flash Jack shot out a hand to snatch the receiver. 'Keegan,' he bit out, features impassive, and as Jack severed eye contact with Ella, she risked a glance at Ian's rigid profile.

Apart from his opening comment he'd made no effort to defend himself, hadn't really been in focus throughout Ella's row with Jack. He'd gone white, Ella registered, her heart reaching the floor as he stubbornly refused to meet her gaze. Her fault. Like

Jack, Ian was blaming Ella. Like Jack, he doubtless had cause. Whichever way she viewed it, Ella was in the wrong. But the fact that Ian had warned her made Jack's condemnation of Ian seem patently unfair. She'd have to explain – but how, since Jack wasn't in the mood to listen?

The phone call over, Jack's contribution little more than three or four terse words of enquiry, he replaced the handset, those speculative blue eyes switching straight back to Ella.

Aware of a subtle change of mood, Ella sat and squirmed, resisting the urge to reach for the cup of coffee she'd made – hours ago now, it seemed – and which sat untouched and probably stone-cold in the middle of the desk. Cold, like Ella's heart.

The silence was unnerving, the relentless tick of the clock on the wall, the tuneless tattoo of Jack's fingers on the desk driving her to screaming pitch. And still he didn't speak.

'Jack – ' Catching a movement out of the corner of her eye, she broke off. Jack's response was electric.

'And where the hell do you think you're going?' he barked, rounding on Ian as he slunk towards the door, defeat written into the lines of his body.

'I – I thought I'd make a start on my packing,' the younger man explained awkwardly, a dull flush darkening his features.

'Why?'

'The cottage. It goes with the job. And since the job no longer exists – '

'Oh, hell, man,' Jack entreated, the merest hint of a thaw in his tone. 'Of course the job exists. Estate manager. And if the best estate manager in the country can look me in the eye and quit, then fine, walk away, Ian. Don't let me stop you.'

'Meaning?' Ian queried warily as Ella held her breath, allowed herself to hope that Jack's anger had burnt itself out.

'Meaning exactly what I say. Your decision, Ian. Though if you really want to see me squirm,' Jack added lightly, the familiar grin beginning to split his features, 'I guess I could always spell it out in words of one syllable.'

'Put it in writing and I might just believe it,' Ian flashed, his own smile spreading as the truth dawned. His glance flicked from Jack to Ella and back again, Ella's almost imperceptible nod of reassurance galvanizing Ian into action. 'Right. Time I went back to work, then. If you're sure . . .'

'I'm sure,' Jack insisted. 'And Ian,' he added unexpectedly, 'thanks. For everything.'

Praise indeed, Ella derided – only silently. And Jack's smile vanished like the wind the moment the door closed to.

'Well?' he queried, features impassive.

'Perfectly well, thank you,' Ella conceded, with deliberate misunderstanding. For if Ian had kept his job, the perpetrator of the crime had still to be sentenced. Ella's responsibility, Ella's decision. And with Ian off the hook she'd be damned if she'd explain – or, heaven forbid, apologize. 'Coffee?' she offered, reaching for the untouched cup.

Jack shot out a hand to stop her – a vice-like grip on her wrist that drove the breath from her body. 'Thank you, but no,' he declined politely. 'Not yet, at least. Not until someone provides the answers to a number of questions. And, since you appear to be the driving force,' he conceded, with another of those smiles designed to set her teeth on edge, 'fire away, Ella. Surprise me.'

'You mean I haven't already?' she stalled, shockingly aware that his grip had slackened, that his thumb was describing erotic circles on the inside of her wrist.

'Oh, yes,' he conceded lightly. 'Once or twice. Walking out, walking in, arranging my life without so much as a by my leave. Given your track record, Ella Keegan, I'm simply relieved to find the house is still standing. So, unless I'm very much mistaken, someone owes me a detailed explanation – hey, Ella?'

Ella Keegan. Ella's cheeks began to glow as the lump of ice around her heart began to melt. The phone call, she decided. Difficult to gauge, really, since Jack's terse replies had given little away, but Lynette Kaye, at a guess, filling Jack in on the late change of plan.

'Well, Ella?'

Definitely mellow, Ella decided, unable to meet his gaze all of a sudden. Not that she had need to. She'd caught the smile in his voice, the murmur of approval, and with that swirling thumb creating currents of heat that spread upwards and outwards she was shockingly aware that they were alone, man and woman, that the angry scene they'd just played out had raised the emotional thermometer.

'Well, what?' she stalled, attempting, gently to pull away. Jack equally gently stopped her.

'Oh, you know,' he murmured vaguely. 'And, since an apology's out of the question, I guess I'll have to take it as read.'

'Apologize?' Ella spluttered, her head jerking up. Apologize? The cheek of the man. 'For two pins, Jack Keegan, I'd wave my magic wand and spirit you back to the desert – for good this time.'

'I can't think why,' he demurred, moving round the desk, coming to a halt beside her. And Ella dropped her gaze again, focusing her mind on the whorls and knots in the grain of the wood, shockingly aware of the man, of his touch, of his unique body scent, even more aware of the need running through her like a brand.

'Jack!' Ella protested as he raised her hand, kissed the delicate skin on the inside of her wrist.

'Can't a man apologize?' he teased. 'Only fair, don't you think? One apology deserves another, and since you did make yours so prettily – '

'I did nothing of the sort,' Ella scorned, her resistance beginning to crumble as Jack's lips began their slow and languorous climb of her arm. 'No, Jack,' she protested automatically, hazel eyes colliding with dancing sapphire pools, and Jack paused, raised his head, smiled again.

And she was drowning, the battle fought and won, Ella's co-operation, like the apology, taken as read. And why not? Ella didn't belong to Jack, but her body remembered every touch, *craved* his touch. One kiss, she reassured herself as the blood turned to water in her veins. A single, stolen kiss. Surely no one could begrudge her that? And if one kiss led to another . . .

'Oh, Jack,' she breathed as he paused, pulled her close, cupped her face in his hands and gazed down at her, a tender smile playing about the corners of his mouth. 'Oh, Jack, I really don't think this is a good idea.'

'Maybe not,' he agreed solemnly. 'But I think you'll find,' he pointed out smokily, punctuating the words with tiny but devastating kisses, 'that unless you give it a try, you'll never know. And, believe me, Ella, that's exactly what you and I are going to do.'

CHAPTER 10

Busy. A full day. An even fuller night. Far too busy for Ella to waste time brooding, and yet the worries were eating away at the back of her mind.

Jack, Paul Geraghty, the batch of last-minute cooking. Because that was something else Ella had promised Geraghty. No outside caterers. All part of the Geraghty paranoia about security – although, short of running a check on staff and guests, that particular condition seemed a gross waste of time. Yet, given Geraghty's influence and muscle, he probably wouldn't think twice about doing precisely that, Ella mused, the thought vaguely alarming.

All worthwhile, she constantly reassured herself, as long as Geraghty kept his promise to attend. If.

D-day. A houseful of guests and two glaringly empty seats at the dinner table. Fliss – and Geraghty. Jack's tight smile spoke volumes. Not so much a dinner as an early supper, with the real business of the evening still to come. The wine would flow later, Ella supposed, but in the meanwhile, if Geraghty did intend putting in an appearance, time was rapidly running out. Another half-hour and she'd have to serve the meal.

She was toying with the idea of removing the extra places when an agitated Katie appeared in the doorway.

'He's here,' she told Ella, her voice brimming with excitement.

'Thank heavens,' Ella breathed, the shadow of the gallows suddenly retreating. 'And Miss Foxwood?'

'Can't make it till tomorrow,' Katie explained. 'Something to do with an airport strike. Apparently.'

Ella swallowed a smile. Better late than never, she silently conceded. And Fliss would know that tonight was strictly business, that Jack was really relying on Fliss to entertain and charm when the conference drew to an end at the end of the second day.

'Wonderful woman,' Jack acknowledged, hugging Ella in a snatched moment of magic in the kitchen. And the fact that he'd taken time away from the important matters of wheeling and dealing didn't escape her notice. 'But how on earth did you manage to change the guy's mind?'

'Oh, you know . . . just turned on the Ella Keegan brand of charm.' She preened, completely oblivious to the Freudian slip of the tongue.

'Oh?' Jack queried, eyes narrowing thoughtfully.

'He's an American,' she explained. 'And I've read that Americans just love playing at lords and ladies.' She smiled, waved an airy hand. 'Take one stately home, a secure private wing with space enough to house that merry band of minders he can't even visit the bathroom without, and then the *pièce de resistance* – the genuine Edward VI four-poster bed.'

'The *what* bed?' Jack demanded incredulously.

'Why, the bed that King Edward slept in when he came to stay in 1548, of course,' Ella told him, eyes wide and innocent.

'Since the house wasn't built in 1548,' Jack drawled, 'as well you know, how on earth do you manage to make that out?'

'Why, simple, sir,' Ella revealed, lowering her voice and adopting an exaggerated Southern States drawl. 'With the king in question the ripe old age of ten at the time, I just made it up on the spur of the moment!'

'Ella – '

'Worry not, Jack,' she reassured him pertly. 'I won't tell if you don't.'

Kiss and tell. Only Jack wouldn't, of course. An easy conscience, Ella decided, lips tightening, the heated scene in the office replaying in her mind.

'Not a good idea, Jack,' she'd repeated – a desperate effort to convince herself, she'd realized later.

Only Jack had simply smiled, dipped his head, run his tongue across her trembling lower lip and smiled again. 'Trust me,' he'd entreated thickly. 'Just a kiss. Only a kiss, I promise you.'

Just a kiss, Jack's mouth melding with hers, Jack's hands roaming her body. And, shameless through and through, Ella had buried the doubts, smothered the pangs of conscience.

Mouth to mouth, body to body, the currents had swirled through her. A snatched moment of pleasure . . . Jack's tongue darting between her parted lips, swirling into the secret moist depths, an erotic exploration of Ella's mouth and tongue as Jack had pulled her close, run his hands the length of her spine and urged her trembling body into the hard lines of his.

Hard. Oh, yes. Ella had smiled. How he wanted her, Jack's need was every bit as urgent as her own. Only they mustn't. And Jack hadn't. Just a kiss, a frustrating moment of pleasure, because, insanity or otherwise, Ella wanted Jack so badly that it hurt.

Hurt. The thought of Jack and Fliss together. Just a few short hours, Ella acknowledged sickly, and Fliss would be lying in Jack's arms, replete with the glow of love.

'Where the *hell* have you been?'

Ella froze, hugging the pile of towels to her chest. Jack's angry words had drifted through the open doorway and stopped her dead.

'Jack, darling – '

'Don't "Jack, darling" me,' he bit out icily. 'You're late, Fliss. Twenty-four hours late. And in another half-hour I'd have given you up for good.'

As Ella had – or maybe she'd simply hoped, knowing full well Jack would be disappointed. Not so much disappointed as angry, as it turned out, and Ella's own sense of timing left much to be desired. An innocent set of events, she acknowledged wryly, draping the towels over the rail in Fliss's sumptuous bathroom and wondering how to wriggle her way out of this without embarrassing them all.

All part of the job, she supposed, cursing the need to double-check Millie's handiwork. For, having cast a critical eye over the dinner table and registered the crumpled napkin, one thing had led to another. Opening the linen cupboard door to discover the fresh pile of towels Millie had forgotten to place in Felicity's bathroom had been just another minor irritation Ella could easily had done without. And, since Millie was conspicuous by her absence, Ella had snatched the offending bale and gone in search of the young maid.

Then she'd had second thoughts. If Millie was sneaking a forbidden cigarette outside the back door, it would probably be quicker to turn a blind eye and do it herself. She had never dreamed she'd inadvertently stumble upon World War Three.

As luck would have it, the field of battle moved from bedroom to sitting room, and, sensing she'd never have a better moment, Ella slipped through to the adjoining dressing room, her clumsy fingers closing round the handle as the buzz of voices rose again.

Spurred on by panic, Ella tugged. Hard. Oh, hell. The door refused to budge, simply wasn't in use, she realized belatedly, leaning back against the woodwork and wondering how on earth she'd explain her presence to a volcanic Fliss.

'What on earth is going on, Jack?' the younger woman berated. 'This is my home, damn you – '

Jack's anger seemed to have blown itself out as the wind changed direction. 'My home, too,' he pointed out calmly.

'I don't expect you to fill it with a posse of hangers-on,' Fliss pointed out tersely, ignoring his remark.

'The pot calling the kettle, Fliss?'

'Meaning?'

'That "posse of hangers-on" you rarely travel anywhere without.'

'Those, Jack Keegan, are my friends.'

'Exactly, and these are my guests – *our* guests,' he countered, the edge to his tone barely detectable.

'Who were booked in at a hotel, as I seem to recall.'

'Just a slight change of plan, my pet. And hardly the end of the world.'

'But you promised,' she accused huffily. 'The house wouldn't be used for business. You promised, Jack.'

'I know, sweetheart. But something important came up and there was a last-minute change of plan. It's a one-off, Fliss,' he reassured her mildly. 'It won't happen again.'

'Hmm. Well, if you say so,' she allowed, clearly not convinced.

'I do. And, since we're running late, isn't it time you were getting dressed?'

'Undressed,' she contradicted him smokily, and Ella's cheeks flamed. 'We haven't made love in weeks.'

'Hardly surprising since we haven't been together for weeks.'

'Exactly. And now that we are – '

A loaded pause, the rustle of clothes, a throaty laugh and Ella closed her eyes, closed her mind. Trapped. Caught between the devil and deep blue sea.

Declare her presence and embarrass them all, or stand and listen while the man she loved made love with another woman? Too cruel. Her hands clenched, nails digging into the palms as she struggled for control. And then a petulant wail brought Ella's numb mind back to the present.

'But, Jack – '

'Later. We're late and we've a houseful of guests,' he reminded tersely.

'*You've* a houseful of guests,' she needled crossly.

'Wrong, Fliss. This is business. And business, don't forget, pays the bills. I'll wait for you downstairs.'

'Ja-ack!' A door clicking shut, a most unlady like curse, the heavy thump of something solid bouncing off the woodwork, and then the sound Ella had been praying for – the noise of the shower.

The splash of water faded as Fliss slammed the bathroom door. Hardly daring to breathe in case the door was suddenly flung open again, Ella tiptoed across the deep pile of the carpet and made her escape.

Close, too close for Ella's shredded nerves, and the cup of strong, sweet coffee was warming, calming.

Progress, she supposed wryly. Not so many years ago she'd have reached for the cooking brandy. And, though she might have escaped for the moment, she knew what would happen later. Jack and Fliss, making up for lost time, while Ella lay rigid in her bed, her body craving the touch of a man who didn't belong to her. Only she couldn't have it. Damned if she did and damned if she didn't.

So, decision time, Ella. No hiding place. You've reached the end of the line, girl. And she ought to have known that staying on in the first place had been an idiotic idea.

'Ella? So it *is* you? I hardly dared hope to believe it.'

Ella froze. Her night for surprises, she acknowledged as a man detached himself from the table and crossed to the alcove where she'd stationed herself in discreet observation. Not that she had need to. The highly polished table gleamed beneath the weight of silver and crystal, Waterford crystal at that, and the vintage wine, carefully selected by Jack, flowed like water, proving the perfect accompaniment to the exquisite creations of food served by Katie and the rest of the team as if to the manner born.

'Stephen! I didn't realize you were staying,' she almost stammered, and yet why should she have? There'd been too much to organize for Ella to supervise each and every arrangement, and not everyone staying tonight had attended day one, she recalled.

She had a sudden awful thought. Stephen might inadvertently give her away. He'd already called out across the room, though with the chink of cutlery on china and the noisy buzz of conversation, Ella's secret was probably safe. For now.

And yet, why not? she mused, rustling up a smile for Stephen, who'd paused, was gazing down at her quizzically. It could be a blessing in disguise and would bring the farce of her position to an end.

'I had an idea you'd taken this job – couldn't resist responding to the summons,' Stephen revealed, in a succinct, if not entirely accurate description of the invitation to join the conference. 'I hope you don't mind?'

'Of course I don't mind, but – '

'You're busy? Yes, of course you are,' he demurred, scanning the room, the magnificent great hall, with its ornate plaster ceilings and oak-panelled walls with their fruit and flower motifs, the perfect backdrop for the table groaning under the weight of food and capable of seating a hundred and still leaving elbow-room a plenty. Dancing blue eyes came back to Ella. 'I guess this is down to you, Ella,' he acknowledged warmly. 'And a first-class job by the look of things.'

'I'm glad you approve. But in the interests of fairness,' she demurred, her smile dimpling, 'I must point out that I was very well trained.'

'And if I could take the credit for this,' Stephen responded, equally lightly, 'I'd be blatantly dishonest. So, how about a drink? Once you're off duty, I mean. Just for old times' sake. A wee night cap in my room, perhaps?'

Ella raised an eyebrow. 'Are you trying to get me the sack?' she challenged, folding her arms in mock indignation.

'If I thought it would bring you back to Bristol,' Stephen allowed, grinning broadly, 'I'd probably give it a try. But I'd say you're happy here?'

Question, not statement, Ella noted, wondering how to answer that with a degree of honesty. The job was everything she'd hoped for, and more, allowing her to pop across the park and see Gramps two or three times a week, and yet the torment of working for Jack was beginning to take its toll. Heaven and hell both. Purgatory, she supposed. And she would have to walk away. Soon.

'I'm happy,' she insisted, crossing her fingers at the tiny white lie.

'Fine. You can tell me about it later. Your room?' he probed, blue eyes twinkling. 'Since mine's clearly off-limits. A sitting room, perhaps? You must have your own quarters, Ella?'

Out of the corner of her eye Ella saw Fliss excuse herself from her place at the head of the table and sashay across the polished wooden floor in a swirl of skirts and indignation.

'A problem, Mrs Andrews-Watson?'

'Not at all, madam. Mr Tolland and I are just renewing our acquaintanceship. Allow me to introduce you. Miss Foxwood – Stephen Tolland.'

'Felicity,' she insisted, flashing Stephen a winning smile. 'Tolland?' Her pert little nose crinkled. 'But of course – the Tolland hotel chain. I knew I'd heard that name before. So – not so much old friends,' she mused, green eyes narrowing thoughtfully as she switched her gaze from Stephen to Ella and back again, 'as employee and employer.'

Pointedly turning her back on Ella, she crooned, 'Do let's join the others,' with an obscene flutter of lashes. 'Your meal must be getting cold, Stephen. I *can* call you Stephen?' she positively simpered.

Despite the shiver of distaste that rippled down her spine, Ella smiled. Fliss *had* done her homework, she acknowledged as a bemused Stephen offered the younger woman an arm, mouthing the single word, 'Later,' over Fliss's head as he led her back to the table. Clever Fliss. Most impressive, and clearly one of the things Jack saw in the girl, discounting the obvious.

And on the subject of the obvious, Ella's mouth tightened. Designer label notwithstanding, that wisp of a dress left little to the imagination and wouldn't have been decent as a nightdress, she concluded sourly. All white lace and promises, it fitted Fliss's slender body like a glove, the style reminiscent of a Flapper's dress but for the tiny shoestring straps. Flat-chested, Ella couldn't help but note bitchily, her own generous curves almost swelling in pride. And yet, since Fliss had hooked him, clearly to Jack's taste.

Eight years, Ella mused. He'd had eight years of freedom, and with his stunning looks and aura of power, not to mention the magnetic draw of money, Jack could pick and choose. Had chosen Fliss, Ella recalled, rubbing salt into the wound. He'd taken his time but he'd finally taken the plunge, was just a few months short of the wedding of the year.

The Honourable Felicity Foxwood of Deighton Hall to Mr Jack Keegan of Sherbrook. At St Paul's, naturally, Ella wouldn't mind betting. Only the best for the Honourable Fliss. Or the dishonourable Fliss? she mused with a stab of alarm. None of Ella's business, she supposed, but in the early weeks of Ella's employment, she'd been sharply aware that the younger woman's bed hadn't always been slept in. None of her business, she'd decided at the time. And none of her business now. Poor Jack. He might just have bitten off more than he could chew.

'Anything wrong, Mrs A?' Katie queried, her plump features frowning.

'Not as far as I know, Katie,' Ella conceded, banishing the shadows. 'In fact, I'd go so far as to say everything's perfect. Mr Geraghty's holding court in the drawing room, brandy balloon in one hand, best Havana cigar in the other, and not a single armed goon in sight. Mr Keegan's like the cat that got the cream, and as for Miss Foxwood – ' She pulled herself up short. As for Miss Foxwood, she'd done everything Jack could have asked of her and more, and only a fool would doubt it. Why, even before the soup plates had been cleared away she'd had Geraghty eating out of her hand like a well-trained canary.

So, unless Ella was mistaken, with Geraghty happy to relax without the presence of his minders, Jack had secured the support he needed. All thanks to Fliss.

'All thanks to you,' Jack insisted, stopping Ella in the hall, his warm smile disarming.

Ella hardened her heart. 'Just part of the Aileen Andrews-Watson service,' she retorted primly, determined to put their relationship back on a formal footing.

'Not the Ella Keegan service this time, then?' Jack queried, frowning.

'No, Jack. Ella Keegan doesn't exist any more – remember?'

'Since I'm looking at the lady in question, large as life and twice as ravishing, you will understand if I'm forced to disagree?'

Ella shrugged. 'Your prerogative, Jack. But a dangerous one to debate in public, surely?'

'Afraid, Ella? That's not like you,' he jeered.

'Just a matter of common sense,' she demurred. 'Why risk rocking the boat at this stage?' she needled. 'Geraghty's happy, thanks to Fliss, and Fliss is happy to bask in your approval.'

'Hardly,' he countered with a deprecating smile, folding his arms and leaning back against the wall, blue eyes coldly mocking. 'But I guess I follow your drift. Worry not,' he entreated in the same mocking tone, 'we're all alone, and there's not a cat in hell's chance of Fliss discovering the truth.'

'But the walls might have ears, Jack, and then all that careful planning would come to nothing.'

'I don't see why.'

'Fliss – and the wrath of a beautiful woman,' Ella reminded him tightly. 'Not so much a woman scorned as hoodwinked in her own home. Try explaining that away with a houseful of curious lookers-on.'

She made to sweep past. Jack's hand on her arm pulled her up sharp.

'Ella?'

She glanced down. Such a gentle restraint, yet skin-to-skin and searing, the golden hairs on the back of his hand standing out against the tan, the tan standing out against Ella's milky white skin. She raised her chin defiantly. 'Jack?'

'I thought we were friends, Ella?'

'What on earth gave you that idea?' Ella scorned, hazel eyes flashing. 'You're my employer, Jack. Nothing more, nothing less.'

'Liar!'

'Like I said,' Ella retorted, colouring, 'your prerogative.'

'And if I chose to prove it? If I touch you, kiss you – '

'Friends don't kiss and touch,' she bit out. 'Friends don't impose. Friends don't overstep the mark. But go ahead, Jack,' she invited. 'Don't let me stop you. By all means take your pleasure.'

'And the pleasure would be all mine, hey, Ella?' he jeered. 'Since you don't react, don't respond . . .'

'To a man with your track record? At the risk of overloading that enormous Keegan ego,' she scorned, 'you're a good-looking man, and naturally I'm flattered – '

'Flattered? *Flattered?*' he all but choked. 'Good God, woman, you *want* me – '

'I want,' she told him icily, shaking herself free, 'to be left alone to do the job I'm paid for. Nothing more, nothing less.'

'And if I refuse?'

'Your prerogative. Your house. Your fiancée. Your problem when I blast the sordid details from the rooftops.'

'You're bluffing, Ella.'

'Am I?'

'Either that or you've changed beyond recognition,' he bit out, and then his head snapped up, as if something had suddenly struck him. 'Oh, Ella, Ella. What have I done?' he asked in anguish.

Since that particular list of transgressions was as long as her arm, Ella was suddenly lost for words, the anger and the hate draining away. No, not hate, never hate. Pathetic and futile it might be, but she loved him. For better or for worse, she inwardly derided, her anxious eyes scanning his face, seeing the pain, understanding the pain.

Because Jack was blaming himself. The Ella he'd known in the early days didn't exist any more; Jack had destroyed her. At least, Ella amended silently, that was how she was reading it. Only Jack was wrong. Of course Ella had changed, but not in the way Jack was imagining. She'd grown up, she'd grown stronger, she'd learned to stand on her own two feet, and, most of all, she'd finally learned to accept herself, warts and all.

She'd purged the guilt but she'd never, ever stopped loving Jack, wouldn't dream of hurting him. Only now she had. Empty threats. She *was* bluffing.

'Jack?'

'Ella?' Polite now, the anguish showing in his features, the distance between them yawning like a chasm. Because Ella had hurt him, had spurned him, and, gentleman through and through, Jack was giving her space.

Surprisingly he made no effort to move away, seemed oblivious to the sudden buzz of noise as the drawing room door behind him swung open. The comings and goings of a small army of waiters and maids pressed into service, courtesy of Katie and the village, clearly didn't impinge.

Watching him, Ella felt her throat tighten, tears stinging the backs of her eyes. Because she loved him? Because she'd lost him? Because, inadvertently or otherwise, she'd hurt him? Heaven only knew – probably the entire pathetic caboodle, she decided, rekindling her sense of humour. Not so much a *My Wife Next Door* comedy show, as a *Cuckoo In The Nest* farce. Ella, not Fliss. Ella didn't belong, and with the benefit of hindsight she should have followed her instincts and gone the moment she'd realized she was working for Jack.

Jack, devastating Jack, with the expensive dinner jacket carelessly unbuttoned, the muscles of the powerful chest rippling beneath the fine lawn fabric of the dress shirt. More formal than she'd ever known, he carried the elegant clothes with ease, the stark combination of black and white setting off the rapidly deepening tan to perfection. A blond Adonis – the collar-length waves of hair bleached to the colour of straw by a relentless sun, eyes like sapphires in the rugged face she loved. Her Jack, only not *her* Jack any longer.

Stephen? she mused, catching a fleeting glimpse of him through the open doorway. Another blond, blue-eyed hunk. Not quite a match for Jack's rugged looks but capable of turning heads, female heads, when he walked into a room. And he had managed to attract the attention of Fliss, Ella recalled, the muscles in her belly tightening. Or maybe the younger woman had simply chosen to belittle Ella in front of a handsome man, thus underlining her own superiority? A hint of the green-eyed monsters, Ella decided, smiling despite herself. Fliss putting her housekeeper down and then swanning back to the bevy of important people on Stephen's arm.

Important? Stephen? Ella's eyes narrowed suddenly, the awful suspicion that Jack had engineered Stephen's presence running through her mind.

'Naturally I was aware he was a previous employer,' Jack conceded off-handedly when she put the thought into words. 'It was on your c.v.'

'So why the invitation?' she challenged. 'Stephen might own a chain of hotels but he's hardly in your league, Jack.'

'I – had my reasons,' he conceded warily.

'Sheer nosiness, to be precise – hey, Jack?' she needled.

'Just natural curiosity,' he soothed. 'After all, I know nothing about what you've been doing with yourself for the past few years.'

'But it's none of your business,' she hissed, the anger back with a vengeance. Better that way. Much easier to keep him at arm's length.

'I don't agree. You're my wife – '

'*Ex*-wife. Soon to be ex-anything else, for that matter. Ex-employee, ex-housekeeper, ex-'

'Lover?' he interrupted.

'We were ex- that years ago,' Ella scorned.

'So sure, Ella. So very sure. And that's another thing,' he mused, rubbing his chin with the back of his hand, blue eyes narrowing. 'I distinctly heard Tolland call you Ella. Ella,' he emphasized grimly. 'Not Aileen.'

'So?

'So, somewhere between his employ and mine,' he mused, folding his arms and leaning back against the wall, 'you changed part of your identity. Now, why, I wonder?'

'I simply took the name I was given at birth – not that it's any of your business,' Ella reminded him huffily.

'But it *is* my business. Anything and everything that affects you is my business.'

'So sure, Jack? So very sure?' she jeered, and Jack's dull flush, visible even in the shadows, was all the proof she needed that she'd scored the bull's eye. 'And how the hell do you make that out?'

'Wife, ex-wife, ex-employee. My responsibility, Ella.'

'Not as far as I'm concerned. It's over, done with. And the moment I walk away from here you can rest assured that you've done your bit and more.'

'But maybe now that I've found you I'm in no particular hurry to let you go.'

Let her go, sever the ties once and for all, relinquish a responsibility he'd had no right to shoulder in the first place. Only Jack, having sipped from the honeypot of power, didn't want to lose control, clearly enjoyed playing God with other people's lives.

'You know something Jack?' Ella conceded harshly. 'I hadn't realized just what a scheming bastard you are until now.'

'Meaning?

'Meaning all this – ' She waved a hand, the gesture itself oozing contempt. 'Wining and dining in style to sweet-talk people into parting with their well-earned money.'

'Sorry to disappoint you, Ella, but it's normal business practice, and *good* practice at that, since it's tax deductible.'

'And Stephen?' she enquired. 'Issuing invitations to the small fry? How does that fit into the Jack Keegan scheme of things? He hasn't the money to invest in your consortium,' Ella reminded him icily, 'so don't insult me now by suggesting you believe it. No,' she acknowledged in the same scathing tone. 'Stephen's here tonight because Jack Keegan couldn't resist throwing Stephen and me together to see what materialized.'

'Ah, yes, but don't forget,' he pointed out slyly, 'you wouldn't have been together if someone hadn't interfered in the first place and switched the venue. Wriggle out of that one, Ella – if you can.'

'I don't need to. The motive doesn't change. Knowing you, you'd simply have changed tactics – ingratiated yourself with Stephen at the hotel, pumped him for information and then issued an open invitation here, if the truth's known.'

'Like I said, my dear, so sure – '

'Jack!'

The sharp hiss of indrawn breath was Ella's. So close, she realized as the younger woman appeared from out of nowhere.

'Fliss! Darling!' Recovering fast, Jack held out a hand, inviting Fliss's presence. And sure enough, Ella noticed, irrationally hurt, Fliss preened, closed the gap between them and slid her hand possessively into Jack's. Ella's sharp gaze didn't miss the ugly flash of triumph in a pair of emerald eyes.

'Just complimenting Mrs Andrews-Watson and her team on a job well done,' Jack explained smoothly, neatly preventing Ella from melting away into the shadows. 'Talking of which . . .'

He paused, pulled Fliss close, dipping his head and allowing his mouth to brush against hers, to linger, to savour, to kiss again as a rigid Ella was forced to stand and watch from the sidelines. 'Well done, darling,' he crooned smokily. 'Everything's gone to plan, and believe me,' he breathed, tugging her away, the dismissive glance he shot at Ella freezing the blood in her veins, 'we'd never have done it without you.'

CHAPTER 11

'Ella?'

'Stephen! Good heavens, you startled me,' she insisted as the colour came and went in her cheeks. Since her thoughts had been miles away, she had visibly jumped.

Stephen smiled, a quizzical note in his voice. 'Not too late for that nightcap, Ella?'

She hesitated. It was well past midnight and she was tired, bone-weary, but she wouldn't sleep now, she realized instinctively. Too many harsh words had seen to that – not to mention that other niggle eating away at her, that unremitting picture running through her mind. Fliss and Jack together, man and woman, naked, kissing, touching, making love.

Not yet, since the party hadn't broken up by any means, but as sure as night followed day it would happen. Too cruel. And yet ridiculous, really, since it must have been happening for months. And Jack was no monk. He wouldn't have slept alone each and every night for the past eight years. Unlike Ella. Foolish, foolish Ella.

Swallowing hard, she forced a smile. 'Too late? Why the night's still young,' she trilled, over-brightly. 'Give me five minutes to check on things here and I'll be with you.'

Two minutes to check everything was tidy in the kitchens, to ensure that taxis had been called for any staff who'd declined to take up the option of staying, and two minutes to head back to the drawing room, cast an enquiring glance around in case there was anything glaringly obvious for Ella to do. Not that she had need to. Technically, at least, she'd been off duty for the past half-hour and people were beginning to drift up to their rooms, replete with food and wine.

So, five minutes she'd promised, five minutes she took, and Stephen's smile of approval was balm to a battered ego.

'Lead on, my lady,' he teased, executing a mock bow before offering his arm.

'Why, this way, my lord,' she obligingly joined in. 'Not quite what you've been used to, I'm sure,' she demurred, 'but if sir doesn't mind roughing it belowstairs – '

'Mrs Andrews-Watson.'

The woman's arctic tone stopped Ella in her tracks.

'Madam?' she enquired politely, acutely aware of her arm linking Stephen's. And then she remembered. She'd done nothing wrong and she'd be damned if she'd stand like a naughty schoolgirl while this bright young thing raised her supercilious eyebrows in tangible disapproval. 'Anything wrong, Miss Foxwood?' she queried pleasantly. 'If there's something you need – ?'

'Thank you, no,' Fliss interrupted coolly. 'I simply wondered where you were going.'

Since they were poised at the top of the stairs, the stairs that led directly to Ella's self-contained flat, Ella was forced to smother the obvious retort that sprang to her lips. 'I was just about to go off duty, madam. Unless you feel it's inconvenient?'

'Not at all. Most of our other guests,' she conceded, with a pointed glance at Stephen, 'have already retired for the night. Talking of which . . .'

'Madam?' Ella probed, sensing what was coming next and angling her head in polite enquiry.

'I do hope, Mrs Andrews-Watson,' Fliss sneeringly observed, 'That you haven't forgotten your position in this house?'

'Good heavens, no,' Stephen interjected, pre-empting Ella's stinging retort with a devastating smile. 'Just a couple of old friends, you know, catching up on the gossip. And since entertaining a lady in my bedroom might be misconstrued . . .'

'How very considerate,' Fliss acknowledged dryly, the venomous glance she shot at Ella a clear indication that, in this case at least, the description of lady didn't apply.

Ella stiffened, only Stephen's reassuring squeeze of an arm persuading her to hold her tongue. 'But there's no need to hide yourself away downstairs,' Fliss chided lightly. 'You're a guest, Stephen.

There's no shortage of rooms in a house this size. And, since the fire's still burning in the green room, under the circumstances it might be more appropriate for Mrs Andrews-Watson to join you there.'

Bitch, Ella mouthed silently as Fliss flounced away, the angry stab of stiletto heels ricocheting eerily around the marble-tiled hall.

'Bitch,' Stephen echoed, surprisingly. And then he grinned. 'The green room, my lady? Or shall we live dangerously?'

Living dangerously won. Ella had no intention of sitting all prim and proper upstairs just to appease Fliss's sense of propriety. Why, the barefaced cheek of the woman. She could hop from one bed to another, despite being engaged, but when it came to Ella –

'Don't let her upset you,' Stephen entreated, sensing Ella's unease.

Reaching Ella's door, he pulled up, taking her face in his hands and gazing down, strange emotions stirring in the depths of his eyes.

He hadn't given up hope, Ella realized, her heart sinking. They might not have parted friends, but Stephen wasn't about to let that come between them, and Ella sighed as Stephen dipped his head, ran his tongue across her lips, allowed the kiss to deepen for a fraction of a second.

'Come on,' he entreated, tugging her inside. 'I don't know about you but I could do with a drink. The stronger the better. Anything at all, in fact,' he added tartly. 'Just to wash away the taste of that woman's poison.'

Whisky for Stephen, coffee for Ella, and the conversation light and easy. Ella's tiredness began to drain away. She'd almost forgotten Stephen was such good company, felt herself begin to relax for what seemed like the first time in weeks as she threw back her head and laughed at the tale he retold of an overweight guest who'd become wedged in the bath resulting in a visit from the fire brigade.

'I shouldn't laugh, really,' Stephen acknowledged, having made himself at home, jacket draped carelessly over the back of a chair, elegant bow tie discarded. 'But the local papers got hold of it and he turned out to be an eminent member of the council, whose extra-marital activities came as shock to no one but his wife.'

'Ah. I take it he wasn't alone at the time?'

'He was by the time the Press arrived,' Stephen countered merrily. 'But it wouldn't have happened in your day, hey, Ella?'

'Certainly not,' she agreed with mock horror. 'Standards, Mr Tolland. What is life in the hotel trade coming to?'

'You could always come back,' he suggested carefully, swirling the amber liquid round and round the bottom of his glass, an over-casual gesture that didn't deceive Ella for a moment. 'You'd whisk the place back into shape in no time.'

'I guess I could at that,' she agreed, glad to know the job was hers if she wanted it. Having parted with him on less than amicable terms, it was a relief to discover Stephen was more than happy to forgive and forget. But if he was about to repeat that other proposal he was destined to be sadly disappointed.

He didn't, instead placing his glass down and pulling her against him on her minuscule settee before kissing her. Thoroughly this time.

Not entirely surprised at this sudden turn of events, Ella forced herself to relax, attempting to respond, testing, remembering the taste of Stephen. So like Jack and yet not at all like Jack. No demands. Not yet, at least, Stephen, like Ella, was seemingly reluctant to test the limits of their relationship. Yet.

There was more easy chatter, and the conversation turned to the conference.

'I might invest at that,' Stephen surprised her by admitting when Ella raised the subject. 'Aunt Hilda died. You remember – the old dear who lived alone on Dartmoor without benefit of running water or electricity? It turned out she was worth a small fortune, and yours truly was the only heir.'

Ella grinned her delight. 'Then all the more reason to invest wisely,' she pointed out, knowing Stephen had long nurtured ambitions of taking his British-based hotel chain into Europe.

'Maybe,' he agreed, refilling Ella's cup before helping himself to coffee from the cafetière on the table. 'But Keegan's no fool. He has a nose for making money. Where Keegan leads today, the rest of the pack follow tomorrow. Intuitive. A very clever guy,' he conceded without rancour. 'Apart from his Achilles' heel.'

'Achilles' heel?' Ella queried warily.

'The Honourable Felicity. A nasty piece of work if ever I saw one.'

'But you don't know her?' Ella probed. 'I mean, you haven't come across her before now?'

'I don't need to. I've met her type in the past. For all the ability to charm, an out-and-out bitch. Pity,' he mused. 'Despite his runaway success, Keegan's a nice guy.'

'Yes.' Ella smiled despite herself. A very nice guy. A wonderful guy. And probably well on the way to making love by now, she realized with a stab of anguish.

'Ella? Is something wrong? Do you want me to go?'

'No!' She closed her eyes for an instant, banishing the moment of pain, and then her lids fluttered open to find Stephen's brow creased with concern. 'No,' she repeated firmly, forcing a smile. 'Not yet, at least. If my reputation's in shreds as far as a certain young lady's concerned,' she pointed out tartly, 'then I'm not about to disappoint her.'

Because if Ella knew Fliss half as well as she thought she did, not content with making the suggestion, the hostess with the mostest would undoubtedly check that her handsome guest in the green room had everything he needed. And he did. Right here belowstairs.

Ella smiled. Easy. All she had to do was keep her mind from straying the length of the house, up the double spiral staircase and into either of the bedrooms in a certain suite of rooms.

'Happy, Ella?' Stephen probed, sensing some of her mood.

'Probably as happy as I'll ever be,' she acknowledged frankly, and, suppressing the shiver of apprehension that trickled down her spine, she knelt on the hearthrug, coaxing the embers of fire back into life with the poker.

Disconcertingly, Stephen joined her, his expression suddenly sombre.

'Stephen – '

'It's okay,' he soothed, cupping her face in his hands and smiling down at her. 'I won't rush you, Ella. No sudden demands on mind or body. Cross my heart,' he insisted, brushing her mouth with his lips before doing precisely that. 'I just want to sit and hold you,' he explained, leaning back against the padded frame of the settee and pulling her close, a protective arm across her shoulder as they studied the pictures in the flames.

'So?' he enquired into the comfortable silence. 'Time to spill the beans. Why doesn't the Hon Fliss like you?'

'Like me?' Ella grinned. 'Now there's an understatement. Who's to know what's running through the dear lady's mind. But is it really so obvious?' she queried sharply.

'Mrs Andrews-Watson,' he clipped, with definite arctic undertones, 'I do hope you haven't forgotten your position in this house.'

Ella giggled. 'With the Hon Fliss to remind me, not to mention keeping a weather eye on my morals, how I could I possibly forget?' she teased. 'It's – nothing personal,' she told him carefully. 'From what I can gather, she had her heart set on a butler.'

'I see. And Keegan overruled her? He's no fool.'

'Wrong, Stephen!' Ella exclaimed, hoping the rush of colour to her cheeks could be explained away by the glow of the fire. 'Jack wasn't here at the time.'

'Jack? My, my, first-name terms with the boss,' he teased. 'Things do sound cosy.'

'I'm on first-name terms with you,' she pointed out primly. 'And I always was, I seem to recall.'

'Ah, yes, my love, but I'm not in the same league as Keegan, and if the lovely bride-to-be happened to overhear she'd skin you alive, hey, Ella?'

'Not to mention the slight matter of hanging, drawing and quartering,' Ella agreed, cradling her head in the comfortable niche of Stephen's shoulder.

Cosy. Nice and easy. None of the turmoil of being with Jack. Just nice and gentle, a silence shared. Jack and Stephen. So very alike and yet so vastly different. Tall, blond, good-looking and with a surprising amount in common when it came down to business. Strange, really. And she'd always had a soft spot for Stephen.

Could she change her mind? she mused. She couldn't even argue that marrying Stephen would take her away from Gramps. Like Jack, Stephen was hell-bent on building an empire. Like Jack, Stephen would see the sense of expanding, would be happy to move to the moon if the potential was there. Bristol, Birmingham, Stafford . . . oh, yes, the potential was there, and with Stephen's latest venture, The Kensington Savana, beginning to give even the largest five-star hotel group a run for its money, she wouldn't mind betting Stephen really was on his way.

Nice and easy? the voice of her conscience scorned. Second best, you mean. And with one failed marriage behind him, Stephen deserved better than that. But there would be no demands, she realized instinctively. Since Stephen was an adoring father already, Ella's infertility wouldn't be a barrier. Second best, she reminded herself. Whichever way she viewed it, she'd still be cheating Stephen. In any case, she recalled, smiling wryly, wasn't she jumping the gun? Stephen hadn't asked her again. Yet.

'More coffee?' she offered, making to rise.

'Not yet awhile,' he demurred, and, since Ella had moved, he twisted round to face her, that solemn expression in his eyes again as his hands closed round her shoulders.

Suppressing the frisson of unease, Ella forced a smile. 'I – '

'Don't,' he entreated softly. 'Don't say a word. Everything's perfect as it is, and I promise you, Ella, I'm not about to spoil things. Trust me, hey?'

Trust. Man and woman. Man kissing woman, woman kissing man. A ritual as old as the hills and as every bit as natural. Mouth to mouth, lips to lips.

Stephen's arms slipping round to hold and enfold. Ella stiffening at the hard body contact.

'Relax,' Stephen soothed, his hands caressing the lines of her back as his mouth feathered kisses from one corner of her mouth to the other and back again. 'I'm not going to hurt you, I promise.'

Just a kiss, nothing more, nothing less. Just a man and a woman alone, and balm for Ella's bruised heart, her battered ego. No demands, no towering emotions. Just touch, taste and taste again, a giving and receiving of pleasure. Stephen's fingers raked through the tight coil of her hair, pulling out the pins, allowing the long, vibrant locks to cascade down her back.

Ella's fingers scrunched through Stephen's glossy waves, so like Jack's, so unlike Jack's. Jack. Ella's mind slipped, the surge of emotion catching her offguard, because suddenly it was Jack she was craving, Jack she was kissing, her fingers tracing the angles and planes of Jack's face as she pushed her body into the hard lines of his.

'Ella – '

The phone rang – the internal phone, Ella noted automatically with an absurd surge of disappointment. And then she realized. Stephen. Not Jack. Stephen. Oh, God. Was she mad? What on earth would Stephen think of her?

Careful to avoid contact with his probing eyes, she pulled herself upright and reached for the receiver, pushing her hair back over her shoulder before taking three or four deep and calming breaths.

'Housekeeper. How may I help you?' she enquired pleasantly, expecting it to be Fliss and too overwrought to cope with the mouthful of her name.

Only it wasn't. It was Jack. And, judging from his tone, it wasn't a social call.

'Ella! Good God, woman,' he blasted viciously, and Ella visibly blanched. 'What took you so long to respond? No – never mind now,' he railed as Ella tried to get a word in edgeways. 'There's no time to waste,' he castigated coldly. 'We need a doctor. Fast. It's Fliss. She's ill. And I only hope for your sake, madam housekeeper, that it isn't what I think it is.'

CHAPTER 12

'Food poisoning? But – are you sure?' Ella queried, smothering the panic, feeling suddenly every bit as ill as Fliss seemed.

'Judging from the symptoms, as sure as I can be,' the doctor stated matter-of-factly, taking the bar of antiseptic soap that Ella proffered with a curt nod of thanks. 'We'll run a few tests just to make sure, but we won't have the results for a day or two. In the meanwhile,' she insisted, drying her hands, 'you'd better make a note of who's eaten what over the past forty-eight hours.'

'Forty-eight hours?' Jack groaned, propping up the jamb of the bathroom door.

'Just standard practice,' the doctor explained, not the middle-aged man in a starched white coat that Ella had vaguely envisaged, but a surprisingly young and attractive woman in a crisp grey linen suit. 'I take it there's just the family involved?'

'Oh, hell,' Jack murmured, his thoughts a mirror image of Ella's.

'Oh, dear,' the doctor echoed, once Jack had filled her in. 'That does put a different complexion on things. Outside caterers?'

There was another raised eyebrow when Ella vehemently shook her head.

'I see. Well, if it's salmonella it's a notifiable disease,' she reminded them, her clipped tones turning frosty. 'And since we can't rule it out altogether, we'd better assume the worst and hope we're being over-cautious. I suppose it's too much to hope you've kept samples of everything?'

'Samples?' Jack queried incredulously.

'For analysis,' Dr Treacy explained. 'The sooner we identify the source, the sooner your fiancée gets the treatment she needs. And if there are other cases . . .'

Ella swallowed hard. Her career, Jack's business, not to mention the risk of death salmonella could pose. An icy shiver ran down her spine. The thought simply didn't bear thinking about.

'I expect you'd like to take those samples now,' Ella murmured, far more calmly than she felt.

'Not my domain,' the doctor explained pleasantly, but – taking the opportunity to check on levels of hygiene, Ella surmised – she obligingly followed as Ella led the way down to the kitchens and the small fridge used solely for that purpose, where an overwrought Ella listened intently as Dr Treacy outlined the procedure for contacting the local environmental health department.

Opening the fridge door, Ella moved to one side.

'As you can see, everything's labelled, and all the utensils were sterilized first.'

The doctor raised an eyebrow. 'Most impressive,' she acknowledged, logging the trays with their scraps of food, a miniature feast that would have done a dolls' house proud. 'You've done well.'

'Not at all,' Ella demurred, the panic beginning to subside as she made a quick mental inventory. 'Every school cook in the country would have known to do the same.'

Salmonella? Surely not, she mused, willing herself to believe it. She'd taken no chances, hadn't used any of the high-risk foods, and, since she'd supervised the cooking herself, she could personally vouch for the standards of hygiene. Colour-coded chopping boards, separate fridges for raw food and cooked, and stainless steel surfaces so squeaky clean the most fastidious of inspectors would be hard-pressed to find fault. And yet there was no denying Fliss was ill.

Fliss. She didn't look ill, so much as green about the gills, Ella realized, with that sinking feeling about her heart again, and, recalling Fliss's earlier reaction to her presence, Ella stiffened.

'What the hell is *she* doing here?' Fliss had demanded, raising her tear-stained face from the pillows to glare across at Ella, who'd paused on the threshold of her bedroom. Dr Treacy's presence behind her had clearly not registered.

Wincing at the venom in her tone, but aware that nothing she could say would improve things, Ella had flushed, watching in mute apology as Jack had crossed the room to regain his place on the edge of the bed.

'Sweetheart, don't fret,' he'd soothed, brushing a damp wisp of hair from her brow in a strangely tender gesture that spoke volumes.

For if she'd doubted it before, the truth was now glaringly obvious to Ella. Jack loved Fliss, had simply been playing games with Ella – teasing, tormenting, amusing himself. And if part of the fun happened to include making love to Ella on the hearthrug, who was Jack to look a gift horse in the mouth? Only she hadn't gone through with it. Precious little consolation, but something to hold onto in the dark hours.

Conscious of two sets of accusing eyes crossing the room to greet her, Ella had moved aside, allowing the doctor past before slipping silently out of the way, opting to wait in Fliss's opulent sitting room.

It was not a long wait by any means; the doctor had coped easily with Fliss's distress. And there was no denying she looked dreadful, eyes luminous green pools in a chalk-white face, her silver-blonde crop plastered to her head, that exquisite designer dress clearly ruined.

The dress. Ella visibly jumped. She'd been too overwrought to notice earlier, but Fliss was lying fully-clothed on top of the bed, or as fully-clothed as that wisp of lace would ever allow. Which meant that she and Jack –

A technicality, Ella conceded bitterly, blinking back the tears. Jack loved Fliss, and in a few short months he'd be proclaiming that love to an indulgent congregation. And then something awful popped into her mind. Fliss *would* be all right, surely? Oh, God. Ella smothered a cry.

'Not your fault, Ella,' Stephen insisted, his fingers threading through hers with a squeeze of reassurance.

'But what if it is?' she wailed with a break in her voice. 'Oh, Stephen – '

'Hush,' he soothed, kissing the top of her head. 'No point in meeting trouble halfway, hey, love?'

He pulled her against him, cradling her close, and, needing something concrete to hold onto, Ella leaned against him, the warmth of Stephen's body helping to take the edge off the chill.

The chill of fear, and the chill of disapproval, Ella acknowledged, her stomach muscles tightening. For if Fliss's illness wasn't bad enough to start with, Stephen's appearance with Ella had compounded the crime. Jack's razor-sharp eyes had missed nothing: Ella's dishevelled state, the crumpled dress, the cascade of hair about her shoulders, not to mention Stephen's own casual appearance.

Aware of the gamut of emotions chasing across Jack's brow – surprise, hurt, contempt, most of all contempt – it had been Ella's turn to stiffen, to blast Jack with the chill of her defiance. Yes, she and Stephen were together, and if Jack didn't like it, Jack could lump it. But no time for silent challenges. Fliss was challenge enough for one night.

'But I want to go to hospital,' Fliss wailed, determined to milk the situation for all it was worth. Or maybe Ella's cynical response was a desperate attempt to mask her own fear. 'I'm ill. I'm dying. I've been poisoned,' Fliss insisted piteously. 'That woman's poisoned me,' she all but spat, pointing an accusing finger at Ella, not quite out of sight thanks to the door swinging open on its hinges.

Ella visibly winced. Jack's grim expression was eloquent proof that he echoed Fliss's concern. More misery as Jack turned back to Fliss, whispered words not meant for other ears – words of love, Ella supposed, hating herself for watching but unable to tear her gaze away as Jack dropped another light kiss on the top of Fliss's head.

'She's overwrought,' the doctor explained in the privacy of the sitting room. 'Another twenty-four hours and she'll probably be as right as rain.'

'Unless,' Jack reminded her grimly with a venomous glance at Ella, 'unless it really is salmonella poisoning?'

The doctor nodded. 'Very true,' she allowed, reaching for her bag. 'But the symptoms are quite mild and I'm hoping it's nothing more than a tummy bug.'

'A tummy bug?' Jack scorned, not bothering to temper his derision. 'A tummy bug? Oh, I see, nothing serious, of course,' he mockingly acknowledged, running his fingers through his hair in anguish. 'Just a little something she's eaten – Fliss and two dozen others,' he said tersely, and then, 'Good

God, woman,' he demanded viciously, turning on Ella, 'what the hell are you trying to do? Ruin me?'

'I – '

'I think our first concern should be the patient,' Dr Treacy cut in mildly.

'Exactly. And I, for one, refuse to take any chances. Hospital,' Jack said grimly. 'If it isn't too much trouble to arrange?'

It was surprisingly easy to arrange, if the patient could afford to pay, and, since money was no object, in no time at all Fliss had been whisked away by private ambulance, a solicitous Jack at her side, leaving Ella the unpalatable task of preparing breakfast for a houseful of guests who might soon be following suit.

'Not your fault, Ella,' Stephen repeated, pulling her close and hugging her. 'The woman's a fraud. If she's suffering from salmonella, then I'll eat my hat.'

'You might have to,' Ella said, gently pulling free. 'I know you're only trying to help, Stephen, but we might as well face it. Fliss is ill, and if it's something she's eaten – '

'But it can't be,' Stephen interjected, features lightening. 'Think, Ella, think. I sat opposite Fliss at dinner and you can take it from me, she barely ate a thing. And when she did condescend to swallow a mouthful,' he added, almost gleefully, 'she chose the same foods I ate. Do I look ill?' he demanded, grinning broadly.

'No-o, but – '

'But nothing,' he insisted, grabbing her hands and swinging her round and round until the room spun dizzily. 'Like I said, the woman's a consummate actress. You mark my words, it's probably nothing more than a touch of wind.'

It was a bit more than a touch of wind, as it turned out, and Ella's sinking heart settled somewhere near the floor.

'It's serious, then?' she probed, swallowing hard as an invisible hand tightened its grip on her throat.

'Food poisoning generally is,' Jack derided. 'But luckily for you Fliss is in good hands. Twenty-four hours on a saline drip and she'll probably be allowed home. Assuming the place hasn't been condemned,' he added with another touch of venom.

Ella smothered a sigh. Her fault, she was more than half convinced – despite Stephen's constant reassurances, despite the seemingly healthy contingent who'd drifted down to breakfast.

A terse meal if ever she'd served one. Ella's anxious eyes had darted from face to face, searching for a hint of a disturbed night, the merest bead of sweat on a pale and furrowed brow. Not even a whisper, she'd finally conceded, resisting the urge to check on the lie-abeds. For ignorance was bliss.

Not true, of course, and so Ella was keeping her fingers crossed. Not to mention a full set of toes. Another twelve hours, twenty-four, thirty-six, and she might just allow herself to believe it, but in the meantime Jack was speaking, had paused, was clearly waiting for Ella's reply.

'I'm sorry,' she conceded, catching sight of herself in the mirror, eyes pools of fear in a much too pale face. Hardly surprising, given the upset, and although she'd had no sleep at all, curiously enough she wasn't the least bit tired. 'I – '

'You don't seem to be listening, Ella,' he castigated coldly. 'But I'm sure you'll be relieved to hear salmonella has been ruled out.'

'Thank heavens,' Ella murmured, not realizing she'd said the words aloud.

'Yes. Thank heavens,' Jack echoed cruelly. 'But since food poisoning has been ruled *in*, you will understand if I don't join the celebrations. Food poisoning, Ella. Understand?'

Ella did. Only too well. Her fault. And if Fliss had succumbed, heaven only knew who would be next. Given her luck, Paul Geraghty, Ella decided, reaching the conclusion that she might as well pack up and leave at once and save Jack – or Fliss – the trouble of sacking her.

'What do you want me to do, Jack?' she queried wearily.

'Just keep the place ticking over, Ella. If it isn't too much trouble,' he niggled pointedly. 'The tests on Fliss have proved inconclusive so we'll simply have to wait for the lab tests on the food. And then – '

And then. End of the road for Ella. And, since it was hardly an endorsement for another job in the trade, she wouldn't dream of holding Stephen to his offer of her job back.

Jack rang off. Lynette Kaye, he'd tersely informed Ella, would handle what he sneeringly termed 'their little problem', using the regulation follow-up calls to make discreet enquiries about the general well-being of the guests.

'All clear,' a cheery Lynette revealed a few days later, after another interminable wait. 'I've managed to contact all but seven, and not a single complaint about the catering. In fact,' she confided warmly, 'apart from Geraghty, who went into raptures about his bed, of all things, the food, and I quote, was "the best thing" about the whole event. But you won't tell Jack I've told you?'

Some hope of speaking to Jack these days, civilly at least, but as Ella replaced the handset, the first glimmer of hope began to burn. Another twelve hours, she calculated swiftly, and she would be in the clear. So – if the source of the infection wasn't to be found at Sherbrook, where on earth had Fliss picked up a tummy bug?

'On the plane?' she mused aloud, amazed the thought had never occurred before.

'Kind of obvious when you think of it,' Lynette agreed, in her second call of the day, and it was music to Ella's ears. 'The moment I called the airline I sensed we were getting warm. Just like the in-flight food, I guess,' she added wryly. 'So – problem solved.'

One problem solved, another to face. Resignation time, Ella? she mused. Jump before you're pushed, girl. Because, despite the happy outcome, as sure as eggs were eggs, Fliss would be looking for a scapegoat.

'Ella?'

'Jack! Oh, God, you nearly frightened the life out me,' she stammered, swinging round, eyes wild, cheeks on fire as she forced herself to meet his gaze, logged the shadows in his eyes.

Thoughtful. Yes, definitely thoughtful, she realized, that sinking feeling around her heart again. So, decision time indeed. Jack's decision. Courtesy of Fliss. Only Ella was damned if she'd go down without a fight.

Untying her apron, she cast a critical eye about the kitchen, an enormous room with an Aladdin's cave of treasure – a mixture of old and new that had fascinated Ella from very first moment. The old-fashioned ranges sat cheek by jowl with the latest in food technology; row upon row of soup tureens and platters that hadn't seen light of day since the Earl of Shrewsbury's visit in 1937, Ella wouldn't mind betting, yet were perfectly in tune with the modern sets of crockery peeping out from the row of glass-fronted cupboards. Hell to keep clean, especially in a kitchen, but better that than open shelves, Ella concluded, beginning to realize how much she'd grown to love the place.

Just like Gramps, she appended, grimacing at the pain she'd cause in throwing away the job of a lifetime at Gramps's old home. Not quite the master of the house in his day, but master of all he surveyed and pleased as Punch to boot, in a cottage in the grounds.

A different cottage now, and not tied to the hall, thank goodness. But still the disappointment to face, courtesy of Ella. Poor Gramps. But she'd do her best to find another job close by, and Gramps, bless him, would understand. Too many lost years for either of them to waste time on futile if-onlys.

So – deep breath, head high, arms folded tight across her chest, Ella raised a single enquiring eyebrow.

'I – '

'Might as well save your breath, Jack,' she interrupted curtly. 'I think I can guess what you've come to say.'

'I doubt it,' he contradicted dryly, the hint of smile playing about the corners of his mouth.

Ella stiffened. 'Fine,' she acknowledged, angling her head in polite enquiry. Only Jack, exasperating Jack, wasn't about to make things easy. So, two long, silent, nerve-stretching minutes later: 'Well?' she demanded.

'Fliss?' he enquired blandly. 'Thank you, Ella, how kind of you to ask. You'll be pleased to know she's on the mend and is hoping to be discharged sometime tomorrow.'

Ella counted to ten. 'You were saying?'

'I was saying . . .?'

Another silent, screaming count to ten. 'I don't know what you were saying,' she pointed out through clenched teeth. 'Since you didn't manage to finish.'

'Didn't manage?' he queried slyly, folding his arms to match hers and regarding her from under hooded lids. 'Or wasn't given the chance?'

'Same difference,' Ella pointed out huffily.

'Same end product, perhaps,' Jack allowed. 'But at the risk of splitting hairs, Ella, not the same difference by a long shot.'

'So?'

'So . . .?' He shrugged, smiled, shrugged again. 'Let's just say, I'm curious to discover how well you can read my mind.'

'Not having been blessed with psychic powers,' she snapped, 'probably not at all. Reassured, Jack?'

'Disappointed, Ella. Very disappointed,' he almost purred. 'Under the Trades' Descriptions Act, it would count as misrepresentation. The reason I'm here?' he reminded her. 'Unless I'm very much mistaken, you were about to tell me why.'

'Just a guess,' she acknowledged warily, vaguely alarmed to note that somewhere along the way Jack had moved a step or two closer. 'A calculated guess. Nothing more, I assure you.'

'Fine.' He smiled again, again seemed to have moved imperceptibly nearer. 'Intuition. Guess-work. Or the powers of Gypsy Rose Ella and her crystal ball . . .' He spread his hands. 'Fire away, Ella,' he smilingly invited. 'Surprise me.'

'Difficult,' she pointed out, licking her dry lips – a nervous gesture that Jack would have caught, caught and understood. Because it wasn't her imagination, she decided. Stealthy as a cat, he'd managed to close the gap between them, and Ella's attempt to retreat was curtailed by the solid bulk of the oil-fired range at her rear. Exit stage left, then, only to be brought up sharp by a nimble piece of footwork that would have served Michael Flatley proud.

'Oh?' he queried pleasantly, and if Jack was aware of the panic in Ella's eyes, he was giving nothing away.

'Since the devil himself would have trouble following the maze of your mind, a mere mortal like myself wouldn't stand a chance, Jack.'

'Ah, yes,' he agreed good-naturedly. 'But that wasn't about to stop you. So, Ella, why not spit it out – get it over with?'

'Maybe I've changed my mind,' she pointed out, aware of the laughter bubbling in his eyes and not in the least reassured.

'Maybe you have at that,' he conceded. 'Being a contrary-minded female. Contrary-minded,' he repeated thoughtfully. 'Or in this case, Ella, a sad case of chickening out.' He shook his head, a slow and mournful reproach that Ella, thoroughly unnerved by the proximity of a most exasperating man, was still hard pressed not to laugh aloud at. 'The prettiest shade of yellow,' he taunted softly. 'A sort of fluffy primrose – you know, that feathery down on an Easter chick. Yellow. The colour of canaries. Or daffodils. Mustard. Topaz. Lemon. Honey. Shall I continue?'

'Pray, do,' she invited, aware that he'd be hard put to come up with many more definitions of the colour yellow, aware too that she'd been wrong, very wrong.

Jack wasn't about to sack her. On the contrary, unless she was very much mistaken, given the gleam in his eye, allowing Ella to walk away was the last thing on his mind. Dangerous. Close. The hairs on the back of Ella's neck prickled out a warning. Infuriating man.

'Hmm. Now, where was I?' he mused, folding his arms, pinning her with his gaze, blue eyes dancing with laughter.

'Tormenting me, as well you know,' she chided, her features softening despite herself. Dangerous. Much better to keep him at a distance. Difficult when he was close enough to touch simply by leaning forwards. The urge to reach out, run her hand along the angle of his jawline, feel the early-morning rasp of stubble beneath her fingers was almost driving her insane.

He looked tired, tired yet relieved. He was simply glad that Fliss was over the worst, Ella reminded herself, suppressing the stab of pain. Fliss. Fliss and Jack. Not Ella and Jack. She'd lost that privilege years ago, had thrown it away along with her self-respect. Only she'd regained her self-respect, the hard-fought battles of her mind and body restoring the remnants of her pride. Pride. And she'd done it alone. No Jack. Because she'd driven him away and now he didn't belong to her.

He didn't belong, and yet the distance between them was non-existent now, the thump of Ella's heart so loud that surely it bounced from wall to wall, ricocheted around the room as it echoed inside her mind?

Aware that moving so much as an inch in any direction would be folly, Ella licked her dry lips, focused her gaze on the buttons of his shirt, achingly aware of the body beneath the straining fabric, the powerful chest with its thick mass of hair, and, desperate for control, she clamped her arms to her sides, her ears straining in vain for the sound of Katie's footsteps as she arrived for the day. Alone. Ella and Jack. Close enough to touch, to kiss –

'No, Jack!' Her head snapped back as if stung, the feather-light touch of his lips against hers almost sheer imagination.

'No?' he queried softly, raising his head, those blue eyes swirling with emotion. He shrugged. 'Fine.' A smile, another eloquent shrug, and then, as Ella smothered the absurd stab of disappointment that he'd capitulated without demur, a single finger traced the outline of Ella's trembling mouth, the touch every bit as devastating as the kiss had been.

Ella closed her eyes – another mistake as Jack slid his hand around the back of her neck, his fingers raking through the carefully woven pleat of hair, pulling out the pins, allowing the thick black waves to tumble freely about her shoulders. Ella's gasp of dismay provoked a throaty laugh.

'Oh, Ella, Ella,' he chided softly. 'You're wasting your time, my lovely. You can freeze, you can refuse to look, you can deny, and yet we both know that underneath that prim and proper exterior there's a flesh-and-blood woman aching to escape. The right word, the right touch, the right man . . . Let yourself go, Ella,' he urged, the words stirring, the touch devastating, the very presence of the man enough to turn her blood to water. Want, need, love – on her part at least. But as for Jack –

'No!' She jerked away from the magic touch, lashing out with her fists, connecting with his shoulders and pushing him away. But Jack simply laughed, pulled her even closer, the iron grip of fingers unnoticed as body collided with body, Ella's gasp an echo of Jack's as the current of heat surged from man to woman and back again. And, though Ella's mind refused to loosen its grip on reality, her body was screaming for the touch, hip against hip, thigh against thigh, Jack's need every bit as urgent as her own.

'No, Jack,' she protested feebly, twisting her head from side to side as she sought to escape the ravage of hungry lips.

'Yes, Ella!' he insisted thickly, his hands sliding upwards in a swift and intimate exploration of her body that kindled fresh needs and fears in Ella's frantic mind. Cupping her face in his hands, he angled his head, tilted Ella's chin, forced her to meet his smouldering gaze. And Ella looked, logged the wealth of emotion and trembled deep inside.

Not hers, she reminded herself. Jack didn't belong to her. But oh, how easy to take the coward's way out and give her body what it craved. Cowardice. Give in to Jack and she'd be chickening out. So easy to give in. But she had to be strong. She had to deny him. How to deny him when she loved him to the point of madness?

'Buttercups,' he tossed out absurdly, reading her mind with devastating accuracy. 'Such a vivid colour, don't you think? Much more vibrant than plain and boring yellow. Just like life, Ella. And there is a choice,' he told her, underlining the words with a solemn nod of the head. 'Plain and boring, Ella – or brimming with fun and excitement. The difference between twenty-four carat gold and a fistful of straw. Shades of yellow,' he goaded. 'A pale imitation – or everything that life can give in full Technicolor glory – '

'In other words, take, take, take, Jack,' Ella cut in as the anger surged. 'The new Jack Keegan motto, and just the thing for the master of the house and all that he surveys,' she scorned with a contemptuous toss of the head. 'And why not?' she needled viciously, eyes pools of hate. 'Given the size of your ego, I'm only surprised you haven't commissioned a coat of arms to nail above that imposing front door. "I am, therefore I take,"' she parodied bitterly. 'Or whatever the hell it comes out as in Latin.'

'I am, therefore I want,' he agreed, his features carved out of granite. 'And what I want, I buy. Buy, Ella, not take. Understand? I pay my way and don't you forget it.'

'And me, Jack? Where do I fit into the Jack Keegan scheme of things? You *pay*, therefore you take?' she sneered, sniffing back the tears – tears of hate and anger she told herself, willing herself to believe it. 'Correction – you pay my wages,' she reminded him icily. 'Nothing more, nothing less. And in future I'd thank you to leave me alone.'

'Leave you alone?' he queried slyly. 'Or leave you to Tolland?'

'None of your business,' she bit back, irrationally pleased that she'd found a buffer at last – because if Jack believed Ella was involved with Stephen, she wasn't about to disabuse him. Let him believe, because the more he believed the more Ella was inclined to give the idea serious thought. Stephen and Ella. Not Ella and Jack. A pipe-dream, maybe, but not an impossibility. And though she had already given Stephen her answer, so much had changed in the intervening weeks that nothing was the same any more. She'd found Jack for a start. Not that she'd been searching, she inwardly derided. And since Jack was engaged to be married . . .

A way out, she realized, at the same time aware she'd be short-changing Stephen. No, not short-changing. Because if she did say yes, then Ella would do everything she could to make him happy. Apart from loving him. Love. Her lips curled in contempt. Look where that fickle emotion had led her: to Jack, away from Jack, and, thanks to an ironic twist of fate, full circle back to Jack. Because she loved him.

Ella swallowed hard as the anger died. A pipe-dream. Safer that way. A way out, if she was brave enough to take it. But braver still if she had the guts to go it alone. Lonely too, she acknowledged. But no risk at all. No hurt, no pain, no love. Just emptiness.

'Ella – '

'Leave it, Jack,' she entreated frigidly. 'Just say whatever it was you came to say and leave me to do the Job that I'm paid for.' And then an awful thought occurred. That scapegoat for Fliss. Just another of life's ironies that Jack would decide to sack her the moment she realized she wasn't ready to walk away. And that was something else that would take a lot of swallowing – only later. Chickening out again, Ella acknowledged, and, despite the tension hanging in the air, a ghost of a smile lit up her features.

'I was wrong, wasn't I?' Jack stated bleakly, seeing the smile and forming his own conclusion.

'Yes, Jack,' Ella told him curtly. 'About a lot of things.'

'Too many to overlook?' he queried, and Ella flushed, registered some strange emotion in the depths of his eyes and moved warily away, began to busy herself with something and nothing – moving about the kitchen, nudging the simmering kettle back onto the central hob and cutting doorstep slices of bread from the crusty loaf she'd placed ready on the bread-board, hours ago now, it seemed.

'Breakfast?' she stalled, recalling that Jack had only just arrived home from the hospital, that early-morning shadow on his face tugging at her heart-strings.

'Too many to overlook?' Jack repeated as Ella emerged from the stone-flagged larder, basin of eggs in one hand, jug of fresh, foaming milk courtesy of Ian in the other.

'Eggs?' she queried. 'Boiled, scrambled, poached? Free-range and guaranteed salmonella-free by the tenant of home farm,' she added without thinking.

'Ella – '

'Oh, hell.' Hardly in the best of taste, given Fliss's illness. Ella flushed. 'I'm sorry, Jack – '

'*You're* sorry? For God's sake, woman,' he almost bellowed. 'How the hell do you think I feel? And no, Ella,' he added curtly, 'I don't want eggs – poached, boiled, scrambled or curdled, thank you very much. And that's how they'll turn out if you don't relinquish that basin.'

'Oh!' Ella flushed again, realized she was clutching the eggs to her chest like a mother hen waiting for her brood to hatch, and placed the offending dish on the table.

'I was wrong, Ella.'

'Yes, Jack,' she replied carefully, not really understanding.

'All part of the Jack Keegan package,' he acknowledged. 'I am, therefore I can't possibly be wrong – ever,' he parodied with a self-mocking smile. 'And, yes, Ella, it takes a lot of facing. Because I'm as human as the next guy – only sometimes I guess I don't believe it.'

'Only sometimes?' Ella couldn't resist teasing.

'As bad as that, huh?' he queried, a broad grin splitting his features.

Sensing a subtle change in atmosphere, Ella dropped her gaze. Bacon? she wondered, since he'd clearly ruled out eggs. Or, recalling how weary he seemed, just a quick cup of coffee before a couple of hours' snatched sleep. And since bang on cue the kettle had begun to sing . . .

'No, Ella,' he insisted tightly when Ella put the thought into words. And then, when Ella simply stood, eyebrows raised in silent enquiry, 'Hell, woman, can't you see I'm trying to say I'm sorry?'

'What for? For protecting the woman you love? For channelling your anger to where it seemed to belong? Hardly the crime of the year, Jack,' she retorted coolly.

'For doubting you. I should have known if wouldn't be down to you.'

'But the obvious one to blame, hey, Jack?'

'Too obvious,' he agreed.

'Occupational hazard,' she reminded him. 'Although so far – touch wood – I guess I've been lucky.'

'Lucky – or meticulous?' Jack challenged softly.

'Just thorough,' Ella allowed. Neurotic, she supposed, if the truth were known – about standards of hygiene, at least. But things could go wrong even in the best run kitchens.

'So – to paraphrase my original question,' Jack said, sneaking up close, whisking the unopened packet of coffee beans away and leaving Ella with nothing to do with her hands. 'What's the verdict, Ella? Forgiveness for a fellow human? Or . . .'

'Or?' Ella probed, belatedly aware that clever Jack had backed her into a corner, that, short of vaulting the now redundant but obviously well-used butcher's block, she was well and truly caught.

'Or maybe . . .' he mused, leaning forwards, resting his hands on the block on either side of her waist and neatly snaring Ella in between. 'Maybe madam would prefer it if sir paid a forfeit?'

Madam wouldn't, but then, contrary-minded females, as Jack had taken the trouble to remind her not so long since, had a habit of changing like the wind, and she had to admit the sort of forfeit Jack clearly had in mind wasn't without appeal.

So easy to give in. So much better for Ella to resist. But how to resist when Jack, wonderful, impossible, irresistible Jack, was smiling down at her, reaching out for her, running his finger across her lips and smiling again at Ella's tremulous reaction? Not a good idea, Ella, she silently chided herself, but when Jack's arms closed around her shoulders, the most natural thing in the world was for Ella to melt against him.

CHAPTER 13

'So you will come, won't you, Ella? Tickets are like gold, but when I realized you were free this weekend I called in a couple of favours. Ella? *Ella*?' he repeated with a touch of impatience. 'I don't believe you've heard a word I've said.'

She banished the cobwebs. 'Sorry, Stephen, guilty as charged,' she admitted with a smile in her voice. 'You were saying?' she prompted pleasantly, threading her fingers through the twisted coil of the phone line and gently disentangling it.

'Oh, nothing much,' Stephen drawled, her lack of attention obviously rankling. 'The weekend?' he prompted testily. 'If you've nothing better planned I thought we could fly to the moon on the back of a dolphin, help ourselves to a dish of cream cheese and then head off through the stars to the far side of the galaxy. How does the eight o'clock shoal sound?'

'Far too early,' Ella admitted, after a moment's stunned silence. Sarcasm? From Stephen? Goodness, she *had* touched a nerve. 'But make it nearer nine,' she responded in like vein, 'and a pod of whales and you're on.'

'Good. That's what I hoped you'd say. The Fireworks Extravaganza,' he reminded her on a lighter note. 'In Hyde Park. I've arranged a suite at my place, so all you have to do is pack your best frock and a suitcase and let me know which train to meet.'

Another stunned silence. London. Not Bristol. Stephen was inviting her to London, to the Kensington Savana, she realized, smothering the panic. And just what did a suite at his place entail? A cosy little twosome in the penthouse? she mused with a shiver of apprehension. Or luxurious isolation – an entire suite of rooms for a solitary female?

London. With Stephen. The charity ball, she recalled belatedly, placing the handset back in its cradle. And, with the Princess of Wales in attendance, the social event of year. Tickets like gold, Stephen had reminded her but easily acquired by a man of influence. A man of influence. Jack. Oh, hell. Ella went cold. Jack . . .

'Just a kiss, my bonny lass,' he'd crooned, stealing another, and then another. 'Just to prove that I'm forgiven, you understand.' And then, the moment he'd come up for air: 'Now, madam, about this forfeit.'

'You mean you haven't just paid it?' Ella had teased, playing with fire and completely unrepentant for once. She'd smiled saucily up at him.

'Little more than a first instalment,' Jack had growled, and, pulling her close, he'd hugged her, his sudden sense of urgency taking her by surprise. Cupping her face in his hands, he'd locked his gaze onto hers, a wealth of emotion swirling in his eyes, a hundred and one questions burning there.

Ella had barely been able to breathe as Jack had dropped his head to kiss her – a bruising brush of lips, his hands sliding the length of her spine, fingers feathering a trail that scorched through the flimsy fabric of her blouse, and she'd been pushing against him, aware of the hardness at Jack's groin, aware of his hands cupping the swell of her buttocks as he'd tugged her even closer, ground his hips against hers, the low moans in the back of Ella's throat a haunting refrain, a poignant refrain.

'Hush, sweetheart,' Jack had crooned, the pressure easing as he took pity, swept his tongue across her soft, inner lip, nibbling, nuzzling, teeth gently biting, soothing and stirring. Lips to mouth, then on to the hollow in her throat and back again, fingers sweeping round to brush the underswell of breasts that ached for Jack's touch.

Her mind had screamed out as the fingers denied her, hell and heaven both as Jack allowed his thumbs to take their place, to trace erotic circles that triggered currents of heat the length of her body. Not blood in her veins any longer but molten lava, and the focus of eruption the twin nubs that had hardened at the mere thought of his touch, thrusting outwards in shameless desperation. Jack's approving chuckle was like music to her ears as he finally allowed the connection.

Body to body the kiss had gone on – Ella conscious of nothing but the man and his unique body scent, the faint trace of aftershave, his mouth exploring hers again as his hands roamed her body, not a curve or a convolution escaping an almost reverent touch – Ella trembling as he reached the curve of her bottom, his hands caressing the swell before moving round to the vee of her groin, the fabric of the plain black skirt a clear irritation, a minor irritation as Jack slid his hands beneath the hem, not quite skin against skin, thanks to self-holding stockings, but skin against skin in an instant as he climbed the quivering flesh of her thighs, reached the flimsy barrier of Ella's panties and then paused.

Mind and body in turmoil, Ella had raised her lids, Jack's smouldering gaze all the reassurance she'd needed, and Ella had smiled, pushed against his hands – another shameless reminder of her need – and it was Jack's turn to groan, to touch, to finger the damp scrap of lace, to pause again.

Hell and heaven both, because still Jack had denied her, fingers touching but withholding, lips exploring, tongue entwined with tongue, teeth nibbling, gently biting, nibbling, lips nuzzling, kissing, sucking, Jack dipping his head to kiss her breasts through the fabric of blouse and bra, the nipples standing dark and proud through the twin layers of material.

'Hell, woman,' Jack had groaned, raising his head, his eyes locking with hers and seeing to the centre of her soul. 'I want you. I'll take you here and now if that's what you want, but, oh, Ella,' he'd insisted thickly. 'It's only a matter of time. You belong to me. And I want you, Understand, Ella – I want you now. Come, feel how much I want you.'

Nodding solemnly, he'd taken her hand in his, guided her fingers to the bulge at his groin, the heat and the hardness shocking her. 'Yours, Ella,' he'd insisted as the thrill of possession had rippled through her mind. 'All yours.'

Not true, Ella had remembered, her fingers caressing, brushing, teasing and refusing to heed the rumblings of truth. Less contrary-minded than spineless. Because, heaven help her, she wanted him. And, yes, Jack wanted Ella. Want. Possession. A man of power. And Ella had walked out on him, had left a crater-sized dent in that ego of his. Not so much revenge as Jack's balm, because ego is a hungry master. It needs feeding. Fliss, Ella, countless dozens of others, Ella had recalled belatedly.

So easy to give in, such sweet release for her body, such torment for her soul. Spineless. Because Jack was simply using her. He loved Fliss. Hadn't Ella witnessed that for herself? And if Fliss didn't exactly return that love, drop for careful drop, she was good for Jack – good at feeding that ego, at entertaining, charming the Paul Geraghty bird from its tree. Ella had to acknowledge that, fighting for control, fighting for the strength to deny him. Jack and Fliss. Not Jack and Ella. Too late for Jack and Ella. But how to be strong with his hands roaming her body, his lips and tongue plundering her mouth?

Resist – how to resist? Now or never, she'd told herself as Jack had tugged her through the door at the far side of the kitchen and out into the corridor that led to the back of the house – left to the tradesman's entrance or right to the housekeeper's den . . . A right turn, or a wrong turn? she'd mocked silently, hysterically, as Jack had paused at the top of the stairs. The stairway to heaven – or hell – and the privacy of Ella's bedroom.

'Ella – ' A smothered curse as a door had slammed close by, followed by the sound of hurrying footsteps.

Katie, Ella had realized, with the scent of panic in her nostrils as the footsteps drew nearer. Katie. Relief and disappointment had jostled in her mind, and yet, with her give away appearance, the panic had surged back with a vengeance. Another thirty seconds and she'd be well and truly caught.

'He says you're to take the week off,' Katie had explained when Ella finally emerged from her bolt-hole, fingers crossed that the distinctive Mercedes SL60 would be missing from its parking space in the yard. 'You've been working too hard, with one thing and another, and with Miss Foxwood convalescing in London there's little enough to do here.

'I can cope,' Katie had insisted, darting Ella a shrewd, assessing glance – or maybe Ella's guilty conscience had simply gone into overdrive? 'It's not like I haven't done it before,' she'd explained, and, leaning forwards, she'd dropped her voice. 'Mrs Murdstone,' she'd gleefully revealed, 'had a bit of problem. The cooking sherry. So many's the time I was left to cope by myself. Besides, with himself and Miss Foxwood in London . . .'

London. Full circle, Ella acknowledged now wryly, beginning to feel caught by forces beyond her control. Not to mention the irony of Mrs Murdstone's little problem. The demon drink. The ex-housekeeper and, once upon a sorry time ago, the present incumbent.

London. Ella swallowed hard. And Jack. And Fliss. And Stephen. Call Stephen and cry off? Coward. Ridiculous in any case. There'd be thousands at the fireworks, hundreds with tickets for the post-extravaganza ball. And if by some fluke she did come face to face with Jack . . . Safety in numbers, she reassured herself. So, no more needless worrying about Jack. Hadn't she worries enough in plenty, with her mind focusing on the implications of that suite of rooms at the Kensington Savana?

'Just for a couple of days, Gramps, if you're sure you don't mind?'

'Mind, love?' The weatherbeaten face creased into a smile. 'To tell you truth, I'm glad. Oh, not that you're going away.' He chuckled, seeing Ella's start of surprise. 'But it's nice to know you'll be out and about enjoying yourself for a change. You've been working too hard,' he chided softly. 'And don't think I haven't noticed.'

Under strict instructions to relax while Gramps made the tea, Ella resisted the urge to plump up the cushions, tweak the cloth back into place on the table.

Relax. Easier said than done, but having Jack's concerns echoed by Gramps was unnerving to say the least. Jack. The grandson-in-law Gramps had never met. Another of life's little ironies, since now they were practically neighbours. Ex-grandson-in-law now, she amended, allowing her eyes to travel around the living room.

Not a single speck of dust, despite the clutter of possessions: the Staffordshire figurines that had been her Grandmother's pride and joy, the well-thumbed books stacked neatly on the table beside the high-backed chair, and, carefully placed to catch the light from the window, the batch of photographs on the sideboard – pride of place given to a youthful Gramps with his bride. As her idle gaze passed onto a photo she hadn't seen before, Ella's smile faltered.

With a feeling of *déjà vu*, she moved across the room, drawn to the faded black and white snap in its new silver frame. Ella, only not Ella. A shiver of excitement ran down her spine.

'Mum?' she said without turning, sensing Gramps had shuffled in from the kitchen.

'Ah, yes.'

Something in his tone made Ella turn her head. Her imagination, maybe, but were Gramps's hazel eyes suspiciously damp? Difficult to know for sure, since he busied himself with the tray he was carrying, that proud head turned away as he lowered the tray, placed the teapot, milk jug, cups, saucers and sugar bowl carefully in the centre of the table, only the slight rattle of cup on saucer betraying him.

Fragile emotions under control, he crossed to stand beside her, taking the photo in both hands and gazing down at the young woman whose frank, engaging smile had reached out to Ella across the room. It was Ella's turn to swallow the lump in her throat as she watched a magic lantern show of memories flick across his well-loved features.

'I was rummaging through the sideboard drawers,' he explained. 'A lifetime of rubbish, if the truth's known, so I thought I'd have a clear-out. I came across this. I didn't realize your gran had kept it,' he explained apologetically. 'So I took it into Stafford last week and had it framed. It's for you, love.'

'Oh, Gramps.' Not just a suspicion of tears this time; Ella's eyes were brimming as she hugged him, the fragile frame coming as a shock. So many lost years, she railed, and, with Gramps nudging eighty, so little time to make up for it all.

'Too short for if onlys, hey, love?' he asked, his thoughts an uncanny parallel of hers. 'But I never could make your gran see it my way.'

'She couldn't forgive Mum?' Ella probed softly.

'She couldn't forgive herself,' he explained, waving Ella to a chair and allowing her to pour the strong brown tea into incongruous delicate china cups.

'Blamed herself for turning her back on your mother in the first place,' he confided, 'then couldn't come to terms with the adoption. And once your mother came home – '

'It was too late,' Ella supplied softly, beginning to understand.

'It was too late,' he echoed, his voice choked with emotion. 'She was ill. Heaven only knows how she'd managed up till then, but we didn't need a doctor to break the bad news. Your mother was ill and she'd come home to die.'

'But she did come home,' Ella reminded him softly, reaching her hand across the red chenille cloth, her fingers closing round Gramps's, squeezing, reassuring, her own tears threatening to fall. 'She came home. Surely that must have helped?'

'Ah, yes, but if she hadn't gone away in the first place,' he railed, eyes suspiciously bright again, 'she'd never have fallen ill.'

'Maybe,' Ella conceded, swallowing hard, and then, glancing back at the photograph, 'She's very pretty. I wish I'd known her, if only for a little while.'

'Too late for if onlys,' Gramps reminded her brusquely. 'And you were lucky. It's never easy for a child without a father, and your mother carried the shame until the day she died. She thought she'd let us down,' he explained in response to Ella's raised eyebrow. 'Couldn't do right for doing wrong. But believe me, Aileen, no matter how it seems, she did more than her best for you.'

'She let me go,' Ella said simply, understanding, forgiving. By giving her baby up for adoption she'd given Ella the chance of a happy family life. 'And now I've come home,' she said softly as Gramps's bony fingers returned her squeeze. 'I've come home. And you've no idea how good that feels.'

'Oh, yes, I have,' he contradicted gruffly. 'But then somewhere deep inside I had this strange notion it would all come right in the end. I only wish your gran could have been here to share it.'

All come right in the end. Jack, Stephen, a weekend in London. And then home to Gramps, or as near as she'd ever be short of moving in. And since the cottage, for all its mod-cons, was little more than a doll's house, Ella was clutching at straws. She'd need a live-in job in the area and soon. But as the train pulled into Euston and she eased her bags from the luggage space between the seats it was a definite case of first things first. And top of the list was Stephen and that suite of rooms.

She took a taxi, having declined Stephen's offer of a lift with the excuse that she didn't know which train she'd be on. Just a little white lie but it had bought her precious moments alone to muster her thoughts.

More precious moments alone in the lift. Mr Tolland had been detained, she'd been informed at once by the smiling desk clerk, but if there was anything she needed, she simply had to ask.

Ella had shaken her head, managed a smile, allowed her small case to be plied free of rigid fingers by the uniformed porter. Aware that she needed a drink, and a stiff drink at that, she'd slipped the coded key card into a pocket and set off in the direction of the bar. The bar. The distinctive aroma of spirits had hit the back of her throat as she'd pulled up short on the threshold. One drink wouldn't harm, she'd reasoned, and in any other mood she'd have been happy to sit and linger over a crisp white wine. But to think she actually *needed* a drink! Oh, no! She wasn't about to embark on that dangerous journey.

A swift about-turn as she headed for the bank of lifts. The twelfth floor. Not quite the penthouse, she reassured herself, but, despite her years in the trade, she had to admit to being impressed. Stephen had done well, would go far. As far as Jack? she mused, hating herself for the comparison. Stephen and Jack. So alike, so much in common, even allowing for Ella, and yet as different as chalk and cheese.

Stephen and Jack. And the awful thought just beginning to dawn was that Stephen's main attraction was his similarity to Jack. She wanted Jack, she couldn't have Jack, and so she'd take the next best thing. Brutal. Only not true, she silently railed, reaching the door to her suite and taking a deep and calming breath.

She didn't love Stephen, couldn't sleep with Stephen, wouldn't cheat Stephen by marrying without love. So – what the hell was she going to do if faced with the stamp of Stephen's presence when she opened the door?

If. The Kensington Savana. The flagship of Stephen's growing empire. And, yes, she couldn't escape his presence. The video screen with its personalized words of welcome, the champagne chilling in the silver bucket, the pair of crystal flutes ready on a tray, the exquisite arrangements of flowers, not to mention the helium balloons filled not with the usual cuddly toys but with the sort of expensive little trifles that men like Jack probably bestowed on women like Fliss over breakfast. Wall to wall opulence. Only not Jack – Stephen. Stephen. His hotel, his invitation, his gifts.

Unconditional? Ella wondered as, heart in mouth, she inspected the rooms behind the various doors. Bathroom – no, two, she amended, not to mention the *en suite* shower in what Ella finally decided was the master bedroom, and, since she'd found no tangible evidence of Stephen anywhere else, she'd clearly reached the end of the line. The master bedroom. A king-sized bed, a bank of walk-in cupboards and not an occupied hanger in sight. A suite of rooms with no strings attached, she finally decided, and, no longer desperate for that drink, made a leisurely inventory of the well-stocked mini bar before helping herself to an orange juice.

Spinning round on her heels, she allowed her gaze to travel the sitting room, where a family of ten wouldn't look out of place, where the royal family itself wouldn't feel out of place, and raised her glass in silent toast. To a pleasant weekend with no strings attached. Or so she hoped.

CHAPTER 14

'Here's to a lovely weekend. To you, Ella, with my thanks.'

Ella raised her glass. 'To you Stephen, with *my* thanks,' she demurred, and then, like a little girl faced with a surfeit of presents, 'Everything's so wonderful – I keep expecting to wake up and discover that I'm dreaming.'

'With this sort of reality, who needs dreams?' Stephen entreated, glancing round and waving an airy hand, taking in the room, the decor, the subtle hint of privilege, the discreet presence of staff alert to each and every need.

Reality. Stephen's reality. Stephen's pride and joy. Ella was forced to smother a smile as she watched him visibly preen.

'Though on second thoughts,' he mused, his gaze coming back to Ella, smouldering eyes sweeping the lines of her body, slowly, assessing, appraising, down and then up, before locking onto hers with almost tangible approval. 'I guess you were right in the first place. But if you really want to thank me,' he added swiftly, 'all it takes is a simple yes. Believe me, you'll make me the happiest guy in the world.'

'Oh?' she queried carefully, taking a tiny sip of her ice-cold wine and allowing it to linger on her tongue for a moment. 'But how can I say yes,' she stalled, 'when I haven't yet heard the question?'

'Oh, but you have,' he reminded her softly. 'You just haven't heard it for a month or so.' And he smiled, nodded, raised his glass again. 'But you will,' he informed her solemnly. 'And soon.'

Ella's smile faltered. She shouldn't have come. No strings attached. Just a subtle touch of blackmail. Unfair, she decided, logging the expression in a set of hungry eyes. No strings attached but a huge disappointment if Ella turned him down. *When*, not if, she silently amended. Unless she could head him off, let him down gently, allow him to guess that he was wasting his time?

Ah, yes, but is he wasting his time? she forced herself to ask. Would she be here now if she'd ruled Stephen out of her life once and for all? Marriage. He'd asked once, he'd ask again, and only a fool would pretend differently. So – might as well face it. Despite the show of nerves, she hadn't yet made up her mind.

Dinner with the boss. One thing less to worry about, she supposed, aware of the glances of speculation even the best trained staff couldn't quite hide. Dinner with the boss in a discreet corner of the restaurant. Cosy, but nothing like as cosy as dinner in her suite would have been. Or Stephen's.

'Hardly the pick of the house in any case,' he'd revealed with a self-deprecating smile over pre-dinner drinks in the bar. 'Just a couple of rooms in the attic.' And, logging Ella's surprise, he'd spread his hands. 'Logic. Since I'm rarely in residence for more than a day or two, it doesn't make sense to tie up the penthouse.'

'Sense?' Ella had teasingly probed. 'Or straightforward economics?'

'You've worked the system,' he'd smilingly reminded her. 'You tell me.'

With Stephen rising by the minute in Ella's estimation, she'd simply nodded her approval, taking the arm that he'd proffered as they made their way across the marble-columned foyer and into the welcoming calm of the restaurant. Subtle lighting, strategically placed banks of plants and the melodic strum of a piano. Opulence without the decadence, and in this area of London it wouldn't come cheap.

'Just sound business investment,' Stephen demurred when Ella put the thought into words. 'London was the obvious place to start my expansion, and with hotels ten a penny it had to be something different. All thanks to you.'

'Me?' Ella queried, nonplussed.

'But of course – don't sound so surprised. You whipped the Bristol Savana into place and provided the perfect template. Quite an achievement, Ella.'

'But the Bristol Savana doesn't exist,' she

pointed out, Stephen's words, not to mention the expression in his eyes, bringing another glow to her cheeks.

'It does now. A change of image, a change of name,' he explained with a touch of pride. 'The Tolland Hotel didn't have quite the right ring, and, given that expensive re-fit, I had to do something to attract the best.'

'Oo-oo!' Ella couldn't help but tease. 'And if that's not out-and-out snobbery, Stephen Tolland, I don't know what is. Attract the best?' she challenged lightly. 'Or keep humble Joe Public from crossing the threshold?'

'Just straightforward economics,' he demurred. 'Identify a market, then target it. But don't worry Ella,' he smilingly entreated. 'Despite how it seems, I haven't sold my soul to the devil. There's room for both, all in the fullness of time.'

'A Savana in every city?' Ella mused, catching his drift at once. 'Cheek by jowl with its more modest counterpart, The Tolland.'

'Got it in one. I always knew you'd go far. Which makes the housekeeper post you've settled for a complete and utter waste.'

'A rose by any other name,' she pointed out, aware that Stephen wasn't so much needling as trying to make sense of Ella's decision. 'The role's quite demanding, as I'm sure you must have noticed.'

'I did. I only hope Keegan appreciates the gem he's acquired.'

'I'm sure he does,' Ella retorted coolly, reaching for her fork.

'Yes. I'm sure *he* does,' Stephen agreed as the temperature dipped. 'But I wouldn't mind betting his brittle fiancée isn't quite so gushing.'

'Fliss – '

'Has eyes as green as that ostentatious emerald she wears – figuratively and literally,' Stephen informed her coldly. 'It must have crossed your mind she wants you out?'

'I can't say that it has,' Ella conceded carefully, the avocado mousse suddenly leaving a nasty taste in her mouth. Or maybe it wasn't so much the food as the unexpectedly bitter flavour of the dialogue.

Stephen smiled, only the light didn't reach his eyes. 'Come off it, Ella, don't pretend you haven't noticed. "Mrs Andrews-Watson,"' he parodied, just as he had that night at Sherbrook, '"do remember your place."'

'Exactly. Belowstairs. And quite right too,' Ella reminded him primly.

'And if *that's* not out-and-out snobbery,' he scorned, 'I don't know what is.'

Bull's eye. But, like Ella's earlier gibe, there was no real sting in the words. A smattering of the truth, perhaps, but that was something else. 'She's the lady of house,' Ella pointed out lightly. 'She's entitled to her foibles.'

'Ah, yes, but does the master of the house happen to agree?'

'I wouldn't know,' she replied, reaching dangerous ground and refusing to be drawn.

'No.' A strange, loaded pause, and then, 'Why on earth are we wasting time discussing Keegan and his poisonous bride-to-be?' he enquired incredulously, pushing his plate away and reaching across to take her hand. 'I must be mad. I'm sorry, Ella,' he murmured contritely. 'I didn't mean to spoil the weekend. But having seen you at Sherbrook, knowing Keegan's gain is my loss, obviously rankles more than I realized. But no more niggles, I promise. Friends?' he queried softly, his threaded fingers holding hers and refusing to allow her to pull away.

Ella swallowed hard. 'If you say so,' she allowed, not really convinced.

'I do,' he insisted, blue eyes pinning her. And then he smiled. 'For now.'

Friends. For now. But until – and if – Stephen popped the question, there was no point in meeting trouble halfway.

No point indeed, given the pace of their leisurely meal, and, since Stephen seemed in no particular hurry to whisk her back upstairs, Ella began to relax, the experience of sharing a first-class meal with a good-looking man a definite boost to her ego. For, despite the screen of greenery, she was acutely conscious of the admiring glances that filtered through the foliage – surreptitious maybe, but no less envious.

The avocado mousse gave way to tiny filo parcels, flakes of haddock in a delicate cheese sauce, served on a bed of rocket leaves, each and every taste mouth – meltingly delicious. A crisp Pouilly Fumé maintained the ambience, and Ella's usual quota stretched just this once to two.

When the fillet steak arrived, medium rare and perfectly pink, Stephen made no comment when Ella refused a glass of red. Chateau Gruaud-Larose, 1982 – a vintage year, she logged automatically, wondering at the occasion. And then it hit her. Ella almost choked on a mouthful of food and was forced to bury her face in her napkin.

Stephen's worried face swam back into focus.

'I'm fine,' she insisted, struggling for control, the knots in her stomach tightening as she stared the truth hard in the face. Occasion? Difficult to miss, really. *She* was the occasion.

'Now had it been the fish course,' Stephen teased, pouring a glass of iced water and sliding it across, giving her time to recover, 'I could have understood it. But bones in a fillet steak?' He assumed an expression of horror. 'I guess that highly expensive chef could be facing the sack.'

'Judging from the evidence so far,' Ella demurred, 'the man's worth a pay-rise – and soon. Thank you, Stephen, that was delicious.'

'Warts and all?' he teased.

'And bony warts at that,' she agreed.

Dessert was another delicious concoction – crême brulée with a scorched crust so transparent it might have passed for stained glass, and the strawberry shortcake arranged around the rim the perfect accompaniment. No room for cheese, despite Ella's need to prolong the meal.

Eleven o'clock, and arm in arm they headed back across the restaurant, the murmur of voices stilling for an instant. A show-stopping couple? she mused. Or just that aura of power that Stephen seemed to have acquired all at once? Power. Yes. Ella's lips tightened. Success plus money equals power. She was beginning to appreciate that. Just as it did with Jack. And an ego to match? she probed, breathing a huge sigh of relief when Stephen headed not for the bank of lifts but for the least crowded of the bars.

'A nightcap, Ella? Or coffee, perhaps?'

And since either could have been served in the privacy of her suite, Ella stifled the suspicion that Stephen wasn't playing so much the solicitous host as a very clever game – lull Ella into a sense of false security and then pounce, repeat the question that was playing on her mind. Unfair, she decided, opting for coffee. All's fair in love and war, and if Stephen was determined to play by an accepted set of rules, who was Ella to demur?

'Goodnight, Ella,' he whispered thirty minutes later, and the twenty-yard journey from lift to bedroom door seemed interminable. 'Sweet dreams.'

A smile, a hand cupping her chin, tilting her face upwards, the merest brush of mouth against mouth and, before she'd even had time to catch her breath, Stephen was halfway to the lifts again.

Breakfast. Those dreams still playing in her mind. And the trill of Stephen's mobile phone cutting short the meal – for Stephen at least.

'Sorry, Ella.' He telescoped the aerial, shoulders raised in a shrug of resignation. 'Problems at Bristol, last-minute touches to the re-fit,' he explained, rising to his feet and allowing his napkin to land in a heap among the crumbs on the table. 'You don't mind if I desert you?'

'At the risk of giving a girl a complex?' she teased, secretly relieved to have the day to herself. 'Go ahead, Stephen. Heaven forbid that I stand in the way of progress.'

'Ah, yes,' he agreed with a strangely knowing smile. 'But I'll be back before you have a chance to miss me, and believe me, giving this particular girl a complex is the last thing on my mind. Seven o'clock,' he reminded her, blue eyes smoky. 'We'll have a bite to eat here before we head into town. You did remember your ballgown?'

'Ballgown? You are teasing?' Ella enquired, Stephen's words triggering another twinge of panic. 'My best frock is what you requested; my best frock will simply have to do.'

He raised a hand to his head in snappy salute. 'Yes, ma'am,' he concurred, eyes dancing. 'But with a figure like yours you could wrap yourself in sackcloth and still make an impression.'

Hmm. A moot point. Lady Godiva had doubtless made an impression riding naked through the streets of Coventry on the back of a horse. But as for Ella's best frock – she folded the newspaper's society page inhalf and propped it up against the teapot.

> Diana, Princess of Wales, seen here wearing a Catherine Walker white lace sheath dress studded with sequins, is expected to draw the crowds at tonight's Fireworks Extravaganza in Hyde Park. Having officially severed ties with all but a handful of charities, the Princess's personal endorsement would be quite a feather in the organizer's cap, and, though her presence at the post-fireworks ball has still to be confirmed, demand for tickets has outstripped all expectations. And, in case you're wondering what you're missing, for a cool nine hundred pounds you too could be tripping the light fantastic with the rich and famous . . .

Nine hundred pounds a ticket? For what amounted to little more than a dinner dance? Ella swallowed hard. Had Stephen taken leave of his senses? She'd always known he was ambitious, but even so . . . But why not? she decided, losing interest in the news and pushing the paper away. The refit at Bristol, the Kensington Savana, the unexpected interest in Jack's holiday village scheme.

If Stephen made a habit of rubbing shoulders with the rich and famous it would only be a matter of time before he got himself noticed. Some clever PR, substantial donations to just the right charities, not to mention whichever political party happened to be in the ascendancy, and Stephen would be set.

And in that case, she realized, respect and condemnation vying for position, her best frock, along with that exclusive scrap of sackcloth, was about to be consigned to the dustbin.

Oxford Street. Designer label outfits at a price she could afford. Leastways, that was the theory. Debenhams, Selfridges and, a desperate last stop, The Store. Ella smothered her disappointment. At these sorts of prices it would be next stop Charity Shop!

And then she spotted the outfit of her dreams being modelled by the mannequin. Perfect. The right size, the right colour, the right style. And more money than Ella thought possible. She tried not to wince as she signed away a chunk of her savings. But just this once it would be worth it. For Stephen's sake.

'Wow! You mean this is your best frock?'

Ella's smile broadened. 'It is now,' she conceded, Stephen's unconcealed delight a boost to her confidence. She gave a theatrical twirl, allowing the filmy pleated skirts to billow outwards, before coming to a halt in front of him. 'Unless you think it's just a trifle low-key?' she couldn't resist teasing, features carefully neutral. 'I don't want to let you down, Stephen, and I know you'd set your heart on that sackcloth.'

'Ella, oh, Ella – dressed like this you'll be the belle of the ball.'

'With Princess Diana stealing the limelight?' Ella scorned. 'Chance would be a fine thing.'

'You don't say,' Stephen drawled, his smouldering gaze instantly sobering. 'At the risk of sounding corny, Ella, I'll only have eyes for you. And I wouldn't mind betting I won't be the only one.'

Difficult to judge in the dark, but the night was still young and only time would tell, Ella realized, shivering despite the velvet cloak – an impulsive purchase in the early days of her marriage. Since evenings like this had been few and far between, the cloak had barely seen the light of day since.

Smiling at the incongruous comparison, Ella allowed Stephen to take her hand, flashed him a smile in the gloom. A shiver of excitement rippled through her as the guest conductor mounted the bandstand to a massive round of applause. There was another surge of applause when the guest of honour appeared with her entourage, took her place in the temporary royal box.

A ringside view for Ella, courtesy of Stephen. The tickets to the extravaganza had probably been yet another small fortune, Ella wouldn't mind betting. Just like her dress. She smothered a pang of conscience. Three months' wages blown on an outfit she'd probably never wear again. With her future in jeopardy, she ought to have had more sense.

There was a flurry of late arrivals as the music struck up, and with Stephen and Ella slightly to the left of centre it was easier to stand, to allow people to shuffle past. Since the two seats next to Ella remained conspicuously empty, Ella didn't bother sitting down until the concert was finally under way.

As the orchestra struck up with the opening bars of Handel's 'Fireworks' Ella sank down onto her cushion – and was immediately sorry when the bob of heads along the row heralded the tardy pair.

Unbelievable. Spectacular bursts of colour in perfect synchronization with the music. The oohs and ahs of the crowd threatened to drown out all but the loudest chords, for the first couple of minutes at least.

The latecomers drew level, Ella smothering a sigh of annoyance as she came to her feet, leaned back to allow them to pass, her eyes riveted on the kaleidoscopic tableau above her head.

'Excuse me. I'm terribly sorry.'

The voice, the distinctive perfume, despite the acrid smell of cordite in the air, the even more distinctive whiff of Aramis as the woman slid past and the man drew level.

'Jack!'

'Well, well, well,' he drawled, his sharp glance flicking from Ella to Stephen and back again. 'How does the phrase go? Small world? It's a small world indeed.'

No time for polite conversation – too much noise, with the orchestra in full swing and the hiss, spit, crackle and ear-numbing explosions of what should have been an out of this world experience for Ella. But the evening was ruined before it began. No. Not true. Damn Fliss. Damn Jack. She wouldn't let them spoil it.

She smiled brightly up at Stephen, ignoring the man to her left, twisting her body away from him. So much easier to admire the patterns of colour and light reflected in the Serpentine, to focus on the sky with its glittering array of jewels, the massive cascades that must surely tumble onto their laps and yet which melted away like iridescent flurries of snow.

Unbelievable – despite the unexpected company. But the night was still young. One of those awful thoughts occurred. No. Even fate wouldn't be that cruel.

Fate would.

'The car wouldn't start,' Jack explained as the crowds began to disperse. Since the park was a heaving mass of humanity, it was much easier to sit and wait for the crush to ease, for the fleet of limousines and taxis to arrive. 'And tonight of all nights,' Jack added wryly, offering Stephen his hip flask, 'there wasn't a single cab to be hailed.'

'If you're going on to the ball,' Stephen offered, pulling generously on the whisky, 'why not tag along with us? There's plenty of room and my driver will be waiting.'

'Why, thank you, Tolland. It's good of you to offer. Yes – '

'No!'

Impasse. Jack's raised eyebrows. Fliss's grim expression.

Say no, Ella implored silently, digging her finger-nails into her palms. Please, say no. She couldn't bear it. To have to make polite conversation with the man she loved while he sat making eyes at his lovely fiancée. To endure Fliss's silent contempt through-out the meal. To keep Stephen's intentions on an even keel.

Stephen. Oh, hell. She ran her fingers through her hair, aware she was ruining the handiwork of the Savana's resident stylist and yet uncaring in her panic. Stephen. He could give her away once and for all. Because the moment he referred to her as Ella, she was doomed.

Decision made – not that it was Ella's to make in the first place. And her nerves were as taut as fiddle strings as the tense group arrived at the exclusive hotel on Park Lane.

'Almost as quick to walk,' Jack remarked plea-santly, his polite conversation in the car having been an attempt to mask Fliss's seething silence.

'In these heels?' Fliss scorned, darting him a glance of pure loathing, and, gathering her skirts in one hand, she swept imperiously up the steps ahead of them.

A flash of apology from Jack. A shrug of under-standing from Stephen.

'See what I mean?' Stephen challenged Ella once the velvet cloak had been safely deposited and lipstick, hair and perfume had been carefully ad-justed. Stalling, she had realized, gazing at her reflection, logging the panic, smothering the panic before going back to face him. 'Flavour of the day you ain't.'

'And if you'd paid a small fortune to rub shoulders with the nobs,' Ella demurred, taking the arm he proffered and smiling broadly up at him, 'you'd be just a teensy bit piqued to find you were slumming it instead with a lowly employee.'

'In your position, Ella,' Stephen allowed dryly, '*I'd* be the one complaining.'

The lowly employee had better luck at dinner. Or maybe the angry Fliss had made her own enquiries, ensuring that Ella and Stephen were seated as far away as possible? An interesting thought but hardly important. Just a huge relief for Ella.

Too nervous to eat, she simply picked at the exquisite morsels of food, Stephen's raised eyebrows speaking volumes. In an effort to calm herself, she downed her glass of wine in one, polished off the second equally swiftly and then, realizing what she'd done, glanced up to find Jack's thoughtful gaze fastened on her face. Ella's cheeks burned with the shame. Even across the sea of heads Jack would have noticed. Jack would know.

Ella was a nervous wreck, and just like in the early days of her marriage, the moment it all grew too much she reached for the bottle.

Not true – but how to convince Jack of that? Why bother trying? she silently scorned. Jack could believe what he liked. She'd had a couple of glasses of wine, and if that made her an alcoholic then half the people present tonight would be ahead of Ella in the queue for drying-out.

'Something wrong?' Stephen probed, bending to nibble at her earlobe as the dessert plates were being cleared. 'If you can't face the dance, we could always go home.'

Home. The Savana. With Stephen. Alone. Too many implications for Ella's churning mind. Hell if she left. Hell if she stayed. But safety in numbers, she finally acknowledged, bringing her troubled gaze back to Stephen, logging his concern – *concern*, she underlined silently. No hint of anything remotely resembling the dreaded seduction.

Home, then – and yet, sensing a strange scrutiny, she felt the hairs on the back of her neck begin to prickle as her gaze slid beyond Stephen and across the room, to lock with the woman whose scornful glance spoke volumes. Ella's chin snapped up.

'Home?' she queried over-brightly. 'At nine hundred pounds a ticket? Not to mention the waste of this rag of a ballgown? Lead on, Stephen,' she insisted with a defiant toss of the head. 'Princess Di has taken to the floor and everyone else is duty-bound to follow suit.'

They did – less of a waltz than an overcrowded shuffle. But with Stephen's body pressed against hers, his solid mass soothing, Ella felt some warmth creep back into her veins.

It was a long night. And with the dancing due to give way to a champagne breakfast, Ella mentally gauged how long it would be before they could leave.

She would have to stay long enough to be seen to be enjoying herself, but not so long that the strain would begin to tell.

Like the fireworks before, the room was a riot of colour, the one or two play-safe 'little black dresses' more than outnumbered by the season's vivid primaries, and oranges and greens so electric it almost hurt to look. And why not? With money clearly no object, the exclusive designer outfits were disposable – an obscene waste in Ella's eyes, but equally none of her business.

Yet in 'playing safe' herself, she hadn't made a conscious decision, had simply fallen hook, line and sinker for the full-length dress of pleated chiffon, with the top so revealing she'd blushed when she'd tried it on. It fitted where it touched, as her adoptive mother would have said, and Ella had loved the delicate cream fabric, the shoulderless, almost backless bodice that moulded to her breasts, gave tantalizing glimpses of Ella's generous cleavage.

An extravagance she could well have done without, but at least the style was classic, the cut superb and, with luck, the dress wouldn't date. Where on earth she'd ever manage to wear it again was anybody's guess, but Ella smiled. Just this once, it didn't matter. If all else failed she'd try it on in the privacy of her bedroom, close her eyes and glide around an imaginary ballroom in time to an imaginary tune, in the arms of imaginary partner.

Jack, she amended as his face swam into view. No, not Jack. Wasn't Jack spoken for, clearly besotted?

Powerless to tear her gaze away from the flesh and blood Jack, who now smiled down at the woman in his arms, Ella almost stumbled. She felt Stephen's grip tighten and pulled herself together with a massive surge of will.

It was hot in the ballroom, despite the full-length windows that opened out onto the terrace, and the bronze mirrored walls reflected the swirl of colour and movement. Since mirrors within mirrors within mirrors created an illusion, seeing double or treble the number of people really present was confusing. And if more than one Jack she could cope with, more than one Fliss was a trial Ella could well do without.

The tempo increased, and a bemused Stephen flashed Ella a silent plea for mercy. Ella smilingly obliged, seizing the chance to slip out of the overheated room and into the powder-pink calm of the Ladies'.

Alone for the first time in hours, Ella took her time, revelling in the peace and quiet, the unobtrusive piped music barely registering as she reapplied her lipstick and pushed a stray lock of hair back into the elegant chignon the Savana's top stylist had created. A quick spray of perfume from the atomizer in her purse – Chanel No. 5, and just one of the 'little trifles' Ella had recovered from the clutch of helium balloons in her room – and she was ready to face the fray.

Not ready for this particular fray, though. Fliss, her expression ugly, stepped deliberately across Ella's path.

'What the hell do you think you're playing at?' she bit out, green eyes spitting flames.

Sensing hers was the advantage, despite the element of surprise, Ella came to a leisurely halt, eyebrows raised in mocking enquiry.

'I'm a guest,' Ella reminded her coolly, the younger woman's anger strangely reassuring. 'There's no law against my attending, surely?'

'You're – '

'Forgetting my place?' Ella cut in pleasantly.

'Wasting your time. You're out of your league. Stephen – '

'Seems happy enough to me.'

'He's amusing himself at your expense. And why not?' Fliss asked gleefully. 'He's only human – a full – blooded male with a man's basic needs. But don't kid yourself, my dear,' she said confidentially, leaning forwards and placing her hand on Ella's arm, its vividly painted talons curling round. Red for danger, Ella noted inconsequentially, resisting the urge to flinch from the touch. 'You're nothing more than Stephen's bit of rough – and cheap enough at half the price.'

'Given the cost of the tickets?' Ella scorned, hanging on to to her temper with a massive surge of will. 'Don't be ridiculous. Besides, if all Stephen wanted was a tumble between the sheets he wouldn't be short of offers.' And there was just the merest hint of a pause before she tagged on slyly, 'Present company included.'

'Meaning?'

'Work it out for yourself,' Ella invited coolly, aware she was playing with fire. Goad Fliss, push her too far, and her job wouldn't last the next five minutes, let alone the next five weeks.

'If you're saying what I think you're saying – '

'Just speaking the truth as I see it – madam,' Ella responded – not a sneer this time but a pointed reminder of the nature of their relationship. 'But you needn't worry. Like all staff worth their salt,' she soothed, shaking free of those vicious red talons and taking a step away, 'when the occasion demands it, I'm the soul of discretion.'

'And is that supposed to reassure me?'

Ella shrugged. 'Knowing you, I doubt you even care,' she conceded. 'But you can take it from me, kiss and tell isn't one of my failings, and neither is servant hall gossip.'

'How very commendable,' Fliss scorned, eyes chips of ice as they rested on Ella. 'Especially as no one in their right mind would choose to believe you.'

'Ah, yes,' Ella acknowledged, smiling despite herself. 'But then they wouldn't have to, would they? Sooner or later,' she pointed out sweetly, 'the lady in question is sure to grow careless and give herself away.'

'Thus speaketh the all-knowing housekeeper,' Fliss jeered, the twin spots of colour in her cheeks eloquent proof that Ella's darts were beginning to hit home. 'See no evil, hear no evil, speak no evil. Quite the paragon of virtue, hey, Mrs Andrews-Watson?'

'In my line of work, Miss Foxwood,' she mockingly conceded, 'I find that it generally pays.'

'Are you threatening me?'

'Threatening?' With her meaning unmistakable, Ella suppressed another surge of temper. How dared she? How dared she imply that Ella would stoop so low? Blackmail. An ugly word for an ugly deed. Ella took another step back, allowed her scornful gaze to travel the length of the younger woman, her nose crinkling in distaste at what she clearly viewed as some noisome thing she'd inadvertently dragged in on the sole of her shoe. 'Oh, no,' she retorted icily. 'Since you've more than enough rope to hang yourself with already, why should I resort to threats? Like I said, it's only a matter of time.'

'You little – '

'Bitch?' Ella queried, baring her teeth in the semblance of a smile. 'That sounds suspiciously like the pot calling the kettle,' she scorned. 'But at least we seem to understand one another.'

'Exactly,' Fliss hissed, leaning forwards, the heavy scent of her perfume catching at the back of Ella's throat. 'You'd better know your place, Mrs Andrew-Watson, or believe me, I'll be watching night and day to make sure you don't forget it.'

'But if I were you,' Ella conceded, saccharine-sweetly, 'I'd be guarding my own back. With one bedroom door much the same as any other,' she pointed out brightly, 'and especially in the dark, an unsuspecting man might just catch his loving fiancée dispensing the sort of favours he'd naturally assumed were his and his alone.'

Fliss flounced away – or as much of a flounce as she'd ever manage given the constrictions of her dress and the ridiculous high heels. Not for Fliss the traditional ballroom attire. Her stark white sheath with its ankle to thigh slash left little to the imagination. Little enough to reveal, Ella noted sourly, her own full breasts almost swelling with indignation. And yet long and lean was the fashionable shape, clearly appealed to men like Jack.

'What the hell have you been saying to upset Fliss?'

'Me?' Waylaid by the fastidious man himself on her way back into the ballroom, Ella raised an innocent eyebrow, logged Jack's thunderous expression and decided she'd had enough for one night. 'I simply pointed out one or two home truths,' she acknowledged coolly, attempting to sweep past.

Jack's hand on her arm pulled her up short. Ella glanced down, her eyes blurring, for a moment seeing not Jack's still tanned hand with its sprinkling of gold hairs but those vivid red talons that had gripped almost to the point of drawing blood.

'Such as?'

'Use your imagination,' she invited coolly, pulling away. 'You know the woman – you must know the way her mind works. The colour green,' she tossed out over her shoulder, recalling a not too distant conversation about shades of a different hue. 'And a snub little nose that's been pushed out of joint.'

'Ella – '

'*Aileen*,' she spat, spinning back to face him, and it was Ella's turn to glare. 'Aileen Andrews-Watson, and don't you forget it.'

'And Tolland?' he bit out, the pulse at his temple beating a wild tattoo that drew Ella's curious gaze. 'Or is Tolland one of the privileged few?'

'Meaning?'

'The truth, madam. Ella or Aileen? And before you rustle up some glib denial, we both know what he calls you. He knows, doesn't he?'

'About us? No, Jack,' Ella told him coldly. 'Stephen knows nothing, and that's the way it's going to stay.'

'Why?'

'Why, what?' she bit back, folding her arms and regarding him warily.

'Why the need to lie?'

'Not lies, Jack, just – '

'The truth, the whole truth and nothing but the truth?' he jeered. 'Ashamed, Ella?'

'Of my behaviour or yours?' she enquired politely.

'Oh, hardly mine,' he reminded her harshly, folding his arms in turn and returning her hatred glare for angry glare. 'Since I wasn't the one who walked away, drank myself stupid – '

Ella's head snapped up as if hit. 'You bastard.'

'If you insist,' he conceded with an ugly curl of the lips. 'Predictable as ever, Ella. You've said it before;

you'll doubtless say it again. I only hope for your sake that whatever the provocation you'll be sober. Take it from me, the insult loses impact otherwise.'

'Stone-cold sober,' she informed him, choking back the tears – tears of hate and anger. 'Just like now.'

'Really?' It was Jack's turn to raise an eyebrow. 'But if seeing is believing, Ella, you're well on the way already. Tell me, my dear,' he entreated confidentially, 'how many glasses does it take these days? A couple with dinner, another couple since, and heaven only knows how many you'd downed before the night began.'

'Three,' she told him frigidly. 'Not that it's any of your business, Jack Keegan. Two white wines and an orange juice.'

'Ah, yes. Two glasses of wine in the space of five minutes. Nothing more, nothing less, hey, Ella?'

'Since you're the one keeping count,' she pointed out coldly, 'you tell me.'

'I don't have to. We both know the truth. But admitting to two is progress indeed. Now, in the bad old days – '

'Exactly,' Ella hissed. 'Over. Past. Gone. And just like our marriage, Jack, my problem with drink is over and done with.'

'If you say so, Ella.'

'I do. But if seeing really is believing,' she countered swiftly, 'why not stick around? Count the sips, the glasses, the bottles, offer Stephen the benefit of your advice when I finally slide beneath the table in an alcoholic haze?'

'Thanks, but no, thanks,' he bit out. 'You're Tolland's responsibility now, thank God.'

'Wrong, Jack. I'm a free woman – and a sober one at that,' she railed. 'And that's the way it's staying.'

She didn't wait for his reply, simply turning on her heels and gliding away, edging her way round the dance floor, the room a blur as she headed for the corner where she and Stephen had been sitting. With Stephen conspicuous by his absence, she pulled up, half-heartedly scanning the couples who shuffled their way around the dance floor, her thoughts in turmoil.

Damn Jack Keegan. For two pins she'd resign here and now, tell him exactly what he could do with the job. She'd manage. She'd done it before and she'd so it again. And with Stephen standing in the wings . . .

Second-best, she inwardly railed, instinctively aware that working for Stephen was no longer an option. It was all or nothing. A partnership in every sense. She didn't love Stephen, wasn't convinced that Stephen loved her, but they'd make a good pair – working together, living together, making love . . . Ella's mind skittered away.

Only Jack, only ever Jack. The thought of spending the night in another man's arms, another man's bed, was strangely unnerving. Ridiculous, she silently whipped herself. She was a grown woman, not a skittish virgin. She'd made love with Jack, craved love with Jack. She needed a man's touch, a man's body. A man, Ella.

Only Jack, only ever Jack.

'Don't tell me Tolland's stood you up?' Jack appeared out of nowhere, the anger and the scorn seemingly forgotten as his hands slipped round, sliding over the curve of her stomach and pulling her into the hard lines of his body. The surge of longing took her by surprise. 'Jack!' she protested, and like a scalded cat she jerked away. Jack's lightening reflex pulled her up short, and, powerless to resist, she dropped her gaze as he reeled her in, one tug, then another, then another, until Ella was standing before him, her eyes fastened on the highly polished floor beneath their feet.

'Oh, Ella!' he chided softly, tucking a finger beneath her chin and tilting her head upwards. 'Oh, Ella, what on earth am I going to do with you?'

And as Ella's troubled eyes locked with his Jack smiled, pulled her onto the dance floor, wrapped his arms around her and held her close. So close she could hear the thump of his heart beneath her cheek, her own agitation clearly matched by his, her own need more than matched by his judging from the hardness at her groin as Jack strained against her.

'Relax,' he murmured against her hair, his hands caressing the trembling expanse of skin on Ella's exposed back and shoulders. 'Just relax. We're alone, alone in the crowd, and I want you to savour each and every moment.'

'Wishful thinking,' Ella scolded, determined to keep her head if the effort nearly killed her. 'You're with Fliss; I'm with Stephen – '

'Hush,' he insisted, touching her mouth with his finger. 'Hush. Believe. Just you and me. Alone.'

'Alone? Oh, Jack,' she berated, struggling for control, aware that a word, a glance, a touch from Jack was enough to ignite her, and equally aware that he could destroy her, that he'd destroyed her once already. 'With five hundred people shuffling by,' she pointed out coolly, his earlier gibe neither forgotten nor forgiven, 'to insist we're alone is nothing short of lunacy.'

And, recalling the hip flask he'd earlier offered Stephen, the chance for revenge was just too good to miss. 'Unless, of course, they're the garbled words of a man who's over-indulged in the whisky?'

CHAPTER FIFTEEN

'Champagne, maybe,' he conceded, smiling, steering her through an open doorway and out onto the terrace. And, since the terrace was a blaze of light, in no time at all he'd managed to find a shadowy alcove, had tucked them both out of sight as he dipped his head to touch her lips. 'And little more than a glass or two, I promise.'

'Stone-cold sober, then?' Ella challenged, weakening despite herself.

'Complete intoxication,' he teasingly contradicted, 'judging from the nectar of your mouth. God, woman,' he groaned in unexpected anguish. 'You've no idea what you do to me. And I was wrong. Each and every word of that revolting accusation. I was hitting out, Ella, and the past was an easy target. If you feel like smacking my face,' he murmured with unexpected humility, 'go ahead. It would make me feel a whole lot better.'

It would have made Ella feel a whole lot better too, only she didn't. Her nerves were in shreds to start with, what with the weekend with Stephen and the threads of doubt about his motives, then this interminable night under the same roof as Fliss and Jack.

Hardly interminable, she amended, and it was hardly the first time. And with another five weeks of her notice to work, another five weeks of wondering, imagining Jack and Fliss together, romping naked through the connecting suites of rooms, kissing, cuddling, making love – Ella flinched as the pain scythed through her, the anguish shadowing her features.

'Ella, oh, Ella,' Jack crooned, seeing the pain and dipping his head to brush his lips against hers.

'No, Jack,' Ella protested, struggling to be free.

'Yes!' he contradicted, cupping her face in his hands and kissing her, the pressure of his lips bruising, branding. The more Ella struggled to pull away, the more the pressure seemed to increase, though Jack's vice-like grip relaxed almost imperceptibly as he sensed the fight draining from her body.

Ella was drowning, her good intentions floundering on a forbidden surge of passion, her mouth opening like the petals of a flower as Jack's tongue swept through, brushing across her sensitive lower lip and triggering a series of explosions, moving on into the moist, dark depths, seeking Ella's tongue and finding Ella's tongue, entwining, exciting, caressing, creating havoc with each and every touch, creating havoc in her mind as he drew away, paused, fastened his solemn gaze onto hers in the half-light thrown up from the lanterns on the terrace and shook his head.

'Ella. My Ella,' he told her, and as Ella shook her head, silently screaming the denials she knew were futile, Jack nodded, allowed his thumb to brush the soft down of her cheek and smiled. '*My* Ella,' he repeated thickly, and he was kissing her, and Ella was responding, the need so urgent, the touch so right that it couldn't possibly be wrong. Fliss, Stephen, the sordid details of the past – all were pushed away, nothing could intrude. They belonged. They'd always belonged.

Hands, magic hands, roamed her body, tracing its curves, the touch of skin on skin a searing trail of delight. The curve of her shoulder, the ridge of her spine – Jack's fingers stroking, exploring, and Ella was lost, her mind refusing to function, her body remembering, needing, craving.

Too wonderful to be wrong. Man and woman. Ella and Jack. Mouth to mouth, lips against lips, tongue seeking tongue. Hunger. A bittersweet craving – because Ella's bruised mind was beginning to function, the knowledge unlooked for and unwanted.

Need. Want. Hunger. Jack's need. Her need too, Ella silently screamed. The need for love, for trust, for tenderness, for love again. Only Ella had thrown it all away. Unfair, she inwardly railed. Blame. Too easy to point the finger of blame. Not Ella, not Jack, just one of life's cruel twists. And yet nothing had changed. She wanted him, she loved him, she needed him, and with Jack's hips grinding against her, Jack's wonderful hardness straining at the fabric of his trousers, straining against her, Ella trembled with the heat of her own desire and knew she was losing the battle.

Time. She belonged to Jack and Jack alone, and sooner or later Jack would take her. Take her, use her, discard her, the voice inside her mind began to chant, over and over. He didn't love her, didn't belong. Time.

'No, Jack,' she protested as his mouth feathered downwards from the column of her neck, reaching the hollow between her breasts. 'Dear God, Jack, no.' No. No. No. The echo in her mind gathered speed as Jack hungrily nudged aside the flimsy fabric of her bodice, exposing her breasts, along with her hardening nipples, to his reverent gaze.

'Hell, woman, you drive me insane,' he murmured, but the sounds of the night began to impinge; the heavy beat of music, the tinkle of laughter, voices, footsteps – footsteps growing louder, the angry stab of stiletto heels.

'Jack?'

The little-girl-lost voice was strangely at odds with Fliss's stony face, barely a fleeting glimpse as Ella shrank against the cold, hard stone. The pause was interminable, Jack's low growl of laughter for Ella's ears alone as he caught her to him, enclosing, protecting, his mouth finding hers again as he kissed her.

To anyone passing by they were just another couple in love, stealing a moment of passion in the shadows of the terrace, and sure enough the footsteps retreated, leaving Ella alone with Jack, alone with her thoughts, alone with the knowledge that Jack was simply playing games.

'Worry not, Ella,' he chided softly, sensing her unease. 'From the back, one white dinner jacket's pretty much the same as any other. Now, *that* stunning little number – '

He broke off, whistled appreciatively under his breath, and a startled Ella glanced down to find her exposed breasts hardening at the look that was almost a tangible caress. The churn of emotion was suddenly all too much, and as Jack reached out to touch her Ella lashed out, pushed him viciously away, folded her arms across her shameful nakedness and blasted him with all the hatred she could muster.

'You bastard. *Bastard*, Jack. And, believe it or not, I'm stone-cold sober.'

'Since I'm not in the habit of taking advantage of even slightly inebriate women,' he drawled, clearly amused, 'yes, Ella, I'm inclined to agree – about your state of health at least.'

'Big of you,' she needled, not bothering to argue the ins and outs of that particular claim. 'But not big enough to face the truth, hey, Jack? An out-and-out bastard. Cheat on Fliss, cheat on me – '

'For your information, madam, I never so much as *looked* at another woman – '

'Tell that one to the tabloids,' she bit out. 'The society page, the gossip page – whichever page I happened to be perusing,' she informed him frigidly. 'There'd be the dashing entrepreneur, smiling for the camera, yet another bright young thing hanging on his arm – '

'Since you were conspicuous by your absence, Ella,' he lazily reminded her, 'I hardly think that counts as infidelity. Irretrievable breakdown,' he added. 'According to law, adultery doesn't exist unless one of the party at least happens to be married.'

'Irrelevant. You're splitting hairs. Given the state of our marriage, it was only a matter of time – '

'And with Mr Watson waiting in the wings,' he reminded her, folding his arms, just the set of his mouth betraying his annoyance, 'that sin wouldn't appear to be mine.'

'You really don't believe that I walked out on you for another man?' Ella demanded incredulously.

He shrugged. 'Who knows?' he queried nastily. 'Who cares? You sure as hell didn't waste much time crawling from my bed to his.'

Ella hit him, the imprint of her hand spreading out across his cheek as, horrified, she stumbled backwards, was brought up sharp by a hand snaking round her wrist and biting deep. 'Touched a nerve, did I?' he bit out, his angry face too close for comfort.

Ella closed her eyes, his nearness unnerving, her sudden need to explain an impulse she mustn't indulge. The truth. She loved Jack, had never stopped loving him, loved him ever now, in the midst of the hate. But tell him the truth and she was doomed.

Because Jack didn't want Ella, didn't need Ella. He never had, never would. But he'd use her all the same. He'd use her, take her, discard her – Jack's decision this time. Because Ella had walked away. Pride. That was all it amounted to, not a shared responsibility. Irretrievable breakdown. No one to blame. Not Jack. Not Ella.

So much easier to blame. And Jack blamed Ella. Fat and frumpy Ella. Fat, frumpy and infertile Ella. Oh, yes, she remembered the words, that dreadful scene when he'd made her face the truth in front of the bathroom mirror. Fat, frumpy, infertile. And drunk. Ella. Ella's fault. Whichever way she viewed it. And if Jack chose to believe she'd left him for another man, so much easier to live with. Ella's fault, not Jack's. Because Jack really had loved her – once.

Aware that Jack was shaking her, Ella opened her eyes. The condemnation in his was a knifeblade twisting in her heart.

'Well, madam?'

'It's the wrong time and place, Jack,' she pointed out calmly, far more calmly than she felt. 'And the inquest took place years ago. Let it go. Let me go. It's over, Jack, and raking over the stone-cold embers of our marriage doesn't help at all.'

Gathering the remnants of her pride, she tugged her crumpled bodice back into place, smoothed the fabric with fingers that shook, and tilted her head in defiance. 'It's over, Jack,' she reminded him, swallowing hard. 'And it's high time you started to believe it.'

She began to walk away, crying inside, aware that she had to walk back into that ballroom and find Stephen, smile and sparkle for Stephen, when all the time she was dying inside, wanting Jack, loving Jack, needing Jack, hating Jack. Love and hate both, and less than a hair's breadth between them. And, since love was surely a fickle emotion, why not simply settle for common sense and the life that Stephen was offering?

'Ella?'

She paused, didn't turn, hardly dared breathe as Jack came up behind, so close she could almost feel his body heat. The urge to lean back, have Jack's arms fold round her, feel Jack's body the length of hers was so fierce she had to dig her nails into the palms of her hands. Aware that Jack was waiting for a word, a sign, an indication, Ella politely inclined her head. 'Jack?'

'About Watson. If he loved you half as much as I did,' he conceded thickly, 'The man was a fool for letting you go. Why, Ella? Why did it have to fall apart?'

Past tense, Ella registered, swallowing the pain. Not that she'd expected any different. 'Simple, Jack,' she conceded softly. 'A simple matter of fate. It just wasn't meant to be. But if it's any consolation . . .' she added, aware that in a strange sort of way this was Jack's attempt to shoulder some of the blame. 'If it's any consolation,' she repeated, blinking back the tears, 'I'll always remember the good times.'

Good times. Life without Jack – or a second chance with Stephen? Decision time, Ella. Because the weekend was drawing to a close and she was shockingly aware that Stephen expected an answer. Ah, yes, but he still hasn't asked, Ella consoled herself, clutching at straws. He will, she countered swiftly, nodding solemnly at her reflection, towelling dry her hair before reaching for her comb. The long tangle of tresses was the least of her problems.

The phone rang, cutting through her musings.

'Good afternoon, sleepyhead,' Stephen chided. 'Or should it be good evening?'

'Given the time a certain young woman arrived home,' Ella reminded tartly. 'I'm only surprised I didn't sleep the clock round.'

'If this is Tuesday, I guess you might have done at that,' Stephen teased.

'If this is Tuesday,' Ella agreed, checking the date on her watch just in case, 'then one of us is horribly late for work and could well be facing the sack.'

'No problem. With my expanding empire, Ella, you can take your pick of jobs. Waitress, maid, porter,' he mused. 'There's sure to be an opening in one of my hotels. Hmm, now let me see, the Stafford Savana, perhaps . . .'

'Stephen – '

'Just a tentative plan, you understand,' he cut in swiftly. 'Depending on your answer. But if lugging suitcases doesn't appeal there's a vacancy for you and you alone. Interested, Ella?'

'I might be,' she conceded carefully, instinctively aware that it wasn't a job Stephen was offering. The Stafford Savana. A tentative plan. Because Stephen knew that Ella was loath to leave the area. Amazing. He'd never asked, never pried, had simply accepted Ella's explanation that her grandfather was old and needed her close.

Not the truth, the whole truth and nothing but the truth, but as much as she'd given. Not so next time. The truth. Because before she married Stephen she'd have to give him the truth about Jack.

'Look, I know you've been married before,' Stephen forestalled her that night over dinner, a cosy meal for two in Ella's magnificent sitting room. 'But that makes two of us. It's no big deal. These things happen, Ella, and if and when you feel like explaining, I'll be happy to listen. If,' he repeated, the blue eyes holding hers a solemn reminder of another set of eyes. Jack's eyes, Jack's easy words.

From the back, Jack had pointed out with blatant unconcern, one dinner jacket is pretty much the same as any other. Just like a man? Ella probed. A set of blue eyes, rugged blond looks and a passion to succeed. So alike and yet so vastly different. Second-best, Ella mused, or a desperate attempt to wipe away the stain of Jack's kisses, Jack's touch?

Difficult to decide, since Stephen seemed determined to give her space, clearly making up for forcing her hand the last time he'd raised the subject.

'It's no big deal,' he repeated, kissing Ella lightly on the mouth, drawing her away from the table and down onto one of the Regency striped sofas, cradling her against his shoulder. 'You know about Louise because I needed to talk about the kids,' he reminded her. 'And with my office walls plastered with snapshots, I could hardly hope to pass for footloose and fancy free.'

The kids. Ten-year-old Stevie, the image of his father, judging from the photographs, and an angelic Lucy, the apple of her father's eye.

'Angelic, my foot,' Stephen derided, replacing the snaps in his wallet and rejoining Ella on the sofa. 'That little madam would try the patience of a saint.'

'And will break a few hearts before she's much older,' Ella observed, swallowing a smile. 'You must miss them, Stephen?'

'Like hell. But they're coming over for Christmas – staying with Mum and Dad for a month. We haven't had a real family Christmas since Lucy was born,' he explained, with a sudden surge of pride, and then, the words carefully casual, 'If you've nothing special planned, Ella, why not tag along?'

'And leave Gramps?' Ella stalled.

'No problem. If you're part of the family, Ella, so is Gramps. But you don't have to decide this minute. Take your time – take all the time in the world.'

All the time in the world. As long as Stephen got the answer he was hoping for.

'Marry me, Ella,' he finally urged, Ella's nerves having reached screaming pitch as the hours ticked away and Stephen stubbornly refused to come to the point.

A clever man, she was beginning to realize. Just like Jack. Because if Stephen had handled it wrong once before, he was determined to learn from his mistakes, determined that this time things would go his way.

'You know it makes sense,' he urged. 'And no,' he added swiftly, putting a finger to her mouth, stopping her from speaking. 'Don't say a word. Not yet. Take your time, Ella. Take as long as you need.'

And Ella nodded, smiled, tilted her head for the kiss she knew Stephen wasn't about to take for granted, her mouth opening beneath his.

The kiss was gentle, tentative almost, as Stephen pulled her close, wrapped his arms around her, and Ella closed her eyes, closed her mind. A man. Pretty much the same as any other. Two eyes, two arms, two legs and all the bits and pieces in clear working order. Jack. Stephen. A man's needs. A woman's needs. The surge of longing caught her unawares.

Oh, God! Hours later and wide awake, Ella, hugged the duvet close, recalling the twin sensations that had gripped her, the tears squeezing out from beneath her lashes and trickling unheeded down her cheeks. Longing and shame.

A man's touch, a man's lips on hers, a man's hands roaming her body. And, heaven help her, Ella had responded. She'd kissed him, pushing her body into the hard lines of his, aware of his hands slipping under the hem of her sweater and caressing the bare skin of her back. A feather-light touch, like the lips that were nuzzling her mouth, tentative, fleetingly unsure.

Leastways, Ella amended with awful clarity, the touch hadn't been unsure, simply his reaction to Ella's sudden surge of passion. Because he hadn't been about to push her too far, risk another rejection.

No chance of rejection with her body primed for love, needing love, a man's love, and if this man had never professed to love her he'd never lied, never let her down.

Oh, so easy. Man and woman, mouth to mouth, body to body. Long, exploring fingers had stroked the underswell of breasts that were screaming out for skin-to-skin contact, thumbs brushing against nipples that could harden at the mere thought of Jack's touch, Jack's knowing gaze. And Ella had pushed herself against the exploring fingers, moving her hips against him, registering his hardness, the need running through her like a flame. Jack. Only not Jack. Stephen.

'No!' She'd pulled away, disbelief shadowing her features, disappointment clouding Stephen's. Shockingly aware of how close she'd come to the point of no return, her mind had soared. Reaching out, she'd cupped Stephen's face in her hands, pulling his head close to hers. 'Thank you,' she'd murmured almost reverently as she'd kissed him, aware that Stephen couldn't possibly comprehend the wealth of emotion that was gripping her. How could he, when Ella herself wasn't sure any more?

She wasn't sure now, eight long, guilt-ridden hours later, and that surge of elation was not even a distant memory. She'd been wrong. And yet for one heart-stopping moment she'd been sure she was laying the ghost of Jack once and for all. She *could* sleep with Stephen. After all, hadn't she come perilously close? Which meant she could marry Stephen. Stephen, not Jack. A marriage of convenience. Give Stephen what he needed, allow Ella to purge the man she loved from her system.

Cheat Stephen? No, no, no, she railed. The truth. Tomorrow she'd give Stephen the truth and take it from there. Because if Stephen could cope with Ella, warts and all, then, if the effort nearly killed her, Ella would make sure that Stephen was never, ever short-changed.

A life without Jack, Ella acknowledged bitterly. And, since life goes on, it was high time she pushed Jack and everything he stood for to the back of her mind.

It was a hurried breakfast – so many unspoken thoughts. Stephen's thoughtful gaze resting on her face, the solemn shake of his head when Ella tried to speak.

'No, Ella,' he smilingly forestalled her. 'Not yet. It's too soon. Because when you finally say yes,' he explained, reaching for her hand, cradling it in his, the expression in his eyes unfathomable, 'we'll both know that it's what you really want.'

When, not if, she noted, the touch of male arrogance rankling. More shades of Jack. Jack, Jack, Jack. And with the doubt continuing to fester, it was a tense drive to the station.

'I can manage,' Ella protested, when Stephen insisted on carrying her bags onto the train.

'I know you can. It's one of the things I love most about you,' he amazed her by admitting. Love, when she'd long given up hope of any man loving her again!

'I'm sorry, what did you say?' she queried, too caught up with that particular novelty to catch what Stephen was saying now. He gave a broad smile as he told her.

'Babies?' Ella went cold, the blood pounding in her ears, drowning out the drone of the tannoy, the shriek of whistles and voices.

'Lots of babies,' Stephen repeated, hugging her, kissing her lightly. 'Since Louise moved to the States I've really missed the kids. But we can stick at a couple if the idea doesn't appeal?'

'At my age?' Ella stalled, feeling her way around an unexpected minefield.

'Fiddlesticks. You're young enough to mother a football team,' Stephen teased, blue eyes twinkling. 'But it was only a thought,' he conceded, Ella's stunned reaction beginning to impinge. 'One baby, two – an all-star eleven.' He shrugged. 'Like I said, you're young enough and we've all the time in the world.'

But all the time in the world simply wasn't enough, Ella acknowledged silently, sinking down into her seat as the train jerked into motion. And how ironic, yet another of life's cruel twists. On the verge of committing herself to Stephen, he had said the one thing guaranteed to make Ella turn him down.

CHAPTER 16

'You mean you were really there, Mrs A? In the same room as Princess Di and rubbing shoulders with all them nobs? I bet the Honourable Fliss wasn't impressed with that.'

'No.' Ella swallowed a smile at the rapid switch in Katie's tone. Awe to derision in the space of half sentence. She wouldn't mind betting The Hon Fliss had been even less impressed at missing out on that champagne breakfast.

But every cloud had a silver lining, and Fliss *had* managed to grab the spotlight, Ella acknowledged, remembering the commotion, the unexpected sight of Fliss sprawled in a heap at the bottom of the steps. Three very shallow steps, Ella had been relieved to note, and, since the younger woman's dignity seemed the major casualty, Ella had bobbed quickly out of sight again. Not so the bevy of reporters with their relentless flashbulbs. Less front-page news than society page gossip – Fliss, in full Technicolor glory, an expression of pain – or an ugly twist of anger – shadowing her features.

'Just a badly sprained ankle,' Jack had explained in a terse early-morning phone call. 'And, since Fliss has been advised to rest it, we'll be staying on here for a day or two.'

The longer the better as far as Ella was concerned. She was aware that her 'rubbing shoulders with the nobs' would have altered the balance of a precarious relationship. Fliss. The woman's dislike of Ella was tangible, to Ella at least, and the thought of another five weeks under the same roof was anything but cosy.

'The lull before the storm,' Katie mused. 'But at least we've a bit more notice this time.'

'Oh?' Ella queried, folding the paper in half and pushing it away.

'A photographic convention. Middle of next month, according to Ian – which reminds me. He's over at the trout farm this morning but should be back by two, and if you can pop into the office later he'll put you in the picture.'

Ian did, and Ella's raised eyebrows prompted a smile. 'I'm as surprised as you,' he conceded, running his fingers through a windswept mop of hair. 'Though on second thoughts I should have seen it coming. The travel fair,' he reminded her. 'And with Geraghty attending quite a coup, all thanks to you. And Jack's no fool, Mrs A. He's sense enough to know when he's sitting on a goldmine.'

'Either that or the lady of house has fallen for the dubious charms of fame,' Ella put in dryly.

'Very true,' Ian acknowledged, catching her drift at once. The efficiency of the staff grapevine never ceased to amaze Ella. 'But since pride normally comes before a fall,' he added, only slightly tongue in cheek, 'I wouldn't mind betting there's a moral there somewhere.'

'Ah. I take it you saw the pictures?' Ella queried, lips twitching imperceptibly.

'Since they were splashed across the front of most of the tabloids,' Ian conceded, grinning broadly, 'difficult not to. Not that I stopped to look, you understand?'

'Oh, heaven forbid,' Ella replied, feigning horror at the thought. 'But if you happen to be passing the kitchens later, drawn by the subtle aroma of freshly brewed coffee, you might just catch a glimpse of the newspaper cutting Katie's pinned to the order board.'

'She hasn't, Mrs A?'

'She has. And heaven help Katie if Himself arrives unannounced and spots it.'

Heaven help Katie or heaven help Ella? Jack's stormy expression was more than eloquent proof that he wasn't amused.

'A snatch of belowstairs gossip?' he queried coldly, crumpling the offending cutting into a ball and dropping it in the bin. 'You disappoint me, Ella. Now, Katie – '

'Isn't to blame,' Ella interrupted. 'My staff, my responsibility, Jack. My apology. I'm sorry,' she conceded, raising her head, her steady gaze locking with his and logging the contempt. 'It shouldn't have happened.'

'Only it did. So, tell me, Ella,' he invited saccharine-sweetly, folding his arms and regarding her from under heavily hooded eyes. 'Since the incident clearly amuses. What exactly happened that night?'

'To Fliss? I've no idea,' she told him brightly. 'But, given those ridiculous heels she insisted on wearing, losing her balance was only a matter of time.'

'Ah, yes, but did Fliss fall or was she pushed?'

'Meaning?'

'Meaning precisely that. And since you were standing right behind her at the time,' he pointed out slyly, 'surely you'd have noticed?'

Ella flushed. 'I'm not sure that I like what you're implying.'

'No. I didn't think you would. Food for thought, my dear. And talking of food,' he added, swinging away, the conversation clearly palling, 'I'd like dinner served at eight. Dinner for three. You, me and Ian. I assume that isn't a problem?'

No more than any other request from the master of the house. But with Fliss electing to stay on in London, at least Ella would be spared the younger woman's scorn. For now.

Aperitifs, and Ella pointedly opted for freshly squeezed orange juice. The atmosphere was strained as Jack made not the slightest effort to put her at her ease, and Ella prayed for the buffering presence of Ian.

The phone rang. Ella angled her head in enquiry, and Jack, equally politely, nodded his assent as Ella rose to take it.

'Sorry, Mrs A,' Ian explained ruefully, and a shiver of alarm ran the length of Ella's spine. 'Something's come up. I'll have to take a raincheck on that dinner. Will you break the news or shall I?'

'Problems, Ian?' Ella queried, her gaze flicking back to Jack, sprawled lazily on one of the sofas, those cool blue eyes suddenly alert.

'Nothing serious,' Ian reassured her. 'Just one of the mares about to foal. The vet's on his way and as far as I can tell everything's fine. At least,' he amended dryly, 'everything's fine at this end.'

'Ian's loss, my gain,' Jack conceded pleasantly when Ella had finished explaining. 'Dinner,' he reminded her, leading the way through to the smaller of the dining rooms and the table set for three. 'A first-class meal with first-class company. What more could a man ask for?'

Knowing Jack, the sun, moon and stars, but with Jack's mood unpredictable to say the least, Ella didn't bother putting the thought into words, instead clearing away the superfluous place before setting out the first course – a layered terrine of spinach, carrot and broccoli which ought to have slid easily down her throat.

Since it was Katie's day off, Ella had produced a meal that could be left ticking over on heated trays and would practically serve itself: chicken breasts poached in red wine with swirls of creamy potatoes to soak up the sauce, followed by brandy snap baskets and fruit on a raspberry coulis.

Jack poured the wine, a crisp dry white followed by a robust red, and Ella's attempt to decline was blatantly ignored. Fine. So Jack was out to prove a point. Two could play at that game, and, though Ella appeared to take several dutiful sips, the level in both glasses remained high.

'So – ' Jack raised his own glass, blue eyes raining scorn as they rested on Ella's face. 'To absent friends?' he queried. 'To Fliss – and Tolland?'

'If you insist,' Ella murmured, privately cursing Ian for his last-minute defection. 'But shouldn't we be discussing business?'

'We should indeed,' he agreed pleasantly, draining his glass and promptly refilling it. 'Estate business. But with my estate manager unavoidably detained we might as well not bother. Worry not, Ella,' he lazily entreated, 'it will keep.'

It would have to, Ella supposed, since Jack had issued the summons, had clearly set his own agenda. Never one for small talk, he turned his attention to the meal, his appetite seemingly unaffected by the tension quivering on the air – a tension that grew with the silence, stretching Ella's nerves to breaking point.

The exquisite food might have been cardboard for all the pleasure it gave, each and every mouthful sticking in her throat. Ella silently fumed. Damn Jack Keegan. He was her employer, nothing more, nothing less, and putting her through hell so that he could score points was out of line.

Focusing her anger, she demolished the brandy-snap basket with a vicious stab of the fork, and, glancing up, found Jack's amused gaze fastened on her face.

'Thank you, Ella. I enjoyed that,' he conceded, his empty plate a glaring contrast to Ella's. 'Yet another masterpiece, and further proof that you're selling yourself short. Housekeeper?' he chided lightly. 'Cook? With your flair for food, you could hold your own in the best hotels in the world. Yet what does Ella Keegan do instead? She buries herself in the depths of the country.'

'Ella Andrews-Watson,' she corrected tersely. 'And, since my work can't be faulted, I don't see there's a problem.'

'The work, or your motives?' he probed. 'For heaven's sake, woman, you're a natural. You're organized, level-headed and clearly not afraid to take risks. The travel fair,' he reminded her. 'Not a hitch, not a hiccup, not a single complaint. Just superb organization. And Geraghty. Believe me, Ella, persuading a man like Geraghty to attend was nothing short of miraculous. Face it, Ella, you're wasted in domestic service.'

Echoes of Stephen, Ella acknowledged wryly, but Jack's hint was unmistakable, and she hadn't time to bask in the back-handed compliment.

'Time to go?' she queried as evenly as possible. 'Let me guess, Jack. You'd like me to leave before Fliss gets back?'

'Wrong, Ella. Or maybe that's wishful thinking on your part. Running away?' he queried slyly. 'Running scared? Or running back to Tolland, in fact?'

'Since a girl has to live,' she pointed out coolly, 'needs a roof over her head and food on her plate, when one job comes to an end it makes sense to look for another.'

'It makes even more sense not to jump to the wrong conclusion,' he told her with an admonitory shake of the head. 'Five weeks you owe me, five weeks I'd like you to do. And don't forget the bills, Ella,' he entreated gravely. 'Electricity, gas, water rates, phone.' He counted them off on his fingers. 'Once you're back in the real world,' he reminded her, 'the list is never-ending. Oh, yes, and don't forget that other little essential,' he crooned, blue eyes oozing derision. 'In a girl's mind at least. The dress bill.'

'Since walking naked through the streets was illegal the last time I checked,' she said sneeringly, 'naturally I need to buy clothes.'

'Ah, yes, but not just any old item, hey, Ella? Take that stunning little number you wore on Saturday evening – '

'None of your damn business,' she bit out, the colour flooding her cheeks.

'No? No, I don't suppose it is,' he conceded with an evil flash of teeth, coming to his feet and towering over her. 'But that doesn't stop a guy from wondering.' He moved swiftly round the table. 'Coffee?' he enquired.

His mood had changed like the wind, and the hairs on the back of Ella's neck prickled out a warning as, solicitous and close, he helped slide back her chair. 'Brandy?' he offered, leading the way into the sitting room. 'Metaxa – your favourite, I seem to recall. No? Fine.' He smiled, shrugged, waited for Ella to settle herself down on one of the easy chairs before taking the one opposite, coffee cup and brandy balloon placed carefully on the table beside him.

Not just any old brandy. Metaxa. A carefully chosen reminder. Greek brandy from a Greek holiday – their honeymoon, in fact. So, just what devious game was Jack playing?

'Life, Ella,' came the amused response when Ella summoned the nerve to challenge him. 'I'm playing at life. Just like you and Tolland, in fact.'

'And Fliss?' she enquired politely. 'Where does Fliss fit into the Jack Keegan scheme of things?'

'You know very well where.'

Yes. Fiancée. Soon to be his wife. Not so much the dutiful kind, Ella decided, lips tightening in unconscious disapproval, as the flighty kind. Poor Jack, if only he but knew it.

'So . . .' Jack paused, palmed his glass, swirled the familiar amber liquid around the balloon and then angled his head in enquiry. 'You and Tolland are an item?'

'Are you asking me or telling me?' Ella stalled, half inclined to repeat that it was none of his damn business.

'Simply weighing all the options, Ella. But, given the cost of those tickets . . .'

'We're – good friends,' she conceded reluctantly, wondering just how long that would last once Stephen had her answer. And it would have to be no, Ella realized starkly – should have realized all along.

'So I noticed,' Jack murmured dryly.

'Jealous, Jack?'

'I could be,' he conceded. 'If I thought that it was serious.'

'What makes you so certain that it's not?'

'Simple, Ella. You love me. Always have, always will.'

'So sure,' she goaded. 'Well, for your information, Mr Arrogance Personified, Stephen has asked me to marry him.'

'I see.' Just that, and a pulse beating an angry tattoo at his temple.

'Do you?' Ella queried coldly, hazel eyes oozing scorn. 'I doubt it.'

Jack shrugged, ignoring the taunt in her words. 'You'll be making it third time lucky, then?' he queried instead.

'Maybe,' Ella conceded warily.

'And maybe not, hey, Ella?' Jack scorned. 'Because Tolland might have asked but you haven't said yes.'

'I haven't said yes – yet,' she allowed, vaguely aware that beneath the sneering words Jack was smarting, simply wasn't sure, that in a perverse kind of way he resented Stephen's place in her life. A typical man, Ella scorned, but silently. He thinks he can have his cake and eat it.

'You haven't said yes, full-stop. If a girl needs time to think, Ella, then a girl isn't sure.'

'But I thought I was sure the last time, Jack,' she reminded him sweetly. 'And look what that got me.'

'Watson, apparently. But since I haven't had the pleasure of his company,' Jack observed, 'I'm hardly in a position to judge.'

'Yes. No.' Ella felt her colour rise, cursed herself for the careless slip of the tongue and vowed to think before she spoke in future. 'More coffee?' she queried, jumping up and crossing to the sideboard. 'More brandy, Jack?'

'What an excellent idea,' he agreed at once. 'But, since it's never very sociable drinking alone, only if you join me, Ella.'

Easy words, an easy smile, yet the challenge was loud in Jack's candid blue eyes. Brandy. The very smell was enough to trigger the memories. The thought of having to sit and cradle a glass, take sips from that glass, was more than Ella could stand.

Aware that Jack was testing, goading, though heaven alone knew why, Ella forced a smile. 'Fine. But if you don't mind, I'll help myself to more wine instead. There's plenty left from dinner.'

Two minutes. Two precious minutes alone in the dining room, and the urge to fill her glass, drain it and fill it again, almost gained the upper hand. Playing into Jack's hands, apparently, though heaven alone knew why he should want to dredge up the sordid mess of her past – unless, of course, he was paying Ella back for some imaginary slight?

Revenge? she mused. Jack's revenge for Ella's walking out? Final proof that the fault was Ella's? Irretrievable breakdown. No fault divorce, no guilty party, no blame. So much easier to blame. Ella. Ella's fault. No babies, no marriage, no love – and transient consolation in the contents of a bottle. Only not any more, she told herself grimly, and, stiffening, returned to Jack's den.

'To absent friends?' she goaded from the security of the chair, raising her glass in defiance. 'To your fiancée, Jack – and mine.'

'Marry in haste, repent at leisure,' he reminded her, lips tightening.

'A salutary lesson,' she agreed. 'So let's hope you heed your own advice.'

'Meaning?'

'Fliss. The next Mrs Keegan. I should hate you to be taken for a ride, Jack.'

'Why, thank you, Ella. And to think, I didn't know you cared.'

'I guess I did at that,' she agreed easily. 'Once.'

'Unkind, Ella,' he chided. 'Unkind and out of character.'

'Well, maybe the worm's turned, Jack. Maybe I'm a hard woman these days. Hard – and sober.' And, raising her glass with a flourish, she placed it to her lips, drained the contents in one and set it carefully down on the table beside her. 'One drink, Jack. Just to be sociable. My decision, and my decision to keep to one. And now, if you don't mind, I'd like another coffee.'

'Be my guest,' he insisted, waving an airy hand. 'Make yourself at home.'

'Not the easiest of tasks,' she pointed out tersely, 'with my host in tormenting mood. Why, Jack, why?'

He smiled, spread his hands. 'I don't – '

'Oh, yes, you do,' she insisted, leaning forwards, the anger that had been simmering beneath the surface finally bursting through. 'You know exactly what you're doing – punishing, needling, goading, hinting, sneering, dangling the bait of the demon drink just to test my reactions. And not just any old drink, Jack. Brandy. Metaxa brandy. What the hell are you trying to do? Push me over the limit, prove yourself right once and for all?'

'Just trying to make you take a long, hard look at yourself,' he conceded mildly.

'What makes you think I didn't do exactly that years ago?' she hissed, aware of the sting of tears – tears of love, tears of hate, tears of frustration.

She dashed them away with the back of her hand, vaguely aware that Jack had moved, had come to kneel before her. His presence was more unnerving than the sneering words, the battery of insults; her self-respect was hanging by a thread. Cry? For Jack? For the man who'd destroyed her. No, no, no! No, because she was wrong, about so many things. The truth, Ella, she needled. Not Jack's fault, not even Ella's, just life dealing out one its loaded hands. Hands. Jack's hands, reaching out, closing round . . .

'Oh hell, sweetheart – '

'No! Leave me alone!' Pushing him away, struggling to be free, the tears coursed down her cheeks. The touch of skin on skin was sending rivers of heat surging through the pain, the handkerchief thrust between her fingers allowing her the dignity of blowing her nose, wiping away the tell-tale stains as she struggled for control.

Jack reached out a finger to brush away a rogue tear, the touch searing, and Ella's sharp hiss of indrawn breath was matched by Jack's as he swore, pulled her into his arms, held her, kissed her.

No, no, no, Ella's mind cried. Yes, yes, yes her body contradicted, and it was Ella's turn to kiss, to touch, to hold; her fingers tracing the angles and planes of his face, the rasp of stubble a wonderfully erotic sensation that created shivers of heat in the depths of her belly. Jack, only Jack, always Jack. Useless to resist. Resist? Deny the nectar of his mouth, the magic of his touch, when each and every inch of her was crying out for satisfaction?

'Ella, my Ella,' he crooned, his lips nuzzling hers, his mouth exploring, and as his tongue slid through into the warm, moist depths Ella gave a gentle nip of teeth, felt Jack's shuddering response beneath her fingers and smiled inside.

Her man. Man and woman. Man and woman alone, with a man and woman's needs, bodies primed for love, screaming out for love. Body to body, the barrier of clothes for the moment not important. So much love, so much wasted time.

Mouth to mouth, lips to lips, skin to skin as arms folded round, holding, enfolding, hands exploring, caressing, fingers stroking. Ella's fingers plunging through the luxuriant mass of his hair as Jack dipped his head, feathered the stem of her neck, mouth to throat and back again, and down, nuzzling the hollow of her throat as magic hands reached her breasts, another feather-light touch that excited and denied as the hands glided away.

'Jack – '

'Hush, sweetheart,' he crooned, raising his head, locking his gaze onto hers. 'Hush. Soon,' he murmured smokily. 'Very soon, I promise.'

Nowhere near soon enough for Ella, but no time to brood as Jack gathered her close, pulled her to her feet, body to body, his hands gliding the length of her spine and over the curve of her bottom, cupping, caressing, tugging her against him. Ella gasped as the hardness at his groin strained against her, provoking a chuckle.

'Oh, yes,' he admitted huskily. 'I want you and you want me every bit as badly – but not yet, Ella. Soon, very soon,' he insisted, fingers stroking, hands stoking, words enflaming. 'For if a beautiful woman is like a first-class meal,' he suggested hoarsely, nibbling at her earlobe, 'I want to savour each and every course. I want *you* to savour each and every course. So relax, Ella,' he entreated, the very words a gentle caress. 'Enjoy, taste, savour, and the moment you think you've tasted your fill – why, then I'll take you on another journey of pleasure.'

Pleasure. So much love. So many lonely nights in the depths of her bed. A stolen moment of pleasure. Just a taste, she acknowledged as the pain scythed through her. Not nearly enough for satiation. For if Jack belonged in the arms of another woman, just for today, just for a single moment of pleasure, he belonged to Ella, and all the lonely tomorrows would be faced in the cold light of day. Today, tonight, if only for a moment, Jack and Ella belonged.

More kisses – the sense of urgency building as Jack explored her mouth, held her face rigid between his fingers and denied the natural movement of her head. Forced to suffer the exquisite torture of Jack's tongue sweeping across the sensitized inner skin of her lips, Ella moved her hips, pushing against him, grinding her hips, gasping as Jack arched his lower body out of range.

Ella's response was instinctive. She reached out to touch, to finger, to stroke, felt the shudder beneath her fingers and trembled. So much power, so much need. Jack's need as he pushed against her hand, the straining fabric of his trousers denying Ella's fingers the satisfaction of closing round him. Jack himself denying her as he slid his hands the length of her spine, over the swell of her buttocks, pulling her urgently back against his male hardness.

'Too soon,' he groaned in anguish, as, hip against hip, he ground her against him. Ella's turn to incite as she angled back from the pivot of her waist, cupping her breasts, offering her breasts, her nipples hardening as Jack nudged her hands away.

'Mine,' he insisted thickly, thumbs brushing against her nipples. 'Only mine.' He bent to kiss, sucking through the fabric, tugging, and the answering tug in the pit of her stomach almost drove her insane.

'Jack! Please, please, please,' she implored.

'Too soon,' he insisted, the laughter gurgling in his throat as he caught her moan of anguish. But he kissed her, savouring the taste of her mouth as his hands ranged her body, into the curves and convolutions in fleeting exploration as his fingers feathered the swell of her aching breasts, flicked across the nub of straining nipples, climbed to trace the angles of her face.

'Oh, Ella,' he growled, a wealth of emotion swirling in the bottomless pools of his eyes. 'Too soon and yet not nearly soon enough. Oh, Ella. You really are the most wonderful woman in the world. And I want you. I want you and I'm going to take you,' he informed her solemnly. 'My bed, or yours, or the rug in front of the fire,' he insisted thickly, 'but we will make love – all night long.

CHAPTER 17

'If you say so,' she murmured provokingly, the battle already fought and lost in her mind. Because she loved him and she wanted him, and she no longer had the strength to resist him.

'Yes, madam, I do!' he growled. And he smiled, and Ella smiled, and then, quick as a flash, she darted away, the gurgle of laughter rising in her throat as she logged the stunned expression on his face.

Reaching the door, she halted, leaned back against the jamb, snapping the buttons of her dress with slow deliberation. And all the time her smoky gaze was fastened on his face.

'Promises, promises,' she teased, allowing the bodice to fall open, to give a tantalizing glimpse of the body beneath. Another electric pause before she nudged the dress from her shoulders, allowing it to drop unheeded at her feet. Clad in nothing but petticoat, bra and pants and the sheerest of stockings, she allowed him to feast his eyes before stepping neatly out of the crumpled heap and, kicking off her shoes, setting off again. 'Come along, Jack,' she taunted over her shoulder. 'What's keeping you?'

'Not so fast,' he growled, snaring her wrist as she reached the end of the corridor. And Ella laughed, raised her face for a kiss, a tantalizing taste of the man she loved, and then she sped away, as fleet as the wind as she headed for the self-contained flat she wouldn't be calling home for much longer.

Smothering the stab of pain, she pressed on, aware that he was gaining on her, though slowly, the kiss-chase all part of the game. Slowing slightly, she snapped the catch of her bra, pulled it free of tingling breasts as she reached the corner, disappeared around it and once there halted, dangling the wisp of lace into the open passageway. It was a red rag to a raging bull, yet the moment the flimsy garment was wrenched from her fingers she was back on the move.

Another fleeting pause at the top of the stairs – a single stocking discarded, its twin twined around the newel post at the bottom. Another kiss, longer, more urgent, with a definite reluctance to let her go, but go she would, twisting free, dancing away, the petticoat trailing from her fingers until, reaching the door to her sitting room, Ella pulled up, breathless, leaning back against the door, the chill of the wood against her almost naked body forgotten in an instant because he'd caught her, was pinning her, kissing her, pushing his body into the lines of hers and he was hard, so wonderfully hard, and nothing else in the whole wide world mattered. Only Jack. Wonderful, wonderful Jack.

'Wonderful, wonderful, woman.' He echoed her thoughts, raising his head, his eyes bottomless pools as they locked onto hers.

He reached behind her for the handle, cupped his hands around her buttocks instead, his growl of frustration as exploring fingers met with lacy black briefs music to her ears. Impatient fingers slid beneath the waistband, cupping her again, skin against skin, kneading, caressing, holding, his mouth fastening onto hers, and it was Ella's turn for frustration as Jack pulled away, snaring her wrist as he prised open the catch before tugging her inside.

'The rug in front of the fire,' she reminded him smokily. 'Or the bed?'

'Why not both?' he challenged thickly, impatiently shedding his clothes.

Ella smiled, stood and watched as jacket, shirt and tie landed in a heap on the floor. His magnificent torso gleamed in the lamplight, muscles rippling like the waves of the sea, and, seeing the mass of gold across his chest, she reached out, running her fingers through the curls, brushing against a nipple, which hardened. Her smile grew tender as she danced out of reach again, tantalizingly close, tantalizingly dressed, tantalizing as she placed her hands upon her hips and pirouetted saucily in front of him, slid her hands upwards to cup her breasts, lean forwards, offer her breasts, rub her thumbs against her dark, thrusting nipples.

'Ella – '

Another gurgle as she swayed out of reach, but Jack had had enough – hadn't had anywhere near enough, except of frustration, and quick as a flash he caught her, snared her wrist, reeled her in, paused, almost touching – almost. His turn to tease, to tantalize, to frustrate as he dipped his head to flick a rigid nipple with his tongue, brush a second with his thumb, fleeting, devastating, and as the heat ran through her she moaned, swayed forwards, her breasts brushing against his chest, a searing contact that was equally fleeting as Jack arched out of reach.

'Jack!'

'Ella?' Blue eyes danced with happiness, with desire, the smokiness increasing as his gaze swept over her, down, down. Her nipples darkened, hardening again as his eyes lingered, seemed almost truly to touch, and moved on, over the plains of her belly.

The currents of heat in the epicentre were growing stronger, coiling outwards and upwards and down to the junction of her legs, to the neat triangle of curls simply made for fingers to thread – his fingers. And she felt the sudden flood of heat and dampness and trembled. Because she loved him, and she wanted him, and the reverence of his gaze told her that Jack wanted her every bit as badly.

'Please, Jack,' she murmured shamelessly, piteously.

'The rug or the bed?' he growled. But he didn't wait for her reply, pulling her against him, kissing her hair, her face, her mouth while his hands slid down the silky skin of her back, urging her into the lines of his body, the barrier of their clothes heightening the tension.

Clothes? Ella's mind smiled. Jack's trousers and her own shameless attire – the tiniest pair of briefs. His hands were reaching the waistband, fingers sliding beneath the waistband, hands cupping the swell of her bottom as he urged her even closer, his hardness straining against her, and she was moving against him, her hips undulating against him, enticing, teasing, stoking the fires – and she wanted him, wanted him naked against her. She reached for the fastening of his trousers and his fingers met hers, threaded through hers, guided hers to snap the fastener and tug, oh, so slowly at the zipper, the heat of him, the thrust of him almost driving her insane.

'Soon,' he murmured as her fingers closed round him, the thrill of her possession awesome. 'Very, very soon.' And he kissed her, softly, tenderly, peeled the last layers of clothing over his long, powerful legs and, dropping to his knees, gazed up at her, his eyes locking with hers, the moment timeless. 'Ella, oh, Ella,' he murmured reverently, and his hands reached out to cup her breasts as lips and mouth and tongue nuzzled the plains of her belly. Ella arched towards him, craving the touch, the taste, her legs turning to water as she sank down beside him.

Face to face, mouth to mouth, body to body, but slowly, savouring the need, stoking the need, the urgency, skin against skin. They were stretched out on the rug, the softly dying embers of the fire giving a roseate glow to their skin and Jack paused, propped himself up on one elbow and gazed down at her – so much emotion in his eyes, so much love reflected in Ella's. And if she flinched at the knowledge that Jack didn't love her, she hastily smothered the pain. He needed her, he wanted her. It was enough. For now.

'Wonderful,' he murmured, his glance reverential as it swept the length of her – not the too-sleek body of the girl he'd married, not the frump she'd become in the dark days. Seeing the wonder in his eyes, the hunger in his eyes, Ella knew that her woman's body pleased him, that the taut skin was everything he remembered and more – taut, tactile, tremulous, a tingling, quivering, shivering mass of nerve-endings.

He dipped his head to kiss her, his tongue swirling through into the moist recesses of her mouth, lips demanding, and, stretched out beside her once more, body to body, he held her, moved against her, touched her, caressed her, denied her.

'Jack, Jack, Jack,' she groaned in anguish, and his throaty growl was music to her ears because soon he would take her – soon, he'd promised, but not too soon. The magic was too powerful to squander in an instant and so the hell went on for Ella – hell and heaven both as magic fingers, magic lips touched and teased, caressed, enticed, lifting her higher and higher as his mouth moved lower and lower, skirted the curls, feathered the soft milky skin of her thighs, down one long, slender leg, nuzzling the instep of first one foot then the other, and then back, up, ever upwards. Pause, electric pause, and Ella held her breath, closed her eyes, anticipated, smiled, trembled – and waited.

A single finger threaded the curls. Pause. Her lids flying open, eyes locking with his. A tremulous smile – Jack's answering smile lighting up her mind. And yet Ella's smile wavered for an instant. Because she was alone with a man, naked with a man, this man whom she loved with each and every inch of her, and she ached to please him, to make it perfect, as perfect for Jack as it was for her.

The finger moved, slid into the secret, sensitive part of her, paused again to savour the warmth, the moistness. But the trembling had already begun, somewhere deep inside, was building, rolling, breaking, the mere touch of Jack's finger enough to trigger the explosions. And then Jack was inside her, moving with her, his body part of hers, the music in her head soaring, the rhythm perfect, the crescendo crashing as the waves began – wave upon wave upon wave of sheer delight that she knew would live with her for ever.

She opened her eyes in the stillness, suddenly shy, a shiver of fear rippling through her as Jack's solemn gaze locked with hers. Regret? The merest hint of an emotion she couldn't identify was masked in an instant and Jack was smiling down, kissing her again, softly, gently.

'My Ella,' he breathed. 'Wonderful, wonderful Ella.' And she buried the pain, the truth – would face that in the cold light of day. Replete, she snuggled into the hollow formed by arm and shoulder, felt his arm close round to hold and enfold, and slept.

Dreams, such wonderful dreams, because she was loving Jack, was touching him, tasting him, needing him, and she moaned, moved instinctively closer, her bottom wriggling into the curve of his stomach, unintentionally inciting. And as something deliciously familiar began to stir into life the realization hit her, hazel eyes snapping open in disbelief.

Better than a dream – heaven on earth. Jack's mouth nuzzling an earlobe, a hand creeping round to cup her aching breast, to brush her hardening nipple, the hardness that was thrusting against the small of her back more than eloquent proof.

'Bed, my lady,' Jack growled. 'The rug was fine for starters but . . .' And he was on his feet, sweeping her into his arms, carrying her across the room and into the bedroom beyond, and Ella laughed out as he dropped her into the soft folds of the duvet, the pause but an instant before he dived to cover her body.

No time to wait, the sudden urgency catching both unawares, and then he was inside her, moving with her, for her, the climax a perfectly timed salvo of explosions, two minds, two bodies, one purpose – an earth-shattering, out-of-this world experience.

Not a good idea, she decided, opening her eyes to find fingers of light beginning to steal across the duvet. But surprisingly no regrets. Only the glaring knowledge that she couldn't stay now – a simple matter of fairness since Jack was engaged to be married, would need time alone with his beautiful fiancée. Oh, yes, and there was the pain. Because he didn't love her, hadn't loved her for years. But no regrets, just an unbelievable night of magic to carry her through the rest of her life. Alone. Now and always.

Jack had left her alone, the single red rose he'd placed on the pillow where his head had lain eloquent proof that he hadn't crept away in shame. Ella smiled. She was happy. Happy and sad both. But most definitely no regrets.

Catching the muffled sound of footsteps, she stacked the pillows behind her and, wriggling into an upright position, drew the duvet under her chin in a belated search for modesty, her heart beating nineteen to the dozen as the door creaked slowly open.

The beloved rugged head popped around the jamb, dancing blue eyes locking with hers. 'And how did madam sleep?' Jack enquired, placing the tray with a flourish on the bedside table. Breakfast in bed, and served by the most devastating waiter a girl could ask for – naked from the waist up at least, chest muscles rippling and deliciously inviting.

'Intermittently,' Ella told him tartly, the sudden shyness vanishing under the warmth of his gaze.

'I can't imagine why,' he teased, perching on the edge of the bed as he poured the freshly perked coffee, passed a cup to Ella before turning his attention to the food – croissants and jam that he shared between them, pulling the soft, sweet bread apart with his hands, sticky fingers brushing against her lips as he fed her mouthful after mouthful.

The tension mounted with every touch, until the very last crumb disappeared, and then Jack growled, caught the matching hunger in her eyes and, stripping off his trousers, climbed in beside her and buried himself in her body.

They slept. The trill of Jack's mobile phone was a strident intrusion. Stirring against her, Jack checked his watch in the light filtering through the curtains, smothered a curse, dropped a light kiss onto Ella's exposed shoulder and padded naked to the sitting room.

Alone and replete, Ella snuggled down into the warmth left by the imprint of his body, allowing the murmur of Jack's velvet voice to lull her back into the land of dreams.

The sudden change of tone jerked her rudely upright.

Suppressing a shiver of fear, she shrugged herself into a robe and padded out to join him.

'Jack? What is it?' she asked as he cut the connection and telescoped the aerial, defeat written into the lines of his body.

He spun round, his expression bleak.

'Was it Ian?' she queried absurdly, an icy finger touching her heart. 'Is it the horse? Didn't the foal survive?'

He shook his head. 'No. Not Ian,' he conceded wearily. 'Fliss.'

'Oh.' Pain. A lifetime of pain. A lifetime of memories. A single night of love to cherish in the dark hours. 'I see.'

'No, Ella,' he contradicted harshly, wild fingers raking his hair. 'Believe me, you don't see at all.'

Pulling the edges of her robe together, she folded her arms across her chest, hugging herself. The ice was beginning to spread, devastating tongues of ice licking through each and every part of her.

'It's all right, Jack,' she reassured him tightly, squeezing back the tears. 'You don't have to explain. Not to me. Fliss – '

'No!' He cut her off, closing the gap between them in two easy strides, his fingers digging deep as he gripped her upper arms. 'No, Ella,' he said starkly. 'You don't understand. It's not what you're thinking. Fliss phoned because her ankle's giving her hell and, since she couldn't sleep, she switched on the radio and caught the latest international news. It's the holiday village complex in the Gulf,' he explained, almost tonelessly. 'It's been overrun by terrorists and Lloyd Raft is missing.'

CHAPTER 18

'Someone's quiet today. Tired, love? Been overdoing things? Or is the news from the Gulf playing on your mind?'

Ella jumped guiltily. Trust Gramps to read it right. She'd been miles away – several thousand miles in fact. It was not so much the news as its absence eating away at her. Jack's calls to the house were intermittent, strained and anything but reassuring. Initially they were told little beyond the stark fact that Lloyd was still alive, that the trail to find him had grown cold and that Jack had no intentions of coming home without him. Or his body. And as for the danger Jack himself was in . . . Ella's mind skittered away.

Glancing across, she caught the shadow of concern in a set of eyes that might have been the blueprint for her own and forced a reassuring smile. 'Sorry, Gramps. Guilty on all counts, I'm afraid. It's been a bit hectic lately.'

'I can imagine, and it can't be easy carrying on as normal when there's so much on your mind. But if it's any consolation, it's my guess you're worrying over nothing. Your Mr Keegan's a fighter, Aileen. He's a survivor. Large as life and twice as brash, from what I've heard, but just the sort to come sailing through without a scratch.'

Her Mr Keegan. The knifeblade twisted. If only. If only she could explain, confide in Gramps – about everything. Soon, she promised herself. The moment Jack was safely home and Ella had made the final break.

'And George says – '

Ella swallowed a smile. Trust Gramps not to miss a chance of bestowing the benefit of his advice on Jack's chief gardener – over a Friday pint at The Bull, if Ella wasn't mistaken. But since Jack's gardener had clearly been singing Jack's praises, along with half the village by the sounds of it, Ella wasn't about to demur. One of life's survivors. Please God, Gramps was right.

'Let me make some tea,' she offered, more for something to do than the need for a drink.

It had been the same back at the house. With Jack away, the photographic conference had been a God-send, keeping mind and body busy and providing a focus for Ella's wayward thoughts.

'Everything goes ahead as planned,' Ian had insisted when it became apparent Jack wouldn't be back to pick up the reins. 'It's the least we can do for Jack.'

Ella had nodded. The fact that they hadn't reached the stage of discussing the finer details, thanks to the horse in foal and Ella's night of love, had clearly slipped Ian's mind. Not that Ian would know, she added hastily, about certain things at least. And she'd smiled at the memory, hugging it to her in a desperate attempt to fill the void of Jack's absence, the void in her heart where the truth lurked – a truth she wouldn't face until Jack was safely home.

Work, work and more work. Ian's words were not so much a spur as a blessed excuse to push herself to the point of exhaustion, to fill her time in an effort to keep that vivid imagination under control.

'The conference was the turning point,' Ian had acknowledged frankly. 'Jack was impressed with the way it all ran – your superb organization. But now, with J.K. Holdings dominating the news, we're really under the spotlight. It's crunch time, Mrs A,' he'd reminded her solemnly. 'It's got to be perfect; we owe it to Jack. And for something on this scale we don't take any chances. Outside caterers for a start.'

'I can cope,' Ella had demurred, though she was aware that it made sense. If Jack was having second thoughts about not using Sherbrook for business, it wouldn't be fair on the staff to expect them to cope single handedly. And once Ella herself had moved on . . .

'I know you can – that's why Jack employs you – but at this rate you'll burn yourself out.'

Good. That was what she'd prefer, not time alone with her thoughts, minutes that seemed like hours, hours that seemed like years, and her imagination working overtime.

'No news is good news,' people were apt to remind her tritely, but with Lloyd apparently held to ransom by an extreme religious sect and Jack heaven alone knew where, no news was anything but good for an overwrought Ella. And then had come the call they'd all been waiting for – Jack's voice music to her ears.

'Lloyd's alive, Ella,' he'd explained, the strain breaking through, despite his efforts to sound optimistic. 'The details are hazy but he's alive, and that's the important thing. We've some trained negotiators flying in tomorrow, and the moment we establish contact with his captors we're ready respond to their demands. Leastways,' he'd amended tersely. 'That's what I'm hoping. The government here take a hard line with terrorists, but the fact that Lloyd's British should help. With a bit of luck we'll have him out before the end of the week.'

Thank heavens, Ella had prayed silently, and, though she'd been relieved to know that Lloyd was safe and well, it was Jack who had dominated her thoughts – Jack who'd already spent so much time in the desert on undercover negotiations, Jack who would now disappear for days on end on the same delicate mission. Because the holiday village scheme was Jack's responsibility, and the terrorists refused to deal with anyone but the boss-man himself.

She'd blinked back the tears, because Jack was safe, for now. Only Jack hadn't finished talking. The words were disjointed, thanks to gremlins on the phone line, but the message was plain. 'You won't leave, Ella. Promise me. I need someone there I can trust. Promise you won't leave before I come home.'

And Ella had promised, her heart freezing over again. Because she would leave, had to leave, and even Jack finally accepted it was only a matter of time. And expediency. He needed her there for now to run things, to help Ian keep an important part of Jack's organization ticking over. Nothing more, nothing less.

Ella checked the time, amazed to discover that the afternoon had flown – a rare snatch of peace with Gramps, even if she hadn't been very good company.

She paused on the doorstep. 'I'll see you next week,' she reminded him, wondering if she'd be able to slip across more often now that the photo convention was over and done with – the calm before the storm of Jack's arrival. And then, the moment Jack walked in, Ella would go. If Jack walked in.

Unbearable thought. An icy trickle ran down her spine. Ella closed her mind. 'I know,' she said impulsively, leaning forwards to kiss him. 'Instead of me coming here, you can come over to Sherbrook. I'll organize a taxi. We can spend a lazy afternoon wandering round the park and then have tea in the great hall. Just you and me. Doesn't that sound grand?'

'Very grand,' he agreed. 'If you're sure that I'll be welcome?' he added doubtfully, eyes suspiciously bright.

Watching him, Ella felt her own eyes start to brim. 'Of course you're welcome,' she insisted, hugging him, holding him, the fragile frame beneath her fingers coming as always, as a shock. 'You'll be visiting me. I live there now, remember?' Though not for much longer, she realized starkly, wondering how on earth she would break the news to Gramps. The truth this time, the truth, the whole truth and nothing but the truth. If Jack came home.

One day at a time, no point in meeting trouble head on. Just work – the outward signs of normality.

'We're snowed under,' Ian explained one day, flicking through the latest batch of enquiries and dropping the letters onto the large, untidy pile spilling out across the table. 'Understandable, I suppose, given the publicity. But I could do with sifting through them, weeding out the doubtfuls, the unsuitables and the downright nosy. The last thing Jack needs when he gets back is a houseful of gawking ghouls.'

And with Jack's decision to utilize the house for business still at the tentative stage, all the more reason not to create any waves.

'I can spare an hour or two,' Ella suggested, closing the household accounts book. 'This afternoon, if you like. Or would you rather we went through them together?'

It was the second of their scheduled monthly meetings and probably their last, although Ian wouldn't know it, and, since Sarah only worked mornings, they had the cosy estate office to themselves.

'Could you? It would be a help,' Ian conceded, clearly relieved. 'I'd do it myself, but with one thing and another I just can't spare the time. I'm already late for the trout farm,' he explained, shrugging himself into his jacket. 'But I could always pop back later, see how you've gone on?'

'Fine.' Ella shuffled the papers into a neat pile and smiled across. 'And since there's no time like the present,' she murmured brightly, 'if you'll pass me three of those box files, Ian, I'll make a start now. How does, yes, no and maybe sound?'

'Perfect. But on one condition, Mrs A.'

'Oh?' she queried warily.

'Take it easy, hey? I know you, and the last thing I need is Jack on my back when the strain begins to tell.'

'It won't,' she reassured him airily. 'Believe me, as far as work goes this is a bit of light relief. Anyway, Jack will never know. If you don't tell, I won't tell.'

'It wouldn't make a penny's worth of difference, Mrs A. You can take it from me – Jack has a nose for that sort of thing.'

Mindful of Ian's words, Ella paced herself, stopping off mid-afternoon to prepare a casserole for supper. Not that she had need to, given the contents of the freezer, but it was a break from the clerical job, the task pretty mundane, simply requiring a bit of common sense and time.

Time. She'd have plenty of that on her hands soon – ought really to be looking for another job. She made a mental note to scour the local papers, see what she could find in the area. Ideally it would need to be residential, Gramps's tiny cottage, even if he was amenable, was far too small for the two of them.

Dorset casserole. The fragrant aroma filled the kitchen, and instead of dividing the contents up – one to cook and one to freeze – Ella gave in to an impulse and put the entire dish in the oven on low.

'We've done well. No . . .' Ian grinned, leaning back in his chair later that day hands raised to the back of his neck as he stretched, allowed taut muscles to relax. 'Correction. You've done well. I'd never have managed a quarter of this alone. And, since we might as well strike while the iron's hot, I'll sort out a few dates now and Sarah can make a start on the provisional bookings tomorrow. Thanks, Mrs A. I know Jack will be pleased.'

Yes. When he returned. The devastating word, 'if', was unspoken but hanging tangibly between them.

'If you're going to work on,' Ella mused, giving Ian's thanks a nod of acknowledgement. 'Why not join me for supper? There's a casserole in the oven. Nothing fancy but more than enough for two.'

'Sounds great. It beats beans on toast at my place any day. Not to mention the platefuls of stodge served down at the pub. If you're sure?' he queried, clearly tempted but just as clearly loath to impose.

Ella nodded. She was sure. With the latest silence from Jack beginning to nudge into day four, she was finding her own company, and her vivid imagination in particular, unnerving.

'When you're ready,' she explained, 'simply follow your nose to my sitting room.'

Forty minutes later, and bang on time as far as Ella was concerned, Ian did precisely that, taking the chair she waved him to with a self-conscious smile. Ella was intrigued. She might have read him wrong, but, if his reactions to Fliss were anything to go by, she'd been sure Ian Sampson was every inch a ladies' man. But there again, she mused, perhaps an older woman like Ella was a whole new experience. Or maybe that firm but gentle rebuff when Ella had first arrived had hit hard?

'To absent friends?' Ian queried, raising his glass of cider. 'Or does that sound insensitive?'

'Sounds fine to me,' Ella acknowledged, responding, taking a long sip of iced water and smiling across the table. 'To absent friends and their safekeeping.'

There was no shortage of things to discuss. Business. A nice, safe, neutral subject – something in common after all. Every other sentence seemed to centre on Jack: when Jack comes home . . . The moment Jack's back . . . Remind me to ask Jack . . . Tell Jack . . . Jack. Jack. And more Jack.

'He will come back, won't he, Ian?' she said at length. There. She'd done it. Brought all her worries out into the open. The need to share her fears with someone, with anyone, in fact, was a luxury she'd long been denied.

'Knowing Jack? What do you think?' he challenged, grinning broadly. 'But there again,' he mused, swirling the golden liquid round and round his glass before darting her a speculative, sideways glance. 'Since you haven't known him long, I can understand the doubt. But you can take it from me, he'll be home, all right – large as life and twice as natural.'

The meal over, they moved away from the table in its window niche and settled themselves in the easy chairs either side of the fire. The hearthrug stretching between them was yet another poignant reminder of Jack. Jack. Such a few short weeks and everywhere she turned seemed to scream of him. A few more weeks and Ella would be moving on. Only this time, she realized, all the bitterness had gone. She loved him and she had that wonderful night to treasure for the rest of her life.

Ian drained his glass and Ella collected the jug he'd left on the table. Having cooked with cider, it had made sense to serve cider with the meal, although Ella, mostly out of habit these days, had kept to water.

Crossing back to Ian, she stooped to refill his glass, smiled as he glanced up and, since he seemed about to speak, she paused, waited, raised a quizzical eyebrow. She was caught completely unawares as his lips brushed against hers. She jerked back and, though thoroughly unnerved, managed to glide away without over reacting.

'I'm sorry – '

'No.' She cut him off with a smile as she regained her seat. 'Don't apologize. Given the difference in age between us, I'm almost flattered.'

'Almost?' He grinned wryly, the awkward moment over. 'I guess that puts me firmly in my place.'

'If you like,' she acknowledged lightly. 'As long as you don't take it to heart.'

'I just thought . . .'

'You thought . . .?'

He had the grace to look ashamed. 'I'm not sure, really. I guess I was testing. The night of the party . . .'

'Ah, yes,' Ella acknowledged dryly. 'You saw me with Jack, put two and two together and jumped to conclusions.'

'Put it this way.' Ian grinned, completely unabashed. 'If Fliss had seen the two of you together that night, she'd definitely have jumped to conclusions.'

'Then it's lucky for Jack that she didn't,' Ella clipped out, blushing at the memory.

Ian was nice, she decided, and the fact that he worked hard spoke for itself, was all the more impressive since Jack wasn't around to witness it. While the cat's away, she mused, thinking of Fliss, remembering Fliss flirting openly with Ian. Yes, she could see that Ian would be tempted, would prove a temptation himself. Young, good-looking, and with those hungry brown eyes a girl could happily drown in. A girl like Fliss . . .

Ella frowned. No. She was wrong. Irrational or otherwise, she had a hunch that Ian was far too loyal to Jack to play around with his fiancée.

Somewhere in the depths of the house a clock chimed the hour. 'Time to go,' Ian declared, checking his watch.

'Coffee?' Ella suggested, knowing that Ian would take the offer for what it was – reassurance that nothing had changed between them, that they could carry on working together without any strain.

He shook his head. 'I've a lot on tomorrow so I really should be going. Thank you. The meal was lovely, not to mention the company.' And there was just the merest hint of hesitation before he added softly, 'Thanks – Ella.'

Her head jerked up, the twin spots of colour in her cheeks a total give-away. 'How do you know my name? No, let me guess,' she supplied woodenly. 'Jack, the night of the party.'

'I – I thought at first I'd imagined it,' Ian admitted carefully. 'But, having seen you together . . .'

'Yes. It's difficult playing at strangers when so much of the past has been shared,' she acknowledged bitterly. 'But you needn't worry, Ian. I shan't rock any boats. The moment Jack comes home, I'm leaving.'

'If that's what Jack wants?' he probed, brown eyes brimming with strange understanding.

'It's what I want,' Ella said tightly.

'Because you love him?'

Her chin snapped up again. 'As obvious as that, hey?' she derided.

'Only with the benefit of hindsight,' Ian reassured her. 'And, since I already had my suspicions, I was probably looking for clues. Tonight – '

'Simply allowed you to put them to the test? How very convenient,' she sneered, more hurt than she cared to acknowledge. 'My invitation must have been a Godsend.'

'No. I came tonight because you asked me – because I guessed you needed the company,' he conceded frankly. 'Just like I did. And when you didn't respond to my kiss everything fell into place. Not deliberate, Ella, I promise you.'

No. Locking glances, reading the truth in Ian's velvet eyes, Ella felt her surge of anger die. Not deliberate. Not even testing. Just insight. He was a rare breed – a sensitive man. He would make someone a wonderful husband one day.

She swallowed hard, her brief nod a tacit acceptance of the truth.

'So you really are going?'

'I must,' she said simply.

'Yes. I guess you must at that. Pity.' A ghost of a smile and then he turned to go, was brought up short by Ella's hand on his arm.

'About Jack – ' she began, hazel eyes softly pleading.

'It's all right, Ella,' Ian reassured her. 'If you don't tell, I won't.'

'So, be honest, Gramps, what do you think? Gone to rack and ruin since your day, I suppose?' Ella teased, slipping her arm through his as they strolled back up the drive.

'It's certainly changed,' he admitted frankly. 'And I'm not sure that I approve of all these new-fangled gadgets. Motorized mowers?' he scorned, though not unkindly. 'Young George Snelling doesn't know he's born. What with rabbits breeding in the trees and moles causing havoc under the croquet lawn – you can take it from me, there was never a dull moment. And as for keeping the grass short – why, a couple of high-tech ponies did the trick back in the good old days.' He chuckled at the memory. 'Progress. Still, there's no denying the place is looking good.'

Croquet. Ella smiled. A touch of nostalgia there, she realized, storing the snippet away and looking on as Gramps crouched, running his fingers through the friable soil.

'It was always a bit on the heavy side,' he explained, a frown of concentration furrowing his brow, 'but this is well mulched by the looks of things.' He let the particles of soil trickle lightly to the ground. 'Aye. It'll do,' he pronounced gruffly, straightening with difficulty. And, though sorely tempted to offer a hand, Ella managed to resist. 'I don't suppose I'd have done better myself.'

Praise indeed, Ella decided as she steered him back towards the house. It was pleasant though chilly in the gardens, the autumn sun a welcome splash of colour that brightened the day but provided little real warmth. And there was the house to see yet – just a brief tour, she decided, not wanting Gramps to overdo it, followed by the *pièce de resistance*, the highlight of his visit: afternoon tea in the great hall, proudly served by a pink-faced, curtsey-dropping Katie.

Ella smiled. She'd need to have a quiet word soon, see what she could do about that 'weakness' in her knees before Jack came home. And, since the girl had come along in leaps and bounds under Ella's charge, maybe, just maybe, Jack would take her advice about that as well. Katie was young for the post, but, given the chance to prove herself, would make a first-class replacement for Ella.

'Who'd have thought it?' Gramps mused, casting a surreptitious glance around the oak-panelled hall. 'Garden boy to this. Eating indoors in my day meant a slab of bread and dripping in the pantry.'

'Why didn't you say?' Ella chided lightly. 'These things can arranged. If I'd known,' she added teasingly, 'we could have eaten belowstairs. All it takes is a wave of my magic wand.'

'Talking of arrangements, I've been thinking.'

'Oh?' Ella mused, the tiny hairs on the back of her neck prickling out a warning.

Gramps set his cake fork carefully down on his plate before bringing his gaze back to Ella. 'I'm finding the cottage a bit much just lately, so I've made some enquiries. Sheltered accommodation. I've little enough to spend my money on and can more than afford the fees. So I've been wondering – about the cottage. I should hate to see it go to strangers,' he explained apologetically, voice not quite steady, eyes suspiciously bright as they rested on Ella. 'And since it's always good to have a bolt-hole,' he added simply, 'if you'd like it, love, you'd be doing me a favour.'

A bolt-hole. Ella's escape. One less thing to worry about. Too small to suit her needs in the long run, but as an interim arrangement – perfect.

'Oh, Gramps,' she breathed, tears stinging the backs of her eyes. 'Thank you. You've no idea how much that helps.'

The door at the far end of the hall swung open and a flustered Katie reappeared. 'What is it, Katie?' Ella queried, another shiver of alarm running down her spine.

'It's Miss Foxwood, Mrs A. She's arrived with a party of friends and she's asking for you. I did try explaining it was your afternoon off – '

'It's all right, Katie,' Ella reassured her, dropping her napkin onto her plate and coming to her feet. 'Leave it with me.' She moved round the table. 'Sorry, Gramps.' She gave a rueful smile as she hugged him, suppressing a surge of annoyance at Fliss's sense of timing. 'Katie will bring some fresh tea,' she reassured him brightly. 'Help yourself to scones and jam. I'll only be a moment.'

A very brief moment since Felicity, never noted for her patience at the best of times, had followed hard on Katie's heels.

'Oh, so this is where you're hiding.' Fliss halted, her slender form framed in the doorway, green eyes darting past Ella, not missing a thing. The small but exquisitely set table in the bay of the leaded window with its magnificent view of the park, the best cutlery, the fine bone china. It was Gramps's treat and, incongruous or not, Ella had been determined to make everything perfect. 'I see.'

'I doubt it,' Ella murmured pleasantly, going forward to meet her. 'Allow me to introduce you – '

'That won't be necessary,' Fliss interrupted rudely. 'If you've quite finished entertaining, my guests require your attention.'

'Certainly, madam. Give me ten minutes and I'll be with you.'

A single eyebrow arched. 'Better make that five,' Fliss murmured frigidly, and, without waiting for a response, spun on her heels and glided away in a cloud of heady perfume.

Five minutes, Fliss had insisted, and five minutes Ella took – just time enough to take leave of Gramps, walk him down the steps to the waiting taxi and wave him out of sight. And wonderful, wonderful Gramps hadn't said a word, not about Felicity, at least, simply hugging Ella and whispering his words of thanks.

'It's been the best afternoon of my life,' he'd insisted. 'Bar none.'

Ella had been choked. It had been pretty special for her too. And now she braced herself. The afternoon wasn't over yet.

'You're fired.'

Ella flushed. 'Any particular reason?' she enquired mildly, beginning to feel like a schoolgirl called before the head for some minor misdemeanour. Though with Felicity stretched out on one of the sofas, idly flicking through the pages of a glossy magazine, that idea quickly lost its impact.

'Take your pick,' she invited coolly. 'Rudeness should do, for a start. Neglect of duty. Oh, yes, and entertaining friends on company time. Not to mention the cost of the food.'

'Not guilty, I'm afraid,' Ella pointed out, holding onto her temper. 'It's my afternoon off, as I'm sure you know, and, since the job's residential, meals are included.'

'Yours. But not your friends'.'

'Fine. I suggest you ask Ian to take it out of my wages.'

'I intend to. In the meanwhile, you'd better start packing.'

'Why?'

'Didn't you hear me? You're fired.'

'Correction, Miss Foxwood. I'm leaving all right, but not until Jack comes home.'

'But I'm asking you to leave. And believe me, Mrs Andrews-Watson,' she murmured, licking the tip of one crimson-taloned finger and turning another page, 'in *Mr Keegan's* absence – ' she emphasized the name coldly '– I have full authority to hire and fire. In case it's slipped your mind,' she sneeringly reminded her, 'I made your appointment in the first place.'

'Maybe so,' Ella acknowledged, not bothering to argue the finer points of that technicality. 'But since I'm already working my notice, you'll simply have to be patient.'

'Working your notice? But I didn't – ' Green eyes narrowed as the younger woman pulled herself up short.

Ella swallowed a smile. Full authority or not, Ella's words had come as a surprise to her.

'Even better,' Fliss acknowledged coldly. 'And since I'm not prepared to be patient, you can go. Tonight.'

Ella shrugged. Put like that, she hadn't much choice, and, though she had promised Jack, now wasn't the time to stand and argue. So, she'd pack an overnight bag, check into a local hotel and contact Ian first thing in the morning. 'If that's what you want,' she murmured coolly. 'I assume you and your guests can manage without me?'

'Perfectly, thank you.'

'And the rest of the staff?' Ella enquired saccharine-sweetly. She was bluffing, of course, wouldn't dream of asking Katie and the others to risk their jobs by walking out with her. But Fliss wouldn't know that.

Chill green eyes narrowed again. 'Are you threatening me?' she challenged icily.

'Not threatening,' Ella countered evenly. 'Merely pointing out the facts. But you're right,' she soothed, with a sudden change of tack. 'In Mr Keegan's absence, naturally you're in charge. I'll be out within the hour.'

'No.'

'No?' Despite the urge to smile, Ella remained impassive.

'I've changed my mind,' Felicity explained curtly. 'Since you are already working your notice, you might as well stay and earn your keep. *Work*,' she emphasized slyly, her cupid's bow of a mouth forming the semblance of a smile. 'Your afternoon off it may have been, my dear, but as of this moment all leave has been cancelled. Any objections?'

'None at all,' Ella demurred.

'Good. In that case, Mrs Andrews-Watson, it's dinner for ten. Eight o'clock sharp.'

Yes, ma'am.

Since Felicity had given no warning of her visit, most of the staff had already gone home, leaving Katie and Ella to set to with a vengeance.

A meal fit for a queen, or in this case a viscount's daughter, plus guests, appeared on the table bang on time.

'Anything else I can do, Mrs A?' an uncomplaining Katie enquired once the debris had been cleared, the pots and pans scoured, the dishwasher loaded and the freshly brewed coffee lay ready and waiting for Ella to carry through to the drawing room.

Ella shook her head. 'Thanks, Katie, but you've done more than your share already,' she insisted. 'And with breakfast for ten on the cards, you'll be back here soon enough. I can manage the rest. Take yourself off home and – ' She broke off, half convinced she was hearing things, but as Katie opened the door to the hallway the ring came again – short, sharp and strident. 'Visitors?' Ella mused, a shiver of apprehension running the length of her spine. 'At this hour of the night?'

'More of madam's friends, most likely,' Katie suggested waspishly, and, shrugging herself out of the coat she'd been buttoning, was off before Ella could stop her. 'It's okay, Mrs A,' she tossed back over her shoulder. 'Leave it to me. Another five minutes won't hurt. If it's important, I'll show them straight through.'

She did. And Ella took one look at Ian's face and almost dropped the tray she was just about to place on the sideboard.

'Ian, darling!' Long legs unravelled themselves from one of the Chesterfields as Fliss danced across the expanse of carpet, raising her face for the kiss Ian dutifully gave. 'What a lovely surprise,' she trilled, Ian's tight expression passing her by completely. 'Come in. Come and meet the gang,' she insisted, and, blissfully unaware of the silence descending on the rest of the room, linked her arm through his as she drew him forwards. 'And since I never know with you,' she chided playfully, 'to what do we owe the honour at this time of night? Business?' she queried with an obscene flutter of lashes. 'Or pleasure?'

'Neither,' he murmured quietly, and, though Fliss was smiling up at him, his solemn gaze had already crossed to lock with Ella's. 'It's Lloyd,' he said simply, a wealth of compassion in the depths of his eyes. 'He's free. They let him go half an hour ago. Lloyd's safe. The terrorists finally agreed to let someone take his place.'

'It's Jack, isn't it?' Ella whispered as the rest of the room retreated.

Ian nodded. 'It's Jack.'

CHAPTER 19

A nightmare. Three weeks of hell. The need to appear cool, calm and in control driving Ella to the brink of madness. Because Jack wasn't hers and she couldn't afford the luxury of giving way – not in public, at least. Unlike Felicity, who milked the situation for all it was worth. Or maybe Ella had simply grown hard, allowing her jealousy of the younger woman to colour her thinking.

Tears, hysterics, histrionics, tempting trays of titbits in her room – none of which were ever returned uneaten, Ella noticed sourly – and, when the isolation palled, poignant displays of bravery, those green eyes carefully shielded behind ultra-dark lenses, the make-up discreet and pale, a delicate wisp of lace clutched in long, tapering fingers and used with nauseating frequency whenever she had an audience. And, since the Press were camped out in droves on the doorstep, there was never any shortage of sympathetic glances.

Even that was blessed relief to Ella – the endless pots of tea, coffee and sandwiches by the plateful, courtesy of a concerned and gracious fiancée, giving Ella something to occupy her mind, drive her body to the point of exhaustion. And, though she'd been photographed more times than she cared to remember, the newshounds had quickly grown tired of repeating questions that Ella had schooled herself not to hear. She was the housekeeper, nothing more, nothing less, and had nothing to offer beyond the trays of food and drinks. Besides, with Fliss on form, bravely providing copy for the tabloids, they had no need of a tight-lipped Ella.

'You'll wear yourself into a frazzle,' Ian pointed out, concern shadowing his eyes. 'You're doing too much, Ella.'

'I'm simply doing the job that I'm paid for,' she countered mildly, forcing a smile. Ella. He rarely used her name, clearly wouldn't risk Fliss overhearing, and the fact that he chose to use it now was enough to bring her to the point of tears. Only she mustn't cry. Give way now and she'd never stop.

'Maybe,' he conceded tersely. 'But I doubt Jack would approve, and I know full well who'll get the blame for driving you too hard. When did you last take an afternoon off?'

'Well . . .' She gave an eloquent shrug of the shoulders. Apart from a snatched hour here and there with Gramps, she'd barely had a moment to herself. And, since Gramps was in the throes of moving, he'd been too busy to notice Ella's neglect, too busy – or too tactful to comment, she realized with a sudden pang of guilt. But with all leave cancelled there wasn't much she could do, short of risking the sack again.

The sack would be a blessed relief in a way, and yet simply being at Sherbrook made Ella feel closer to Jack. And, though she could have explained it to Ian, something held her back. The thought of causing trouble between Jack's fiancée and his right-hand man, she supposed. And it would cause friction, Ella realized that instinctively.

'Exactly. Point made,' Ian chided softly, watching the shadows chase across her brow. 'You don't remember and neither do I. So, you and I are going for a drive. Today. I'll pick you up at two. And that, Ella,' he insisted fiercely, 'is an order. Fliss and her bevy of spineless hangers-on will just have to manage without you for once.'

'Going for a drive? With Ian? But why?' Fliss enquired incredulously when Ella carried in the lunchtime tray of coffee.

'Nothing special. Just for a breath of air, I suppose,' Ella conceded, flushing, that schoolgirl feeling back with a vengeance. Because having to ask for time off had been bad enough without having to explain why. 'Is there a problem?'

'Only the impression you'll be giving – out on a jaunt and enjoying yourselves while Jack's held captive in some hellhole. Still,' she conceded huffily, green eyes raining scorn, 'I'm sure Ian knows what he's doing.'

Spending an hour or two with me, Ella could have retorted, but didn't, catching her drift at once. A touch of the green-eyed monsters, she decided. Sheer pique that Ian preferred Ella's company to hers, that *any* man could prefer Ella's company to hers. Or maybe Fliss was so used to being the centre of attention she simply couldn't cope when the spotlight moved away?

'He will come home,' Ian reassured her, having stopped the car in the middle of nowhere, intuitively understanding her need to simply sit and think. 'Hell, woman, you know the man. He has the gift of the gab. Drop Jack in the middle of the ocean and he'd talk a man-eating shark into bringing him back safe.'

'It's camels in a desert he's in need of,' she riposted, smiling despite herself. 'But just to know that he's alive and well would help.'

'He will be,' Ian insisted. 'Believe me, if things had gone wrong, we'd have heard by now.'

Yes. And in a strange sort of way, Ella would have known. Jack was alive – she had to believe it. But the moment he came home Ella would have to leave. Yet another of life's little ironies, she acknowledged as the knifeblade twisted. Because Jack would be coming home to Fliss.

'She'll never hold him,' Ian observed, uncannily reading her thoughts. 'She's in love with an idea, the money, the trappings of power. And with Plumpton gambling away the family seat, Jack's simply the means to an end.'

'Maybe,' Ella allowed, hating the idea that Fliss could ever hurt him. 'But she's everything Jack needs just now. She's young, full of fun, a breath of fresh air.' Not to mention every man's concept of beauty. Oh, yes, and fertile. Mustn't forget that, she tagged on silently, bitterly. Babies for Jack. The one thing Ella couldn't give him.

'And you?' Ian probed softly. 'Where do you fit in?'

'Nowhere. I'm a mistake – the face from the past,' she reminded him bitterly. 'I'd no idea Jack was lord and master of Sherbrook, and he sure as hell didn't expect to walk in and find me holding the fort.'

'Exactly. Fate.'

'Coincidence,' she countered, staring rigidly ahead. Having lost Jack, she'd searched for the family she'd never known, had found Gramps and, naturally enough had wanted to be close to him, never dreaming she'd land right back in the middle of that nightmare.

One nightmare over, another begun. Until Jack came home. And then she really would be alone, that single night of love something precious to cling to in the dark hours. 'And since I couldn't hold Jack,' she reminded Ian, with a curious lack of emotion, 'I'm the last one qualified to comment on Fliss and her motives.'

'Maybe,' Ian acknowledged, darting her a shrewd, assessing glance. 'So what went wrong?' he mused. 'You're two of the nicest people I know, and from where I'm looking you suit one another down to the ground. It seems such a waste if you love the guy.'

And I do. Always have, always will. But Jack loves Felicity now. He's engaged to Fliss, will marry Fliss, make babies with Fliss. Babies. 'It – wasn't Jack's fault,' she hastily reassured him. 'Not even mine, I'm beginning to see. Though that's not how it seemed at the time. It was – just one of those things.' She stalled, aware that Ian would listen, would try to understand, wouldn't judge. But she simply couldn't risk slicing open wounds that hadn't had the chance to heal. 'And water under the bridge now.'

'Gone but not forgotten.'

'No.' She smiled. 'You know the guy. Once met, forever smitten – for me at least.'

'In that case, Ella, why not stay and fight?'

'Because I love him,' she acknowledged frankly. 'Those circumstances, Ian,' she reminded him tightly. 'You can take it from me, nothing's changed.' She loved him, could live without the babies. She'd long come to realize that. It was life without Jack that seemed so unbearable.

They drove on, the sun coming out to greet them, cheer them on their way, and, though they'd been gone well over the couple of hours she'd cleared with Fliss, Ella wasn't sorry when Ian pulled the car off the road and into a café car park.

'What would you like to eat?' he asked, settling Ella at a cosy window table overlooking the canal with its ribbon of brightly coloured narrow boats – moored for the winter, Ella supposed.

'Just a pot of tea, please,' she murmured with an apologetic shrug of the shoulders. The mere thought of food was enough to make her queasy. Nerves, she decided, and worry over Jack.

A single eyebrow rose. 'You're losing weight,' Ian accused, ordering himself an enormous plateful of sausage, egg and chips with bread and butter. Stodge, she noted wryly, and, along with beans on toast, Ian's staple food. 'Jack's going to take one look at those luminous eyes in a much too pale face,' he chided softly, 'and flay me alive.'

'I'm a big girl now,' she reminded him, equally mildly, Ian's concern bringing a lump to her throat. 'I decide when I'm hungry.' Only she wasn't, had been off her food for days, waves of nausea striking without warning.

The first time it had happened she'd had the ludicrous thought that she was pregnant. The idea had been amusing in a bitter sort of way, since her chances of conceiving were remote, and, if by some miracle she did, she'd been told by more specialists than she cared to remember that she'd never carry a child to term. No. Not morning sickness, all-day sickness. Worry, she told herself. The moment Jack walked in safe and sound it would be sure to disappear.

'Home, then?' Ian asked as they emerged into the rapidly falling dusk. 'Or maybe we should find ourselves an olde worlde pub and treat ourselves to a brandy?'

'And risk the wrath of the lovely Fliss? Surely not?' Ella scorned lightly.

Which was how twenty minutes later they came to find themselves propping up the bar in Ian's local – Gramps's local too, until he moved out at the weekend. And Ella stifled another twinge of conscience at the fact that she hadn't been able to help.

'You'll get us both sacked,' Ella pointed out, eschewing the brandy in favour of a fruit juice. 'And then you'll be sorry.'

'Not half as sorry as Fliss when she's forced to rustle up food for ten at the drop of a hat. And, since Katie and Millie finish at five on Thursdays, that's a distinct possibility. Unless, of course,' he mused, brown eyes full of dancing lights, 'the super-efficient housekeeper left something prepared on the off chance she'd be late?'

'You know,' Ella confided as a gurgle of laughter rose in her throat, 'the super-efficient housekeeper clean forgot. Careless of me, I'd say.'

'Oh, very,' he agreed solemnly, draining his glass. 'And, since we might as well be hung for a sheep as a lamb, let's make it the same again all round.'

Since Ian was driving, he stuck to shandy for the rest of the evening – the nicest evening she'd spent in ages, Ella decided as the driveway lights of Sherbrook came into view.

They were late, and she had more than a sneaking suspicion she'd find herself carpeted first thing in the morning. Another angry scene, she acknowledged, but, since Ian had mooted the afternoon off, Fliss would be powerless to act. Leastways, Ella amended, her lips forming the ghost of a smile as she tiptoed down to her sitting room, that was the theory.

The theory lasted a whole sixty seconds.

'Where the hell have you been?'

Ella pulled up short, her startled gaze colliding with the younger woman's stormy one, and, despite the surge of anger that Felicity had chosen to let herself in, uninvited and unwelcome, Ella's voice was curiously flat.

'I don't suppose "out" would cover it?' she murmured, dropping her handbag onto a chair and darting her a cool, defiant glance. Logging the set of Felicity's mouth, Ella's heart sank. She was more tired than she'd realized, the string of sleepless nights beginning to take their toll, and, having arrived home mellow from a pleasant afternoon and evening, she'd hoped to be able to sleep for once.

'No, "out" *doesn't* even begin to cover it. An afternoon off you applied for – a couple of hours. And by my reckoning that makes you six hours overdue.'

'Take it up with Ian,' Ella suggested in the same mild tone as she shook herself out of her coat. 'He arranged it and he is my manager.' Not strictly true, of course, since Ian and Ella had different, if slightly overlapping areas of responsibility.

'Exactly. Your manager, not your employer.'

'Meaning?'

'Meaning me.'

'Ah, yes. I think I'm beginning to see. Let me guess – you want me to leave?'

'Got it in one.'

'Fine.' Ella shrugged. 'We'll discuss it in the morning.'

'We'll discuss it now.'

'You're the boss,' Ella conceded flippantly. 'Apparently.'

Green eyes narrowed at once. 'My, my,' Felicity drawled, moving close, so close the cloying scent of her perfume caught in the back of Ella's throat. 'Miss Prim and Prissy isn't quite what she seems. Evenings out with Ian clearly don't suit you, my dear, if this is the mood they leave you in.'

'Only one,' Ella reminded acidly. 'And I was perfectly happy until I walked in.'

'If you say so,' Felicity countered. 'But that's still one evening too many as far as I'm concerned. You're here to work, not fraternize.'

'Socialize,' Ella contradicted. 'And in my free time at that.'

'Not any more, Mrs Andrews-Watson. As of nine o'clock tomorrow morning, you're surplus to requirements.'

'Nice of you to let me stay the night. Or does a silver service breakfast figure high in those careful calculations?' Ella queried dryly.

'Since my guests missed out on dinner, thanks to you, naturally you'll be serving breakfast.'

'Will I?' Ella challenged softly.

The other woman's head snapped up. 'For someone who's just lost her job,' she pointed out coolly, 'you're surprisingly self-assured. References, my dear. And severance pay – not that it amounts to much. And, since you work a month in hand, four weeks' wages.'

'Which you're about to withhold?'

'Maybe, maybe not,' Felicity conceded, her lips forming the semblance of a smile. 'Let's just say, it all depends.'

'On breakfast?' Ella queried incredulously.

'On breakfast.'

Ella swallowed a smile. Breakfast. Only it was more than that. Felicity had an image to keep up and her lady of the manor façade had already taken a dent – the thought of rolling up her sleeves two meals running clearly unthinkable. But, since the money was legally Ella's, and would be paid in time, the threat was an empty one.

Without a word, she crossed to the table in its window niche, reaching for the pen and pad she kept at hand. Still without speaking, she flicked through the pages of her diary. It took less than twenty seconds to locate the number, scribble it down, tear the sheet off the pad.

Straightening, she turned to meet Felicity's puzzled gaze. 'It's the catering firm we employed for the photo convention,' Ella explained, passing it across. 'You'd better give them a ring.'

'I don't see why.'

Ella smiled. 'You will,' she informed her sweetly, heading for her bedroom door. 'Goodnight, Miss Foxwood. See you in the morning – maybe,' she tagged on provokingly.

Fliss darted forwards. 'Oh, no, you don't,' she rasped, her hand gripping Ella's arm, the vivid red talons digging cruelly into the skin. 'You stay right there. I haven't finished yet.'

Hazel eyes narrowed at once. 'Maybe not, but I have,' Ella retorted icily, the anger that had been simmering beneath the surface beginning to break through as she glanced from Felicity's thunderous face to the hand that detained her and back again.

And somewhere along the way her subconscious noted the enormous emerald ring that Jack had given her, more than eloquent proof of his love for this woman, this woman whom Ian insisted would never be able to hold him. And the knowledge hurt, and the hurt fuelled the anger and the anger refused to be tamed.

'I've heard enough – more than enough,' Ella rasped, jerking free of the richly jewelled claw. 'You've sacked me once too often, madam, and there's not a thing you can say or do that will make a scrap of difference. You don't own me,' she reminded her frigidly. 'And I don't owe you so much as the time of day. Like I said, see you in the morning – maybe.'

'You bitch! You can't – do you hear me? I won't let you.'

Ella halted, spun round on her heels, eyebrows raised in enquiry. 'A word of advice,' she murmured quietly, though her insides were churning and fresh waves of nausea had begun to ripple through her. 'In future, leave the hiring and firing to Ian. Or Jack – always assuming he's stupid enough to marry you – '

Felicity hit her, the rifle crack sound of her open palm connecting with Ella's cheek hanging on the air.

Ella stumbled backwards as the room began to spin, and she was fighting the nausea, fighting the urge to let go, to let the blackness enfold her. She was going to fall, she realized. She was falling – falling, slipping away into the blackness. And then frantic fingers were clutching at her shoulders, hands she hadn't the strength to reject were lowering her carefully into a chair. Ella closed her eyes, shutting out the room the woman, the knowledge that she was alone, never so alone.

A lifetime passed before she raised her leaden lids, brought the room back into focus. 'You shouldn't have done that.'

'No. I'm sorry.'

She looked it, too, Ella decided, logging the stricken face and smiling despite herself. Poor Felicity. They were fighting over Jack, if only she knew it. Because Ella loved Jack, and Jack loved Fliss. Only Ella shouldn't have blown up, should never have allowed the other woman to goad her.

Jack's fiancée, Jack's bride, and, in Jack's absence, Ella's boss. And for once in her life, Fliss, beautiful, spoiled Felicity Foxwood, was lost for words, looked absurdly young standing in the middle of Ella's sitting room, twisting that ostentatious ring round and round her finger.

'Let me make you a drink.'

'I – '

'No, please, I insist. It's the least I can do,' Fliss urged, already darting away.

Ella closed her eyes again. Progress indeed. Being waited on hand and foot by the grand lady herself. And surely she'd misheard. What had Fliss said? *Please*. There was hope for the woman yet, Ella decided, and maybe, just maybe, Ian's perception was wrong and Felicity and Jack really would make it.

Tea. Scalding hot and sweet – much too sweet for Ella, who didn't take sugar in tea to start with.

'Good for shock,' Felicity explained as if reading her mind.

Ella nodded. Yes. And, with her cheek still stir-rings from Felicity's swipe, quite a shock at that.

'I'll say goodnight then. If you're sure you'll be all right?'

'I'm fine,' Ella insisted, and, glancing across, seeing a wealth of remorse in the younger woman's eyes, felt her first stirrings of pity. Had things been different, Ella might even have grown to like her, was beginning to see why Jack was so besotted. Vulner-able. Yes. Absurd though it seemed, that just about summed Fliss up.

Felicity reached the door as the phone began to ring, the sound cutting through the silence, and Ella jerked upright in the chair, the splash of hot tea barely registering. At this time of the night it had to be important, and she went hot, then cold, the colour flooding her cheeks before draining away, leaving behind the vivid stain of the handprint.

'May I?' Felicity enquired, angling her head.

'Be my guest,' Ella invited, suppressing the urge to dash across and snatch up the handset, the tightly clenched fingers her only sign of nerves.

On the outside looking in, she could only watch as Felicity spoke into the mouthpiece, paused, listened, spoke again – short, sharp questions that an overwrought Ella didn't understand, was screaming out to understand. Her nails dug cruelly into her palms as Felicity cut the connection and turned, leaning back against the sideboard, a wealth of emotion chasing across her face.

'It was Ian,' Felicity murmured softly, incredulously, her exquisite features beginning to soften. 'Jack's safe. They set him free an hour ago and by this time tomorrow he'll be on his way home. Isn't that the most wonderful news in the world?'

CHAPTER 20

The most wonderful news in the world. Jack was coming home and Ella was leaving. Because that was what they'd agreed. Hell and heaven both. But he was safe and that was the important thing.

Another sleepless night – hardly worth the effort of going to bed, given the time it had been when Felicity had left, the angry scene forgotten as Ella had taken control, phoned the airport, booked Felicity onto the first available flight and then helped her to pack.

Yet another of life's little ironies: Ella standing at the top of the steps to see her out of sight, not waving exactly, as the taxi had sailed down the driveway, but her love and prayers silently winging their way across the miles.

'You look dreadful,' Ian brutally informed her, having dropped by early to share the latest news. 'I thought you'd be over the moon.'

'I am. I just didn't sleep, that's all. Too many things running through my mind.'

'And the rest. Fliss,' he reminded her, accepting the cup of coffee Ella pushed across the table. 'Since she answered the phone – the housekeeper's phone,' he emphasized grimly, 'at that time of night, I'd guess it wasn't a social call.'

'No.' Ella smiled. 'Let's just say we managed to reach an understanding. And, since the house isn't big enough for both of us, I'll soon be on my way.'

'But you will hang on until Jack flies in?'

'I – yes, I suppose so,' she conceded flatly.

'But you'd rather not?'

'I promised,' she explained tightly. And it would be good to see him, to see for herself that he was safe and well. Heaven and hell. Because then she would go.

'And then what happens?' Ian probed, brown eyes pools of velvet.

'Who knows?' Ella trilled, smiling brightly across. And then his face swam out focus as the tears welled.

More tea. She was awash with the stuff, was beginning to hate the smell of it, found the taste strangely metallic.

'Better now?'

'Better now,' she agreed, and, just to prove that she was back in control, she added lightly, 'Till the next time.'

'Talking of which, it must be time for the news. You don't mind if I switch your TV on?'

'I'd be positively cross if you didn't,' she conceded. She'd caught the first bulletin of the day herself, just a one-line statement that had told her nothing new, but was a precious snippet to hold onto, and tangible proof that she hadn't been dreaming.

Sure enough, Jack was top of the bill.

'. . . was released late last night and is reported to be safe and well and eager to be home after his first decent night's sleep in weeks,' the newsreader revealed. 'Jack Keegan of J.K. Holdings is said to have negotiated his own release, with far-reaching implications for the tourist trade in the Gulf. We're hoping to bring you further details later on in the bulletin . . .'

'What did I tell you? That man could talk his way out of Alcatraz.'

'What does it mean, "far-reaching implications for the tourist trade"?' Ella queried, the after-image of Jack plastered across the screen embedded in her mind.

'Alcohol,' Ian explained. 'It's a Moslem country and alcohol's taboo. The place is idyllic – sun, sand, sea and completely undeveloped. A paradise on earth just waiting for someone like Jack to transform it.'

'But?' Ella queried, pretty sure she'd worked the answer out for herself.

Ian shrugged. 'No booze, no tourists,' he explained. 'No tourists, no profits. But Jack knew the risks involved. He stands to lose millions if the deal falls through, but if it goes ahead – '

'Jack gets first pick of all the prime sites,' Ella interrupted dryly.

'Precisely. And if I know Jack, that's exactly what will happen.'

Ella didn't care. She just wanted him home, wanted to see for herself that he was safe and sound. And though she spent the day hovering from TV to radio and back again, waiting for news, desperate for news, she was destined to be disappointed. Patience. He was safe, that was all that mattered for now.

And in between there was work: beds to change, sheets to launder – but no meals to cook, thank goodness, since Felicity's house guests had developed some tact and, in the absence of their hostess, headed back to the bright lights. And the packing. Her own cases this time – precious little really, since all her jobs had been residential. No clutter, no store of mementoes, just the rocking horse Jack had bought the first time she'd been pregnant – an absurd piece of sentiment she'd be unable to part with. Oh, yes, and the memories, wonderful memories of her night of love.

'All set?' Ian asked, having popped back in to catch the six o'clock news.

'As set as I'll ever be,' Ella agreed, butterflies chasing round and round her insides as she took the chair opposite.

'. . . and today's main item comes from our reporter in the Gulf of Oman. Jack Keegan, the British entrepreneur who was released late last night, made a surprise decision not to hold a Press Conference. Instead, Mr Keegan, in surprisingly good health given the ordeal of the past few weeks, is on his way by Jeep to Muscat to catch the first flight to Britain.

'Details of his release are still hazy but it would appear that a tough government line on terrorism is likely to benefit the country immensely. Despite strict controls on alcohol, the deal should open the door to tourists and the expected flood of foreign currency will be worth its weight in oil.

'Mr Keegan is reported to be relieved that his pioneering scheme is back on course for an early completion but for now his priority is simply to go home. Hardly surprising, since "home" for the multi-millionaire property developer is a former stately home in the heart of the Staffordshire countryside. Sherbrook . . .'

Aerial pictures of the hall switched to Felicity leaving the plane at Muscat and then on to the departure lounge, and a pushing, shoving, jostling crowd with Jack at the centre, large as life and twice as natural, grinning, hair dishevelled and bleached by the sun, his tanned face showing just the faintest hint of the strain he'd been under. Ella's heart turned somersaults in her breast.

'Mr Keegan, how does it feel to be free . . .?'

'. . . to be heading for home?'

'What did you miss most, Mr Keegan . . .'

'How were you treated . . .?'

A rapid fire of questions came too fast for Jack to answer, came too close to the terror of the weeks he'd endured, and so Jack simply nodded, smiled, carried on.

'Any message for the folks back home, Mr Keegan?'

He halted then, practically swallowed up by the circle of thrusting microphones, the battery of cameras, and then he was back in focus, his rugged face dominating the screen.

'Just give them my love,' he said, the simple words music to Ella's ears.

'Anyone in particular, Mr Keegan?'

'Your fiancée, perhaps?'

'You'll be pleased to know she's on her way – that her plane has just landed.'

'Quite a reunion, hey, Mr Keegan?'

'When's the wedding to be?'

'Are you looking forward to the big day?'

'Come on, Mr Keegan. Give us a break. You must have a date in mind?'

'Soon,' Jack replied, smiling broadly, fielding the questions. 'As soon as we can arrange it. I've already waited more than long enough to make the woman I love my wife.'

'Anywhere special in mind for the honeymoon, Mr Keegan?'

'The Gulf Of Oman, perhaps?'

'Oh, I can think of somewhere better than that,' he countered, grinning broadly.

'Anywhere we know, Mr Keegan? Some other slice of paradise you're keeping to yourself?'

'I certainly am,' he informed them, informed the whole world. 'Bed.'

Bed. With Fliss. Given their enforced separation, his enforced celibacy, it was hardly surprising Jack didn't make it back to Sherbrook for the weekend. He phoned, of course, the moment his plane touched down in London, and the strain in his voice tugged at Ella's heartstrings.

'I'm coming home,' he told her fiercely. 'Promise me, Ella, you will be there when I get home?'

When? Two days? Three? What did it matter? But the waiting was tearing her apart. Because she'd promised, and until Jack came home Ella couldn't leave, was simply left to brood, to imagine, to want. To know that she'd lost him, that he hadn't been hers in the first place. And the pictures in her mind's eye were unremitting: Jack with Fliss, Jack kissing Fliss, Jack touching Fliss, Jack making love to her over and over again.

The waiting was a nightmare. Limbo.

Oh, she filled her time, just as she had while Jack was missing – dusting rooms that the maids had left pristine, polishing silver that shone like a mirror before she'd begun, filling the freezers with food enough to feed a marching army.

She even managed to visit Gramps, proudly installed in his new flat, his independence maintained with his own front door but with communal rooms when he needed company, panic buttons in case of any problems and a resident warden to keep a discreet weather eye.

And then onto the cottage. She'd all but moved in – her meagre possessions quickly arranged, the cottage unnaturally quiet without Gramps. But all hers. The moment Jack came home.

When Jack came home. Better than if, she consoled herself. A million times better than if.

'Ella?'

'Jack! Oh, Jack!' Stealing up on Ella in the kitchen, he kissed her, hugged her. Ella held him close, wanting him, crying tears of joy, tears of relief. Because he was home and he was safe. And then she remembered. He wasn't hers. Ella froze.

'What is it?' he asked, sensing her change of mood.

She pushed herself free of his embrace, her body screaming out to feel his arms around her. She was cold, so very cold. Because Jack had come home and Ella would have to leave. Only fair since Jack loved Felicity, and even if Jack could play around, Ella couldn't stomach the deception. He wasn't hers and so she'd go. A clean break. Better that way. And soon.

'You – didn't bring Fliss?' she queried, busying herself with some mushrooms, peeling and slicing automatically, her eyes fixed rigidly on the task in hand. Since she'd already eaten, this casserole was simply something concrete to help fill the time.

'She's staying on in London for a while,' he explained in a tight voice.

'Pining for the bright lights?' Ella needled, the words unintentionally ironic as she added tartly, 'After her enforced incarceration in the depths of the country.'

'Hardly,' Jack murmured, wincing as, too late, Ella recalled the ordeal he'd just endured. 'But, since she has been away for a while, there were one or two things she needed to sort out.'

Her trousseau, presumably, Ella acknowledged silently, bitterly. Little enough for the honeymoon if Jack's broadcast to the world could be believed. Bed.

More pictures flashed through her mind; man and woman, bodies entwined, Ella and Jack, Fliss and Jack. Her mind skittered away, remembering, wanting, hating as strong arms folded round to draw her back. So easy to melt against him, have his lips nuzzling at her temples while stroking fingers filled her with heat. Ella pulled away.

'Don't. Don't touch me, Jack,' she said tightly. 'Please don't touch me.'

'But – why?' he asked incredulously. 'I've come home, Ella. I need you.'

Oh, sure. Celibacy. And now no Fliss. Nice and convenient, and how clever of Jack to have planned it. He wanted Ella all right, and why not? She'd been eager enough the last time, so – might as well face it – a tumble between the sheets with Fliss, a long, lazy weekend followed by a hint that she might like to sort out a few minor details, like order a wedding dress or plan a champagne reception. And then, having dealt with the loving fiancée, make time for the loving ex-wife. Clever. Very clever. Only Ella wasn't playing.

'You want me,' Jack insisted, the hurt in his eyes tearing her apart. Hurt, bewilderment, pain. Because he wanted Ella and Ella wasn't about to settle for Felicity's leavings.

She hardened her heart. 'Wrong, Jack. I'm independent now. I've worked my notice and I'm free to go. You're home, I'm leaving,' she reminded him dully, unfastening her apron and wiping damp palms on a cloth. 'Now. It's what we agreed.'

'But – where the hell will you go at this time of night?'

'A hotel?' she suggested tartly.

'If you must.'

'As a matter of fact, no,' she conceded, her mouth softening at the thought. 'I don't have to. I'm not entirely alone in the world, believe it or not.'

'Meaning?'

'Nothing. Nothing for you to worry about,' she informed him briskly. 'I'll simply phone for a taxi and be out of your hair.' Out of his life – for good this time.

'Out of my hair – or out of my bed?'

'Wishful thinking, Jack,' Ella scorned. I – '

'But of course,' he interrupted, blue eyes boring into hers – the most vivid blue in the world set against the tan. 'Of course, that's it. You're running away – from me. You want me. You want me, damn you. We made love. You *wanted* me.'

'Don't sound so surprised,' she jeered. 'You are a man of experience. Fliss, me, doubtless a dozen others. And yes,' she conceded frankly, 'I wanted you – then. But in the cold light of day I realized I'd made a mistake. Face it, Jack, it happened but it was wrong.'

'But you enjoyed it?' Half-query, half-statement, and the doubt in his voice tugged at her heart.

'Naturally. And so did you. Hence the need for a repeat performance.'

'Do you have to make me sound like a prize stallion?'

'Hired out to service the mare?' she jeered. 'With me incapable of falling. Or should that be foaling?' she quipped with bitter irony. 'Falling pregnant' – a common enough expression that managed to make the whole wonderful idea sound like a catastrophe. 'Such a waste, don't you think?' she heard herself goading. 'Where I'm concerned.'

'No! Never that. No, Ella,' he insisted, snatching at her upper arms, tugging her close, shaking her almost. 'I wanted you, just you, always you. The babies – '

'Weren't meant to happen, Jack. Not your fault. Not mine.'

'And me and you, Ella? Where do we fit in?'

Ella shrugged, her gaze faltering. There was so much love swirling in her eyes that she couldn't risk looking him in the face, couldn't bear to see the hurt. 'We happened. Past tense, Jack. You've got your life, I've got mine – '

'Precisely. Your life. Your *life*,' he repeated bitterly. 'Life without Jack. Life with Tolland – hey, Ella?'

So easy to lie, to keep him at that distance, and yet pointless in a way. They were in the same business, and, with Jack's holiday village scheme firmly back on course, Stephen would be involved. Ella *could* lie, but it would be a short-lived piece of fiction. And then Jack would know. Ella forced back the tears. Pride. It was all she had left. And she couldn't bear Jack to know the truth.

'Well, Ella?' Terse words, accusing eyes, biting fingers.

'You're wrong.'

'Don't lie. Not now. Not to me. After everything we've been through. Good God, woman – '

'No, Jack!' She jerked herself free, taking a step away, eyes shooting flames – because she loved him, needed him, wanted him, and Jack, devastating Jack, wanted her. *Want*, she underlined cruelly. Not love. And she wasn't about to settle for second-best.

'No, Jack,' she repeated flatly. 'I'm not going back to Stephen – not today, not tomorrow, not ever. In fact,' she added softly, willing him to understand, to hear the words, to take the words at face value, 'since Stephen and I never were an item, not in the way that you mean, going back simply wasn't an option. But then, going back never is, hey, Jack?'

'But – ' He ran his fingers through his hair, a gesture of despair that Ella willed herself to resist, knowing the slightest sign of weakness would damn her for ever – in her own eyes at least. Pride. She had to hang onto that self-respect. Heaven knew, she'd fought long and hard to regain it. 'I don't understand.'

No. Poor Jack. Arrogant Jack. He *didn't* understand, she silently scorned, love, pain, bitterness battling in her mind. He wanted Ella; Ella didn't want him – ergo, there must be another man around someplace. And yet demolish the myth of the other man and Jack Keegan's ego couldn't swallow the implications. Jack's problem, not hers, Ella told herself, seeing the pain, the doubt, the million and one thoughts swirling in the depths of troubled blue eyes. The doubt, and then a dawning incredulity.

Jack's face hardened, and, watching him, Ella smothered a spurt of alarm, suppressed the urge to put distance between them – a lot of distance.

'Ah, yes,' he mused, almost as if talking to himself. 'Of course. I should have realized sooner,' he purred, the soft words at odds with the hatred blasting out from arctic features. 'Clever, clever, Ella. Tolland was a smokescreen – nothing more, nothing less. Congratulations, Ella. I've always known you were devious, but this time you really have excelled yourself.' And he angled his head, that frigid gaze pinning her, refusing to allow her to look away. 'You bitch, you cold-hearted, calculating little bitch.'

Her head snapped up. 'Devious?' she queried absurdly, crying inside, dying inside, Jack's sneering condemnation the final insult. No more pain. She'd already suffered enough. She mustn't let Jack's bitter words hit home.

He nodded. 'Devious. Remember the brandy, Ella? All those bottles stashed neatly out of my sight? Devious. And nothing's changed. Because that's how Ella Keegan's mind works when she wants something badly. She plots and schemes until she gets what she wants, and heaven help anyone she tramples on the way. Devious. Once it was the drink and now it's a man. Watson.'

'And how do you work that out?' Ella scoffed, smothering the urge to laugh. Laugh when she was close to crying – and yet some of Jack's anger was beginning to make sense.

'You know. Don't pretend you don't. Watson. Watson, not Tolland. And that's what this is all about, isn't it, Ella? Your ex-husband. Look me in the face and deny it if you dare.'

She dropped her gaze. The truth. Jack's version. Ella Keegan, bitch of the year, playing one man off against another while all the time angling for a third. Ella Keegan – or Ella Watson? And somewhere in between the truth lurked – a truth she had to hide from Jack.

'Well?'

Ella licked her lips, glancing across through the veil of her lashes. 'I – '

'Watson,' Jack clipped. 'A simple yes or no will suffice. And the fact that you haven't denied it speaks for itself,' he sneeringly observed. 'Still, having flown halfway across the world to hear it, I might as well hold out for the truth. The truth, Ella, the whole truth and nothing but the truth – always assuming you know what that means.'

'Don't add lies to my list of sins, Jack,' she castigated coolly. 'The truth, the whole truth and nothing but the truth,' she acknowledged grimly. 'Fire away, Jack, but don't blame me if you don't get the answers you need.'

'My problem, Ella, and I'll cross that bridge if and when I reach it. So . . .' He smiled, an ugly snarl of teeth, as he leaned against the worktop, folded his arms, allowed his insolent gaze to wander the lines of her body. 'About Watson?'

Ella nodded warily.

'Just a simple yes or no, Ella. Is he the reason you gave up the job in Bristol?'

'I – '

'You're stalling, Ella,' he frigidly reminded her. 'And you can take it from me, it doesn't look good. Is Watson the reason you moved to Stafford?' he repeated, and, tiring of the game of verbal ping-pong, he reached out, tucked a vicious finger beneath her chin and forced her reluctant gaze to lock with his. 'Is he?' he hissed. '*Is he?*'

And because Jack had pushed her, goaded her, judged her, Ella returned his gaze unblinkingly and gave him the truth. 'Yes.'

'So – I might have known. I *should* have known,' he rasped as Ella flinched, that finger beneath her chin biting deep for a fraction of an instant, the contempt in his eyes as he finally released her almost more than she could stand. 'Oh, yes. Fool that I am, I should have guessed. Which leads me neatly round to the sixty-four thousand-dollar question. Why, Ella?' he demanded, and then the anger gave way to sheer disbelief as the truth dawned. 'You little fool,' he castigated viciously. 'You love him. After everything he's put you through, you're still carrying a torch for your ex-husband.'

'For your information, Jack,' she told him softly, willing him to understand yet achingly aware that he couldn't. 'I never stopped loving him and I doubt I ever will.'

He flinched. His pain Ella's pain. Because she'd given him the truth and she'd hurt him. Because she loved *him*, had never, ever stopped loving *him*. But Jack was luckier than Ella. She was living with a broken heart. All Jack had to face was a bit of hurt pride.

CHAPTER 21

Hours, days, weeks. Time blurred. So much to take on. Explaining it all to Gramps, moving into the cottage, living without Jack. Wanting Jack, loving him, needing him, scrupulously avoiding the announcement column in *The Times*, and, since Sherbrook was little more than a stone's throw away, refusing point-blank to buy a local paper. Just in case.

'Bed', he'd announced to the world. Jack couldn't wait to marry the woman he loved. A Christmas wedding? Ella mused, wondering if even a short wait would prove too long for a man who'd been to hell and back again. But, irrespective of the forthcoming nuptials, bed, bed, bed and more bed. Jack and Fliss. Over and over in Ella's fertile mind.

But if Ella was alone, she was also achingly aware she was merely treading water. She had the rest of her life to plan and yet she was living in limbo, even the thought of another job put in abeyance. Time enough later, she decided, stifling the panic, wondering how on earth she'd cope. But she was a grown woman; she had her savings and a roof over her head, thanks to Gramps, and she'd manage.

She stepped down off the bus, the handles of the plastic carriers biting deep into the soft flesh of her fingers. She'd almost taken her bicycle, would have enjoyed the sting of the crisp November air against her cheeks, but she'd wanted to get the shopping over and done with and the basket on the bike held next to nothing. Besides, she was being careful – over-cautious maybe, if the doctor was to be believed, but better safe than sorry.

Leaving the main road behind, she breathed a huge sigh of relief. Almost there. The cottage had been a Godsend, but with the boundaries of Sherbrook just a half-mile hike across the fields she wouldn't be able to relax until she was safely inside with the front door closed firmly behind her.

So near, so far, and yet clearly ridiculous. Because if Jack did choose to venture out of doors, he'd be zooming back and forth in his powerful Mercedes. A lone pedestrian huddled into the folds of a warm but shabby coat wouldn't merit so as much as a glance as he passed through the village.

Rounding the corner of the lane, Ella halted, the breath leaving her body. A Mercedes SL60 was parked outside the cottage. A metallic blue Mercedes. Oh, no. She swung round, hoping and praying he wouldn't have seen her, that his sharp blue eyes wouldn't be trained on the driver's mirror, allowing the approach to the cottage to be covered from both directions.

A door slamming behind her, footsteps, another faint hope demolished.

'Ella! Please, Ella.'

She was rushing, half running, dropping the bags in her haste to get away – a waste of time in any case, since he rapidly out-paced her and her treacherous body responded as he pulled her up short.

'Ella, oh, Ella,' he chided softly, the piercing blue eyes boring into her, surely seeing to the centre of her soul.

'What do you want, Jack?' she asked, the blood pounding in her ears, her heart beating nineteen to the dozen. So much for taking things easy. The way she'd been going she'd have managed the four-minute mile!

'Just being neighbourly,' he explained enigmatically. 'Which is more than I can say for you. Coffee?' he prompted silkily. 'Or tea for two in your cosy-looking cottage. Always assuming you remembered to buy the milk?'

'I remembered,' she acknowledged curtly. 'Though heaven knows if it's survived the journey home.'

'The journey home?' he pointedly challenged. 'Or the unscheduled flight?'

'Coffee,' she reminded him, refusing to rise to the bait. And, shaking herself free of his grip, began to retrace her steps.

'Allow me,' he insisted, retrieving her bags and inspecting the contents. 'Scrambled eggs for supper,' he murmured with a solemn shake of the head. 'Or a nice, fluffy omelette. Throw in the cheese and you'll have hit on my favourite. I don't suppose a starving neighbour could wangle an invitation?' he added hopefully.

'Well done, Jack. You got it right first time,' she retorted curtly, leading the way inside. 'Thank you, I'll take care of those.' And, taking the bags and brooking no denials, she shooed him through the door and into the tiny lounge. 'Sit down, why don't you? Make yourself at home.'

Stalling. Waiting for the kettle to boil, she unpacked the shopping – surprisingly intact apart from the yellow slime collecting in the cardboard egg box. Not even salvageable for an omelette, she decided ruefully, dropping the soggy carton into the bin, and, since Jack would surely come to find her if she didn't appear soon, she straightened, picked up the tray and, taking the biggest breath of her life, pushed open the door.

'Coffee,' she offered, pressing the plunger on the cafetière and pouring him a cup. 'Help yourself to cream and sugar.'

'What about you?' he asked as Ella's cup rattled in its saucer. Nerves – the sort of nerves Jack would notice and would understand only too well.

'Thank you. I'd rather stick to tea.' Herb tea, since the common or garden breakfast stuff, not to mention her favourite Earl Grey, still left that metallic taste in her mouth – along with lots of other foods, she acknowledged silently, wondering when it would pass.

The infusion was hot and she sipped it warily, eyeing Jack from beneath a veil of lashes. He was looking tired, she decided, and surprisingly pale since the tan had faded, allowing the strain to show through. It couldn't have been easy, living on his wits, living on his nerves, wondering if each day would be his last. No ring, Ella noted, the surge of relief taking her by surprise. And he would be wearing a wedding ring if Ella knew Fliss. So – the sixty-four thousand-dollar question.

'Why are you here, Jack?'

He drained his cup, put it carefully in its saucer, placed it equally carefully down on the table. 'I've come to see you.'

'Really? I can't imagine why,' she murmured, stifling the panic. He surely couldn't know? No one did, not even Gramps, and yet give it a few more months and the world and its brother would doubtless see for themselves. And then, since Jack clearly didn't mean to give her an answer, 'How did you find me?'

'Elementary, my dear Mrs Andrews-Watson. I simply followed the trail of clues.'

'Oh?'

'Fliss. Something about a cosy meal for two in the great hall with – quote – "a man old enough to be your grandfather".'

'And?'

'You. Your interest in the history of the place. Just natural curiosity, I assumed, when I found you engrossed that day in the library. As luck would have it, I remembered the volume in question – and the year you'd been perusing.'

'So, clever Jack Keegan puts two and two together and bingo?'

'Hit the jackpot,' he agreed, a fleeting smile lighting up his features. 'And I couldn't believe it when the trail led here, to a cottage right under my nose. So, tell me, Ella, just to put the record straight. Your Mr Watson, the Mr Watson of Andrews-Watson fame – ex-husband, Ella, or grandfather?'

'You mean you don't know?'

'As a matter of fact, no,' he conceded. 'Doubtless I could have made a few enquiries, but, believe it or not, I'm not in the habit of prying.'

'How very noble,' Ella sneered, hitting out, hating him – hating him for sitting there so cool, calm and collected while her insides were churning. 'But, silly me, I almost forgot. You're part of the nobility these days, Jack.'

'Am I? And how do you work that out?'

'Felicity. Wedding bells. A viscount for a father-in-law. I assume the arrangements are all in place?'

'Special licence,' he agreed solemnly. 'The moment she says yes.'

'Not doing things in style, Jack?' Ella scorned, hitting out again, the relief that he wasn't married tempered by that tiny but devastating word 'yet'. 'And after such a touching public proposal, too. What *is* the woman playing at?'

'Like so many of the species, Ella,' he lazily informed her. 'Playing hard to get. But you can take it from me, she's worth the wait.'

'I'm sure you're right,' she murmured politely.

'I know I am.'

Yes. Ella swallowed hard. Hardly a wait in any case, since Fliss was already sharing his life, his bed. Bed. Making love. Making babies. Jack was entitled to know.

But not yet, she told herself, hugging the knowledge to her. Too soon. Sheer superstition on her part, maybe, but, given the disappointments of the past, Ella wasn't about to take any chances. So Jack would be the first to know – the moment Ella allowed herself to believe it. Recalling the day she'd been told, she smiled . . .

'Pregnant? But – are you sure?' she'd queried absurdly, politely, her heart beating so loud that-surely she'd misheard?

The doctor had smiled – not Gramps's ancient practitioner, whose retirement surely hadn't come a moment too soon, but a new broom with a computerized filing system and a surgery fitted with all mod cons and a warm and cheery waiting area a far cry from the dingy room Ella had imagined from the one or two snippets Gramps had let drop.

'No doubt about it, Mrs Andrews-Watson. The signs are unmistakable even at this early stage. But you must have had an idea?'

An idea? Oh, yes. She could recognize the signs. After all, she'd been pregnant before often enough. She'd known; she simply hadn't wanted to believe it. More heartbreak and yet another of life's little ironies. To conceive Jack's baby and then be forced to sit around and wait for the inevitable.

'Not necessarily,' the doctor had countered when Ella's tearful explanation had ground to a soggy halt. 'Until we run the tests I can't say for sure, but we've made a lot of progress over the past few years and, believe it or not, your medical history sounds all too familiar. Antiphospholipid syndrome – APS for short.'

He'd smiled, seeing the expression on Ella's face, the fleeting flash of hope, and then he'd nodded, his fingers climbing a rack of pamphlets until he found what he was looking for and, folding it open, passed it across for Ella to read. Ella had blinked, the block of ice around her heart beginning to thaw – a very slow thaw, because Ella was afraid, afraid to believe that he was giving her hope.

'APS: a clotting disorder . . . known to destroy areas of the placenta . . . a major cause of recurrent miscarriage . . .' Ella had read and read again, only half understanding the medical jargon.

'And the treatment?' she'd asked simply, raising her head and reading the truth in a set of wise, grey eyes.

The doctor's smile had broadened. 'Believe it or not, a controlled dose of aspirin.'

A controlled dose of other drugs too – anticoagulants, for starters – and the sooner the treatment could begin, the better . . .

Alone in her thoughts, Ella smiled. At less than eight weeks pregnant at the time, for once her timing had been perfect.

'I could be wrong,' Jack murmured, shrewd blue

eyes narrowing as they rested on Ella's face. 'But a certain ex-housekeeper looks like the cat that got the cream.'

Ella. Her baby. Not the full cream, she could allow, since she'd never be entitled to Jack, but quite a consolation prize – once she allowed herself to believe in it.

Flushing guiltily, she jumped up, rattling the cups and saucers back onto the tray. As she reached the door to the kitchen Jack's voice sliced across to halt her.

'Ella?'

She swung round, angling her head in polite enquiry.

'I was wrong, wasn't I?' he queried tightly. – 'I was a fool to hope. Husband or grandfather. I was clutching at straws. It's been the husband all along. You love him?'

'You know I love him,' she admitted tightly. 'I've told you I love him. I've never, ever stopped loving him.'

'Yes. I just – ' He broke off, shrugged, fished the car keys from his pocket as he stood up to leave. 'Don't let him hurt you, Ella,' he murmured softly.

'It's too late for that,' she tossed out bitterly. 'Since he's marrying someone else – and soon.' *Special licence*, she tagged on silently, Jack's earlier words tearing her apart. *The moment she says yes.*

There. She'd done it. She was hurting and she'd lashed out at the man she loved. She watched the shadows chase across his face through a blur of tears and couldn't bear to look any longer. Because she loved him, and she'd lost him, and she'd already given away more than she'd intended.

Choking back the tears, she pushed on the door, allowed it to swing to behind her, all but dropping the tray in her need to hang onto the threads of self-control. Rigid fingers clutched the edge of the draining board as the creak of the door behind told her she wasn't alone.

'Ella?'

She froze. 'Go home, Jack,' she murmured tightly. 'Doubtless the lovely Fliss will be wondering where you are.'

'I doubt it,' he murmured dryly. 'With the boutiques of Paris and Rome beckoning like a magnet.'

'Ah, yes. The trousseau. Only the best for Fliss, hey, Jack?'

'Apparently. Hence the Christmas wedding. You did catch the announcement?' he queried matter-of-factly.

'Special licence, *you* said,' she needled, absurdly hurt that he'd been lying. 'The moment she says yes.'

'Very true, Ella,' he agreed solemnly, bridging the gap between them in two easy strides. 'But, since I haven't yet popped the question, I can hardly hope for an answer. Remiss of me, I'd say.'

As he halted behind her Ella stiffened, the tiny hairs on the back of her neck prickling out a warning. 'Don't,' she murmured as he touched her – a fleeting touch of fingers brushing aside her hair.

'Any particular reason?' he queried softly, his breath a warm flutter on her skin – skin that tingled at the touch, at the mere thought of Jack touching, kissing, nibbling.

'Don't play games with me, Jack. Leave me alone. Leave me in peace. Don't – '

'Kiss you?' he queried, doing precisely that. 'Touch you?' he murmured, his hands sliding around her waist as he tugged her into the hard lines of his body. 'Want you?' he growled, pulling her close, and Ella gasped. The hardness at his groin was unmistakable, the heat running through her like a brand. 'Need you?' he breathed, his lips nibbling her earlobes as his hands slid upwards to touch her breasts, a feather-light-brush of fingers that turned her blood to water. 'Need you?' he repeated huskily. 'Just like you need me?'

'No!' She jerked away, cheeks on fire, eyes spitting flames. 'I don't want you. I don't need you. And you sure as hell don't need me, Jack Keegan. That Christmas wedding,' she spat, 'clearly can't come soon enough. Four weeks and then you're caught – hook, line and sinker. And, in the meanwhile, wasting an idle hour with me isn't on the agenda. I'm off-limits, Jack Keegan. No touching, no kissing, no sex.'

'An idle hour? Oh, no,' he told her solemnly, folding his arms and watching her carefully. 'That's not what I'm suggesting. Believe me, I was thinking more along the lines of a lifetime.'

'What's the matter, Jack?' Ella demanded. 'Missing Fliss – or missing out on the comforts of her bed?

While the cat's away, the mouse will play?' she scorned. 'And a cunning plan at that,' she acknowledged bitterly. 'Your mistress cosily installed in a cottage right under your nose. Because that's what you're suggesting. Only you're wrong. I don't want you, I don't need you, and one night of wonderful sex isn't an open invitation to the delights of my bedroom.'

'Most definitely wonderful,' he agreed, lips twitching almost imperceptibly. 'Delightful, delicious, and devastatingly wonderful. But only on condition that you marry me.'

'I beg your pardon?' she queried politely.

'Marriage. That special licence. It's all set. All it takes is for you to say the word.'

'Me?' she challenged incredulously.

'You,' he agreed solemnly. 'Only you, only ever you, I promise.'

'And Fliss?'

'Why settle for me and a wing in a stately home when someone equally rich can offer a string of castles?'

Another stab of pain. Too cruel.

'Second-best, Jack?' Ella jeered, choking back the tears. 'Well, I hope it hurts. I hope it hurts like hell,' she told him, the knifeblade twisting in her belly. 'Because that's how I feel. Second-best. Second choice. Good enough to marry because the woman you love has turned you down and your gullible ex-wife can supply the goodies in bed. Only I can't, remember? Sex, undoubtedly,' she needled, 'if I'm stupid enough to let you.' And, crossing her fingers at the tiny white lie, she tagged on grimly, 'But not the babies.'

'Only you, Ella. Only ever you,' he repeated, and he closed the gap between them as Ella backed away, was brought up sharp by the draining board. The minuscule kitchen, despite its mod-cons, provided no place to hide; her escape route to the lounge was effectively blocked by Jack's massive presence. 'Ella, Ella, I want you,' he murmured, hands closing round her upper arms as he held her. 'Only you. Only ever you.'

And he was kissing her – tiny kisses raining down on her eyelids, trailing the angles and planes of her face, the corners of her mouth – and Ella was rigid in his arms, the needs of her body battling with the needs of her mind. Second-best. Only ever second-best. Because Fliss had turned him down and Ella would save him the trouble of breaking in another bed-mate. Good in bed. Good sex. Wonderful sex. But no love.

'No! No, no, no!' she railed, balling her fists and hitting him, hitting out blind, struggling to be free. 'No, Jack! No! No! No!'

And she was crying, the tears pouring unheeded down her cheeks as he swore softly under his breath, pulled her against him, cradled her head against his chest. The heaving sobs choked her, the hate and the bitterness pouring out once and for all. Because she loved him, and, yes, she could hate him, fleetingly, when the pain proved too much, but she loved him far too much ever to hate him for long.

'Marry me, Ella,' he urged softly when the tears had subsided.

Second-best bride. Tempting, even knowing the truth. Ella was sorely tempted, especially with a baby on the way. Jack's baby. Marry Jack. A lifetime spent with Jack. Because she loved him. Second-best. Better than nothing, she tried to console herself. But she was lying. She loved him. She couldn't settle for second-best.

'I can't marry you, Jack,' she told him quietly, pulling free, searching for a tissue to wipe away the residue of tears and forced to settle for a snatch of kitchen roll. 'I love my ex-husband, remember? Always have, always will.'

'But *I'm* your ex-husband,' he pointed out with a curious lack of emotion.

'Well, ye-es,' she agreed warily, careful to keep her back turned.

'The one and only ex-husband, Ella. The man you love. Always have, always will. He doesn't exist, does he, the elusive Mr Watson?'

'Oh, yes, he does,' she told him, seizing the question like a lifeline and smiling despite herself as Gramps's weatherbeaten face swam into her mind. And, suddenly back in control, she spun round, eyes bright, the smile lighting up her eyes. 'Oh, yes, he does,' she repeated, hurting him, hurting herself more. 'Believe me, Jack, he exists, and I love him more than words can say.'

'I see.' Just that – oh, and the weariness settling like a cloud on his shoulders. Because she'd hurt him. Like Fliss, she'd hit him where it hurt – his pride.

He turned to go – for good, Ella realized instinctively, aware that she couldn't let him walk away with bitterness festering between them, equally aware that it was safer this way. No turning back. No moment of weakness. Simply let him go. Only she couldn't.

'Jack?'

He stopped. His turn to angle his head politely.

'About Fliss. I'm sorry it didn't turn out the way you hoped.'

'Oh, but it did,' he acknowledged with a fleeting smile. 'I didn't love Fliss; she didn't love me. But letting her down lightly was proving a bit a problem. Coming home a hero from the Gulf thankfully brought it to a head. We were on the rocks, and for once even Fliss had sense enough to see it.'

'And the woman you loved?'

'Love, Ella. Always have, always will,' he admitted with another devastating smile. 'Believe it or not, I'm looking at her.'

Nothing. No reaction. Not even the blink of an eye. Because Ella's mind had seized up, his words rattling round inside her head in a meaningless jumble.

Watching her, Jack shrugged, moved away, into the lounge and through to the tiny hall that led to the front door.

'Jack! No! Wait!' she called out hysterically, her legs like jelly, the words refusing to form on her lips. And, spotting the photograph of Gramps on the sideboard, she darted across, grabbed the frame, all but thrust it under Jack's nose. 'Gramps,' she explained, only didn't explain, since he clearly hadn't a clue what she was saying. 'My grandfather, Jack. Peter Watson. I love him. I love you. I love you both. Don't go. Please don't go.'

'Are you saying what I hope you're saying?' he queried as the truth began to dawn.

She nodded, the tears brimming – tears of happiness this time, because Jack had gathered her to him, was kissing her, touching her, holding her, needing her, just as she had need of him.

And the moment the kiss came to an end, and since they happened to be standing at the bottom of the stairs, it seemed the most natural thing in the world to climb the stairway to heaven, hand in hand, slowly, unhurriedly, through into Ella's tiny bedroom, where Jack's head collided with the ceiling. Only he didn't seem to notice, having eyes only for Ella, the smoky expression in his eyes making the blood boil in her veins.

'Are you sure?' he murmured, reaching out, fingers already snapping the buttons of her blouse as Ella reached up to loosen the knot of hair at the nape of her neck, allowing the long black tresses to tumble freely about her shoulders.

'I'm sure,' she told him huskily, the moment of doubt that it might hurt the baby banished in a trice. Her baby, her man, her future. And it *was* going to happen, she realized with a blinding flash of instinct.

Blouse, skirt, petticoat, tights. The clothes lay where they dropped, quickly followed by Jack's shirt, socks and trousers, and Ella trembled as she stood almost naked before him, saw the hunger in his eyes and trembled all over again. Her man. Her Jack. Her love.

'I love you,' he told her solemnly, reaching for the catch at the front of her bra. And as her breasts spilled free he gasped, his eyes darting from her face to her breasts and back again. 'Oh, woman, I really do love you.'

'Me – or my body?' she challenged, but she was teasing, smiling, as Jack was, was suddenly in his arms, the touch of skin on skin sending currents of heat surging through her. And then it was Ella's turn to gasp as his hands moved down, down to the swell of her buttocks, over the swell of her buttocks, to tug her even closer, his need shocking her, the hardness eloquent proof of his need, his love. And then his hands slid beneath the lace of her panties, cradling the tingling skin of her bottom as Ella moved against him, creating fresh needs and currents in her own sensitized body.

'Oh, no, you don't,' he growled as she made to pull away, but Ella simply laughed, allowing herself to fall onto the bed, her open arms eloquent invitation as Jack dived to cover her, his lips claiming hers, his tongue sweeping through into the warm, moist depths of her mouth.

And then he was moving down, raining tiny kisses down the column of her neck, down again to the valley between her breasts where he lingered a while, savouring, nuzzling, tasting, the proudly thrusting nipples proving a diversion as his mouth fastened on first one and then the other while devastating fingers kneaded the tingling flesh.

Journey resumed, his lips moved over the soft swell of her belly, his tongue swirling into the hollow of her navel in an erotic sweep of warmth and wetness that left her trembling uncontrollably, and still he moved lower, his fingers easing the lace of her panties over her hips, discarding the panties, threading the curls, parting the curls.

And she was writhing, wanting, begging, needing, the warmth and the dampness eloquent proof of her need. Jack growled, continued to touch, to taste, to deny, bringing her time and time again to the point of explosion, so near, so far, denying her, stoking, teasing, tantalizing, enflaming, hands and tongue both, until she simply couldn't bear it any longer and shamelessly she reached for him, felt his need and trembled all over again.

Guiding him inside her, she gasped as he thrust, and again, and again, and still he denied her, the pace building, the rhythm quickening until they reached the point of no return, wave after wave after wave of mind-blowing, atom-splitting emotion.

'You do love me, Ella?' he asked, a lifetime later.

'Do you need to ask?' she queried softly, cradled in his arms, her face against his chest, the comforting beat of his heart beneath her cheek everything she needed and more.

'No. Not any more. I just like to hear you say it,' he told her smokily.

'I love you, Jack. I love you, I love you, I love you. Your turn now,' she prompted saucily.

'I love you, woman. Now and always,' he added, hugging her fiercely. 'And, fool that I am, I nearly lost you – again.'

'And me cosily installed right under your nose. I doubt it,' she told him frankly. 'Fate, my love. We belong. Always have, always will.'

More kisses – languid, tender, reassuring.

'Tell me about Gramps,' he urged, stroking the delicate skin of her cheek with the back of his thumb. 'Doesn't he live here, too? And in that case, my love,' he queried languidly, 'shouldn't we get dressed? I should hate to start off badly with my newly discovered grandfather-in-law.'

'He doesn't. You won't. And he isn't – yet,' she explained, taking each point in turn.

'He isn't what?' he queried, puzzled.

'Your grandfather-in-law. Only nearly.'

'How nearly?'

'That special licence,' she reminded him. 'How soon can it be arranged?'

'Tomorrow soon enough?' he probed.

'Hmm . . . I guess I can wait until tomorrow,' she conceded. 'Besides, I need to see Gramps, ask him to give me away. How about you?'

'My best man? Oh, Ian, of course – despite the rumours about cosy afternoon drives with my lovely wife-to-be the moment my back was turned. And, since the man clearly has second sight, he made a point of sending his love. Hang on a minute, now that

I come to think of it,' he mused, propping himself up on an elbow and gazing sternly down at her, 'he referred to you as Ella. Just how cosy *were* these afternoons out?' he demanded mock-severely.

'Just one,' Ella reassured him. 'Not counting supper at my place, of course,' she tagged on provokingly. 'Jealous, my love?'

'As hell. But I guess I'll learn to live with it. Talking of which . . .'

'Hmm?'

'Sherbrook. It's too big for two and yet too perfect to lose. But you were right about its potential. So, I was wondering. How does a self-contained flat in the East Wing sound, leaving the rest for business? Unless you'd rather keep things as they are?' he added doubtfully.

'Jack, I'd live in the housekeeper's pantry as long as it made you happy.'

'I'm not sure Katie would approve,' he pointed out, features impassive.

'Katie?'

'The housekeeper. You were a hard act to follow but the girl's shaping up well – all thanks to you.'

Ella smiled. Having walked out the way she did, she hadn't even made the suggestion, she realized, with a sudden pang of guilt.

No time to brood, not with Jack's thumb idly brushing against her nipple, his growl of delight music to her ears as her body reacted, the spark igniting at once, the flames spreading through her. Only Jack, impossible, wonderful, frustrating man that he was, refused to give her what she wanted –

touching, fingers probing, lips nuzzling, exploring, mouth, neck, breasts.

Down ever lower, a trail of tantalizing kisses the length of one leg, all the way to the tip of each and every toe, and then back up the other, slowly, languidly, lazily. His tongue was lapping at the curls at the junction of her legs, his hands stroking the swell of her belly. Not a very big swell, Ella could allow, easily overlooked in the heat of the moment. But –

A sudden pause. He raised his head, blue eyes boring into hers. 'You're pregnant?'

She nodded, eyes bright, her smile tremulous. 'I'm pregnant.'

'But – oh, hell, sweetheart!' He jerked upright, kneeling beside her in an instant as he cradled her face in his hands. 'The baby – you should have said – we shouldn't – '

'Hush, love,' she reassured him, kissing him, her tongue sliding into the warm, moist depths of his mouth as she eased her body back into the hard lines of his. 'We should. Doctor's orders,' she insisted, moving against him. 'Trust me.'

And he did. And they did.

'Later, madam,' he chided softly, raising his head, all the love in the world pouring out from those piercing blue eyes, 'you and I are going home so that I can keep an eye on you. And tomorrow,' he reminded her, hugging her fiercely, 'we make this relationship legal once and for all.'

'Pity, really,' she murmured provokingly, feature impassive.

'Oh?' he murmured warily.

'If the master of the house had registered Sherbrook for weddings,' she pointed out saucily, 'it would have saved us the bother of getting out of bed!'

'You, madam, are shameless,' he growled, kissing her.

'Complaining, my love?'

'Only about the time we've lost. But we've a lifetime ahead of us to make up for it all, and, having put the thought in my head, I'll give you three guesses what's running through my mind.'

She glanced down, saw his manhood stirring into life and smiled slyly up at him. 'A cold shower?' she suggested, and quick as a flash she was out of the bed, heading for the bathroom, an outraged Jack hot on her heels.

And sure enough he caught her in the shower, a wonderfully warm shower, the water cascading over them as man and woman, body to body, gave love, gave pleasure, great waves of pleasure that rolled, gathered momentum, reached a towering apex and then exploded into a billion droplets of love.

QUESTIONNAIRE

Please tick the appropriate boxes to indicate your answers

1 Where did you get this Scarlet title?
Bought in supermarket ☐
Bought at my local bookstore ☐ Bought at chain bookstore ☐
Bought at book exchange or used bookstore ☐
Borrowed from a friend ☐
Other (please indicate) ____________________

2 Did you enjoy reading it?
A lot ☐ A little ☐ Not at all ☐

3 What did you particularly like about this book?
Believable characters ☐ Easy to read ☐
Good value for money ☐ Enjoyable locations ☐
Interesting story ☐ Modern setting ☐
Other ____________________

4 What did you particularly dislike about this book?
____

5 Would you buy another Scarlet book?
Yes ☐ No ☐

6 What other kinds of book do you enjoy reading?
Horror ☐ Puzzle books ☐ Historical fiction ☐
General fiction ☐ Crime/Detective ☐ Cookery ☐
Other (please indicate) ____________________

7 Which magazines do you enjoy reading?
1. ____________________
2. ____________________
3. ____________________

And now a little about you –
8 How old are you?
Under 25 ☐ 25–34 ☐ 35–44 ☐
45–54 ☐ 55–64 ☐ over 65 ☐

cont.

9 What is your marital status?
Single ☐ Married/living with partner ☐
Widowed ☐ Separated/divorced ☐

10 What is your current occupation?
Employed full-time ☐ Employed part-time ☐
Student ☐ Housewife full-time ☐
Unemployed ☐ Retired ☐

11 Do you have children? If so, how many and how old are they?

____

____

12 What is your annual household income?

under $15,000	☐	or	£10,000	☐
$15–25,000	☐	or	£10–20,000	☐
$25–35,000	☐	or	£20–30,000	☐
$35–50,000	☐	or	£30–40,000	☐
over $50,000	☐	or	£40,000	☐

Miss/Mrs/Ms ______________________________
Address ______________________________

____

____

Thank you for completing this questionnaire. Now tear it out – put it in an envelope and send it to:

Sally Cooper, Editor-in-Chief

USA/Can. address
SCARLET c/o London Bridge
85 River Rock Drive
Suite 202
Buffalo
NY 14207
USA

UK address/No stamp required
SCARLET
FREEPOST LON 3335
LONDON W8 4BR
Please use block capitals for address

MAHOU/4/97

Scarlet titles coming next month:

CAROUSEL Michelle Reynolds

When Penny Farthing takes a job as housekeeper/nanny to Ben Carmichael and his sons, she's looking for a quiet life. Penny thinks she'll quite like living in the country and she knows she'll love the little boys she's caring for . . . what she doesn't expect is to fall in love with her boss!

BLACK VELVET Patricia Wilson

Another SCARLET novel from this best-selling author! Helen Stewart is *not* impressed when she meets Dan Forrest – she's sure he's drunk, so she dumps him unceremoniously at his hotel! Dan isn't drunk, he has flu, so their relationship doesn't get off to the best start. Dan, though, soon wants Helen more than he's ever wanted any other woman . . . but is she involved in *murder?*

CHANGE OF HEART Julie Garratt

Ten years ago headstrong Serena Corder was involved with Holt Blackwood, but she left home because she resented her father's attempts to control her life. Now a very different Serena is back and the attraction she feels for Holt is as strong as ever. But do they have a future together . . . especially as she wears another man's ring!

A CIRCLE IN TIME Jean Walton

Margie Seymour is about to lose her beloved ranch, when she finds an injured man on her property. He tells her not only that he is from the 1800s, but that *he*, not she, owns the ranch! It's not long before feisty Margie Seymour is playing havoc with Jake's good intentions of returning to his own time as soon as he can!